THE OLD COUNTRY

Collected Stories of
Sholom Aleichem

THE OLD

COUNTRY

TRANSLATED BY

JULIUS AND FRANCES BUTWIN

with Illustrations by Ben Shahn

DE LVXE ILLVSTRATED EDITION

CROWN PUBLISHERS, INC.

NEW YORK

CONTENTS

*The design on the front cover of the book is Sholom Aleichem's
signature, a combination of English and Yiddish script.*

FOREWORD

YEARS ago when Sholom Aleichem came to New York, Mark Twain was among the first to visit him. "I wanted to meet you," he said, "because I understand that I am the American Sholom Aleichem." History does not record the answer of the man who is called variously "the Jewish Mark Twain," "the Jewish Dickens," "the modern Heine."

There should be an end to these comparisons. Sholom Aleichem was none of these things. He was like no one else. He was unique, a genius whose writings are the perfect expression of a people, their mind, their heart, their wit and above all their special idiom.

But there is no need to describe the quality of Sholom Aleichem's work. Here are the stories. Read them and see for yourself. There are twenty-seven stories in the book. I think you'll wish there were more.

There are more. For Jewish literature rejoices in a large body of work by Sholom Aleichem. In all, he wrote some three hundred stories, five novels, many plays, and a number of other works. And we may hope that in time all this work will be translated into English.

Sholom Aleichem is the pen name of Solomon Rabinowitch who was born in 1859 in Pereyeslav which is in the Ukraine. He died in New York in 1916 and is buried in Mt. Carmel

Cemetery in Brooklyn. His grave has become a shrine and every year many Jews go there to pay homage to him.

If anyone were to ask me how my husband and I came to do this translation, I would say that it was by pure accident. Neither of us had harbored the project before, or thought of it, for that matter. Nothing led up to it. One day we were talking to so-and-so and this-and-that happened. But if you asked Tevye, whom you will meet soon, or better yet, Tevye's wife Golde, she would laugh at this glib explanation. How did we come to do it? It was *bashert* of course. It was fated. It had been inscribed in the heavenly books and so it came to pass. And who can say that Tevye's wife is completely wrong, and that accidents may not be accidents after all, but only the means by which a series of seemingly unrelated events are suddenly brought into focus?

The work of translating these stories was a delight and a challenge at the same time. Often what was entirely right and simple and flavorsome in Yiddish completely missed fire when translated literally. Some stories just could not be transplanted and had to be abandoned. Sometimes we had to use translators' license with the exact wording. This we did in *A Page from the Song of Songs* and to some extent in *The Enchanted Tailor,* stories which depend a great deal on mood and atmosphere. Others that were carried forward by action and incident like *The Miracle of Hashono Rabo* and *The Convoy* follow the original almost word for word. In a few stories we left out passages that seemed to us irrelevant or outdated. This we did in *The Fiddle* where we omitted an elaborate description of the informer, and in *The Lottery Ticket* where a whole digression occurs that has no bearing on the story. We never tampered with the main flow of the story, and we never changed the substance of a beginning or an ending. A number of words which occur over and over and which have no equivalent in English were retained in the original Yiddish. Those are words descriptive of occupations like *melamed* and *shochet* and others which are almost self-explanatory in their context. Chief among these words is *shlimazl* which means literally a person of little luck.

The choice of stories was for the main part our own. We selected those that appealed to us most and those we thought would appeal to the English reader. Some we rejected for a definite reason, because of some special problem of translation as in the monologues which depend almost entirely on the teller's idiom, or when the story turned on some phrase that was completely untranslatable. Some of the stories seemed to us to be outdated, though there were surprisingly few of those. Others centered about a complicated religious ritual which would have needed a whole essay to explain. In many cases we chose among several stories similar in type.

One of the most wonderful and at the same time the most maddening things about these stories is the utter simplicity of their language. You ask yourself over and over, how can such a limited vocabulary be such a perfect instrument for expression? It isn't the fact that it portrays a simple people. Compared to the people of a Steinbeck or a Hemingway, these are virtuosos of the intellect. Words are their chief weapon, their joy and their ornament. But it isn't the variety of words at their command so much as the way they are put together that makes their speech distinctive—the way a phrase is chopped off or inverted or repeated with slight variations. It is like spoken Yiddish which depends for its drama on the inflection of the voice, on a pause, a raised eyebrow or a shrug of the shoulder. These things are difficult to transmit into another language, but when you feel that you've succeeded you experience the real thrill of creation.

While the language is simple, it is often violent and earthy. We had to compromise with this earthiness. Take just the small matter of the Yiddish curse. There are as many types of curses as there are people cursing, but the hardest to explain is the mother cursing her child. The child may be crying because he is hungry. The mother bursts out, "Eat, eat, eat. All you want to do is eat. May the worms eat you. May the earth open up and swallow you alive." This mother loves her child, she is only pouring out the bitterness that's in her heart in the only way she knows. But in translation she sounds like a monster. When the wayward son-in-law Menachem Mendel comes home for Passover and his mother-in-law and his wife shower curses on his head he is not offended. He knows his wife is happy to see him because as soon as she is through cursing, she bursts into tears.

We encountered our greatest problem in working on the Tevye stories. They are all in the first person and they all depend for their effect on Tevye's manner of expressing himself. In fact, they *are* Tevye. Tevye is the perfect *shlimazl* and also the perfect *kasril,* the man whom nothing in life can down. He considers himself a man of great learning and erudition—that is what makes his life bearable—and his speech is practically a series of Hebrew quotations from the Holy Books, most of which are, of course, misquotations, hilariously funny to the reader who could understand them, but otherwise meaningless. The problem was not only how to untangle these misquotations, but also how to render mistakes in one language within another language into a third language. We simply had to omit many passages. In others we used Biblical diction to approximate the Hebrew. Of course, some of the pungency and flavor of this most delightful and most completely realized of all of Sholom Aleichem's characters was lost in translation.

I would like to emphasize that throughout this work we made no attempt to be academic or perfectionist. These stories are not for the Hebraist or the Yiddish scholar. They are not especially for those who can read and enjoy the original. Rather, they are intended for the many Jews and non-Jews who, through a barrier of language, have had no access to the work of the most interesting and most beloved of Yiddish writers. They are intended for the general reader to whom they may open a new field of human experience.

Both of us came from the Old Country, I more recently than my husband, but it was he who had the deeper sense of identification with the past. He was brought to America at the age of one from Walkowisk in Lithuanian Russia. For forty years—that is, all of his life—he lived in a middle-sized city in Mid-America. He walked its streets as a native, he knew its buildings and people, its history and politics intimately. The tempo of this life suited him. And yet his roots were elsewhere. He used to say that he knew the geography of Walkowisk as well as that of St. Paul. Here was his grandfather's mill, there the Long Street, here the *cheder* where his father used to teach as a young man. And that mill, that street, that *cheder* could just as well have been in Kasrilevka or Verebivka, in Boiberik or Haschavata. For all of those towns, real or mythical, in White Russia or the Ukraine, in Galicia or Lithuania, belong to the same country to which our parents and grandparents referred when they spoke of *in der heim* or home.

One Sunday last November, which turned out to be the last day of his life, my husband was talking about his grandparents. He told how his grandfather used to take him walking by the river; how he loved watching his grandmother roll out the thin yellow sheets of dough for noodles. He said, "For me they were the ideal grandparents." And I think that in a restricted but no less real sense the life they represented was to him an ideal life. He was aware of its limitations, its misery and hardship, but he also understood its dignity, its warmth, and most particularly its humor. He was a product of all these things. And it gave him rare pleasure to be able through these translations to interpret that life to his contemporaries.

So that finally, these stories are intended for those to whom The Old Country is only a name remembered from childhood and for those to whom it represents a whole complex of emotions, of words and pictures, of smells and sounds, for which they have no common frame of reference. If we have succeeded truly in bringing Sholom Aleichem to Americans, if we have succeeded in clarifying and sharpening only a few of those sounds and smells and pictures, if we have lit up only a corner of that vast and wonderful country of the heart we call The Old Country, our work has been well worth doing.

F. B.

St. Paul, March 1946

THE OLD COUNTRY

The Town of the Little People

THE town of the little people into which I shall now take you, dear reader, is exactly in the middle of that blessed Pale into which Jews have been packed as closely as herring in a barrel and told to increase and multiply. The name of the town is Kasrilevka. How did this name originate? I'll tell you:

Among us Jews poverty has many faces and many aspects. A poor man is an unlucky man, he is a pauper, a beggar, a *schnorrer,* a starveling, a tramp, or a plain failure. A different tone is used in speaking of each one, but all these names express human wretchedness. However, there is still another name—*kasril,* or *kasrilik.* That name is spoken in a different tone altogether, almost a bragging tone. For instance, "Oh, am I ever a *kasrilik!*" A *kasrilik* is not just an ordinary pauper, a failure in life. On the contrary, he is a man who has not allowed poverty to degrade him. He laughs at it. He is poor, but cheerful.

Stuck away in a corner of the world, isolated from the surrounding country, the town stands, orphaned, dreaming, bewitched, immersed in itself and remote from the noise and bustle, the confusion and tumult and greed, which men have created about them and have dignified with high-sounding names like Culture, Progress, Civilization. A proper person may take off his hat with respect to these things, but not these little people! Not only do they know nothing of automobiles, modern travel, airplanes—for a long time they refused to

1

believe in the existence of the old, ordinary railroad train.
"Such a thing could not be," they said. "Why," they said, "it's
a dream, a fairy tale. You might just as well talk of merry-go-
rounds in heaven!"

But it happened once that a householder of Kasrilevka had
to go to Moscow. When he came back he swore with many
oaths that it was true. He himself had ridden in a train to
Moscow, and it had taken him—he shrugged his shoulders—
less than an hour. This the little people interpreted to mean
that he had ridden less than an hour and then walked the
rest of the way. But still the fact of the train remained. If a
Jew and a householder of Kasrilevka swore to it, they could
not deny that there was such a thing as a train. It had to be
true. He could not have invented it out of thin air. He even
explained to them the whole miracle of the train, and drew
a diagram on paper. He showed them how the wheels turned,
the smokestack whistled, the carriages flew, and people rode
to Moscow. The little people of Kasrilevka listened and
listened, nodded their heads solemnly, and deep in their hearts
they laughed at him. "What a story! The wheels turn, the
smokestack whistles, the carriages fly and people ride to Moscow—and then come back again!"

That's how they all are, these little people. None of them
are gloomy, none of them are worried little men of affairs, but
on the contrary they are known everywhere as jesters, story-
tellers, a cheerful, light-hearted breed of men. Poor but cheerful. It is hard to say what makes them so happy. Nothing—
just sheer joy of living. Living? If you ask them, "How do you
live?" they will answer, with a shrug and a laugh. "How do
we live? Who knows? We live!" A remarkable thing—
whenever you meet them they are scurrying like rabbits, this
one here, that one there. They never have time to stop. "What
are you hurrying for?" "What am I hurrying for? Well, it's

like this. If we hurry we think we might run into something—earn a few pennies—provide for the Sabbath."

To provide for the Sabbath—that is their goal in life. All week they labor and sweat, wear themselves out, live without food or drink, just so there is something for the Sabbath. And when the holy Sabbath arrives, let Yehupetz perish, let Odessa be razed, let Paris itself sink into the earth! Kasrilevka lives! And this is a fact, that since Kasrilevka was founded, no Jew has gone hungry there on the Sabbath. Is it possible that there is a Jew who does not have fish for the Sabbath? If he has no fish, then he has meat. If he has no meat, then he has herring. If he has no herring, then he has white bread. If he has no white bread, then he has black bread and onions. If he has no black bread and onions, then he borrows some from his neighbor. Next week, the neighbor will borrow from him. "The world is a wheel and it keeps turning." The Kasrilevkite repeats this maxim and shows you with his hand how it turns. To him a maxim, a witty remark, is everything. For an apt remark he will forsake his mother and father, as the saying goes. The tales you hear about these little people sound fabulous, but you may be sure they are all true.

For instance, there is the story of the Kasrilevkite who got tired of starving in Kasrilevka and went out into the wide world to seek his fortune. He left the country, wandered far and wide, and finally reached Paris. There, naturally, he wanted to see Rothschild. For how can a Jew come to Paris and not visit Rothschild? But they didn't let him in. "What's the trouble?" he wants to know. "Your coat is torn," they tell him.

"You fool," says the Jew. "If I had a good coat, would I have gone to Paris?"

It looked hopeless. But a Kasrilevkite never gives up. He thought a while and said to the doorman: "Tell your master that it isn't an ordinary beggar who has come to his door, but

a Jewish merchant, who has brought him a piece of goods
such as you can't find in Paris for any amount of money."

Hearing this, Rothschild became curious and asked that the
merchant be brought to him.

"*Sholom aleichem,*" said Rothschild.

"*Aleichem sholom,*" said the merchant.

"Take a seat. And where do you come from?"

"I come from Kasrilevka."

"What good news do you bring?"

"Well, Mr. Rothschild, they say in our town that you are
not so badly off. If I had only half of what you own, or only a
third, you would still have enough left. And honors, I imagine,
you don't lack either, for people always look up to a man of
riches. Then what do you lack? One thing only—eternal life.
That is what I have to sell you."

When Rothschild heard this he said, "Well, let's get down
to business. What will it cost me?"

"It will cost you—" here the man stopped to consider—"it
will cost you—three hundred *rubles.*"

"Is that your best price?"

"My very best. I could have said a lot more than three hundred. But I said it, so it's final."

Rothschild said no more, but counted out three hundred
rubles, one by one.

Our Kasrilevkite slipped the money into his pocket, and said
to Rothschild: "If you want to live for ever, my advice to you
is to leave this noisy, busy Paris, and move to our town of
Kasrilevka. There you can never die, because since Kasrilevka
has been a town, no rich man has ever died there."

And then there is the story of the man who got as far as
America . . . But if I started to tell all the tales of these little
people I'd have to sit with you for three days and three nights

and talk and talk and talk. Instead, let us pass on to a description of the little town itself.

Shall I call it a beautiful little town? From a distance it looks —how shall I say it?—like a loaf of bread thickly studded with poppy seed. Some of the houses are built on the slope of a hill, and the rest are huddled together at the base, one on top of the other, like the gravestones in an ancient cemetery. There are no streets to speak of because the houses are not built according to any plan, and besides, where is there room for such a thing? Why should there be vacant space when you can build something on it? It is written that the earth is to be inhabited, not merely to be gazed at.

Yet, don't be upset. There are some streets—big streets, little streets, back streets and alleys. What if they happen to twist and turn uphill and downhill and suddenly end up in a house or a cellar or just a hole in the ground? If you are a stranger, never go out alone at night without a lantern. As for the little people who live there, don't worry about them. A Kasrilevkite in Kasrilevka, among Kasrilevkites, will never get lost. Each one finds the way to his own house, to his wife and children, like a bird to its own nest.

And then in the center of the city there is a wide half-circle, or perhaps it is a square, where you find the stores, shops, market stands, stalls and tables. There every morning the peasants from the surrounding countryside congregate with their produce—fish and onions, horseradish, parsnips and other vegetables. They sell these things and buy from the little people other necessities of life, and from this the Kasrilevkites draw their livelihood. A meager one, but better than nothing. And in the square also lie all the town's goats, warming themselves in the sun.

There also stand the synagogues, the meeting houses, the

chapels and schools of the town where Jewish children study the Holy Writ. The noise they and the rabbis make with their chanting is enough to deafen one. The baths where the women go to bathe are also there, and the poorhouse where the old men die, and other such public institutions. No, the Kasrilev-kites have never heard of canals or water works or electricity or other such luxuries. But what does that matter? Everywhere people die the same death, and they are placed in the same earth, and are beaten down with the same spades. Thus my Rabbi, Reb Israel, used to say—when he was happiest, at a wedding or other celebration, after he had had a few glasses of wine and was ready to lift up the skirts of his long coat and dance a *kazatsky* . . .

But the real pride of Kasrilevka is her cemeteries. This lucky town has two rich cemeteries, the old and the new. The new one is old enough and rich enough in graves. Soon there will be no place to put anyone, especially if a pogrom should break out or any of the other misfortunes which befall us in these times.

But it is of the old cemetery that the people of Kasrilevka are especially proud. This old cemetery, though it is overgrown with grass and with bushes and has practically no upright head-stones, they still value as they might a treasure, a rare gem, a piece of wealth, and guard it like the apple of their eye. For this is not only the place where their ancestors lie, rabbis, men of piety, learned ones, scholars and famous people, including the dead from the ancient massacres of Chmelnitski's time—but also the only piece of land of which they are the masters, the only bit of earth they own where a blade of grass can sprout and a tree can grow and the air is fresh and one can breathe freely.

You should see what goes on in this old cemetery a month before the New Year, during the "days of weeping." Men and women—mainly women—swarm up and down the paths to their ancestors' graves. From all the surrounding country they come to weep and to pour their hearts out at the holy graves. Believe me, there is no place where one can weep so freely and with such abandon as in "the field" of Kasrilevka. In the synagogue a person can weep pretty freely too, but the synagogue doesn't come up to the cemetery. The cemetery is a source of income for the Kasrilevkite stonecutters, innkeepers, cantors and sextons, and the month before the New Year is, for the paupers thereabouts and the old women and the cripples, the real harvest time.

"Have you been in 'our field' yet?" a Kasrilevkite will ask you cheerfully, as though he were asking if you had been in his father's vineyard. If you haven't been there, do him a kindness, and go down into "the field," read the old, half-obliterated inscriptions on the leaning tombstones and you will find in them the story of a whole people. And if you happen to be a man of feeling and imagination then you will look upon this poor little town with its rich cemeteries and repeat the old verses:

"How beautiful are your tents, O Jacob; how good are your resting places, O Israel."

The Inheritors

THE Maiers and the Schnaiers . . .

Actually there was only one Maier and one Schnaier. They were twins and they looked so much alike that there were times when it was impossible to tell which of the two was Maier and which was Schnaier. As babies, the story goes, a queer thing happened to them. They were almost exchanged—and it is possible that they really were exchanged. This is how it happened.

Their mother, you may know, was a tiny woman and quite frail, but very fruitful. Every year without fail she gave birth to a child, but the sickly infant barely lingered through its first twelve months and then died. This went on until she finally stopped having children and thought she would never have another. But in the end a miracle happened. In her old age the Lord blessed her again, and this time with twins. And since it was too hard for her to suckle two babies, she had to hire a wet nurse. What else was there to do? A Kasrilevkite —no matter how poor he may be—will never throw a child of his into the streets or give it to a stranger to raise, unless, God forbid, the child be an orphan.

Having hired the nurse, the mother took Maier for herself (he was older than Schnaier by half an hour) and she gave Schnaier to the nurse. But since the nurse was herself not such a healthy woman, neither Maier nor Schnaier got too much milk. Both babies were equally starved; they screamed all night long; tore the house apart with their noise. It happened one day that the women were bathing the babies, naturally in one basin. They undressed them and put them into the hot water. Then, adding fresh water to the basin, they watched the children, red and bloated, splashing their little hands and feet, rolling about like beetles, enjoying themselves hugely. When they were through bathing them they took the babies out, wrapped them in a sheet (naturally one sheet) and put them to bed (naturally one bed) to dry. But when they started to dress them again, they couldn't tell which was Maier and which was Schnaier. And an argument took place between the two women.

"Look here, I could swear that this is Maier and this is Schnaier."

"How could you say that? This one is Maier and that one is Schnaier. Can't you see?"

"Do you think I'm dreaming? Either you're crazy, or just out of your head!"

"Good Lord! Can't you tell by their eyes that this is Maier and that is Schnaier? Look at those two eyes of his!"

"A fine argument! What do you want him to have—three eyes?"

Well, one of them kept insisting that Maier was Schnaier and Schnaier was Maier, and the other that Schnaier was Maier and Maier was Schnaier. Until at last the men came in and offered a solution. After all, they were men, with superior brains.

"Do you know what?" they suggested. "Try nursing the babies and we shall see. The one who takes his mother's breast must be Maier and the one who takes the nurse's must be Schnaier. That's simple enough."

And so it happened. As soon as the babies snuggled up to the breast, they each began to suck hungrily, smacked their lips, kicked their legs and made sounds like hungry puppies.

"A miracle of God!" said the men, with tears in their eyes. "See how the Almighty has created His world!"

And as a final test they decided to change the babies and see what would happen. The poor infants were torn away from their breasts and changed about, Schnaier taking Maier's place and Maier Schnaier's. And what do you suppose happened? Do you think they stopped sucking? They sucked as hard as ever!

From that time on they gave up trying to tell them apart. Let them be Maier-Schnaier and Schnaier-Maier. And they were given the name of the Maiers and the Schnaiers, as though each one was both a Maier and a Schnaier. More than once it happened in *cheder* that Maier was whipped when Schnaier should have got the whipping, or the other way around, Schnaier was punished for Maier's misdeeds. And in order to avoid hard feelings, the rabbi hit on this scheme (do they not say where there is learning there is wisdom?):

"You know what, children? Both of you stretch out. Then there will be no argument that I beat this one or that one. It will all remain in the family . . ."

But much, much later—after their *Bar Mitzvah,* when the Maiers and Schnaiers had reached manhood—something happened that made it possible to tell them apart a mile away even at night. What wonders God can devise! The brothers began to sprout beards (they must both have begun to smoke cigars too early) and on Maier's cheeks and upper lip there appeared black hairs (black as ink) and on Schnaier's face red hairs (red as fire). These beards grew as if the devil possessed them (they must both have continued to smoke cigars), so that by the time they were married they both had full beards. Did I say beards? Feather dusters was more like it. A black duster and a red one, that looked as if someone had glued them on.

Great are the works of the Lord, and His wonders are without end. For who knows what would have come to pass after their weddings if the beards, too, had been alike? In the confusion, even the wives might not have known which one of the brothers they had married . . . I do not know how it is with you in the big cities, but here in Kasrilevka it has never yet happened that husbands and wives should start exchanging each other. It is possible that there are husbands among us who would not object to this, but they know their wives and they know what they would get from them. However, all this is beside the point. The real story begins now.

Up till now we have concerned ourselves only with the Maiers and Schnaiers, that is with Maier and Schnaier, and we have become slightly acquainted with their mother and nurse, but we have not said a word about their father, as though they had never had a father. God forbid! Such a thing may have happened to others, but never to our kind of people. We have, thank God, no homes for foundlings where children are raised by strangers. It has never happened among us that a child should grow up and not know who his real father was. And if such a thing has happened, it has happened somewhere in Odessa or in Paris or in faraway America . . . As for Kasrilevka, I can swear that such a thing has never happened, and if it did, it happened to some servant girl or some other unfortunate maiden who was led astray by accident, through no fault of her own—an unhappy victim of another's lust . . .

In short, the Maiers and Schnaiers had a father, and a very fine father, too. He was a virtuous and an honest man named Reb Shimshen, and he had a magnificent beard, long and rich and luxurious. In fact, it could be said without exaggeration that Reb Shimshen had more beard than face. And for that reason he was known in Kasrilevka as Reb Shimshen Beard.

And this Reb Shimshen was—I don't even know what he was. But you can be sure that all his life he struggled and sweated for a meager living, waged constant warfare against poverty. Sometimes he overcame poverty; sometimes poverty overcame him, as is usual with Kasrilevkites, who are not afraid of want, but thumb their noses at it . . .

And Reb Shimshen lived out his life and finally he died. And when he died he was given a handsome burial. Almost the whole town followed his remains to the cemetery.

"Who is it that died?"

"Haven't you heard? Reb Shimshen."

"Which Reb Shimshen?"

"Reb Shimshen Beard."

"A great pity. So Reb Shimshen Beard is gone from us too."

That is what they said in Kasrilevka and mourned not so much for Reb Shimshen himself as for the fact that with his death there was one person less in Kasrilevka. Strange people, these Kasrilevkites! In spite of the fact that they are so poor that they almost never have enough for themselves, they would be pleased if no one among them ever died. Their only comfort is that people die everywhere, even in Paris, and that no one can buy his way out. Even Rothschild himself, who is greater than royalty, has to get up and go when the Angel of Death beckons.

Now let us turn back again to the Maiers and Schnaiers.

As long as Reb Shimshen was alive the Maiers and Schnaiers lived as one, brothers in body and soul. But when their father died they became enemies at once, ready to tear each other's beards out. Perhaps you wonder why? Well, why do sons ever fight after a father's death? Naturally, over the inheritance. It is true that Reb Shimshen did not leave behind any farms or woodlands, houses or rental property, and certainly no cash. Nor did he leave any jewelry, silver or furniture to his children —not because he was mean or avaricious, but simply because he had nothing to leave. And yet don't think that Reb Shimshen left his children absolutely nothing. He left them a treasure that could be turned to money at any time, a treasure that could be pawned, rented or sold outright. This treasure we speak of was the seat he had had in the old Kasrilevka Synagogue, a seat along the east wall right next to Reb Yozifel, the Rabbi, who was next to the Holy Ark. It is true that Kasrilevka wits have a saying that it is better to have an acre outside than a seat inside, but that is only a saying, and when the Lord is kind and a person does have his own seat, and along the east wall at that, it's not so very bad—and certainly better than nothing . . .

In short, Reb Shimshen left behind a seat in the old Kasrilevka Synagogue. But he forgot one small detail. He didn't indicate who was to inherit the seat—Maier or Schnaier.

Obviously Reb Shimshen—may he forgive me—did not expect to die. He had forgotten that the Angel of Death lurks always behind our backs and watches every step we take, else he would surely have made a will or otherwise indicated in the presence of witnesses to which of his two sons he wanted to leave his fortune.

Well, what do you suppose? The very first Saturday after they arose from mourning, the quarrel began. Maier argued that according to law the seat belonged to him, since he was the older (by a good half-hour). And Schnaier had two arguments in his favor: first, they were not sure which of the two was older because according to their mother's story they had been exchanged as infants and he was really Maier and Maier was really Schnaier. In the second place, Maier had a rich father-in-law who also owned a seat along the east wall of the synagogue, and since the father-in-law had no sons the seat would eventually be Maier's. And when that happened Maier would have two seats by the east wall and Schnaier would have none whatever. And if that was the case, where was justice? Where was humanity?

When he heard of these goings-on, Maier's father-in-law, a man of means, but one who had made his money only recently, entered the battle. "You've got a lot of nerve!" he exclaimed. "I am not forty yet and I have every intention of living a long time, and here you are, dividing up my inheritance already. And besides, how do you know that I won't have a son yet? I may have more than one, see!" he stormed. "There is impudence for you!"

So their neighbors tried to make peace between them, suggested that they determine how much the seat was worth and then have one brother buy his share from the other. That sounds reasonable enough, doesn't it? The only trouble was that neither brother wanted to sell his share. They didn't care a thing about the money. What was money—compared to stubbornness and pride?

"How can one's own brother be so pigheaded as to keep a person away from his rightful seat?" "Why should you have our father's place, and not I?" It became a matter not so much of having things his own way as it was of preventing the other from having his. As the saying is: If I don't, you don't either. And the rivalry between the Maiers and the Schnaiers increased in fury. Stubbornness gave way to cunning as each tried to outwit the other!

The first Sabbath Maier came early and sat down in his father's seat; and Schnaier remained standing throughout the services. The second Sabbath Schnaier came first and occupied his father's place, while Maier remained standing. The third Sabbath Maier got there still earlier, spread himself out in the seat, pulled his *tallis* over his head, and there he was . . .

The next time it was Schnaier who hurried to get there first, sat down in the coveted seat, pulled his *tallis* over his face— and just try to budge him! The following week Maier was the first to get there . . . This went on week after week till one fine Sabbath both of them arrived at the same time—it was still dark outside—took their posts at the door of the synagogue (it was still shut) and glared at each other like roosters ready to tear each other's eyes out. It was like this that long ago the first two brothers stood face to face in an empty field, under God's blue sky, full of anger, ready to annihilate one another, devour each other, spill innocent blood . . .

But let us not forget that the Maiers and Schnaiers were young men of good family, respectable and well behaved—not rowdies who were in the habit of assaulting each other in public. They waited for Ezriel, the *shammes,* to come and open the door of the synagogue. Then they would show the whole world who would get to their father's seat first—Maier or Schnaier . . .

The minutes passed like years till Ezriel arrived with the keys. And when Ezriel, with his tangled beard, arrived he was not able to reach the door because the brothers stood against it—one with the left foot, the other with the right foot, and would not budge an inch.

"Well, what's going to happen?" said Ezriel casually, taking a pinch of snuff. "If the two of you insist on standing there like mean scarecrows I won't be able to open the door and the synagogue will have to remain closed all day. Go ahead and tell me: does that make sense?"

Apparently these words had some effect, because the Maiers

and Schnaiers both moved back, one to the right, the other to the left, and made way for Ezriel and his key. And when the key turned in the lock and the door swung open, the Maiers and Schnaiers tumbled in headlong.

"Be careful, you're killing me!" yelled Ezriel the *shammes,* and before he could finish the words the poor man lay trampled under their feet, screaming in horror: "Watch out! You're trampling all over me—the father of a family!"

But the Maiers and Schnaiers cared nothing for Ezriel and his family. Their only thought was for the seat, their father's seat, and jumping over benches and praying stands they made for the east wall. There they planted themselves firmly against the wall with their shoulders and the floor with their feet and tried to shove each other aside. In the scuffle they caught each other's beards, grimaced horribly, gritted their teeth and growled: "May the plague take you before you get this seat!"

In the meantime Ezriel got up from the floor, felt to see if any of his bones were broken, and approached the brothers. He found them both on the floor clutching each other's beards. At first he tried to reason with them.

"Shame on you! Two brothers—children of the same father and mother—tearing each other's beards out! And in a Holy Place at that! Be ashamed of yourselves!"

But Ezriel gathered that at the moment his lecture was in vain. Actually, his words added fuel to the flame so that the two children of one father became so enraged that one of them clutched in his fist a tuft of black hair (from Maier's beard) and the other a tuft of red (Schnaier's beard); blue marks showed on both faces and from the nose of one streamed blood.

As long as it was merely a matter of pulling beards, slapping and pummeling each other, the *shammes* could content himself with reading a lecture. But when he saw blood streaming, Ezriel could stand it no longer, for blood, even though only from a punched nose, was an ugly thing fit for rowdies and not God-fearing men.

He wasted no time, but ran to the tap, grabbed a dipper of water, and poured it over the two brothers. Cold water has always—since the world was created—been the best means of reviving a person. A man may be in the greatest rage, but as soon as he gets a cold bath he is strangely refreshed and cool; he comes to his senses. This happened to the Maiers and the Schnaiers. At the unexpected shower of cold water to which Ezriel had treated them, they woke up, looked each other in the eyes, and grew ashamed—like Adam and Eve when they had tasted of the forbidden fruit of the Tree of Knowledge and saw their nakedness . . .

And that very Saturday night the Maiers and Schnaiers went together with their friends and neighbors to the home of Reb Yozifel, the Rabbi, to have the dispute settled.

If Kasrilevka had not been such a tiny place, stuck away in a forgotten corner, far from the great world, and if newspapers and periodicals had been printed there, the world would surely have come to know the works of our Rabbi, Reb Yozifel. The papers would have been full of tales about him and his wisdom. The great, the wise and the famous of the world would have traveled far to see him in person and to hear from his own lips the words of wisdom. Photographers and painters would have made portraits of him and spread them to the four corners of the earth. Interviewers would have plagued him, given him no rest. They would have asked him all his views —what his favorite dishes were, how many hours a day he slept, what he thought about this and that, about cigarette smoking and bicycle riding . . . But since Kasrilevka is a tiny place stuck away in a forgotten corner, far from the world, and papers and periodicals are not printed there, the world knows nothing of the existence of Reb Yozifel. The papers never mention his name. The great, the wise and the famous do not come to him, photographers and painters do not make pictures of him. Interviewers leave him alone. And Reb Yozifel lives his life quietly, modestly, without noise or fanfare. No one knows anything about him except the town of Kasrilevka, which marvels at him, glories in his wisdom, and pays him great honor (of riches there is little in Kasrilevka, but honor they will give one as much as he deserves). They say that he is a man who modestly conceals his wisdom and it is only when you come to him for judgment that you find out how deep he is, how profound, how sharp. Another Solomon!

With the Sabbath over and the benedictions completed, the Maiers and Schnaiers came to Reb Yozifel to have their dispute settled, and there they found the house already full of people. The whole town was anxious to hear how he would settle it, how he would divide one seat between two brothers.

First he gave both sides a chance to unburden themselves. Reb Yozifel works according to this theory: that before the verdict is handed down the litigants should have the right to say anything they want to—because after the verdict all the talking in the world won't help. After that he let Ezriel, the *shammes,* talk. After all, he was the chief witness. And then other townspeople had their turn—everyone who had the public welfare at heart. And they talked as long as they wanted. Reb Yozifel is the kind of person who lets everyone talk. He is something of a philosopher. He feels this way about it: that no matter how long a person talks, he will have to stop some time.

And that is just what happened. They talked and talked and talked, and finally stopped talking. And when the last person

was through, Reb Yozifel turned to the Maiers and Schnaiers and spoke to them quietly, calmly, as his custom was.

"Hear ye, my friends—this is my opinion. According to what I have heard from you and from all the other citizens it is apparent that both of you are right. You both had one father, and a very noble father, too—may he enjoy the blessings of Paradise. The only trouble is that he left you only one seat in the synagogue. Naturally, this seat is very dear to both of you. After all—it is something to own one's seat along the east wall of the old, old Kasrilevka Synagogue. You can't dismiss that with a wave of the hand. What then? Just as it is impossible for one person to use two seats, so it is impossible for two people to use a single one. On the contrary, it is much easier for one person to use two seats than for two to use one."

And so with example and precept he went on to explain the difficulty of the situation.

"But there is one way," he continued, "in which each of you can sit along the eastern wall in adjoining seats. I have come upon this solution after much reflection. And this is what I have to say. My seat in the synagogue is right next to the one your father left. One of you can have my seat and then both of you brothers can sit next to each other in peace and amity, and you will have no need to quarrel any more. And if you will ask what will I do without a seat? then I will answer you with another question: "Where is it written that a Rabbi or any other man, for that matter, must have his own seat and especially at the east wall, and at the old Kasrilevka Synagogue at that? Let us stop to consider. What is a synagogue? A house of prayer. And why do we go to the synagogue? To pray. To whom? To the Almighty. And where is He found? Everywhere. All the world is filled with His glory. If that is the case, then what difference does it make whether it is east

or north or south, whether it is near the Ark or by the door?
The important thing is to come to the synagogue and to pray.
"Let me give you an example. Once there was a king . . ."
And there followed another of Reb Yozifel's parables of the
two servants who began to tear each other's beards in the presence of the king. And they were sent away with this admoni-
tion: "If you want to tear each other's beards, go outside and
do it as much as your heart desires, but do not defile my
palace . . ."

Thus Reb Yozifel chided them gently, and then he said, "Go
home now, my children, in peace and let your father be an
advocate in heaven for you, for us, and for all Israel."

Thus the Rabbi handed down his verdict and all the people
went home.

The following Sabbath, the Maiers and Schnaiers came to the
synagogue and stationed themselves near the door. No matter
how much they were entreated by the *shammes* on one side and
the Rabbi on the other, they refused to occupy the seats by the
east wall.

If there is anyone who would like to have his own seat by
the east wall in the old, old Kasrilevka Synagogue, the seat next
to Reb Yozifel, the Rabbi, at a reasonable price, let him go to
Kasrilevka and see the children of Reb Shimshen Beard, either
Maier or Schnaier, it does not matter which. They will sell it
to you at any price you say, because neither of them uses that
seat any more. It stands there—unoccupied.

What a waste!

Tevye Wins a Fortune

Who raiseth up the poor out of the dust,
And lifteth up the needy out of the dunghill.
—PSALMS, 113:7.

IF YOU are destined to draw the winning ticket in the lottery, Mr. Sholom Aleichem, it will come right into your house without your asking for it. As King David says, "It never rains but it pours." You don't need wisdom or skill. And, on the contrary, if you are not inscribed as a winner in the Books of the Angels, you can talk yourself blue in the face—it won't help you. The *Talmud* is right: "You can lead a horse to water, but you cannot make him drink." A person slaves, wears himself to the bone, and gets nowhere. He might as well lie down and give up his ghost. Suddenly, no one knows how or for what reason, money rolls in from all sides. As the passage has it, "Relief and deliverance will come to the Jews." I don't have to explain that to you. It should be clear to both of us that so long as a Jew can still draw breath and feel the blood beating in his veins, he must never lose hope. I have seen it in my own experience, in the way the Lord dealt with me in providing me with my present livelihood. For how else should I happen to be selling cheese and butter all of a sudden? In my wildest dreams I had never seen myself as a dairyman.

Take my word for it, the story is worth hearing. I'll sit down for a little while here near you on the grass. Let the horse

do a little nibbling meanwhile. After all, even a horse is one
of God's living creatures.

Well, it was in the late spring, around *Shevuos* time. But I
don't want to mislead you; it may have been a week or two
before *Shevuos,* or—let's see—maybe a couple of weeks after
Shevuos. Don't forget, this didn't happen yesterday. Wait! To
be exact, it was nine or ten years ago to the day. And maybe
a trifle more.

In those days I was not the man I am today. That is, I *was*
the same Tevye, and yet not exactly the same. The same old
woman, as they say, but in a different bonnet. How so? I was
as poor as a man could be, completely penniless. If you want
to know the truth I'm not a rich man now either, but compared with what I was then I can now really call myself a man
of wealth. I have a horse and wagon of my own, a couple of
cows that give milk, and a third that is about to calve. We
can't complain. We have cheese and butter and fresh cream
all the time. We make it ourselves; that is, our family does.
We all work. No one is idle. My wife milks the cows; the
children carry pitchers and pails, churn the butter. And I myself, as you see, drive to market every morning, go from *datcha*
to *datcha* in Boiberik, visit with people, see this one and that
one, all the important businessmen from Yehupetz who come
there for the summer. Talking to them makes me feel that I am
somebody, too; I amount to something in the world.

And when Saturday comes—then I really live like a king!
I look into the Holy Books, read the weekly portion of the
Bible, dip into the commentaries, Psalms, *Perek,* this, that,
something else . . . Ah, you're surprised, Mr. Sholom Aleichem! No doubt you're thinking to yourself, "Ah, that Tevye
—there's a man for you!"

Anyway, what did I start to tell you? That's right. Those
days. Oh, was Tevye a pauper then! With God's help I starved

to death—I and my wife and children—three times a day, not counting supper. I worked like a horse, pulling wagonloads of logs from the woods to the railroad station for—I am ashamed to admit it—half a *ruble* a day. And that not every day, either. And on such earnings just try to fill all those hungry mouths, not counting that boarder of mine, the poor horse, whom I can't put off with a quotation from the *Talmud*.

So what does the Lord do? He is a great, all-powerful God. He manages His little world wisely and well. Seeing how I was struggling for a hard crust of bread, He said to me: "Do you think, Tevye, that you have nothing more to live for, that the world has come to an end? If that's what you think, you're a big lummox. Soon you will see: if I will it, your luck can change in one turn of the wheel, and what was dark as the grave will be full of brightness." As we say on *Yom Kippur,* the Lord decides who will ride on horseback and who will crawl on foot. The main thing is—hope! A Jew must always hope, must never lose hope. And in the meantime, what if we waste away to a shadow? For that we are Jews—the Chosen People, the envy and admiration of the world.

Anyway, this is how it happened. As the Bible says, "And there came the day . . ." One evening in summer I was driving through the woods on my way home with an empty wagon. My head was bent, my heart was heavy. The little horse, poor thing, was barely dragging its feet. "Ah," I said to it, "crawl along, *shlimazl*! If you are Tevye's horse you too must know the pangs of hunger . . ." All around was silence, every crack of the whip echoed through the woods. As the sun set the shadows of the trees stretched out and lengthened —like our Jewish exile. Darkness was creeping in and a sadness filled my heart. Strange, faraway thoughts filled my mind, and before my eyes passed the images of people a long time dead. And in the midst of it all I thought of my home and

my family. And I thought, "Woe unto us all." The wretched
dark little hut that was my home, and the children barefoot
and in tatters waiting for their father, the *shlimazl*. Maybe
he would bring them a loaf of bread or a few stale rolls. And
my wife, grumbling as a wife will: "Children I had to bear
him—seven of them. I might as well take them all and throw
them into the river—may God not punish me for these words!"

You can imagine how I felt. We are only human. The
stomach is empty and words won't fill it. If you swallow a
piece of herring you want some tea, and for tea you need sugar.
And sugar, I am told, is in the grocery store. "My stomach,"
says my wife, "can get along without a piece of bread, but
if I don't take a glass of tea in the morning, I am a dead woman.
All night long the baby sucks me dry."

But in spite of everything, we are still Jews. When evening
comes we have to say our prayers. You can imagine what the
prayers sounded like if I tell you that just as I was about to
begin *Shmin-esra* my horse suddenly broke away as if possessed
by the devil and ran wildly off through the woods. Have you
ever tried standing on one spot facing the east while a horse
was pulling you where *it* wanted to go? I had no choice but
to run after him, holding on to the reins and chanting, "*God
of Abraham, God of Isaac, and God of Jacob.*" A fine way
to say *Shmin-esra*! And just my luck, at a moment when I
was in the mood to pray with feeling, out of the depths of my
heart, hoping it would lift my spirits . . .

So there I was, running after the wagon and chanting at the
top of my voice, as if I were a cantor in a synagogue: "*Thou
sustainest the living with loving kindness* (and sometimes with
a little food) *and keepest thy faith with them that sleep in the
dust.* (The dead are not the only ones who lie in the dust;
Oh, how low we the living are laid, what hells we go through,
and I don't mean the rich people of Yehupetz who spend their
summers at the *datchas* of Boiberik, eating and drinking and

living off the fat of the land . . . Oh, Heavenly Father, why does this happen to me? Am I not as good as others? Help me, dear God!) *Look upon our afflictions.* (Look down, dear God! See how we struggle and come to the aid of the poor, because who will look out for us if you don't?) *Heal us, O Lord, and we shall be healed.* (Send us the cure, we have the ailment already.) *Bless this year for us, O Lord, our God, with every kind of produce* (corn and wheat and every other grain, and if you do, will I get anything out of it, *shlimazl* that I am? For instance, what difference does it make to my poor horse whether oats are dear or cheap?)."

But that's enough. Of God you don't ask questions. If you're one of the Chosen People you must see the good in everything and say, "This too is for the best." God must have willed it so . . .

"*And for slanderers let there be no hope,*" I chant further. The slanderers and rich scoffers who say there is no God—a fine figure they'll cut when they get *there.* They'll pay for their disbelief, and with interest too, for He is one who "breaketh his enemies and humbleth the arrogant." He pays you according to your deserts. You don't trifle with Him; you approach Him humbly, pray to Him and beg His mercy. "*O Merciful Father, hear our voice, pay heed to our lamentations. Spare us and have mercy upon us* (my wife and children too—they are hungry). *Accept, O Lord, thy people Israel and their prayer, even as you did in the days of the Holy Temple, when the priests and the Levites . . .*"

Suddenly the horse stopped. In a hurry I finish *Shmin-esra,* lift up my eyes, and behold two mysterious creatures coming toward me out of the forest, disguised or at least dressed in the strangest fashion. "Thieves," I thought, but corrected myself at once. "What is the matter with you, Tevye? You've been driving through this forest for so many years by day and by night; why should you suddenly begin to worry about thieves?"

And swinging my whip over my head, I yelled at the horse,
"Giddap!"

"Mister!" one of the two creatures called out to me. "Stop!
Please stop! Don't run away, Mister, we won't do you any
harm!"

"An evil spirit!" I said to myself, and a second later, "You
ox, Tevye, you ass! Why should evil spirits come to you all of a
sudden?" And I stop the horse. I look the creatures over from
head to foot: they are ordinary women. One elderly with a silk
shawl on her head and the other a younger one with a *sheitel.*
Both flushed and out of breath.

"Good evening," I cry out loud, trying to sound cheerful.
"Look who's here! What is it you want? If you want to buy
something, all I have is a gnawing stomach, a heart full of
pain, a head full of worries, and all the misery and wretchedness in the world."

"Listen to him going on," they say. "That's enough. You
say one word to a man and you get a lecture in return. There
is nothing we want to buy. We only want to ask: do you
know where the road to Boiberik is?"

"To Boiberik?" I say, and let out a laugh, still trying to
sound cheerful. "You might as well ask me if I know my
name is Teyve."

"Oh? So that's what they call you—Tevye? Good evening,
then, Mr. Tevye. What is there to laugh at? We are strangers
here. We are from Yehupetz, and we are staying at a *datcha*
in Boiberik. This morning we went out for a short walk in
the woods, and we've been wandering ever since, going round
and round in circles. A little while ago we heard someone
singing in the forest. At first we thought it was a highwayman,
but when we came closer and saw it was only you, we felt
relieved. Now do you understand?"

"Ha-ha!" I laughed. "A fine highwayman! Have you ever
heard the story about the Jewish highwayman who waylaid

a traveler in the forest and demanded—a pinch of snuff? If you'd like, I could tell it to you . . ."

"Leave that for some other time," they said. "Right now, show us how to get back to Boiberik."

"To Boiberik?" I said again. "Why, this is the way to Boiberik. Even if you don't want to, you couldn't help getting there if you followed this path."

"Oh," said they. "Is it far?"

"No, not far. Only a few *versts*. That is, five or six. Maybe seven. But certainly not more than eight."

"Eight *versts*!" they both cried out, wringing their hands and all but bursting into tears. "Do you know what you're saying? Only eight *versts*!"

"What do you want me to do about it?" I asked. "If it were up to me, I'd have made it a little shorter. But people have to have all sorts of experiences. How would you like to be in a carriage crawling up a hill through mud in a heavy rain, late Friday afternoon and almost time to light the candles for the Sabbath? Your hands are numb, you're faint with hunger . . . And crash! The axle breaks!"

"You talk like a half-wit," they said. "You must be out of your head. Why do you tell us these old-wives' tales? We're too tired to take another step. We've had nothing to eat all day except for a glass of coffee and a butter roll in the morning, and you come bothering us with foolish tales."

"Well, that's different," I told them. "You can't expect a person to dance before he's eaten. The taste of hunger is something I understand very well. You don't have to explain it to me. It's quite possible that I haven't even seen a cup of coffee or butter roll for the past year . . ." And as I utter these words a glass of steaming coffee with milk in it appears before my eyes, with rich, fresh butter rolls and other good things besides. "Oh, *shlimazl*," I say to myself, "is that what you've been raised on—coffee and butter rolls? And a plain piece of bread with herring isn't good enough for you?" But there, just to spite me, the image of hot coffee remained; just to tempt me the vision of rolls hovered before my eyes. I smelled the odor of the coffee, I savored the taste of the butter roll on my tongue —fresh and rich and sweet . . .

"Do you know what, Reb Tevye?" the women said to me, "Since we are standing right here, maybe it would be a good idea if we jumped into your wagon and you took us home to Boiberik. What do you say?"

"A fine idea," I said. "Here am I, coming *from* Boiberik, and you're going *to* Boiberik. How can I go both ways at the same time?"

"Well," they said, "don't you know what you can do? A wise and learned man can figure it out for himself. He would turn the wagon around and go back again—that's all. Don't be afraid, Reb Tevye. You can be sure that when you and the Almighty get us back home again, we'll see to it that your kindness won't go unrewarded."

"They're talking Chaldaic," I told myself. "I don't understand them. What do they mean?" And the thought of witches and evil spirits and goblins returned to me. "Dummy, what are you standing there for?" I asked myself. "Jump into the wagon, show the horse your whip, and get away from here!" But again, as if I were under a spell, these words escaped me: "Well, get in."

The women did not wait to be asked again. Into the wagon they climb, with me after them. I turn the wagon around, crack the whip—one, two, three, let's go . . . Who? What? When? The horse doesn't know what I'm talking about. He won't move an inch. "Ah-ha," I think to myself. "Now I can see what these women are. That's all I had to do—stop in the middle of the woods to make conversation with women!" You get the picture: on all sides the woods, silent, melancholy, with night coming on, and here behind me these two creatures in the guise of women. My imagination runs away with me. I recall a story about a teamster who once was riding through the woods by himself when he saw lying on the road a bag of oats. He jumped down, heaved the heavy sack to his back and just managed to tip it into the wagon, and went on. He rode a *verst* or two, looked around at the sack—but there was neither sack nor oats. In the wagon was a goat, a goat with a beard. The teamster tried to touch it with his hand, but the goat stuck out his tongue—a yard long—and let out a wild, piercing laugh and vanished into air . . .

"Well, what's keeping you?" ask the women.

"What's keeping me? Can't you see what's keeping me? The horse doesn't want to play. He is not in the mood."

"Well, you've got a whip, haven't you? Then use it."

"Thanks for the advice," I say. "I'm glad you reminded me. The only trouble with that is that my friend here is not afraid of such things. He is as used to the whip as I am to poverty," I add, trying to be flippant, though all the time I am shaking as if in a fever.

Well, what more can I tell you? I vented all my wrath on the poor animal. I whipped him till with God's help the horse stirred from his place, and we went on our way through the woods. And as we ride along a new thought comes to plague me. "Ah, Tevye, what a dull ox you are! You have always been good for nothing and you'll die good for nothing. Think! Here something happens to you that won't happen again in a hundred years. God Himself must have arranged it. So why didn't you make sure in advance how much it is going to be worth to you—how much you'll get for it? Even if you consider righteousness and virtue, decency and helpfulness, justice and equity and I don't know what else, there is still no harm in earning a little something for yourself out of it. Why not lick a bone for once in your life, since you have the chance? Stop your horse, you ox. Tell them what you want. Either you get so much and so much for the trip, or ask them to be so kind as to jump off the wagon at once! But then, what good would that do? What if they promised you the whole world on a platter? You have to catch a bear before you can skin it . . .

"Why don't you drive a little faster?" the women ask again, prodding me from behind.

"What's your hurry?" I say. "Nothing good can come from rushing too much." And I look around at my passengers. I'll swear they look like women, just plain ordinary women, one with a silk shawl, the other with a *sheitel*. They are looking at each other and whispering. Then one of them asks: "Are we getting closer?"

"Closer, yes. But not any closer than we really are. Pretty soon we'll go uphill and then downhill, then uphill and down-hill again, and then after that we go up the steep hill and from then on it's straight ahead, right to Boiberik."

"Sounds like a *shlimazl*," says one to the other.

"A seven-year itch," the other answers.

"As if we haven't had troubles enough already," says the first.

"A little crazy too, I'm afraid," answers the other.

"I must be crazy," I tell myself, "if I let them pull me around by the nose like that."

And to them I say, "Where do you want to be dropped off, ladies?"

"Dropped off? What do you mean—dropped off? What kind of language is that?"

"It's only an expression. You hear it among coarse and im-polite drovers," I tell them. "Among genteel people like us we'd say it like this: 'Where would you wish to be transported, dear ladies, when with God's help and the blessings of Provi-dence we arrive at Boiberik?' Excuse me if I sound inquisitive, but as the saying goes, 'It's better to ask twice than to go wrong once.' "

"Oh, so that's what you mean?" said the women. "Go straight ahead through the woods until you come to the green *datcha* by the river. Do you know where that is?"

"How could I help knowing?" I say. "I know Boiberik as well as I know my own home. I wish I had a thousand rubles for every log I've carried there. Last summer I brought a couple of loads of wood to that *datcha* you mention. Somebody from Yehupetz was living there then, a rich man, a millionaire. He must have been worth at least a hundred thousand *rubles*."

"He still lives there," they tell me, looking at each other, whispering together and laughing.

"In that case," I said, "if you have some connections with the man, maybe it would be possible, if you wanted to, that is, if you could say a word or two in my behalf . . . Maybe you could get some sort of job for me, work of some kind. I know a man, a young fellow called Yisroel, who lived not far from our village—a worthless good-for-nothing. Well, he went off to the city, no one knows how it happened, and today, believe it or not, he is an important man somewhere. He makes at least twenty *rubles* a week, or maybe even forty. Who knows for sure? Some people are lucky, like our *shochet's* son-in-law. What would he ever have amounted to if he hadn't gone to Yehupetz? It is true, the first few years he starved to death. But now I wouldn't mind being in his boots. Regularly he sends money home, and he would like to bring his wife and children to Yehupetz to live with him, but he can't do it, because by law he isn't allowed to live there himself. Then how does he do it? Never mind. He has trouble aplenty, only if you live long enough . . . Oh, here we are at the river, and there is the green *datcha*!"

And I drive in smartly right up to the porch. You should

have seen the excitement when they saw us. Such cheering and shouting! "Grandmother! Mother! Auntie! They've come home again! Congratulations! *Mazl-tov!* Heavens, where were you? We went crazy all day! Sent messengers in all directions. . . . We thought—who can tell? Maybe wolves, highwaymen—who knows? Tell us, what happened?"

"What happened? What should happen? We got lost in the woods, wandered far away, till a man happened along. What kind of a man? A *shlimazl* with a horse and wagon. It took a little coaxing, but here we are."

"Of all horrible things! It's a dream, a nightmare! Just the two of you—without a guide! Thank God you're safe!"

To make a long story short, they brought lamps out on the porch, spread the table, and began bringing things out. Hot samovars, tea glasses, sugar, preserves, and fresh pastry that I could smell even from where I was standing; after that all kinds of food: rich fat soup, roast beef, goose, the best of wines and salads. I stood at the edge of the porch looking at them from a distance and thinking, "What a wonderful life these people of Yehupetz must live, praise the Lord! I wouldn't mind being one of them myself. What these people drop on the floor would be enough to feed my starving children all week long. O God, All-powerful and All-merciful, great and good, kind and just, how does it happen that to some people you give everything and to others nothing? To some people butter rolls and to others the plague?" But then I tell myself, "You big fool, Tevye! Are you trying to tell Him how to rule His world? Apparently if He wants it that way, that's the way it ought to be. Can't you see? If it should have been different it would have been? And yet, what would have been wrong to have it different? True! We were slaves in Pharaoh's day, too. That's why we are the Chosen People. That's why we must have faith and hope. Faith, first of all in a God, and hope that maybe in time, with His help, things will become a little better . . ."

But then I hear someone say, "Wait! Where is he, this man you've mentioned? Did he drive away already—the *shlimazl*?"

"God forbid!" I call out from the edge of the porch. "What do you think? That I'd go away like this—without saying anything? Good evening! Good evening to you all, and may the Lord bless you. Eat well, and may your food agree with you!"

"Come here!" they said to me. "What are you standing there for in the dark? Let's take a look at you, see what you are like! Maybe you'd like a little whiskey?"

"A little whiskey?" said I. "Who ever refused a drink of whiskey? How does it say in the *Talmud*? 'God is God, but whiskey is something you can drink!' To your health, ladies and gentlemen."

And I turn up the first glass. "May God provide for you," I say. "May He keep you rich and happy. Jews," I say, "must always be Jews. And may God give them the health and the strength to live through all the troubles they're born to . . ."

The *nogid* himself, a fine looking man with a skullcap, interrupts me. "What's your name?" he asks. "Where do you hail from? Where do you live now? What do you do for a living? Do you have any children? How many?"

"Children?" I say. "Do I have children? Oh . . . if it is true that each child were really worth a million, as my Golde insists, then I should be richer than the richest man in Yehupetz. The only thing wrong with this argument is that we still go to bed hungry. What does the Bible say? 'The world belongs to him who has money.' It's the millionaires who have the money; all I have is daughters. And as my grandmother used to say, 'If you have enough girls, the whole world whirls.' But I'm not complaining. God is our Father. He has His own way. He sits on high, and we struggle down below.

What do I struggle with? I haul logs, lumber. What else should I do? The *Talmud* is right, 'If you can't have chicken, herring will do.' That's the whole trouble. We still have to eat. As my old grandmother—may she rest in peace—used to say, 'If we didn't have to eat, we'd all be rich.' "

I realized that my tongue was going sideways. "Excuse me, please," I said. "Beware of the wisdom of a fool and the proverbs of a drunkard."

At this the *nogid* cries out, "Why doesn't somebody bring something to eat?" And at once the table is filled with every kind of food—fish and fowl and roasts, wings and giblets and livers galore.

"Won't you take something?" they say. "Come on!"

"A sick person you ask; a healthy person you give," I say. "Thanks, anyway. A little whiskey—granted. But don't expect me to sit down and eat a meal like this while there, at home, my wife and children . . ."

Well, they caught on to what I was driving at, and you should have seen them start packing things into my wagon. This one brought rolls, that one fish, another one a roast chicken, tea, a package of sugar, a pot of chicken fat, a jar of preserves.

"This," they say, "take home for your wife and children. And now tell us how much you'd want us to pay you for all you did for us."

"How do I know what it was worth?" I answer. "Whatever you think is right. If it's a penny more or a penny less I'll still be the same Tevye either way."

"No," they say. "We want you to tell us yourself, Reb Tevye. Don't be afraid. We won't chop your head off."

I think to myself, "What shall I do? This is bad. What if I say one *ruble* when they might be willing to give two? On the other hand, if I said two they might think I was crazy. What have I done to earn that much?" But my tongue slipped and before I knew what I was saying, I cried out, "Three *rubles!*"

At this the crowd began to laugh so hard that I wished I was dead and buried.

"Excuse me if I said the wrong thing," I stammered. "A horse, which has four feet, stumbles once in a while too, so why shouldn't a man who has but one tongue?"

The merriment increased. They held their sides laughing.

"Stop laughing, all of you!" cried the man of the house, and from his pocket he took a large purse and from the purse pulled out—how much do you think? For instance, guess! A ten-*ruble* note, red as fire! As I live and breathe . . . And he says, "This is from me. And now, the rest of you, dig into your pockets and give what you think you should."

Well, what shall I tell you? Fives and threes and ones began to fly across the table. My arms and legs trembled. I was afraid I was going to faint.

"*Nu,* what are you standing there for?" said my host. "Gather up the few *rubles* and go home to your wife and children."

"May God give you everything you desire ten times over," I babble, sweeping up the money with both hands and stuffing it into my pockets. "May you have all that is good, may you have nothing but joy. And now," I said, "good night, and good luck, and God be with you. With you and your children and grandchildren and all your relatives."

But when I turn to go back to the wagon, the mistress of the house, the woman with the silk shawl, calls to me, "Wait a minute, Reb Tevye. I want to give you something, too. Come back tomorrow morning, if all is well. I have a cow— a milch cow. It was once a wonderful cow, used to give twenty-four glasses of milk a day. But some jealous person must have cast an evil eye on it: you can't milk it any more. That is, you can milk it all right, but nothing comes."

"Long may you live!" I answer. "Don't worry. If you give us the cow we'll not only milk it—we'll get milk too! My wife, Lord bless her, is so resourceful that she makes noodles out of almost nothing, adds water and we have noodle soup. Every week she performs a miracle: we have food for the Sabbath! She has brought up seven children, though often she has nothing to give them for supper but a box on the ear! . . . Excuse me, please, if I've talked too much. Good night and good luck and God be with you," I say, and turn around to leave. I come out in the yard, reach for my horse—and stop dead! I look everywhere. Not a trace of a horse!

"Well, Tevye," I say to myself. "This time they really got you!"

And I recall a story I must have read somewhere, about a gang of thieves that once kidnapped a pious and holy man, lured him into a palace behind the town, dined him and wined him, and then suddenly vanished, leaving him all alone with a beautiful woman. But while he looked the woman changed into a tigress, and the tigress into a cat, the cat into an adder.

"Watch out, Tevye," I say to myself. "No telling what they'll do next!"

"What are you mumbling and grumbling about now?" they ask.

"What am I grumbling about? Woe is me! I'm ruined! My poor little horse!"

"Your horse," they tell me, "is in the stable."

I come into the stable, look around. As true as I'm alive, there's my bony little old nag right next to their aristocratic horses, deeply absorbed in feeding. His jaws work feverishly, as if this is the last meal he'll ever have.

"Look here, my friend," I say to him. "It's time to move

along. It isn't wise to make a hog of yourself. An extra mouthful, and you may be sorry."

I finally persuaded him, coaxed him back to his harness, and in good spirits we started for home, singing one hymn after another. As for the old horse—you would never have known him! I didn't even have to whip him. He raced like the wind. We came home late, but I woke up my wife with a shout of joy.

"Good evening!" said I. "Congratulations! *Mazl-tov, Golde!*"

"A black and endless *mazl-tov* to you!" she answers me. "What are you so happy about, my beloved bread-winner? Are you coming from a wedding or a *bris*—a circumcision feast—my goldspinner?"

"A wedding and a *bris* rolled into one," I say. "Just wait, my wife, and you'll see the treasure I've brought you! But first wake up the children. Let them have a taste of the Yehupetz delicacies, too!"

"Are you crazy?" she asks. "Are you insane, or out of your head, or just delirious? You sound unbalanced—violent!" And she lets me have it—all the curses she knows—as only a woman can.

"Once a wife always a wife," I tell her. "No wonder King Solomon said that among his thousand wives there wasn't one that amounted to anything. It's lucky that it isn't the custom to have a lot of wives any more!"

And I go out to the wagon and come back with my arms full of all the good things that they had given me. I put it all on the table, and when my crew saw the fresh white rolls and smelled the meat and fish they fell on it like hungry wolves. You should have seen them grab and stuff and chew—like the Children of Israel in the desert. The Bible says, "And they did eat," and I could say it, too. Tears came to my eyes.

"Well," says my helpmate, "tell me—who has decided to feed

the countryside? What makes you so gay? Who gave you the drinks?"

"Wait, my love," I say to her. "I'll tell you everything. But first heat up the samovar. Then we'll all sit around the table, as people should now and then, and have a little tea. We live but once, my dear. Let's celebrate. We are independent now. We have a cow that used to be good for twenty-four glasses a day. Tomorrow morning, if the Lord permits, I'll bring her home. And look at this, my Golde! Look at this!" And I pull out the green and red and yellow banknotes from my pockets. "Come, my Golde, show us how smart you are! Tell me how much there is here!"

I look across at my wife. She's dumbfounded. She can't say a word.

"God protect you, my darling!" I say to her. "What are you scared of? Do you think I stole it? I am ashamed of you, Golde! You've been Tevye's wife so many years and you think that of me! Silly, this is *kosher* money, earned honestly with my own wit and my own labor. I rescued two women from a great misfortune. If it were not for me, I don't know what would have become of them."

So I told her everything, from *a* to *z*. The whole story of my wanderings. And we counted the money over and over. There were eighteen *rubles*—for good luck, you know—and another eighteen for more good luck, and one besides. In all—thirty-seven *rubles*!

My wife began to cry.

"What are you crying for, you foolish woman?" I ask.

"How can I help crying when my tears won't stop? When your heart is full your eyes run over. May God help me, Tevye, my heart told me that you would come with good news. I can't remember when I last saw my Grandmother Tzeitl—

may she rest in peace—in a dream. But just before you came home I was asleep and suddenly I dreamed I saw a milkpail full to the brim. My Grandmother Tzeitl was carrying it under her apron to shield it from an evil eye, and the children were crying, 'Mama . . .' "

"Don't eat up all the noodles before the Sabbath!" I interrupt. "May your Grandmother Tzeitl be happy in Paradise— I don't know how much she can help us right now. Let's leave that to God. He saw to it that we should have a cow of our own, so no doubt He can also make her give milk. Better give me some advice, Golde. Tell me—what shall we do with the money?"

"That's right, Tevye," says she. "What do you plan to do with so much money?"

"Well, what do you think we can do with it?" I say. "Where shall we invest it?"

And we began to think of this and that, one thing after another. We racked our brains, thought of every kind of enterprise on earth. That night we were engaged in every type of business you could imagine. We bought a pair of horses and sold them at a profit; opened a grocery store in Boiberik, sold the stock and went into the drygoods business. We bought an option on some woodland and made something on that, too, then obtained the tax concession at Anatevka, and with our earnings began to loan out money on mortgages.

"Be careful! Don't be so reckless!" my wife warned me. "You'll throw it all away. Before you know it, you'll have nothing left but your whip!"

"What do you want me to do?" I ask. "Deal in grain and lose it all? Look what's happening right now in the wheat market. Go! See what's going on in Odessa!"

"What do I care about Odessa? My great-grandfather was

never there, and so long as I'm alive and have my senses, my children will never be there, either!"

"Then what *do* you want?"

"What do I want? I want you to have some brains and not act like a fool."

"So you're the brainy one! You get a few *rubles* in your hand and suddenly you're wise. That's what always happens."

Well, we disagreed a few times, fell out, had some arguments, but in the end this is what we decided: to buy another cow— in addition to the one we were getting for nothing. A cow that would really give milk.

Maybe you'll say, "Why a cow?" And I'll answer, "Why not a cow?" Here we are, so close to Boiberik, where all the rich people of Yehupetz come to spend the summer at their *datchas*. They're so refined that they expect everything to be brought to them on a platter—meat and eggs, chickens, onions, pepper, parsnips—everything. Why shouldn't there be someone who would be willing to come right to their kitchen door every morning with cheese and butter and cream? Especially since the Yehupetzers believe in eating well and are ready to pay?

The main thing is that what you bring must be good—the cream must be thick, the butter golden. And where will you find cream and butter that's better than mine?

So we make a living . . . May the two of us be blessed by the Lord as often as I am stopped on the road by important people from Yehupetz—even Russians—who beg me to bring them what I can spare. "We have heard, Tevel, that you are an upright man, even if you are a Jewish dog . . ." Now, how often does a person get a compliment like that? Do our own people ever praise a man? No! All they do is envy him.

When they saw that Tevye had an extra cow, a new wagon, they began to rack their brains. "Where did he get it? How did he get it? Maybe he's a counterfeiter. Maybe he cooks alcohol in secret."

I let them worry. "Scratch your heads and rack your brains, my friends! Break your heads if you begrudge me my small living."

I don't know if you'll believe my story. You're almost the first person I've ever told it to.

But I'm afraid I've said too much already. If so, forgive me! I forgot that we all have work to do. As the Bible says, "Let the shoemaker stick to his last." You to your books, Mr. Sholom Aleichem, and I to my pots and jugs . . .

One thing I beg of you. Don't put me into one of your books, and if you do put me in, at least don't tell them my real name.

Be well and happy always.

A Page from the Song of Songs

BUZIE is a name. It is a diminutive of Esther-Libbe. First Esther-Libbe, then Libuzie, then Buzie. She is a year older than I, or maybe two years, and together we are not quite twenty years old. Now, I ask you, how old am I and how old is she? But that is not important. Instead let me give you a short sketch of her life.

My older brother Benny lived in a village, where he owned a mill. He was a wonder at shooting, riding and swimming. One summer day while bathing in the river, he drowned. Thus the old adage that the best swimmers drown was borne out. He left the mill, two horses, a young widow and a child. The mill was abandoned, the horses were sold, the widow remarried and moved to some distant place, and the child was brought to us.

That child was Buzie.

That my father should love Buzie as his own is easy to understand, and that my mother should watch over her like an only daughter is natural. In her they found a comfort for their great sorrow. But that has nothing to do with me. Then why is it that when I come from *cheder* and find Buzie not at home my food is flat and tasteless? And why is it that when Buzie comes in the darkest corners are suddenly lit up? And why is it that when Buzie speaks to me I drop my eyes? And when Buzie laughs at me I weep?

And when Buzie . . .

All through the winter I had been looking forward to the Passover holidays. Then I would be free from *cheder,* free to play with Buzie, free to run outdoors with her. We would run down the hill to the river's edge, where I could show her how the ducklings learn to swim. When I try to tell her about it she only laughs at me. Buzie doesn't believe a thing I tell her. She doesn't believe that I can climb to the top of the highest tree—if I only wanted to. She doesn't believe that I can shoot—if I only had a gun to shoot with. She never says she doesn't believe, she only laughs at me. And I hate nothing more than to be laughed at. But when Passover comes, the beautiful, free days of Passover, when we can run outdoors away from the watchful eyes of my parents, then I will show her such wonders that they will take her breath away.

The wonderful time, the most joyous time of the year, has come.

Buzie and I are dressed in our holiday clothes. Everything we have on twinkles and shines and crackles. I look at Buzie and I am reminded of the *Song of Songs* which I studied before Passover with my rabbi. Verse after verse, it comes back to me:

"Behold, thou art fair, my beloved, thou art fair; thy eyes are as doves, thy hair is a flock of goats that comes down from Mount Gilead.

"Thy teeth are like a flock of white lambs that come up from the river, all are alike; the same mother bore them.

"Thy lips are like a thread of scarlet; thy speech is full of sweetness."

Why is it that when you look at Buzie you are reminded of the *Song of Songs?* Why is it that when you study the *Song of Songs* Buzie comes into your thoughts?

We are ready to go. I can hardly stand still. My pockets are full of nuts. My mother gave us all we wanted. She filled our pockets and told us we could play with them to our hearts' content. But she made us promise not to crack any before Passover.

"Are you ready?" says Buzie.

I jump for the door. Away we go. The nuts make a drumming sound, they rattle as we run. At first we are dazzled by the brilliance outside. The sun is high up already; it is looking down on the other side of town. The air is free and fresh, soft and clear. Here and there on the hill beyond the synagogue there sprouts the first grass of spring, tender, quivering, green . . . With a scream and a flutter of wings a straight line of swallows flies over our heads and again I am reminded of the *Song of Songs:* "The flowers appear on the earth; the time of the song of birds has come and the voice of the turtle is heard in our land."

I feel strangely light. It seems to me that I have wings. Any minute now I will rise into the air and fly.

From the town strange sounds arise—a roaring, a boiling, a seething. It is the day before Passover, a rare and wonderful day. In one instant the world is transformed. Our yard is a king's court. Our house is a palace. I am a prince and Buzie is a princess. The logs of wood piled about our door are the cedars and cypresses that are mentioned in the *Song of Songs.* The cat that lies near the door warming herself in the sun is a roe or a young hart that is mentioned in the *Song of Songs.* The women and the girls who are working outdoors, washing and cleaning and getting ready for the Passover are the daughters of Jerusalem mentioned in the *Song of Songs.* Everything, everything is from the *Song of Songs.*

I walk about with my hands in my pockets and the nuts rattle. Buzie follows me step by step. I cannot walk slowly, I am treading on air. I want to fly, to swoop, to soar, like an eagle. I start running and Buzie runs after me. I leap onto the pile of logs and jump from one log to another. Buzie jumps atter me. I jump up, she jumps up; I jump down, she jumps down. Who will get tired first? I guessed it.

"How-long-will-you-keep-it-up?" asks Buzie all out of breath.

And I answer her in the words of the *Song of Songs:*

" 'Till the morning breeze come and the shadows flee away.' There! You are tired and I am not!"

I feel proud that Buzie cannot keep up with me. I gloat over her and at the same time I am sorry for her. My heart aches for her, because I imagine she is unhappy. That is Buzie—full of gaiety one moment, and the next she is hiding in a corner, quietly weeping. At times like these nothing helps. No matter how much my mother tries to comfort her, how much my father caresses her, she continues to cry. For whom does she cry? For her father who died when she was a baby? For her mother who married and went off without as much as a goodbye? Ah, that mother of hers. When you mention her mother her face turns fiery red, as though she were ashamed of her. She never says an unkind word about her, but she looks unhappy. I cannot bear to see Buzie looking so wretched. I sit near her on the logs and try to distract her thoughts.

Rolling a few nuts about, I start:

"Guess what I could do if I wanted to."

"What could you do?"

"If I wanted to, all your nuts would be mine."

"Would you win them away from me?"

"No. We wouldn't even start playing."

"Well then, would you take them away from me?"

"No. They would come to me by themselves."

She raises her eyes to me, her blue eyes, eyes straight out of the *Song of Songs*. I say, "You think I am joking. Well, I know a certain language, I know some magic words . . ."

She opens her eyes wider. I explain, feeling grown and important, all puffed up with pride. "We boys know a lot of things. There is a boy in *cheder*, Shaike, who is blind in one eye—he knows everything. He even knows *Kabala*. Do you know what *Kabala* is?"

"No. How should I know?"

I am suddenly lifted to the seventh heaven because I can give her a lesson in *Kabala*.

"*Kabala*, silly, is a useful thing. By means of *Kabala* I can make myself invisible. With *Kabala* I can draw wine from a stone and gold from a wall. With the help of *Kabala* you and I, just as we are sitting here, could rise to the clouds and above the clouds . . ."

To fly up to the clouds with Buzie and above the clouds, and fly away with her, far, far off over the ocean—that has been one of my fondest dreams. There, beyond the ocean, begins the land of the dwarfs who are descended from King David's time. These dwarfs are kindly little people who live on sweets and almond milk, play all day long on little flutes and dance in a ring, are afraid of nothing and are kind to strangers. When someone arrives from our world they give him food and drink and shower him with costly garments and gold and silver ornaments and before he leaves they fill his pockets with diamonds and jewels which lie about in their streets as trash does in ours.

"Really? Like trash in the streets?" asked Buzie, wonderingly, when I once told her about the dwarfs.

"Don't you believe it?"

"Do you?"

"Why shouldn't I?"

"Where did you hear about it?"

"In *cheder*, of course."

"Oh, in *cheder*!"

Lower and lower sinks the sun, painting the sky a fiery gold.

. . . The gold is reflected in Buzie's eyes. They swim in molten gold.

I want very badly to impress Buzie with Shaike's ability and with the wonders I can perform by means of *Kabala*. But Buzie won't be impressed. Instead she laughs at me. She looks at me with her mouth half-open and all her pearly teeth showing, and laughs.

Annoyed, I ask, "Don't you believe me?"

Buzie laughs again.

"You think I am boasting. That I am making up lies."

Buzie laughs harder. I have to repay her for this. I know how, too.

"The trouble with you is that you don't know what *Kabala* is. If you knew, you wouldn't laugh. By means of *Kabala,* if I wanted to, I could bring your mother down here. Yes, I can. And if you begged me very hard I could bring her tonight, riding on a broomstick."

At once she stops laughing. A cloud crosses her lovely, bright face and it seems to me that the sun has suddenly disappeared and the day is done. I have gone too far. I have wounded her tenderest feelings. I am sorry I had ever started this. How can I make up to her now? I move closer to her. She turns away from me. I want to take her hand and speak to her with the words of the *Song of Songs:* "Return, return O Shulamite, turn back to me, Buzie . . ."

Suddenly a voice calls out, "Shimek, Shimek!"

Shimek—that's me. My mother is calling me, to go to the synagogue with my father.

To go with Father to the synagogue on the Eve of Passover is one of the pleasures of life. Just to be dressed in perfectly new clothes from head to foot and to show off before one's friends. And the services—the first evening prayer, the first benediction

of the holiday season! What delights the Lord has provided
for his Jewish children.

"Shimek! Shimek!"

My mother is in a hurry. "I am coming! I am coming right
away, I just have to tell Buzie something, just one little thing!"

I tell her just one thing. That what I told her was not true.
To make other people fly by means of *Kabala* is impossible.
But I myself—I can fly, and I will show her right after the
holidays. I will make my first attempt then. I will rise up
here from these very logs where we are now sitting, and in
one moment I will be above the clouds. From there I will turn
to the right—there, see—there where everything ends and the
Frozen Sea begins . . .

Buzie listens, absorbed in my story. The sun, about to sink,
sends its last rays to kiss the earth.

"What," asks Buzie, "do you mean by the Frozen Sea?"

"Don't you know what the Frozen Sea is? That's far in the
north. The water is as thick as jelly and as salty as brine. Ships
cannot go there, and people who are caught in it never return."

Buzie looks at me wide-eyed. "Then why are you going
there?"

"Am I going to touch the sea, you silly thing? I'll fly high up
over it, like an eagle, and in a few minutes I shall be on dry
land. That is where the twelve high mountains begin that
belch fire and smoke. I shall stop on the tip of the twelfth
mountain and walk from there for seven miles till I come to
a thick forest. I will cross several forests till I come to a small
lake. I shall swim across the lake and count seven times seven.
Out of the ground will spring a dwarf with a long white beard.
He will say to me, 'What is your wish?'

"And I will say to him: 'Lead me to the Queen's daughter!'"

"Which Queen's daughter?" asks Buzie, startled.

"The Queen's daughter," I explain, "is the beautiful princess who was snatched away from under the wedding canopy, bewitched, and carried far, far away and locked up in a crystal palace for seven years . . ."

"What is she to you?"

"What do you mean—what is she to me? I have to set her free, don't I?"

"You have to set her free?"

"Who, then?"

"You don't have to fly so far, believe me. You don't have to fly so far," says Buzie, and takes my hand. Her small, white hand is cold. I look into her eyes and see in them the last faint reflection of the gold that is draining from the sky.

Slowly the day is going, the first beautiful day of spring is passing away. Like a spent candle the sun goes down. The noises that we heard all day are dying too. There is hardly a person to be seen in the street. From the windows of the houses there wink the flames of candles lit for Passover Eve. A strange, a holy stillness surrounds us, and Buzie and I feel ourselves slowly merging with this stillness.

"Shimek! Shimek!"

This is the third time my mother has called me. As if I didn't know myself that I had to go to the synagogue! I'll stay only another minute, not more than a minute. But Buzie hears her too, pulls her hand out of mine, jumps to her feet and begins to push me.

"Shimek, your mother is calling you. You'd better go. It's late. Go."

I am getting ready to go. The day is done, the sun has been snuffed out. All the gold has turned to blood. A cool breeze has sprung up. Buzie keeps pushing me toward the house. I throw a last quick look at her. Her face has changed and it has a different, an unearthly beauty in the twilight. The thought of the bewitched princess flits through my head. But Buzie won't allow those thoughts. She keeps pushing me ahead. I start slowly to go and I look back just once at the bewitched princess who has now completely merged with the weird Passover twilight, and I stand rooted in one spot. But she waves her hand at me, bidding me to go, to go quickly. And it seems to me that I hear her speaking in the words of the *Song of Songs:*

"Make haste, my beloved, be thou like a gazelle or a young hart upon the mountain of spices."

Two Dead Men

(A Tale for *Purim*)

YOU may think this is a strange title for a *Purim* tale; *Purim*—when it is fitting and proper for a Jew to act the drunkard and a storyteller to play the fool! Reader, I know that today is *Purim* and you are supposed to act the drunkard and I the fool; and nevertheless I'll give you a story about two dead men. That's final. All I can do for you is give you this advice: if your nerves are weak, don't read this tale before going to sleep.

I

Chlavne, a short, dark, heavy-set man, had always loved a drink. Fortunately he was brought up in a decent and temperate home, or he would surely have grown up a drunkard. I do not guarantee that it was only his upbringing that saved him from a drunkard's fate. It is possible that in spite of that he might have been able to outdrink a squad of cannoneers, if only he had the means. But his wife Gittel managed all his finances and did not let him have a *groschen* to spend. Wherever money was involved Gittel took care of it. The work itself, the labor that earned their bread, was done by Chlavne (he was, alas, a shoemaker), but when the work was finished it was Gittel who delivered it and collected the money. And

51

naturally Chlavne was not pleased with this state of affairs. "What do you think I am? A thief—or what?"

That is what Chlavne said to his wife Gittel, and he received a clear, unequivocal answer on the spot.

"Heaven forbid! Who said you were a thief? All you are is a soak. Do you dare tell me you aren't?"

To deny it outright was not easy. And yet to go ahead and confess that he loved to take the bitter drop was not so agreeable either. So he took refuge in a pun, as he frequently did, because Chlavne the shoemaker was fond not only of a glass of brandy, but also of a quip, a pun, a pithy saying, for he was a true Kasrilevkite. So he scratched his beard, looked up at the ceiling, and said:

"Listen to the woman! All she can say is soak. Soak! If I have a bottle in my hand, do I ever soak anybody with it? All I do is drink it."

"Oh, go to the devil!" his wife sputtered.

"Together with you, beloved, I'd go through the fires of hell."

"Here, go with this!" cried Gittel, and from the other side of the room she heaved a boot at him. This, too, Chlavne caught with a laugh, and he replied with a quip, as always.

And what did he do when Gittel came home with some money, and handed him a few *groschen* to go buy thread and wax and brushes? He became soft as butter and sweet as honey. And his respect for women in general and Gittel in particular rose immediately. He stroked his high, white forehead (all shoemakers have high, white foreheads) and mused thoughtfully, philosophically:

"I can't understand what a wise man like King Solomon had against you women. Do you know what King Solomon said about women? Or don't you?"

"Who cares what King Solomon said? You go to the market

for thread and wax and brushes. And see that you don't lose your way in some tavern."

At this far-fetched idea, Chlavne burst out laughing.

"Next you'll be telling me not to wear my heavy mittens in July, or eat *matzo* on *Yom Kippur*! Which way is the market place and which way are the taverns? And besides, who would think, in the middle of the week, on a working day, of going off for a drink?"

But even while he was talking he was counting the money Gittel had given him by transferring it, coin by coin, from one hand to the other, and looking philosophically up at the ceiling with one eye closed, was figuring out exactly how much he would need for thread, how much for wax, and how much for brushes. And with a deep, deep sigh he quietly went out of the house, and straight to the tavern.

II

Who was that wise man, that sage, who after deep thought announced that on *Purim* all drunkards are sober? I doubt if he knew what he was talking about. Why should a drunkard miss his chance on a day when it is fitting and proper for everybody to get drunk as a lord? The first to protest against a notion like that would have been Chlavne the shoemaker. How eagerly he awaited that one day! What agony he suffered before it came! And when it finally arrived he went to the synagogue with everybody else, to settle his account with Haman and hang him up on a gallows fifty ells high together with his ten sons. And afterwards, instead of going home to taste the festive *hamantash* he stopped off for a while at the homes of one or two of his shoemaker friends, old comrades of the bottle, for a holiday toast. "May the good Lord spare

Haman and his ten sons for another year so we can get together next *Purim* and hang them again on a fifty-ell gallows and take another drink in their honor. Amen."

And after this series of toasts our hero became so foggy that no matter how far he went, no matter how many corners he turned, he was unable to find his way home. It began to look as if the street in which he lived had decided to play hide-and-go-seek with him. There it was in front of him, winking to him with all the flickering candles in all the small windows, and when he took another step he found himself bumping his forehead into a wall. Where did the wall come from? As long as he could remember, there had never been a wall here in the middle of the street. Someone must have put up a woodshed here. Imagine the impudence—building woodsheds right in the middle of the street! Who would dare do a thing like that? It must have been Yossi the *nogid's* doings. But he'd never get away with it!

"As sure as my name is Ahasuerus, King of Persia!" cried Chlavne, and he reached up both hands to tear down the wall that Yossi the *nogid* had dared to build right in the middle of the street. But just then the wall moved away, Chlavne lost his balance, and stretched himself out like a baron, full length in the famous Kasrilevka mud.

And there let us leave him for a while, till we have introduced you to the second hero of our tale, a man who was known in our town by the glorious and opulent name of—Rothschild.

III

He was given the name of Rothschild in Kasrilevka obviously because he was the poorest man in town. Though poor people were as numerous in Kasrilevka as the stars in heaven, a pauper as completely wretched and miserable as he could not be duplicated even there. There is a proverb (it must have originated in Kasrilevka) that it takes a special kind of luck to be that unlucky. And as you know, every proverb is founded on truth.

Who this man Rothschild was and where he came from I cannot tell you. He was a pauper—that much you know already. And his occupation was—walking. And I don't mean walking from house to house, asking for alms. His walking was aimless. All day long he walked through the deep mud, with short, quick strides like a very busy man in a great hurry. He paused only when somebody stopped him.

"Greetings. And where are you going, Mr. Rothschild?"

Rothschild stopped, wiped the sweat off his forehead with his sleeve, looked with strangely frightened eyes at the person who spoke to him and his thin, yellow, hungry face wrinkled up into a sort of smile, as he answered so softly that he could barely be heard:

"Nowhere. I keep going . . . Maybe the good Lord will send something my way."

And having explained all this, he resumed his march with short, rapid strides. And the person who had stopped him remained standing a while looking after him, then shrugged his shoulders, spit into the mud, and laughed.

"There is a *shlimazl* for you!"

As long as this poor man had been known as Rothschild no one in Kasrilevka had ever seen him approach anyone with a plea for food, a request for drink or lodging, although every one knew very well that he was always hungry and had no place to lay his head. In Kasrilevka, there are experienced authorities on the subject of hunger, one might even say specialists. On the darkest night, simply by hearing your voice, they can tell if you are simply hungry and would like a bite to eat, or if you are really starving. No doubt they have their symptoms to judge by, like doctors who prod you here and there and can tell if you are slightly indisposed or if you are on the verge of giving up your ghost.

If we are to distinguish between the various degrees of hunger, between those who are simply hungry and those who are dead hungry, we must say without hesitation that our hero Rothschild was in the rank of the dead hungry. He was a man who frequently went along for days on end with nothing at all in his mouth. And more than once he would surely have passed out right on the broad highway if some kind soul had not of his own accord noticed that here was that unfortunate wretch, Rothschild. If you gave him something he did not refuse it, but if you asked him if he was hungry he never answered. And if you asked if he was very hungry he still did not answer, but his yellow, emaciated face wrinkled up into something like a smile and his frightened eyes looked down, apparently ashamed that a person could ever be as hungry as he was, and a weak little sigh stole out unwillingly. And who knows what that sigh meant?

The Kasrilevkites, who loved a jest, gave him something to eat first, but afterwards could not refrain from teasing him.

"Mr. Rothschild, tell us the truth. How many millions do you have and where do you hide them all?"

Rothschild lowered his frightened eyes, wrinkled his starved, waxen features, smiled weakly and said nothing.

And younger wags, who had no respect for anyone, came close to him, pulled at his sleeve.

"Well, well! The great *M'sieu* Rothschild himself! And how are things on the Paris Bourse?"

Again Rothschild lowered his eyes. What was there to say?

Even the youngest of the lot, little school children, not much more than toddlers, did not let him pass. They made up a song about him:

Rothschild is a gentleman
Rolling in riches.
There's nothing he lacks
But a pair of britches.

He was especially afraid of these little children and he ran
away from them with his short quick strides. The children ran
after him, they would not stop singing. And hearing them,
their parents shouted:

"Go away, you scamps, you scoundrels! Go back to *cheder*!
Go back to school, you tramps!"

It is possible that there would have been plenty of people
in Kasrilevka to look after him and he would not have had
to hunger at all. But who is to blame if this penniless wretch
would rather die than hold out his hand for help? And besides,
is Kasrilevka expected to support every pauper who comes her
way? Do not the people have troubles and heartaches and
anxieties enough of their own in their struggle for a livelihood?
They thank the Lord that they are able to survive the day and
live through the week with their wives and children.

And yet—let the truth be known—when the Holy Sabbath
came around, Rothschild was provided for. All Kasrilevka
was in the synagogue that day, and Rothschild was in front
of their eyes. And seeing him there, would the people let him
go hungry—on the Sabbath? After all, an extra person at the
table means only that you lay another spoon. So one family
or another would take him home. And if the feast was not so
rich it was no tragedy. His stomach was tolerant. At least he
sat at a table with other Jews. In front of them were a few
slices of Sabbath bread, some fish bones and the brass candlesticks from the night before. All these things, taken together
with the singing and chanting after the meal, had such an

attraction for him that he was ready to forget all the fine dishes, the appetizers and the desserts that human fancy has invented in order to lure us and lead us more deeply into Gehenna.

Great is the power of the Holy Sabbath! On that day you would scarcely recognize the householder of Kasrilevka, or his guest, the derelict Rothschild.

IV

Having fasted the whole day according to custom, the good householders of Kasrilevka finally saw the sun sinking and hastened to the synagogue to celebrate the *Purim* services, to chant the *Book of Esther* and take revenge on Haman. And having hurried through the final prayers standing on one foot, the hungry Kasrilevkites rushed out in a body the quicker to come home and the quicker to break the fast, each one under his own grapevine and his own fig tree, with a fresh, warm *hamantash* full of poppyseed. And in their great haste and desire to partake of food they completely forgot about Rothschild, as if there had never been a Rothschild in the whole world. And Rothschild, seeing that everyone was hurrying, hurried off too, with his short strides, over the muddy roads and alleys of the blessed Kasrilevka, without knowing where he was going.

Running past the half-fallen and dimly lighted shacks and cottages, from time to time our hungry hero stole a glance through a window and saw cheeks and jaws and necks, chewing and grinding and swallowing. What the bulging cheeks enclosed, what the jaws were grinding and the necks were swallowing, he could not see, but he felt fairly certain that it must be those sweet and fresh and wonderful triangular *hamantashen,* stuffed with honeyed poppyseed that melted in your mouth and tasted like something in Eden. And something woke inside of Rothschild and pulled at his heart and said to him, "Fool, why do you wander around in the darkness? Open one of those doors, go into the house and say, 'Good evening and a happy *Purim*. Do you have something that a person can break his fast with? It is the third day now since I have eaten anything.'" And Rothschild became frightened by his boldness. Such a thought had never come to him before—to force his way into a stranger's house like a thief! And lest his Evil Spirit take hold of him again he turned from the houses directly into the middle of the road where the mud was deepest, and in the darkness collided with something soft and broad and alive, and before he could regain his balance fell headlong over our hero number one—Chlavne the shoemaker.

Let us leave our Rothschild alone for a while and find out how Chlavne the shoemaker was doing.

V

Chlavne the shoemaker (we beg his pardon a hundred times for letting him lie in the mud so long) did not feel nearly as wretched in his new surroundings as the reader would imagine. It is an old-established trait of man to adapt himself to his surroundings, no matter how unfavorable they might be. As soon as he found that before resuming his journey he was destined to pause a while in this bed of mud, the famous Kasrilevka mud, he saw to it that he did it like a man, productively, and not idly and wastefully. Without rest and without pause he proceeded to pour his wrath out on the wealthy of the earth, and especially on Yossi the *nogid*. Did Yossi think that he, Chlavne, was drunk? He swore on his honor that he was not. Who could have started that rumor that he, Chlavne, was a drunkard? It must have been that wife of his, Vashti.

And having said the name Vashti, Chlavne the shoemaker became silent and thoughtful. This name—Vashti—came back to his mind again and again like nails being hammered into a shoe. He remembered quite clearly that his wife's name used to be Gittel—and now suddenly it was Vashti! How did that happen? Gittel—Vashti? And it was not only her name. Everything else about her was changed, too. She was dressed like a queen with a golden crown, and everything she wore from head to foot was gold. He decided that this was not the time to start a fight with her. With a beauty like that you made your peace. And he pulled himself through the mud, closer and closer to her; but she drew away. She spurned him. Apparently because of his other passion, drink. The devil take her! She was too proud to have people think that her husband was a drunkard!

"May I never live to get up from this spot if I ever let another drop of brandy touch my lips!" he swore. "Do you hear, Vashti? If you don't believe me, here is my hand. I prommise . . ."

And Chlavne stretched out his thick, blackened hand with its stubby black fingers in the mud—and he was surprised to find that Vashti's hand was wet and cold and Vashti's fingers were damp and slippery. It was impossible to put one's arms around a woman like that. And once more he held out his arms, and embraced—the bony, shivering body of the unhappy Rothschild.

VI

Philosophers tell you that many things can happen as a result of a shock. A woman can have a miscarriage because of a sudden fright. If the shock is great enough a person can go

out of his mind, and in some cases—Heaven forbid!—it has
even been suggested that it was possible for a drunkard to become suddenly sober. So say the philosophers. And therefore
we should not be too much surprised to learn that as soon as
our hero, Chlavne the shoemaker, had embraced the unfortunate Rothschild, he too became sober. That is, not entirely sober,
not sober enough to pick himself out of the mud and stand
like a man, but enough to make him regain his senses one by
one. First of all, through his sense of touch, he became aware
that Vashti was a man with a beard. Then, with the return
of his sense of hearing, he made out these words distinctly:
"*Shma Yisroel!* Help! Help! Save me!" Through his sense
of sight he became aware that the two of them were lying in
the mud, in the thick, suffocating Kasrilevka mud. But try
as he might, he could not distinguish the person who was in
his arms, for just then the moon had hidden behind a thick
cloud and the dark night had spread its sable wings over all
of Kasrilevka.

Rothschild too began slowly to collect his thoughts. His
deathly fear gradually disappeared, and together our heroes
recovered their speech. And what they said shall now be repeated, word for word:

Chlavne: Who are you?

Rothschild: It's me.

Chlavne: What are you doing here?

Rothschild: Not a thing.

Chlavne: How the devil did you get here?

Rothschild: I don't know.

Chlavne: Don't you know anything at all? What are you?
One of us? A shoemaker?

Rothschild: No.

Chlavne: What then? A businessman?

Rothschild: Oh, no! No!

Chlavne: Then what on earth are you? Do you know? What *are* you?

Rothschild: I'm . . . I'm . . . dead . . . hungry . . .

Chlavne: So that's the story! You're dead hungry, and I'm dead drunk. But wait! If I'm not mistaken, aren't you Mr. Rothschild? Of course. I knew you at once. If that's the case, Brother Rothschild, maybe it would be a good idea if you helped me crawl out of this mud, and then if you are strong enough the two of us can go to my house and have a bite to eat. Something tells me that there is some sort of holiday being celebrated today. *Simchas-Torah? Purim?* I'm not sure which, but I know it's a holiday. If all the kings of the east and west insisted that it wasn't, I'd . . . I'd spit in their faces!

It took a little while before the two of them managed to drag themselves out of the mud, and with great effort they started on their way, each one holding on to the other. That is, Rothschild was doing his best to keep Chlavne upright, because so far only the shoemaker's head had sobered up. His feet still went this way and that. And when they came to . . .

But at this point let us leave both of our heroes, and let us glance for a moment into the home of Chlavne the shoemaker, to see how his wife Gittel was getting along.

VII

No matter how much she may be criticized by cynics, no matter how much the humorists may joke about her, a wife is still a wife. As soon as it was dark, Gittel began to get things ready for her husband who ought to be coming home soon from the synagogue after his long day of fasting. In his behalf she spread a festive tablecloth and brought out those things that Chlavne loved so well—a bottle and a glass. It is possible that the bottle held no more than a single glassful, or perhaps in recognition of the holiday enough for two glasses. On the other hand, the *hamantash* which she placed on the table was a huge one. It was a giant of a *hamantash*, rich and golden, with honeyed poppyseed oozing out of its three corners. It cried aloud to be eaten. You could almost hear it plead: "Chlavne, where are you? Chlavne, come eat me!" But Chlavne did not hear. At that moment he was sitting with the other shoemakers pouring long drinks in honor of the holy *Purim*.

In vain did the shoemaker's wife look out of the window, in vain did she listen for a sound at the door. Every step she heard outside sounded like Chlavne's. But Chlavne was not walking just then. Chlavne was stretched out in the deep mud, whispering to Vashti. Gittel thought all the thoughts that a wife could ever think about her husband, but when it became really late she tore her jacket off its hook, threw it over her shoulders, and went out to search for Chlavne. She did not find him. The shoemakers with whom he had stopped to take a few drinks in honor of the holiday swore that they hoped they would not live till next *Purim* if Chlavne had not hurried straight home from the synagogue. And they swore that not one of them had so much as touched a single drop that evening. That is, unless—so said the shoemakers—he had met up some-where with Shimen-Wolf . . .

At the mention of this name Gittel very noticeably trembled. This man, this Shimen-Wolf, was responsible for so many of her troubles . . .

Shimen-Wolf was also a shoemaker, and his greatest passion was the same as her husband's. But how could you compare Chlavne to him? He was notorious throughout that part of the country—he was known by only one name—Shimen-Wolf the Drunkard. The story is that he inherited this trait from his father, who had died of drink. One holiday long ago he drank so much that he caught fire inside and was burned to death. This had happened to Shimen-Wolf, too, on one occasion, but they had put out the fire in time and he was saved. Gittel could not believe that her husband had gone off with this drunkard. After all, he had given her his hand and sworn on his pair of *tfillin* that as long as he lived he would never have anything to do with Shimen-Wolf. Because she had insisted on this oath a feud had broken out at the time between Chlavne's Gittel and Shimen-Wolf's Hanna-Zissel. The feud had started with plain words which led to taunts and ended with something not at all pleasant to narrate: the two women became tangled up in each other's hair, and it was with the greatest difficulty that they were pulled apart alive. Since then they had not spoken to each other, and when they met somewhere by accident they stepped to the side of the road and spit three times, as one did when one encountered an evil spirit.

Gittel did not know what to do. Should she go to that shrew Hanna-Zissel to find out about her husband, or shouldn't she? She was afraid a new scandal might come of it. But the Lord himself came to her aid. Before she had time to move one way or the other she saw someone draped in black coming her way. She looked closer in the darkness and saw that it was Hanna-Zissel. Both women were ready to spring to the side of the road and spit three times, as always, but some strange power took hold of them and they began to talk. The conversation was short but to the point:

"What are you doing out here so late?"

"And what are you doing?"

"I'm looking for my husband."

"So am I."

"Where can they be?"

"I wish I knew."

"Mine was at the synagogue just a while ago."

"So was mine."

"Maybe they went somewhere together."

"It looks like it."

And both women let out a deep sigh, and continued on their way, one this way, the other that . . .

VIII

Sad and dejected, Gittel came home again, glanced at the *hamantash* on the table, and it seemed to her that the *hamantash* looked back at her and said: "What's the matter with Chlavne?" In her grief she threw herself on the bed and lay there so long that she fell asleep. She dreamt that someone knocked on the window and called her by name. Without moving she asked, "Who is that?" And she received the answer that it was Hanna-Zissel and the *shammes* of the burial society who had come to her for a shroud. Gittel felt so faint that she could not understand where she got the strength to ask as coldly as she might ask the butcher for a chicken-wing: "Were they burned to death?" "Yes, they were burned to death." "Both together?" "Together."

In terror she sat up and heard something stirring on the other side of the door, as if several hands were passing over it. She was barely able to ask:

"Who is that?"

"Us."

"Who is us?"

"Unlock the door and you'll see."

"The door is unlocked."

"But we can't find the handle."

Gittel recognized her husband's voice. She sprang to the door, opened it, and saw two creatures covered with mud like some fiends from the depths of the earth. At this sight she leaped back.

"Happy *Purim,* my Gittel," said one of them, staggering into the room without letting go of his companion. "I'll swear that my name isn't Chlavne," he went on, "that you'll never guess who has come to see you. You have two guests for *Purim,* Gittel. Two dead men . . . God in heaven, Gittel, why do you look so scared? . . . Yes, we are dead, but we do not come from the Other World. One of us is dead drunk, the other dead hungry. And which is drunk and which is hungry you'll have to guess for yourself . . .

"What are you staring for, Gittel? Don't you know who this is? It's Rothschild. May Reb Yossi sink into the earth together with the Kasrilevka mud! Rothschild is so covered with the mud that you can't recognize him. You'd think he'd been rolling around in a pigsty."

Chlavne looked around the room, looked long at the table.

"Do you know, Gittel? You're a wise and thoughtful woman. Compared to you, Vashti is a silly little hen. You've put a bottle on the table, I see. Something must have told you what a holiday the whole world is celebrating today, and how we ought to celebrate it—with a prayer and a drink and a *haman-tash.* To your health, Rothschild! May the Lord save Haman for another year, so we can hang him again with his ten sons on one gallows, fifty ells high!

"Gittel—why don't you say amen?"

The Clock that Struck Thirteen

THE clock struck thirteen.

That's the truth. I wasn't joking. I am telling you a true story of what happened in Kasrilevka, in our own house. I was there.

We had a hanging clock. It was an ancient clock that my grandfather had inherited from his father and his father's father straight back to the days of Count Chmelnitzky.

What a pity that a clock is a lifeless thing, mute and without speech. Otherwise what stories it could have told and told. It had a name throughout the town—Reb Nochem's clock—so unfaltering and true in its course that men came from all directions to set their own clocks and watches by it. Only Reb Leibesh Akoron, a man of learning and philosophy, who could tell time by the sun and knew the almanac by heart, said that our clock was—next to his little watch—just so much tin and hardware, not worth a pinch of snuff. But even he had to admit that it was still a clock. And you must remember that Reb Leibesh was the man who, every Wednesday night, climbed to the roof of the synagogue or to the hilltop nearby, before the evening prayers, to catch the exact moment when the sun went down—in one hand his watch, and in the other— his almanac. And just as the sun sank below the housetops he muttered to himself: "On the dot!"

He was always comparing the two timepieces. Walking in without so much as a Good Evening, he would glance up at our hanging clock, then down at his little watch, then over to his almanac, again at our clock, down to his watch, over to the almanac, several times, and away he went.

Only one day when he came in to compare the two timepieces with his almanac, he let out a yell, "Nochem! Quick! Where are you?"

My father, more dead than alive, came running. "What—what's happened, Reb Leibesh?"

"You are asking me?" shouted Reb Leibesh, raising his little watch right up to my father's face, and pointing with his other hand up to our clock: "Nochem, why don't you say something? Can't you see? It's a minute and a half fast! A minute and a half! Cast out the thing!" He hurled the words like an angered prophet with a base image before him.

My father did not like this at all. What did he mean, telling him to cast the clock out? "Where is it written, Reb Leibesh, that my clock is a minute and a half *fast*? Maybe we can read the same sentence backward—that your watch is a minute and a half *slow*. How do you like that?"

Reb Leibesh looked at my father as at a man who has just said that Sabbath comes twice a week or that the Day of Atonement falls on Passover. Reb Leibesh didn't say a word. He sighed deeply, turned around, slammed the door and away he went.

But we didn't care. The whole town knew that Reb Leibesh was a man whom nothing could please. The best cantor you ever heard sounded like a crow; the wisest man was—an ass; the best marriage—a failure; the cleverest epigram—a dull commonplace.

But let us return to our clock. What a clock that was! Its chimes could be heard three doors away. Boom . . . boom . . . boom . . . Almost half of the town ordered its life according to it. And what is Jewish life without a clock? How many

things there are that must be timed to the minute—the lighting
of the Sabbath candles, the end of the Sabbath, the daily prayers,
the salting and the soaking of the meat, the intervals between
meals . . .

In short, our clock was the town clock. It was always faithful
to us and to itself. In all its existence it never knew a repair
man. My father, himself, was its only master. He had "an
intuitive understanding of how it worked." Every year before
Passover he carefully removed it from the wall, cleaned the in-
sides with a feather duster, took out from within a mass of
spiderwebs, mutilated flies which the spiders had lured inside,
along with dead cockroaches that had lost their way and had
met their sad fate there. Then, cleaned and sparkling, he hung
the clock on the wall again, and it glowed. That is, they both
glowed, the clock because it had been polished and cleaned,
and my father—because the clock did.

But there came a day when a strange thing happened. It was
on a beautiful cloudless day when we were sitting at the noon-
day meal. Whenever the clock struck I liked to count the
strokes, and I did it out loud.

"One, two, three . . . seven . . . eleven, twelve, thirteen . . ."
What . . . thirteen!

"Thirteen!" cried my father, and burst out laughing. "A
fine mathematician you are—may the evil eye spare you. Whoever heard of a clock striking thirteen?"

"Thirteen," I said. "On my word of honor. Thirteen."

"I'll give you thirteen smacks," cried my father, aroused.
"Don't ever repeat such nonsense. Fool! A clock can't strike
thirteen."

"Do you know what," my mother broke in, "I'm afraid that
the child is right. It seems to me that I counted thirteen, too."

"Wonderful," said my father. "Another village heard from."
But at the same time he too began to suspect something.

After dinner he went to the clock, climbed on a stool, and prodded around inside until the clock began to strike. All three of us counted, nodding our heads at each stroke: "One, two, three . . . seven . . . nine . . . eleven, twelve, thirteen."

"Thirteen," repeated my father, with a look in his eye of a man who had just beheld the wall itself come to life and start talking. He prodded once more at the wheels. Once more the clock struck thirteen. My father climbed down from the stool pale as a sheet and remained standing in the middle of the room, looking down at the floor, chewing his beard and muttering to himself, "It struck thirteen . . . How is that? What does it mean? If it was out of order it would have stopped. What then?"

"What then?" said my mother. "Take down the clock and fix it. After all, you're the expert."

"Well," agreed my father, "maybe you're right." And taking down the clock he busied himself with it. He sweated over it, he worked all day over it, and at last hung it back in its place. Thank the Lord, the clock ran as it should, and when midnight came we all stood around it and counted each stroke till twelve. My father beamed at us.

"Well," he said, "no more thirteen."

"I've always said you were an expert," my mother said. "But there is one thing I don't understand. Why does it wheeze? It never used to wheeze like this before."

"You're imagining it," my father said. But listening carefully, we heard the clock wheeze when it got ready to ring, like an old man catching his breath before he coughs—"wh-wh-wh"—and then the boom . . . boom . . . boom. But even the boom itself was not the boom of olden days. The old boom had been a happy one, a joyous one, and now something sad had crept in, a sadness like that in the song of an old, worn-out cantor toward the end of the Day of Atonement . . .

As time went on the wheezing became louder and the ringing more subdued and mournful, and my father became
melancholy. We could see him suffering as though he watched
a live thing in agony and could do nothing to help it. It seemed
as though at any moment the clock would stop altogether.
The pendulum began to act strangely. Something shivered
inside, something got caught and dragged, like an old man
dragging a bad leg. We could see the clock getting ready to
stop forever. But just in time, my father came to the decision
that there was nothing wrong with the clock itself. What was
wrong was the weight. Not enough weight. And so he fastened to the weight the pestle of my mother's mortar—a matter
of several pounds. The clock began to run like a charm, and
my father was happy again, a new man.

But it didn't last long. Again the clock began to fail. Again
the pendulum began to act strangely, swinging sometimes fast
and sometimes slow. It was heartrending, it tore you apart, to
see the clock languish before your eyes. And my father, watching it, drooped also, lost interest in life, suffered anguish.

Like a good doctor devoted to his patient, considering every
known treatment or possible remedy, my father tried every way
imaginable to save the clock.

"Not enough weight, not enough life," said my father, and
attached to the weight more and more objects. First an iron
frying pan, and then a copper pitcher, then a flatiron, a bag
of sand, a couple of bricks . . . Each time the clock drew
fresh life and began to run. Painfully, with convulsions, but
it worked. Till one night when a catastrophe took place.

It was a Friday night in winter. We had just eaten the Sabbath meal of delicious spicy fish with horseradish, fat chicken
soup with noodles, pot roast with prunes and potatoes, and had
said the grace that such a meal deserved. The candles were
still flickering. The servant girl had just brought in the freshly

roasted sunflower seeds, when in came Muma Yenta, a tooth-less, dark-skinned little woman whose husband had abandoned her years ago and gone off to America.

"Good Sabbath," said Muma Yenta, breathless as usual. "I just knew you'd have sunflower seeds—the only trouble is—what can I crack them with? May my old man have as few years to live as I have teeth in my mouth . . .

"M-m-m," she went on, faster and faster, "I can still smell your fish, Malka . . . What a time *I* had getting fish this morning, with that Sarah-Pearl—the millionairess—standing next to me at the market. I was just saying to Menasha the fishman, 'Why is everything so high today?' when Sarah-Pearl jumps up with, 'Quick, I'm in a hurry. How much does this pickerel weigh?' 'What's your rush?' I say to her. 'The town isn't on fire. Menasha won't throw the fish back into the river. Among the rich,' I let them know, 'there is plenty of money but not much sense.' Then she goes and opens her mouth at me. 'Paupers,' says she, 'shouldn't come around here. If you have no money you shouldn't hanker after things.' What do you think of her nerve? What was she before she married —a peddler herself—standing in her mother's stall at the market?"

She caught her breath and went on: "These people and their marriages! Just like Abraham's Pessel-Peiseh who is so de-lighted with her daughter just because she married a rich man from Stristch, who took her just as she stood, without dowry. Wonderful luck she has. They say she is getting to look a sight. The life those children lead her . . . What do you think—it's so easy to be a stepmother? God forbid! Look at that Hava for instance. A good, well-meaning soul like that. But you should see the trouble she has with her stepchildren. The screaming you hear day and night, the way they talk back to her. And what's worse—pitch-patch—three smacks for a penny . . ."

The candles begin to gutter. The shadows tremble on the walls, they mount higher and higher. The sunflower seeds crackle. All of us are talking, telling stories to the company at large, with no one really listening. But Muma Yenta talks more than anybody.

"Listen to this," she lets out, "there is something even worse than all the rest. Not far from Yampola, a couple of miles, some robbers attacked a Jewish tavern the other night, killed everyone in the family, even an infant in a cradle. The only one left was a servant girl asleep on top of the oven in the kitchen. She heard the shrieks, jumped down from the oven, and looking through a crack in the door, saw the master and mistress lying murdered on the floor in a pool of blood. She took a chance—this servant girl—and jumped out of the window, running all the way to town yelling, 'Children of Israel, save us! Help! Help! Help!'"

Suddenly, in the midst of Muma Yenta's yelling, "Help! Help!"—we hear a crash—bang—smash—boom—bam! Immersed in the story, all we could think was that robbers were attacking our own home, and were shooting at us from all sides—or that the room had fallen in—or a hurricane had hit us. We couldn't move from our seats. We stared at each other speechless—waiting. Then all of us began to yell, "Help! Help! Help!"

In a frenzy my mother caught me in her arms, pressed me to her heart, and cried, "My child, if it's going to happen, let it happen to me! Oh . . ."

"What is it?" cries my father. "What's happened to him?"

"It's nothing. Nothing," yells Muma Yenta, waving her arms. "Be quiet." And the girl runs in from the kitchen, wild-eyed.

"What's the matter? What's happened? Is there a fire? Where is it?"

"Fire? What fire?" shouts Muma Yenta at the girl. "Go

burn, if you want to. Get scorched, if you like." She keeps
scolding the girl as if it's all her fault, then turns to us.

"What are you all making this racket for? What are you
frightened of? What do you think it is? Can't you see? It's
just the clock. The clock fell down. Now do you know? Everything you could imagine was hung on it—a half a ton at
least. So it fell down. What's strange about that? You
wouldn't have been any better yourself . . ."

At last we come to our senses. We get up from the table one
by one, go up to the clock and inspect it from all sides. There
it lies, face down, broken, shattered, smashed, ruined forever.

"It is all over," says my father in a dull voice, his head bent
as if standing before the dead. He wrings his hands and tears
appear in his eyes. I look at him and I want to cry too.

"Hush, be quiet," says my mother, "why do you grieve?
Perhaps it was destined. Maybe it was written in heaven that
today, at this minute, the end should come. Let it be an atonement for our sins—though I should not mention it on the Sabbath—for you, for me, for our children, for our loved ones, for
all of Israel. Amen. *Selah*."

All that night I dreamed of clocks. I imagined that I saw our
old clock lying on the ground, clothed in a white shroud. I
imagined that I saw the clock still alive, but instead of a pendulum there swung back and forth a long tongue, a human
tongue, and the clock did not ring, but groaned. And each
groan tore something out of me. And on its face, where I used
to see the twelve, I saw suddenly number thirteen. Yes,
thirteen. You may believe me—on my word of honor.

Home for Passover

TWO times a year, as punctually as a clock, in April and again in September, Fishel the *melamed* goes home from Balta to Hashtchavata to his wife and children, for Passover and for the New Year. Almost all his life it has been his destiny to be a guest in his own home, a most welcome guest it is true, but for a very short time, only over the holidays. And as soon as the holidays are over he packs his things and goes back to Balta, back to his teaching, back to the rod, to the *Gamorah* that he studies with the unwilling small boys of Balta, back to his exile among strangers and to his secret yearning for home.

However, when Fishel does come home, he is a king! Bath-Sheba, his wife, comes out to meet him, adjusts her kerchief, becomes red as fire, asks him quickly without looking him in the eye, "How are you, Fishel?" And he answers, "How are *you*?" And Froike, his boy, now almost thirteen, holds out his hand, and the father asks him, "Where are you now, Ephraim, in your studies?" And Reizel, his daughter, a bright-faced little girl with her hair in braids, runs up and kisses him.

"Papa, what did you bring me for the holidays?"

"Material for a dress, and for your mother a silk shawl. Here, give Mother the shawl."

And Fishel takes a new silk (or maybe half-silk) shawl out of his *tallis*-sack, and Bath-Sheba becomes redder than ever, pulls her kerchief low over her eyes, pretends to get busy around

the house, bustles here and there and gets nothing done.
"Come, Ephraim, show me how far you've got in the
Gamorah. I want to see how you're getting along."

And Froike shows his father what a good boy he has been,
how well he has applied himself, the understanding he has of
his work and how good his memory is. And Fishel listens to
him, corrects him once or twice, and his soul expands with
pride. He glows with happiness. What a fine boy Froike is!
What a jewel!

"If you want to go to the Baths, here is a shirt ready for you,"
says Bath-Sheba, without looking him in the eye, and Fishel
feels strangely happy, like a man who has escaped from prison
into the bright, free world among his own people, his loved
and faithful ones. And he pictures himself in the room thick
with steam, lying on the top ledge together with a few of his
cronies, all of them sweating, rubbing each other and beating
each other with birch rods and calling for more, more . . .

"Harder! Rub harder! Can't you make it harder!"

And coming home from the bath, refreshed, invigorated,
almost a new man, he dresses for the holiday. He puts on his
best gabardine with the new cord, steals a glance at Bath-Sheba
in her new dress with the new silk shawl, and finds her still
a presentable woman, a good, generous, pious woman . . .
And then with Froike he goes to the synagogue. There greetings fly at him from all sides. "Well, well! Reb Fishel! How
are you? How's the *melamed?*" "The *melamed* is still teaching." "What's happening in the world?" "What should happen? It's still the same old world." "What's doing in Balta?"
"Balta is still Balta." Always, every six months, the same
formula, exactly the same, word for word. And Nissel the
cantor steps up to the lectern to start the evening services. He
lets go with his good, strong voice that grows louder and
stronger as he goes along. Fishel is pleased with the perform-

ance. He is also pleased with Froike's. The lad stands near him and prays, prays with feeling, and Fishel's soul expands with pride. He glows with happiness. A fine boy, Froike! A good Jewish boy!

"Good *yom-tev!* Good *yom-tev!*"

"Good *yom-tev* to you!"

They are home already and the *seder* is waiting. The wine in the glasses, the horseradish, the eggs, the *haroses,* and all the other ritual foods. His "throne" is ready—two stools with a large pillow spread over them. Any minute now Fishel will become the king, any minute he will seat himself on his royal throne in a white robe, and Bath-Sheba, his queen, with her new silk shawl will sit at his side. Ephraim, the prince, in his new cap and Princess Reizel with her braids will sit facing them.

Make way, fellow Israelites! Show your respect! Fishel the *melamed* has mounted his throne! Long live Fishel!

The wits of Hashtchavata, who are always up to some prank and love to make fun of the whole world (and especially of a humble teacher) once made up a story about Fishel. They said that one year, just before Passover, Fishel sent a telegram to Bath-Sheba reading like this: *Rabiata sobrani. Dengi vezu. Prigotov puli. Yedu tzarstvovat.* In ordinary language this is what it meant: "Classes dismissed. Purse full. Prepare *kneidlach.* I come to rule." This telegram, the story goes on, was immediately turned over to the authorities in Balta, Bath-Sheba was searched but nothing was found, and Fishel himself was brought home under police escort. But I can tell you on my word of honor that this is a falsehood and a lie. Fishel had never in his life sent a telegram to anyone. Bath-Sheba was never searched. And Fishel was never arrested. That is, he was arrested once, but not for sending a telegram. He was arrested because of a passport. And that not in Balta but in Yehupetz, and it was not before Passover but in the middle of summer. This is what happened.

Fishel had suddenly decided that he would like to teach in Yehupetz that year, and had gone there without a passport to look for work. He thought it was the same as Balta, where he needed no passport, but he was sadly mistaken. And before he was through with that experience he swore that not only he but even his children and grandchildren would never go to Yehupetz again to look for work . . .

And ever since that time he goes directly to Balta every season and in the spring he ends his classes a week or two before Passover and dashes off for home. What do you mean—dashes off? He goes as fast as he can—that is, assuming that the roads are clear and he can find a wagon to take him and he can cross the Bug either over the ice or by ferry. But what happens if the snows have melted and the mud is deep, there is no wagon to be gotten, the Bug has just opened and the ferry hasn't started yet because of the ice, and if you try to cross by boat you risk your very life—and Passover is right in front of your nose? What can you do? Take it the way a man does if he's on his way from Machnivka to Berdichev for the Sabbath, or from Sohatchov to Warsaw—it's late Friday afternoon, the wagon is going up a hill, it's getting dark fast, suddenly they're caught in a cloudburst, he's dead hungry—and just then the axle snaps! It's a real problem, I can assure you . . .

Well, Fishel the *melamed* knows what that problem is. As long as he has been a teacher and has taken the trip from Hashtchavata to Balta and from Balta to Hashtchavata, he has experienced every inconvenience that a journey can offer. He has known what it is to go more than halfway on foot, and to help push the wagon too. He has known what it is to lie together with a priest in a muddy ditch, with himself on bottom and the priest on top. He has known how it feels to run away from a pack of wolves that followed his wagon from Hashtchavata as far as Petschani—although later, it is true, he found out that it was not wolves but dogs. . . . But all these calamities were nothing compared with what he had to go through this year when he was on his way to spend the Passover with his family.

It was all the fault of the Bug. This one year it opened up a little later than usual, and became a torrent just at the time when Fishel was hurrying home—and he had reason to hurry! Because this year Passover started on Friday night—the beginning of Sabbath—and it was doubly important for him to be home on time.

Fishel reached the Bug—traveling in a rickety wagon with a peasant—Thursday night. According to his reckoning he should have come there Tuesday morning, because he had left Balta Sunday noon. If he had only gone with Yankel-Sheigetz, the Balta coachman, on his regular weekly trip—even if he had to sit at the rear with his back to the other passengers and his feet dangling—he would have been home a long time ago and would have forgotten all about the whole journey. But the devil possessed him to go into the marketplace to see if he could find a cheaper conveyance; and it is an old story that the less you pay for something, the more it costs. Jonah the Drunkard had warned him, "Take my advice, Uncle, let it cost you two *rubles* but you'll sit like a lord in Yankel's coach—right in the very back row! Remember, you're playing with fire. There is not much time to lose!" But it was just his luck that the devil had to drag an old peasant from Hashtchavata across his path.

"Hello, Rabbi! Going to Hashtchavata?"

"Good! Can you take me? How much will it cost?"

How much it would cost—that he found it necessary to ask; but whether or not he would get home in time for Passover— that didn't even occur to Fishel. After all, even if he went on foot and took only tiny steps like a shackled person, he should have been able to reach Hashtchavata in less than a week . . .

But they had hardly started out before Fishel was sorry that he had hired this wagon, even though he had all the room in the world to stretch out in. It became apparent very soon that at the rate at which they were creeping they would never be able to get anywhere in time. All day long they rode and they rode, and at the end of the day they had barely got started. And no matter how much he kept bothering the old peasant, no matter how many times he asked how far they still had to go, the man did not answer. He only shrugged his shoulders and said, "Who can tell?"

It was much later, toward evening, that Yankel-Sheigetz overtook them, with a shout and whistle and a crack of the whip—overtook them and passed them with his four prancing horses bedecked with tiny bells, and with his coach packed with passengers inside, on the driver's seat, and some hanging onto the rear. Seeing the teacher sitting alone in the wagon with the peasant, Yankel-Sheigetz cracked his whip in the air again and cursed them both, the driver and the passenger, as only he could curse, laughed at them and at the horse, and after he had passed them he turned back and pointed at one of the wheels:

"Hey, *shlimazl*! Look! One of your wheels is turning!"

"Whoa!" the peasant yelled, and together the driver and passenger climbed down, looked at every wheel, at every spoke, crawled under the wagon, searched everywhere, and found nothing wrong.

Realizing that Yankel had played a trick on them, the peasant began to scratch the back of his neck, and at the same time he cursed Yankel and every other Jew on earth with fresh new curses that Fishel had never heard in all his life. He shouted louder and louder and with every word grew angrier and angrier.

"*Ah, shob tubi dobra ne bulo!*" he cried. "Bad luck to you, Jew! I hope you die! I hope you never arrive! Every one of you die! You and your horse and your wife and your daughter and your aunts and your uncles and your cousins and your second-cousins and—and—and all the rest of your cursed Jews!"

It was a long time before the peasant climbed into his wagon again and was ready to start. But even then he was still angry; he couldn't stop yelling. He continued to heap curses at the head of Yankel-Sheigetz and all the Jews until, with God's help, they came to a village where they could spend the night.

The next morning Fishel got up very early, before dawn, said his morning prayers, read through the greater part of the *Book of Psalms,* had a *beigel* for breakfast, and was ready to go on. But Feodor was not ready. Feodor had found an old crony of his in the village and had spent the night with him, drinking and carousing. Then he slept the greater part of the day and was not ready to start till evening.

"Now, look here, Feodor," Fishel complained to him when they were in the wagon again, "the devil take you and your mother! After all, Feodor, I hired you to get me home for the holidays! I depended on you. I trusted you." And that wasn't all he said. He went on in the same vein, half pleading, half cursing, in a mixture of Russian and Hebrew, and when words failed him he used his hands. Feodor understood well enough what Fishel meant, but he did not answer a word, not a sound, as though he knew that Fishel was right. He was as quiet and coy as a little kitten until, on the fourth day, near Petschani, they met Yankel-Sheigetz on his way back from Hashtchavata with a shout and a crack of the whip and this good piece of news:

"You might just as well turn back to Balta! The Bug has opened up!"

When Fishel heard this his heart sank, but Feodor thought that Yankel was making fun of him again and began to curse once more with even greater vigor and originality than before. He cursed Yankel from head to foot, he cursed every limb and every bone of his body. And his mouth did not shut until Thursday evening, when they came to the Bug. They drove right up to Prokop Baraniuk, the ferryman, to find out when he would start running the ferry again.

And while Feodor and Prokop took a drink and talked things over, Fishel went off into a corner to say his evening prayers.

The sun was beginning to set. It cast its fiery rays over the steep hills on both sides of the river, in spots still covered with snow and in spots already green, cut through with rivulets and torrents that bounded downhill and poured into the river itself with a roar where they met with the running waters from the melting ice. On the other side of the river, as if on a table, lay Hashtchavata, its church steeple gleaming in the sun like a lighted candle.

Standing there and saying his prayers with his face toward Hashtchavata, Fishel covered his eyes with his hand and tried to drive from his mind the tempting thoughts that tormented him: Bath-Sheba with her new silk shawl, Froike with his *Gamorah,* Reizel with her braids, and the steaming bath. And fresh *matzo* with strongly seasoned fish and fresh horseradish that tore your nostrils apart, and Passover borsht that tasted like something in Paradise, and other good things that man's evil spirit can summon . . . And no matter how much Fishel drove these thoughts from his mind they kept coming back like summer flies, like mosquitoes, and they did not let him pray as a man should.

And when he had finished his prayers Fishel went back to Prokop and got into a discussion with him about the ferry and the approaching holiday, explaining to him half in Russian, half in Hebrew, and the rest with his hands, how important a holiday Passover was to the Jews, and what it meant when Passover started on Friday evening! And he made it clear to him that if he did not cross the Bug by that time tomorrow— all was lost: in addition to the fact that at home everybody was waiting for him—his wife and children (and here Fishel gave a heart-rending sigh)—if he did not cross the river before sunset, then for eight whole days he would not be able to eat or drink a thing. He might as well throw himself into the river right now! (At this point Fishel turned his face aside so that no one could see that there were tears in his eyes.)

Prokop Baraniuk understood the plight that poor Fishel was in, and he answered that he knew that the next day was a holiday; he even knew what the holiday was called, and he knew that it was a holiday when people drank wine and brandy. He knew of another Jewish holiday when people drank brandy too, and there was a third when they drank still more, in fact they were supposed to become drunk, but what they called that day he had forgotten . . .

"Good, that's very good!" Fishel interrupted with tears in his voice. "But what are we going to do now? What if tomorrow—God spare the thought . . ." Beyond that poor Fishel could not say another word.

For this Prokop had no answer. All he did was to point to the river with his hand, as though to say, "Well—see for yourself . . ."

And Fishel lifted his eyes and beheld what his eyes had never before seen in all his life, and he heard what his ears had never heard. For it can truthfully be said that never before had Fishel actually seen what the out-of-doors was like. Whatever he had seen before had been seen at a glance while he was on his way somewhere, a glimpse snatched while hurrying from *cheder* to the synagogue or from synagogue to *cheder*. And now the sight of the majestic blue Bug between its two steep banks, the rush of the spring freshets tumbling down the hills, the roar of the river itself, the dazzling splendor of the setting sun, the flaming church steeple, the fresh, exhilarating odor of the spring earth and the air, and above all the simple fact of being so close to home and not being able to get there—all these things together worked on Fishel strangely. They picked him up and lifted him as though on wings and carried him off into a new world, a world of fantasy, and he imagined that to cross the Bug was the simplest thing in the world—like taking a pinch of snuff—if only the Eternal One cared to perform a tiny miracle and rescue him from his plight.

These thoughts and others like them sped through Fishel's head and carried him aloft and bore him so far from the river bank that before he was aware of it, night had fallen, the stars were out, a cool wind had sprung up and had stolen in under his gabardine and ruffled his undershirt. And Fishel went on thinking of things he had never thought of before—of time and eternity, of the unlimited expanse of space, of the vastness of the universe, of the creation of heaven and earth itself . . .

It was a troubled night that Fishel the *melamed* spent in the hut of Prokop the ferryman. But even that night finally came to an end and the new day dawned with a smile of warmth and friendliness. It was a rare and balmy morning. The last patches of snow became soft, like *kasha,* and the *kasha* turned to water, and the water poured into the Bug from all directions . . . Only here and there could be seen huge blocks of ice that looked like strange animals, like polar bears that hurried and chased each other, as if they were afraid that they would be too late in arriving where they were going . . .

And once again Fishel the *melamed* finished his prayers, ate the last crust of bread that was left in his sack, and went out to take a look at the river and to see what could be done about getting across it. But when he heard from Prokop that they would be lucky if the ferry could start Sunday afternoon, he became terrified. He clutched his head with both hands and shook all over. He fumed at Prokop, and scolded him in his own mixture of Russian and Hebrew. Why had Prokop given him hope the night before, why had he said that they might be able to get across today? To this Prokop answered coldly that he had not said a word about crossing by ferry, he had only said that they might be able to get across, and this they could still do. He could take him over any way he wanted to —in a rowboat or on a raft, and it would cost him another half ʽuble—not a *kopek* more.

"Have it your own way!" sobbed Fishel. "Let it be a rowboat. Let it be a raft. Only don't make me spend the holiday here on the bank!"

That was Fishel's answer. And at the moment he would have been willing to pay two *rubles,* or even dive in and swim across —if he could only swim. He was willing to risk his life for the holy Passover. And he went after Prokop heatedly, urged him to get out the boat at once and take him across the Bug to Hashtchavata, where Bath-Sheba, Froike and Reizel were waiting for him. They might even be standing on the other side now, there on the hilltop, calling to him, beckoning, waving to him . . . But he could not see them or hear their voices, for the river was wide, so fearfully wide, wider than it had ever been before.

The sun was more than halfway across the clear, deep-blue sky before Prokop called Fishel and told him to jump into the boat. And when Fishel heard these words his arms and legs went limp. He did not know what to do. In all his life he had never been in a boat like that. Since he was born he had never been in a boat of any kind. And looking at the boat he thought that any minute it would tip to one side—and Fishel would be a martyr!

"Jump in and let's go!" Prokop called to him again, and reaching up he snatched the pack from Fishel's hand.

Fishel the *melamed* carefully pulled the skirt of his gabardine high up around him and began to turn this way and that. Should he jump—or shouldn't he? On the one hand—Sabbath and Passover in one, Bath-Sheba, Froike, Reizel, the scalding bath, the *seder* and all its ceremonial, the royal throne. On the other hand—the terrible risk, almost certain death. You might call it suicide. Because after all, if the boat tipped only once, Fishel was no more. His children were orphans. And he stood with his coat pulled up so long that Prokop lost his patience and began to shout at him. He warned him that if Fishel did not jump in at once he would spit at him and go across by himself to Hashtchavata. Hearing the beloved word Hash-tcha-va-ta, Fishel remembered his dear and true ones again, summoned up all his courage—and fell into the boat. I say "fell into" because with his first step the boat tipped ever so slightly, and Fishel, thinking he would fall, drew suddenly back, and this time he really did fall, right on his face . . . Several minutes passed before he came to. His face felt clammy, his arms and legs trembled, and his heart pounded like an alarm clock: tick-tock, tick-tock, tick-tock!

As though he were sitting on a stool in his own home, Prokop sat perched in the prow of the boat and coolly pulled at his oars. The boat slid through the sparkling waters, and Fishel's head whirled. He could barely sit upright. No, he didn't even try to sit. He was hanging on, clutching the boat with both hands. Any second, he felt, he would make the wrong move, any second now he would lose his grip, fall back or tumble forward into the deep—and that would be the end of Fishel! And at this thought the words of Moses' song in *Exodus* came back to him: "They sank as lead in the mighty waters." His hair stood straight up. He would not even be buried in consecrated ground! And he made a vow . . .

But what could Fishel promise? Charity? He had nothing to give. He was such a poor, poor man. So he vowed that if the Lord brought him back home in safety he would spend the rest of his nights studying the Holy Writ. By the end of the year he would go, page by page, through the entire Six Orders of the *Talmud*. If only he came through alive . . .

Fishel would have liked to know if it was still far to the other shore, but it was just his luck to have sat down with his face to Prokop and his back to Hashtchavata. And to ask Prokop he was afraid. He was afraid even to open his mouth. He was so sure that if he so much as moved his jaws the boat would tip again, and if it did, where would Fishel be then? And to make it worse, Prokop became suddenly talkative. He said that the worst possible time to cross the river was during the spring floods. You couldn't even go in a straight direction. You had to use your head, turn this way and that. Sometimes you even had to go back a little and then go forward again.

"There goes one as big as an iceberg!" Prokop warned. "It's coming straight at us!" And he swung the boat back just in time to let a huge mass of ice go past with a strange roar. And then Fishel began to understand what kind of trip this was going to be!

"Ho! Look at that!" Prokop shouted again, and pointed upstream.

Fishel lifted his eyes slowly, afraid to move too fast, and looked—looked and saw nothing. All he could see anywhere was water—water and more water.

"There comes another! We'll have to get past—it's too late to back up!"

And this time Prokop worked like mad. He hurled the boat forward through the foaming waves, and Fishel became cold with fear. He wanted to say something, but was afraid. And once more Prokop spoke up:

"If we don't make it in time, it's just too bad."

"What do you mean—too bad?"

"What do you think it means? We're lost—that's what."

"Lost?"

"Sure! Lost."

"What do you mean—lost?"

"You know what I mean. Rubbed out."

"Rubbed out?"

"Rubbed out."

Fishel did not understand exactly what these words meant. He did not even like the sound—lost—rubbed out. He had a feeling that it had to do with eternity, with that endless exist' ence on a distant shore. And a cold sweat broke out all over his body, and once again the verse came to him, "They sank as lead in the mighty waters."

To calm him down Prokop started to tell a story that had happened a year before at this same time. The ice of the Bug had torn loose and the ferry could not be used. And just his luck one day an important-looking man drove up and wanted to go across. He turned out to be a tax officer from Ouman, and he was ready to pay no less than a *ruble* for the trip. Half-way across two huge chunks of ice bore down upon them. There was only one thing for Prokop to do and he did it: he slid in between the two chunks, cut right through between them. Only in the excitement he must have rocked the boat a trifle too much, because they both went overboard into the icy water. It was lucky that he could swim. The tax collector apparently couldn't, and they never found him again. Too bad . . . A *ruble* lost like that . . . He should have collected in advance . . .

Prokop finished the story and sighed deeply, and Fishel felt an icy chill go through him and his mouth went dry. He could not say a word. He could not make a sound, not even a squeak

When they were halfway over, right in the middle of the current, Prokop paused and looked upstream. Satisfied with what he saw, he put the oars down, dug a hand deep into his pocket and pulled out a bottle from which he proceeded to take a long, long pull. Then he took out a few black cloves and while he was chewing them he apologized to Fishel for his drinking. He did not care for the whiskey itself, he said, but he had to take it, at least a few drops, or he got sick every time he tried to cross the river. He wiped his mouth, picked up his oars, glanced again upstream, and exclaimed:

"Now we're in for it!"

In for what? Where? Fishel did not know and he was afraid to ask, but instinctively he felt that if Prokop had been more specific he would have added something about death or drowning. That it was serious was apparent from the way Prokop was acting. He was bent double and was thrashing like mad. Without even looking at Fishel he ordered:

"Quick, uncle! Lie down!"

Fishel did not have to be told twice. He saw close by a towering block of ice bearing down upon them. Shutting his eyes, he threw himself face down on the bottom of the boat and trembling all over began, in a hoarse whisper, to recite *Shma*

Yisroel. He saw himself already sinking through the waters. He saw the wide-open mouth of a gigantic fish; he pictured himself being swallowed like the prophet Jonah when he was escaping to Tarshish. And he remembered Jonah's prayer, and quietly, in tears, he repeated the words: "The waters compassed me about, even to the soul; the deep was round about me. The weeds were wrapped about my head."

Thus sang Fishel the *melamed* and he wept, wept bitterly, at the thought of Bath-Sheba, who was as good as a widow already, and the children, who were as good as orphans. And all this time Prokop was working with all his might, and as he worked he sang this song:

> *"Oh, you waterfowl!*
> *You black-winged waterfowl—*
> *You black-winged bird!"*

And Prokop was as cool and cheerful as if he were on dry land, sitting in his own cottage. And Fishel's "encompassed me about" and Prokop's "waterfowl," and Fishel's "the weeds were wrapped" and Prokop's "black-winged bird" merged into one, and on the surface of the Bug was heard a strange singing, a duet such as had never been heard on its broad surface before, not ever since the river had been known as Bug . . .

"Why is he so afraid of death, that little man?" Prokop Baraniuk sat wondering, after he had got away from the icefloe and pulled his bottle out of his pocket again for another drink. "Look at him, a little fellow like that—poor, in tatters . . . I wouldn't trade this old boat for him. And he's afraid to die!"

And Prokop dug his boot into Fishel's side, and Fishel trembled. Prokop began to laugh, but Fishel did not hear. He was still praying, he was saying *Kaddish* for his own soul, as if he were dead . . .

But if he were dead would he be hearing what Prokop was saying now?

"Get up, Uncle. We're there already. In Hashtchavata."

Fishel lifted his head up slowly, cautiously, looked around on all sides with his red, swollen eyes.

"Hash-tcha-va-ta?"

"Hashtchavata! And now you can give me that half-*ruble*!"

And Fishel crawled out of the boat and saw that he was really home at last. He didn't know what to do first. Run home to his wife and children? Dance and sing on the bank? Or should he praise and thank the Lord who had preserved him from such a tragic end? He paid the boatman his half-*ruble*, picked up his pack, and started to run as fast as he could. But after a few steps he stopped, turned back to the ferryman:

"Listen, Prokop, my good friend! Come over tomorrow for a glass of Passover brandy and some holiday fish. Remember the name—Fishel the *melamed!* You hear? Don't forget now!"

"Why should I forget? Do you think I'm a fool?"

And he licked his lips at the thought of the Passover brandy and the strongly seasoned Jewish fish.

"That's wonderful, Uncle! That's wonderful!"

When Fishel the *melamed* came into the house, Bath Sheba, red as fire, with her kerchief low over her eyes, asked shyly, "How are you?" And he answered, "How are *you?*" And she asked, "Why are you so late?" And he answered, "We can thank God. It was a miracle." And not another word, because it was so late.

He did not even have time to ask Froike how he was getting along in the *Talmud,* or give Reizel the gift he had brought her, or Bath-Sheba the new silk shawl. Those things would have to wait. All he could think of now was the bath. And he just barely made it.

And when he came home from the bath he did not say anything either. Again he put it off till later. All he said was, "A miracle from heaven. We can thank the Lord. He takes care of us . . ."

And taking Froike by the hand, he hurried off to the synagogue.

The Enchanted Tailor

ONCE there was a man named Shimmen-Eli who lived in Zolodievka, a little town in the district of Mazapevka, not far from Haplapovitch and Kozodoievka (between Yampoli and Strishtch on the road that runs from Pischi-Yaboda through Petchi-Hvost to Tetrevitz and from there to Yehupetz). And he was known as Shimmen-Eli *Shma-Koleinu,* (the Hebrew for "Hear our voice, O Lord") because in the synagogue he shouted louder, swayed more vigorously, chanted and warbled with greater emotion than anyone else. By trade Shimmen-Eli was a tailor; not, you understand, a master tailor who sewed according to the latest fashion books, but a mender of great skill who excelled at darning holes and making patches that could never be detected, in turning a garment inside out and making the old look like new. He could take a threadbare coat and turn it into a gabardine, the gabardine into a pair of trousers, cut the trousers into a jacket, and the jacket into something else again.

This was by no means such easy work, but Shimmen-Eli *Shma-Koleinu* was an artist at it, and Zolodievka being a poor town where a new garment was a rare thing, Shimmen-Eli was held in high esteem. His only drawback was that he could never get along with the rich men of the town. He was always interfering in public affairs, defending the rights of the poor, speaking out bluntly about the town philanthropists, calling the tax-collector a blood-sucker and

93

cannibal, and the rabbis and *shochtim* who worked together with the tax-collector a band of thieves, murderers, scoundrels and highwaymen. Let the devil take them all, together with their fathers and grandfathers and Uncle Ishmael . . .

Among his fellow workers Shimmen-Eli was considered a man of great and esoteric learning, for he was always full of quotations. He quoted passages from the Bible, which some of them knew, from *Gamorah* and *Midrash* which they had heard about, and from other commentaries whose existence they had never even suspected. No matter what the occasion, he had a Hebrew quotation at the tip of his tongue. If the quotation was usually garbled, if the beginning did not match the ending, and if none of it suited the occasion, that is not for us to judge.

In addition to his learning he had a voice that was not so bad, though possibly a little too shrill. He knew all the tunes and traditional renderings of all the prayers by heart, and he loved to lead the services in the Tailors' Chapel, where he was president—an office that brought him more grief than honor. A box in the ear, a slap in the face, was not uncommon at the Tailors' Chapel, and the president was usually at the receiving end.

Although Shimmen-Eli had been wretchedly poor all his life, a pauper actually, nevertheless he did not let his poverty get the best of him. On the contrary, he always said, "The poorer I am, the better I feel. The hungrier I am, the louder I sing. As the *Gamorah* says . . ." And here he let fly one of his famous quotations, one part Hebrew, one part Chaldaic, and the rest as often as not a knock-kneed, staggering Russian.

In appearance Shimmen-Eli was short and homely, with pins and needles sticking out all over him and bits of cotton batting clinging to his curly black hair. He had a short beard like a goat's, a flattened nose, a split lower lip and large black eyes

that were always smiling. His walk was a little dance all his
own and he was always humming to himself. His favorite
saying was, "That's life—but don't worry."

And Shimmen-Eli was blessed with sons and daughters of all
ages—mainly daughters. And he had a wife named Tsippa-
Baila-Reiza who was his exact opposite; a tall, strong, red-faced,
broad-shouldered woman, a regular Cossack in appearance.
Ever since the day of their wedding she had taken him in
hand and never loosened her hold. She was the head of the
house, and her husband had the greatest respect for her.
She had only to open her mouth and he trembled. In the
Tailors' Chapel it was said openly that Shimmen-Eli may
have patched the pants, but his wife wore them. At times,
when they were alone, she was not above giving him a good
slap in the face. This slap Shimmen-Eli would put into his
pocket, and comfort himself with his favorite quotation:
"That's life—but don't worry. The Bible says, 'And he shall
rule over thee,' but it means nothing. Let all the kings of
East and West do what they will, it won't help."

II

And it came to pass that one summer day Shimmen-Eli's
wife, Tsippa-Baila-Reiza, came home from the market with
her basket of purchases, flung down the bunch of garlic, the
few parsnips and potatoes that she had bought, and cried
out angrily, "The devil with it! I'm sick and tired of it all.
Day after day, day after day, I break my head trying to think
what to cook for dinner. You need the brains of a prime
minister to think of something new. Every day it's dumplings
and beans, beans and dumplings. May God forgive me for
complaining, but look at Nechama-Brocha, will you—a
pauper like that, without a *kopek* to her name or a whole

dish in her cupboard—and *she* has to have a goat! Why is it? Because her husband, though only a tailor, is still a man! So they have a goat, and if there is a goat in the house you can have a glass of milk for the children, you can cook porridge with milk, you can make a milk soup for dinner, noodles and milk for supper, and besides you can count on a pitcher of sour cream, a piece of cheese, a bit of butter. Think of it. If we only had a goat!"

"You're quite right, I'm afraid," said Shimmen-Eli mildly. "There is an ancient law that every Jew must own a goat. Let me quote you . . ."

"What good are your quotations?" cried Tsippa-Baila Reiza. "I tell you about a goat and you give me quotations. I'll give *you* a quotation in a minute and you'll see stars! He feeds me quotations, that breadwinner of mine, the *shlimazl*. I wouldn't trade all your quotations and all your learning for one good borsht with cream! Do you hear?"

With broad hints like this Tsippa-Baila-Reiza plagued her husband constantly, until Shimmen-Eli promised her on his word of honor that from then on she could rest easily. With God's help she would get a goat.

"But how?" asked Tsippa-Baila-Reiza.

"Don't worry," answered Shimmen-Eli.

From that time on Shimmen-Eli began to save his *groschens*. He denied himself many necessary things, pawned his Sabbath gabardine, and by the greatest economy managed to save up a few *rubles*. It was decided that he should take the money and go over to Kozodoievka to buy a goat. Why to Kozodoievka? For two reasons. First of all, because Kozodoievka was famous for its goats, as the name implies—*koza* meaning goat in Russian. And secondly, because Tsippa-Baila-Reiza had heard from a neighbor of hers with whom she had not been on speaking terms for a number of years, and who in turn had heard it from her sister who lived in Kozodoievka and who had visited her not long before, that there was a *melamed*, a teacher, in that town, named Chaim-Chana the Wise (because he was such a fool) who had a wife named Tema-Gittel the Silent (because she was so talkative), and this Tema-Gittel owned two goats, both giving milk.

"Now, I ask you," said Tsippa-Baila-Reiza, "why should she have two goats, both of them giving milk? What harm would there be if she had only one? There are plenty of people who don't have even half a goat. And yet they live."

"You are quite right, my wife," said Shimmen-Eli. "That is an old complaint. As the saying goes . . ."

"There he goes again! Another quotation!" interrupted his wife. "You talk about a goat and he comes to you with a quotation. Take my advice. You go to that *melamed* in Kozodoievka and tell him this: 'It has come to our attention that you have two goats, both giving milk. What do you need two goats for? For pets? And since you don't need the two, why don't you sell one of them to me? Will it hurt you?' That's the only way to talk to these people, you understand?"

"Of course I understand. Why shouldn't I?" said Shimmen-Eli. "For my good money do I have to beg them? With money you can get anything in the world. 'Silver and gold,' said our wise men, 'make even pigs clean.' The only thing that's bad is not to have any money at all. As Rashi says, 'A poor man is like a dead man.' Or as it is written elsewhere, 'Without fingers you can't even thumb your nose.' Or, as another passage so appropriately puts it, '*Abracadabra . . .*'"

"Another passage! Another quotation! My head rings with his quotations! Oh, why don't you sink into the earth!"

cried Tsippa-Baila-Reiza. "May you be buried nine feet deep!"
And once more she instructed her husband how to approach
the *melamed,* how to feel him out, and how to close the deal.

But suppose he didn't want to sell his goat? ... Why
shouldn't he want to sell it? Why should he have two goats,
both of them giving milk? There are so many people who
don't have even half a goat. Well, do these people die?
They manage to live.

And so on and so on, in the same vein.

III

And when it was light, our tailor arose from bed, said his
prayers, took his staff and a rope, and started off on foot.

It was Sunday, a bright, warm, summer day. Shimmen-Eli
could not remember when he had seen a beautiful day like
this before. He could not remember the last time that he had
been out in the open country. It had been a long time since
his eyes had beheld such a fresh green forest, such a rich
green carpet sprinkled with many-colored flowers. It had
been a long time since his ears had heard the twitter of
birds and the fluttering of small wings, such a long time
since he had smelled the odors of the fresh countryside.

Shimmen-Eli *Shma-Koleinu* had spent his life in a different
world from that. His eyes had beheld entirely different scenes:
A dark cellar with an oven near the door, with pokers and
shovels leaning against it, and nearby a slop-basin full to
the brim. Near the oven and the basin, a bed made of three
boards, with a litter of small children on it, half-naked, barefoot, unwashed, always hungry.

His ears had heard entirely different sounds: "Mother, I
want some bread! Mother, I'm hungry!" And above these

sounds the voice of Tsippa-Baila-Reiza herself: "You want to eat? May you eat worms! Together with that father of yours, the *shlimazl*! Oh, dear God in heaven!"

And his nose was accustomed to entirely different odors: the odor of damp walls that dripped in winter and molded in summer; the odor of sour dough and bran, of onions and cabbage, of wet plaster, of fish and entrails; the odor of old clothes steaming under the hot iron . . .

And now, having for the moment escaped from that poor, dark, unhappy world into the fragrant, unaccustomed brightness, Shimmen-Eli felt like a man who on a hot summer day dives into the ocean. The water lifts him up, the waves lap around him, he floats blissfully, deeply inhaling the fresh, salty air. He had never known anything like this before.

Shimmen-Eli walked slowly along thinking to himself, "What harm would it do if every workingman could come out here at least once a week, here in the open country, and enjoy the freedom of God's great world? Ah, what a world, what a world!" And Shimmen-Eli began to hum and then to sing under his breath. "Oh, Lord, Thou hast created Thine own world out beyond the town. Thou hast decreed that we, Thy people, should live in Zolodievka, huddled together in stifling quarters. And Thou didst give us woe and troubles, illness and poverty. These things Thou gavest us, O Lord, in Thy boundless mercy . . ."

Thus sang Shimmen-Eli under his breath, and he wanted to throw himself down on the grass, look up at the blue sky and taste just for a moment the sweetness of God's great world. But he remembered that he had work to do and he said to himself, "Enough, Shimmen-Eli, you have loitered enough. On your way, brother! It is time to go! You will rest, God willing, when you come to the Oak Tavern, where

your kinsman, Dodi Rendar, will give you a drink. As the passage goes: 'A drop of whisky gladdens man's life' . . ."
And Shimmen-Eli *Shma-Koleinu* hurried on.

IV

On the road from Zolodievka, half way to Kozodoievka, there stands a guest house called the Oak Tavern. This tavern has a power, the power of a magnet, which draws to itself all travelers who pass by. Whether they are going from Zolodievka to Kozodoievka or from Kozodoievka to Zolodievka, they all stop at the Oak Tavern, if only for a few minutes. No one has ever discovered the secret of this. Some say it is because the host, Dodi Rendar, is such a likable fellow and so hospitable. That is, for money he will give you a good glass of whisky and the best of food. Others say that it is because Dodi, although not a thief himself, has dealings with all the thieves in the vicinity, and at the same time protects all his customers from thieves. But since this is only a rumor, perhaps we had better say no more about it.

This Dodi we speak of was a coarse fellow, fat and hairy, with a large belly, a bulbous nose, and the voice of a wild boar. He had nothing to worry about. He made a good living, owned several cows, was a widower without any ties. He had no learning whatsoever; he scarcely knew the difference between a Bible and a prayer book. And for this reason Shimmen-Eli was ashamed of him. He considered it a disgrace that he, a learned man and president of his synagogue, should have such a coarse and ignorant lout for a relative. And Dodi, for his part, was ashamed to have a worthless tailor for a kinsman. Thus each one was ashamed of the other. And yet, when Dodi caught sight of Shimmen-Eli, he greeted him handsomely, not because he respected his kinsman, but because he feared his loud mouth.

"Oh," he said cheerfully, "look who's here! How are you, Shimmen-Eli? How is your Tsippa-Baila-Reiza? And how are the children?"

" 'What are we and what have we been?' " answered Shimmen-Eli, with a quotation. "How should we be? 'Who shall perish in an earthquake and who in a plague?' Sometimes better, sometimes worse . . . The important thing is, we're still alive. As it is written, '*Abracadabra* . . .'

"But how are *you*, my dear kinsman? What is new here in the country? How are your *vareniki* this year? I remember the ones you served a year ago with your drinks. *Vareniki*, that's what's important to you. The Holy Books mean nothing; you never look into them. Ah, Reb Dodi, Reb Dodi, if your father, my Uncle Gedalia-Wolf—may his soul rest in peace— were to arise now and see his son living in the country among peasants, he would die all over again. Ah, what a father you had, Reb Dodi! He was a good and pious man . . . Ah, yes, no matter what we begin with, we always arrive at death. Come, Reb Dodi, give me a drink. As Reb Pimpon says in his sixth book of commentaries, '*Kapota bimashken,*' 'Pawn your shirt, and buy yourself a drink.' "

"So!" said Dodi, bringing him a glass of whisky. "So you're throwing the Bible at me already! Leave that for later, kinsman. First tell me, Shimmen-Eli, where are you traveling to?"

"I am not traveling," said Shimmen-Eli with a shrug. "I am just taking a walk. As we say in our prayers, 'If you have legs you can walk.' "

"If that's the case," said Dodi, "then tell me, my dear friend, where are you walking to?"

"To Kozodoievka," said Shimmen-Eli, making a face. "To
Kozodoievka to buy goats. As it is written, 'Thou shalt buy
thyself goats.'"

"Goats?" asked Dodi in surprise. "How does a tailor come
to be dealing in goats?"

"That's just a way of talking," said Shimmen-Eli. "What
I meant actually was just one goat, that is, if the Lord has
mercy and sends me the right kind of goat, one that won't
cost too much. As far as I'm concerned, I don't want a goat,
but my dear wife, Tsippa-Baila-Reiza—you know what she's
like when she makes up her mind—has decided once for
all that she must have a goat. And a wife, you have always
maintained, must be obeyed. That's an old law. It's in the
Talmud. You remember what the *Talmud* says . . ."

"About these things," said Dodi, "you are better informed
than I am. You know well enough that I'm not even on
speaking terms with the *Talmud*. But there is one thing I'd
like to know, dear kinsman. How do you happen to be such
an authority on goats?"

"The same way you're an authority on prayers!" said
Shimmen-Eli angrily. "What does an innkeeper know about
holiness? And yet when Passover comes, you recite the *Yom
Kippur* prayers as well as you can, and get by with it!"

Dodi the innkeeper understood the jibe. He bit his lip
and thought to himself, "Wait, wait, you worthless tailor,
you. You're a little too smart for your own good today.
You're showing off your knowledge too much. You'll get
a goat from me yet, and you'll be sorry!"

And Shimmen-Eli brought the conversation to an end
by asking for another drink of that strong brew that is a
cure for all troubles.

The truth can no longer be held back. Shimmen-Eli loved
an occasional drink. But a drunkard he was not. God forbid!

When was he able to buy enough whisky to become a drunkard? And yet he had this weakness: when he took one drink he had to have a second. And with the second he became quite jolly. His cheeks grew red, his eyes shone, his tongue loosened and wagged without stopping.

"Speaking of guilds," said Shimmen-Eli, "the one I belong to is the Tailors' Guild. Our emblem: Shears and Iron! Our people," he said, "have this one trait: we all like honors. At our synagogue, for instance, the least little shoemaker would like to be a chairman of something. If nothing else, then at least of the water basin. Says I, 'My friends, have it your own way. I can live without being president. Elect any shoemaker you want. I don't care for the honor and I don't want the headaches.' But they say, 'Nonsense! Once you've been elected you can't get out of it!' So I say, 'It is written in our Holy *Torah:* "Thou shalt take thy beatings and be a leader amongst men . . ."'

"But there! I've talked too much already. It's getting late. I forgot all about my goat. So goodbye, Reb Dodi, be well. Say your prayers, and look after your *vareniki.*"

"Don't forget," replied Dodi. "On your way back, if God permits, you must come in again."

"If God permits and allows and wills it," said Shimmen-Eli. "After all, I am human, nothing but flesh and blood. Where else should I stop? And as for you, be sure there is whisky on hand, and a bite to eat. In the meantime, goodbye. And remember our motto: Shears and Iron!"

V

And Shimmen-Eli *Shma-Koleinu* departed from the Oak Tavern in an exalted mood, cheerful as he could be. And he arrived in Kozodoievka without mishap. And as soon as he

came there he began to inquire where he could find the
melamed, Chaim-Chana the Wise, who had a wife Tema-
Gittel the Silent and two goats. He did not have to search
very long, since Kozodoievka is not such a large town that
a person can get lost in it. The whole town lies spread out
before your view. Here are the butchers' stalls with the cleavers
and the dogs. Here is the marketplace where women go
from one poultry-stand to another, picking up the chickens,
and pinching and feeling them.

"What do you want for this hen?"

"Which hen? Oh, this one! That isn't a hen, it's a rooster."

"So let it be a rooster. But what do you want for it?"

And two steps farther along is the yard of the synagogue
where old women sit over small baskets of pears, sunflower-
seeds and beans; where the teachers conduct their classes and
children recite their lessons out loud; and where goats—big
goats, little goats, goats of all descriptions—jump about,
pull straw off the roofs, or else sit on the ground warming
themselves in the sun and chewing the cud. And only a few
steps beyond that is the bath house, with its dark, smoke-
stained walls. And beyond that, the pond covered with a
green scum full of leeches and croaking frogs. The pond
shines in the sun, sparkles like diamonds—and smells to high
heaven. And on the other side of the pond is nothing but
earth and sky. That is all there is to Kozodoievka.

When the tailor arrived at Chaim's house, he found him
sitting over the *Gamorah* in his *tallis-kot'n* and skullcap, leading his pupils in a loud recitation:

"And—when—the—goat—saw—the—food—that—had—been
—left—on—the—barrel—she—went—after—it—greedily . . ."

"'*Abracadabra d' barbanta,*'" said Shimmen-Eli *Shma-
Koleinu* in his own Chaldaic, and quickly translated it into
plain Yiddish. "Good morning to you, Rabbi, and to all your

pupils. You are in the midst of the very subject about which I have come here to see your wife, Tema-Gittel, namely, a goat. True, if it depended on me, I would not be buying one, but my dear wife Tsippa-Baila-Reiza has set her heart on one once for all: she must have a goat. And a wife, you will tell me, should be obeyed. The *Gamorah* says so . . . But why are you staring at me like that? Because I am a plain workingman? 'Happy are ye who toil with your hands!'

"No doubt you have heard of me. I am Shimmen-Eli of Zolodievka, member of the Tailors' Guild and president of our synagogue, though I never asked to be chosen. 'I can get along without the honor,' I told them, 'and you keep the beatings for yourselves.' But they shouted, 'It's too late! Once we've picked you, you can't get out of it! A king and a leader you shall be to us. You'll *be* our leader, and you'll *get* the beatings!'

"But here I've been talking, and I almost forgot to greet you properly. How do you do, my Rabbi! How do you do, my boys! A fine crew of imps and mischief-makers, I see. Anxious to get on with your studies. Am I right?"

Hearing these words, the children began to pinch each other under the table and to giggle surreptitiously. They were, indeed, pleased with the interruption. They would have liked such visitors every day. But Chaim-Chana the Wise was not so pleased. He disliked to be interrupted when he was teaching. So he called in his wife Tema-Gittel and he himself returned with his pupils to the goat which had gotten hold of the food on the barrel. And again they began to chant at the tops of their voices:

"And—the—Rabbi—decreed—that—the—goat—must—pay—for—the—food—and—for—the—damage—to—the—barrel."

Shimmen-Eli, seeing that there was no use talking to the *melamed*, turned to his wife, Tema-Gittel the Silent.

"Here I am," said Shimmen-Eli. "As you see, a plain workingman. You may have heard of me, Shimmen-Eli of Zolodievka, member of the Tailors' Guild and president of our synagogue (though I didn't ask for the honor). I have come to see you about one of your goats. For my part I wouldn't be buying a goat now, but since my dear wife Tsippa-Baila-Reiza has made up her mind that she has to have a goat . . ."

Tema-Gittel, a tiny woman with a nose like a bean that she was always wiping with her two fingers, listened as long as she could, and then interrupted:

"So you want one of my goats, do you? Well, let me tell you this, my dear man. I'm not interested in selling the goat. For let's not fool ourselves: why should I sell it? For the money you offer? Money is round. It rolls away. But a goat is always a goat. Especially a goat like mine. Did I call it a goat? A sweetheart, that's what it is! How easy it is to milk her! And the amount of milk she gives! And how cheap it is to feed her! What does she eat? A measure of bran once a day, and for the rest she nibbles the straw from the roof of the synagogue. Still, if you're ready to pay what it's worth, I might think it over. Money is—how do you say it?—a temptation. If I get enough money I can buy another goat. Although a goat like mine would be hard to find. Did I call it a goat? A sweetheart, I tell you! But wait, why waste words? I'll bring the goat in and you'll see for yourself."

And Tema-Gittel ran out and came back leading a goat and carrying a pitcher full of milk that the goat had given that same day.

At the sight of the milk the tailor could not keep from licking his lips.

"Tell me, my dear woman, how much do you ask for this goat of yours? Remember, if it's too much, I'm not interested. You see, I don't even want the animal, but since my wife, Tsippa-Baila-Reiza, has set her heart . . ."

"What do you mean—how much?" burst out Tema-Gittel, wiping her tiny nose. "Let's hear first what you're willing to pay. But let me tell you, no matter how much you pay, you'll be getting a bargain. Because if you buy my goat . . ."

"Listen to that!" interrupted the tailor. "Why do you suppose I'm buying it? Because it's a goat! Naturally! I'm not looking for a snake, am I? Though to tell you the truth, I'd never have thought of buying a goat if my wife hadn't . . ."

"That's what I'm telling you," Tema-Gittel interrupted in her turn and began to recount the virtues of her goat again. But the tailor did not let her finish. They kept interrupting each other until anyone listening to them would have heard something like this:

"A goat? A sweetheart, not a goat . . . I would never be buying a goat . . . A measure of bran . . . Set her heart on it . . . Money is round . . . So easy to milk . . . Tsippa-Baila-Reiza . . . What does she eat? . . . Once for all . . . Straw from the roof of the synagogue . . . A wife must be obeyed . . . A goat? A sweetheart, not a goat!"

At this point Chaim-Chana broke in. "Maybe you've said enough about goats already? Who ever heard of such a thing? Here I am, right in the midst of a point of law, and all I hear is goat, goat, goat, goat! Heavens above! Either sell the goat, or don't sell the goat, but stop talking about it. Goats, goats, goats, goats, goats. My head is ringing with goats!"

"The Rabbi is right," said Shimmen-Eli. "Where there is learning there is wisdom. Why do we have to talk so much? I have the money and you have the goat. That should be enough. Three words can settle it. As it is written . . ."

"What do I care what's written?" said Tema-Gittel softly, arching herself like a cat and brushing her hand back and forth over her lips. "Just tell me what you want to pay."

"What should I say?" Shimmen-Eli answered as softly. "Who am I to say? Ah, well, it looks as if I've wasted a trip.

Apparently I'm not buying a goat today. Forgive me for bothering you . . ."

And Shimmen-Eli turned to go.

"Now, look here, my good man," said Tema-Gittel, catching him by the sleeve. "What's your hurry? Is there a fire
somewhere? It seems to me we were talking about a goat . . ."

At last the *melamed's* wife named her price, the tailor named
his; they haggled back and forth, and finally agreed. Shimmen-
Eli counted out the money and tied the rope around the goat's
neck. Tema-Gittel took the money, spit on it to ward off the
Evil Eye, wished the tailor luck, and muttering softly looked
from the money to the goat, from the goat to the money. And
she led the tailor out with many blessings.

"Go in good health, arrive in good health, use the goat in
good health, and may God grant that she continue to be as
she has been up to now. No worse. May you have her a long
time, may she give milk and more milk, and never stop giving milk."

"Amen," said the tailor and started to leave. But the goat
would not budge. She twisted her head, reared up her hind
legs, and bleated shrilly, like a young cantor trying to impress
his congregation.

But Chaim-Chana came to the rescue with the rod he used
on the boys, and helped to drive the goat out of the house.
And the children helped along by shouting: *"Koza! Koza!*
Get out, *koza!"*

And the tailor proceeded on his way.

VI

But the goat had no desire to go to Zolodievka. She thrust
herself against the wall. She twisted and turned and reared
her hind legs. And Shimmen-Eli pulled at the rope and gave

her to understand that all her kicking and bucking was useless. He said to her:

"It is written that out of necessity must thou bear thy exile. Whether thou wilt or not; nobody asks thee. I, too, was once a free Soul, a fine young man with a starched shirt and shiny boots that creaked and clattered as I walked. What more did I need? A headache? But the Lord said unto me, 'Get thee out of thy country. Crawl, Shimmen-Eli, into thy sack. Marry Tsippa-Baila-Reiza. Beget children. Suffer all thy days and thy years. For what art thou but a tailor?'"

Thus Shimmen-Eli addressed the goat, and pulling her by the rope, he went on his way, quickly, almost at a run. A warm breeze ruffled the skirts of his patched gabardine, stole under his earlocks and stroked his little beard. It brought to his nostrils the fragrance of mint, of rosemary, and other herbs and flowers whose heavenly odors he had never smelled before. And in a spirit of ecstasy and wonder he began the afternoon prayers, very handsomely, with a noble chant like a cantor performing in the presence of an admiring congregation. Suddenly—who knows how?—an Evil Spirit came to tempt him, and whispered these words into his ear:

"Listen to me, Shimmen-Eli, you fool, you! Of all things, why burst into song? It is almost evening, you haven't had a thing in your mouth all day (except two small glasses of whisky), and you gave your kinsman your word of honor that on your way home with the goat, if all was well, you would stop to have a bite with him. It was a promise, so you'll have to keep it."

And Shimmen-Eli finished his prayers as fast as he could. Then he made his way to Dodi Rendar's tavern, entering with a joyful greeting on his lips.

"Good evening to you, dear kinsman, Reb Dodi. I have news for you. Congratulate me. 'I have dwelt with Laban . . .'

I have a goat. And such a goat! Straight from goatland! A goat such as our fathers and forefathers had never known. Look her over, Reb Dodi, and give us your opinion. After all, you're a man of experience. Well, make a guess. How much should I have paid for it?"

Dodi put up his hand to shield his eyes from the setting sun, and like a true expert appraised the goat—at exactly double the figure that Shimmen-Eli had paid. At which Shimmen-Eli was so flattered that he slapped the innkeeper soundly on the back.

"Reb Dodi, dear kinsman, long life to you! This one time you didn't guess right! You were all wrong!"

Reb Dodi pursed his lips and shook his head in speechless admiration, as if to say, "What a bargain! You certainly put one over that time!"

Shimmen-Eli in his turn bent his head sideways, and with a quick gesture as if he were pulling a needle out of his vest and threading it hastily, said, "Well, Reb Dodi, what do you say now? Do I know how to look after my own affairs, or don't I? Why, if you saw how much milk she gave, you would die on the spot!"

"I'd rather see you die," said Dodi in a friendly tone.

"Amen," said Shimmen-Eli. "The same to you. And now, if I'm such a welcome guest, take my goat, Reb Dodi, and put her in the barn where no one can steal her. In the meantime I'll say my evening prayers, and then the two of us will make a toast and take a bite to eat. As the *Megila* says, 'Before eating, one is not disposed to dance.' Is that in the *Megila,* Reb Dodi, or is it somewhere else?"

"Who knows? If you say so, it must be so. After all, you're the scholar around here."

When he had finished his prayers, the tailor said to Dodi, " 'Let me swallow, I pray thee, some of this red, red pottage;

for I am faint . . .' Come, my kinsman, pour out something out of that green bottle, and let us drink of it, for our health's sake. Good health, that is our first concern. As we say in our prayers every day: 'Cause us to lie down in peace and health . . .' "

Having taken a couple of drinks and a little to eat, our tailor became very talkative. He talked about his home town of Zolodievka, the community in general and his synagogue and Tailors' Guild ("Shears and Iron our emblem!") in particular. And in the process of his discourse he denounced all the leading citizens of the town, the well-to-do and influential men, and swore that as sure as his name was Shimmen-Eli, every one of them deserved to be sent to Siberia.

"You understand, Reb Dodi?" he rounded out his dissertation. "May the devil take them, these givers of charity! Is it their own money they give? All they do is suck the blood of us poor people. Out of my three *rubles* a week they make me pay twenty-five *kopeks*! But their time will come, never fear. God shall hold them to account! Although to tell you the truth, my cherished wife, Tsippa-Baila-Reiza, has long told me that I am worse than a *shlimazl,* a fool and a coward, because if I only wanted to use it, I could hold a strong whip over them! But who listens to one's wife? After all, I have something to say, too. Does not our Holy *Torah* tell us: '*V'hu yimshol b' cho?*' Shall I translate that for you, kinsman? '*V'hu*—and he, that is, the husband'—'*yimshol*—shall rule!' But instead, what happens? What should happen? Since you have started pouring, so pour a little more. Remember what the Bible says: '*Abracadabra d' barbanta!*' "

The more Shimmen-Eli talked, the more he wandered. His eyelids drooped and soon he was leaning against the wall and nodding. His head was bent sideways, his arms were crossed over his chest, and in his fingers he held his thin little beard like a man deep in thought. Had it not been for the fact that he was snoring out loud, a snore that was at once a whistling, a wheezing and a blowing, no one in the world would have dreamt that he was asleep.

But though he dozed, his brain worked busily, and he dreamed that he was home at his workbench with a strange garment spread out in front of him. Was it a pair of trousers? Then where was the crotch? There was no crotch. Was it an undershirt? Then why did it have such long sleeves? Then what could it be? It had to be something. Shimmen-Eli turned it inside out—it was a gabardine. And what a gabardine! Brand new, soft and silky to the touch, too new to be made into something else. But out of habit he took a knife out of his vest pocket and began to look for a seam. Just then Tsippa-Baila-Reiza rushed in and began to curse him:

"What are you ripping it for? May your entrails be ripped out! You green cucumber, you fine kidney bean! Can't you see it's your Sabbath gabardine that I got for you with the money I earned from the goat?"

And Shimmen-Eli remembered that he had a goat, and he rejoiced. Never in his life had he seen so many pitchers of milk, so many cheeses, and so much butter—crocks and crocks of butter! And the buttermilk, the cream, the clabber! And rolls and biscuits baked with butter, sprinkled with sugar and cinnamon! What appetizing odors! Never in his life had he smelled such odors. And then another odor crept in—a familiar one—pugh! He felt something crawl over his neck, under his collar, around his ears and over his face. It crawled right up to his nose. He reached out his fingers and caught a bedbug. He opened first one eye, then the other, stole a look toward the window . . . Good heavens, day was breaking!

"What do you think of that! I must have dozed off!"
Shimmen-Eli said to himself and shrugged his shoulders.
He woke up the innkeeper, ran out into the yard, opened the
barn, took the goat by the rope, and started for home as
quickly as he could, like a man who is afraid that he will
miss—the Lord alone knows what.

VII

When Tsippa-Baila-Reiza saw that it was late and that
her husband was not yet home, she began to wonder if some
evil had not befallen him. Perhaps robbers had attacked him
on the way, murdered him, taken his few *rubles* away and
thrown him into a ditch; and here she was, a widow for
the rest of her days, a widow with so many children. She
might as well drown herself. All that night she did not shut
her eyes, and when the first cock crowed at dawn she pulled
on her dress and went outside and sat down on the door-
step to wait for her husband. Maybe God would have mercy
and send him home. But what could you expect from a
shlimazl when he goes off by himself, she thought; and she
planned the welcome that he so richly deserved.

But when finally he appeared with the goat following on
the rope behind him—both of them tied to the rope, the
goat around the neck and Shimmen-Eli around the waist—
she was so relieved that she greeted him affectionately:

"Why so late, my little canary, my almond cake? I thought
you had been robbed and killed on the way, my treasure."

Shimmen-Eli loosened the rope around his waist, took the
goat into the house, and breathlessly began to tell Tsippa-
Baila-Reiza all that had happened to him.

"Behold, my wife, the goat which I have brought to you.
A goat straight from goatland. The kind of goat that our

forefathers dreamt about but never saw. She eats only once a day, a measure of bran, and otherwise she nibbles the straw from the roof of the synagogue. Milk she gives like a cow, twice a day. I saw a full pail with my eyes, I swear. Did I call it a goat? A sweetheart, not a goat. At least that's what Tema-Gittel said. And such a bargain! I practically stole it from her. Six and a half *rubles* was all I paid. But how long do you think I had to bargain with the woman? Actually she didn't want to sell the goat. All night long I had to fight with her."

And while he spoke, Tsippa-Baila-Reiza thought to herself: "So Nechama-Brocha thinks she's the only person in town who amounts to something! She can have a goat and the rest of us can't? Now watch her eyes pop out when she sees Tsippa-Baila-Reiza with a goat too! And Bluma-Zlata? And Haya-Mata? Friends they call themselves, well-wishers. May they have only half the misfortune they wish me!"

And meanwhile she made a fire in the stove and began to prepare some buckwheat noodles for breakfast. And Shimmen-Eli put on his *tallis* and *tfillin* and started the morning prayers.

It was a long time since he had prayed with such feeling. He sang like a cantor on a holiday and made so much noise that he woke the children. When they found out from their mother that their father had brought home a goat and that she was cooking noodles with milk, they screamed with joy, sprang out of their bed still in their nightgowns, and taking each other's hands, started to dance in a circle. And while they danced, they sang this song they had just made up:

> *"A goat, a goat, a little goat!*
> *Papa brought a little goat!*
> *The goat will give us mi-i-lk*
> *And Mama will make noodles!"*

Watching his children dancing and singing, Shimmen-Eli expanded with pleasure. "Poor children," he thought, "so eager for a little milk. That's all right, my children. Today you'll have as much milk as you want. And from now on you'll have a glass of milk every day, *kasha* with milk, and milk with your tea. A goat is really a blessing. Now let Fishel charge as much for his meat as he wants to. He always gave us bones instead of meat, so let him choke on his bones. What do I need his meat for if we have milk? For the Sabbath? For Sabbath we can buy fish. Where is it written that a Jew must eat meat? I have not seen a law on that anywhere. If all good Jews only listened to me, they would all buy themselves goats."

With these thoughts Shimmen-Eli *Shma-Koleinu* put away his *tallis* and *tfillin,* washed himself, made a benediction over a slice of bread, and sat down to wait for the noodles. Instead, the door flew open and in rushed Tsippa-Baila-Reiza with an empty pail, sputtering with anger, her face aflame. And a shower of curses began to descend on the head of poor Shimmen-Eli—not curses but burning stones. Fire and brimstone poured from Tsippa-Baila-Reiza's mouth.

"May your father, that drunkard, move over in his grave and make room for you!" she cried. "May you turn into a stone, a bone! May you end in hell! I could shoot you, hang you, drown you, roast you alive! I could cut you, slice you, chop you to pieces! Go, you robber, murderer, apostate! Take a look at the goat you brought me! May a scourge descend upon your head and arms and legs! God in heaven! Dear, true, loving Father!"

That was all that Shimmen-Eli heard. Pulling his cap down over his eyes, he went out of the house to see the misfortune that had befallen him.

Coming outside and seeing the goat tethered to the gatepost calmly chewing her cud, he stood fixed in his tracks, not knowing what to do or where to turn. He stood there thinking and thinking, and at last said to himself, " 'Let me die with the Philistines!' I'll get even with them yet, that *melamed* and his wife! They found the right person to play tricks on! I'll show them a few tricks they won't forget. He looked so innocent, too, that *melamed*: he didn't want anything to do with the whole transaction. And this is what he did to me . . . No wonder the children laughed when the rabbi led me out with the goat and his wife wished all that milk onto us . . . Milk I'll give them! I'll milk the blood out of those holy Kozodoievkites, those cheats, those swindlers!"

And once more he set out for Kozodoievka, with the intention of giving the teacher and his wife what they had coming . . .

A little later, passing by the Oak Tavern and seeing the innkeeper in the doorway, with his pipe between his teeth, our tailor burst out laughing.

"What are you so happy about?" asked the innkeeper. "What are you laughing for?"

"Listen to this," said the tailor, "and maybe you'll laugh, too." And he roared as though ten devils were tickling him. "Well, what do you think of my luck? Everything has to happen to me! You should have heard what I got from my wife this morning—what Pharaoh's chariots and horsemen got from the Lord. She served it up in every kind of dish, and I had to take it on an empty stomach. If I could only pass it on to the *melamed* and his wife! Believe me, I'll never let them get away with it. It will be an eye for an eye and a tooth for a tooth. I don't like to have people play tricks like this on me. But come, Dodi, put this cursed goat into the barn for a few minutes, and then pour me a drink. I'm a troubled man. I need a little strength before I face those people again.

"Ah, Reb Dodi, here's to your health. We're still men,

that's the main thing. And remember what we are enjoined in the Bible: 'Do not worry . . .' You can be sure that I'll give them something to think about before this morning is over. I'll show them how to play tricks on a member of the Tailors' Guild ('Shears and Iron' our emblem!)."

"Who told you it was a trick?" asked the innkeeper innocently, puffing away at his pipe. "Maybe you made a mistake in picking the goat?"

Shimmen-Eli nearly sprang at the innkeeper's throat. "Do you know what you're saying? I came and asked for a goat that would give milk, even as Jacob asked for Rachel. And I was tricked just as he was!"

Dodi puffed at his pipe, shrugged his shoulders, and threw up his hands as if to say, "Is it my fault? What can I do about it?"

And once more Shimmen-Eli took his goat and went on his way to Kozodoievka. And his anger burned within him.

VIII

And the teacher labored with his pupils, still on the same section in the *Gamorah* dealing with damages and injuries. Their voices resounded over the whole synagogue yard:

"The—cow—swung—her—tail—and—she—broke—the—pitcher!"

"Good morning to you, my Rabbi, and to you boys, and to all Israel," said Shimmen-Eli. "Give me a minute of your time, I pray you. The cow won't run away, and the broken pitcher surely will not mend itself!

"That was a fine trick you played on me, Rabbi. No doubt it was a joke, but I don't like such jokes. It's too much like that story about the two men who were taking their bath one Friday afternoon, stretched out on the top ledge at the bath house. Said one of the men to the other, 'Here is my besom. Whip me with it.' And the other, taking the besom, beat him till he was bleeding. Said the first, 'Listen, my friend! If I have wronged you and you want to pay me back now while I am naked and helpless, that is very well. But if you are doing it as a joke, I want to tell you: I don't care for such jokes!' "

"What is the point of that?" asked the *melamed,* taking off his glasses and scratching his ear with them.

"This is the point. Why did you trick me that way—giving me a goat like this? For that kind of trick," he said, showing him an open hand, "you may get something in return! You needn't think you're dealing with just anybody! I'm Shimmen-Eli of Zolodievka, member of the Tailors' Guild and president of our synagogue ('Shears and Iron' our emblem!)."

The tailor was so excited that he shook all over, and the *melamed,* putting on his glasses, stared at him in amazement. The whole room rocked with laughter.

"Why do you look at me like a crazy fool?" demanded the tailor angrily. "I come here and buy a goat from you, and you send me home with—the devil alone knows what!"

"You don't like my goat?" the teacher asked, slowly.

"The goat? If that's a goat, then you're the governor of this province."

The boys burst into laughter anew. And at this point Tema-Gittel the Silent came in and the real battle started. Shimmen-Eli yelled at Tema-Gittel and Tema-Gittel yelled back. The *melamed* looked from one to the other, and the boys laughed louder and louder. Tema-Gittel shrieked, Shimmen-Eli roared, with neither yielding, till Tema-Gittel caught the tailor by the hand and pulled him out through the door.

"Come!" she cried. "Come to the rabbi. Let the whole world see how a Zolodievka tailor can persecute innocent people—slander them!"

"Yes, let's go," said Shimmen-Eli. "Certainly let the world see how people who are considered honest, even holy, can rob a stranger and ruin him. As we say in our prayers, 'We have become a mockery and a derision . . .' And you come too, *melamed*."

Whereupon the *melamed* put on his plush hat over his skull-cap, and the four of them went to the rabbi together—the tailor, the *melamed*, his wife, and the goat.

When the delegation arrived, they found the rabbi saying his prayers. When he was through, he gathered up the skirts of his long coat and seated himself on his chair, an ancient relic that was little more than feet and armrests, shaky as the last teeth of an old man.

When he had finished hearing both parties, who had hardly let each other talk, the rabbi sent for the elders and the *shochet* and the other leading citizens of the town, and when they arrived he said to the tailor:

"Now be so kind as to repeat your story from beginning to end, and then we'll let her tell hers."

And Shimmen-Eli willingly told his story all over again. He told them who he was—Shimmen-Eli of Zolodievka, member of the Tailors' Guild and president of the synagogue (though he needed that honor like a headache). Harassed by his wife, Tsippa-Baila-Reiza, who was suddenly determined to have a goat, he had come to Kozodoievka, and there had bought from the *melamed* an animal that was supposed to be a goat. But it turned out that these people had taken away his money and passed off on him the devil alone knew what—possibly as a joke, but he, Shimmen-Eli, hated such jokes. "No doubt you have heard," he said, "the story of the two men who were taking their bath on a Friday afternoon . . ."

And the tailor, Shimmen-Eli, repeated the story of the bath, and the rabbi and the elders and the other leading citizens nodded their heads and smiled.

"Now that we have heard one side," said the rabbi, "let us hear the other."

At this Chaim-Chana the Wise arose from his seat, pulled his plush hat down over his skullcap, and began:

"Hear me, O Rabbi, this is my story, just like this. I was sitting with my pupils, sitting and studying, I was studying the Order of Injuries, that's what we were studying. *Bubi-Kama?* Yes, *Bubi-Kama.* And there walks in this man from Zolodievka, and he says he's from Zolodievka, from Zolodievka, you understand, and he greets me and tells me a long story. He tells me that he's from Zolodievka, a Zolodievkite, that is, and he has a wife whose name is Tsippa-Baila-Reiza. Yes, I'm sure it's Tsippa-Baila-Reiza. At least so it seems to me. Isn't that it?"

And he leaned over to the tailor questioningly, and the tailor, who had been standing all this time with his eyes shut, fingering his little beard, his head a little to one side, swaying back and forth, answered, "That is true. She has all three names, Tsippa and Baila and Reiza. She has been called by these names as long as I have known her, which is now— let's see—about thirty years. And now, my dear friend, let's hear what else you have to say. Don't go wandering. Get down to business. Tell them what I said and what you said. In the words of King Solomon, 'Beat not around the bush.' "

"But I don't know anything about it. I don't," said the *melamed,* frightened, and pointed to his wife. "She talked to him. She did the talking. She made the deal with him. I don't know anything."

"Then," said the rabbi, "let's hear what you have to say." And he pointed to the *melamed's* wife.

Tema-Gittel wiped her lips, leaned her chin on one hand and with the other began to tell her side of the story. She talked quickly, without stopping for breath, and her face grew redder and redder as she spoke.

"Listen to me," she said. "Here is the real story of what happened. This tailor from Zolodievka is either crazy or drunk or just doesn't know what he's talking about. Have you ever heard of such a thing? A man comes to me all the way from Zolodievka and fastens himself to us like a grease spot. He won't leave us alone. He insists: I must sell him a goat. (As you know, I had two of them.)

"The tailor makes a speech. He himself would not be buying a goat, but since his wife Tsippa-Baila-Reiza has set her heart on a goat, and a wife, he says, must be obeyed . . . Do you follow me, Rabbi? So I told him, 'What difference does that make to me? You want to buy a goat? I'll sell you a goat. That is, I wouldn't sell it for any amount, for what is money? Money is round. It rolls away, but a goat remains a goat, and especially a goat like this. It's a sweetheart, not a goat. So easy to milk! And the milk she gives! And what does she eat? Once a day a measure of oats, and for the rest some straw from the roof of the synagogue.'

"But thinking it over, I decided: after all, I have two goats, and money is a temptation. Anyway, at this point my husband told me to make up my mind, and we agreed on the price. How much do you think it was? May my enemies never have any more than we asked for that goat. And I gave him the goat, a treasure of a goat. And now he comes back, this tailor does, and tries to tell me that it's not a goat. It doesn't give milk. Do you know what? Here is the goat. Give me a milk pail, and I'll milk her right here in front of your eyes."

And she borrowed a pail from the rabbi's wife and milked the goat right there in front of their eyes, and she brought the milk to each one separately to see. First, naturally, to the rabbi, then to the elders, then to the other leading citizens, and finally to the assembled populace. And such a clamor arose! Such a tumult! This one said, "We must punish this Zolodievka tailor. Let him buy drinks for us all." Another said, "Punishing him like this is not enough. We ought to take away the goat." Still another said, "The goat is a goat. Let him keep it. Let him enjoy it to a ripe old age. What we ought to do is give him a few good kicks and send him and the goat both to the devil!"

When he saw this turn of events, Shimmen-Eli quietly slipped out of the rabbi's house, and disappeared.

IX

The tailor hastened away from the angry multitude like a man running from a fire. From time to time he looked back to see if anyone was following him, and he thanked the Lord for having escaped without a beating.

When he approached the Oak Tavern, Shimmen-Eli said to himself: "He'll never get the truth out of me."

"Well, what happened?" asked Dodi with feigned interest.

"What should happen?" said Shimmen-Eli. "People have respect for a man like me. They can't play tricks on me. After all, I'm not a schoolboy. I showed them a few things. I had a little discussion with the *melamed* too, about a few points in the *Gamorah,* and we found out that I knew more than he did. Anyway, to make a long story short, they begged my pardon and gave me the goat I had bought. Here she is. Take her for a little while, my kinsman, and then give me a drink."

"He is not only a braggart," thought Dodi to himself, "but

a liar as well. I'll have to play the same game once more and see what he'll say next time."

And to the tailor he said: "I have just the thing for you— a glass of old cherry wine."

"Cherry wine!" said Shimmen-Eli and licked his lips in anticipation. "Bring it out and I'll tell you what I think of it. Not everyone knows what good wine is."

When he had drained the first glass, the tailor's tongue began wagging again. He said, "Tell me, dear kinsman, you're no fool and you have dealings with many people. Tell me, do you believe in magic, in illusions?"

"For instance?" asked Dodi, innocently.

"Why," said Shimmen-Eli, "*dybbuks,* elves, evil spirits of all sorts, wandering souls . . ."

"What makes you ask?" said Dodi, puffing at his pipe.

"Just like that," said Shimmen-Eli, and went on talking about sorcerers, witches, devils, gnomes, werewolves.

Dodi pretended to listen attentively, smoked his pipe, and then he spat and said to the tailor, "Do you know what, Shimmen-Eli? I'll be afraid to sleep tonight. I'll tell you the truth: I have always been afraid of ghosts, but from now on I'll believe in *dybbuks* and gnomes as well."

"Can you help yourself?" said the tailor. "Try not believing! Just let one good gnome come along and start playing tricks on you—upset your borsht, pour out your water, empty all your pitchers, break your pots, tie knots in the fringes of your *tallis kot'n,* throw a cat into your bed and let it lie on your chest like a ten-pound weight . . ."

"Enough! Enough!" begged the innkeeper, spitting to ward off spirits. "Don't ever tell me stories like that so late at night!"

"Goodbye, Reb Dodi. Forgive me for teasing you. You know I'm not to blame. As the saying is, 'The old woman had no troubles . . .' You know that saying, don't you? Well, good night . . ."

X

When the tailor returned to Zolodievka he walked into the house boldly, determined to give his wife a piece of his mind; but he controlled himself. After all, what can you expect from a woman? And for the sake of harmony he told her this story:

"Believe me, Tsippa-Baila-Reiza, in spite of what you think, people have to look up to me. I wish you could have seen what I gave that *melamed* and his wife! It was as much as they could take. And then I dragged them off to the rabbi and he ruled that they must pay a fine, because when a man like Shimmen-Eli comes to buy a goat from them, he deserves the greatest consideration, for this Shimmen-Eli, says the rabbi, is a man who . . ."

But Tsippa-Baila-Reiza did not want to hear any more about the praise that had been showered on her husband. What she wanted was to see the real goat he had now brought with him, so she took her pail again and ran out of the house. But it was not long before she came running back, speechless with anger. Catching Shimmen-Eli by the collar, she gave him three good shoves, pushed him out of the house, and told him to go to the devil together with his goat.

Outside, a crowd of men, women and children quickly gathered around the tailor and his goat, and he told them the story of the goat which in Kozodoievka had given milk, but every time he brought her home was no longer a she-goat. With many oaths he swore that he himself had seen the full pail of milk that she had given in the rabbi's house. More and more people came by, examined the goat with deep interest, listened to the story, asked to have it repeated, and wondered greatly at it. Others laughed and teased him, still others shook their heads, spat on the ground, and said, "A fine goat that is. If that's a goat, then I'm the rabbi's wife!"

"What, then is it?" asked the tailor.

"A demon, can't you see? It's possessed. It's a *gilgul*."

The crowd caught the word *gilgul,* and soon they all began to tell each other stories about spirits and ghosts, incidents that had occurred right here in Zolodievka, in Kozodoievka, in Yampoli, in Pischi-Yaboda, in Haplapovitch, in Petchi-Hvost, and other places. Who had not heard the story of Lazer-Wolf's horse that had to be taken out beyond the town, killed, and buried in a shroud? Or about the fowl which had been served up for a Sabbath dinner, and when it was placed on the table began to flap its wings? Or many other such true and well-known happenings?

After several more minutes of this, Shimmen-Eli pulled once more at his rope and proceeded again on his way to Kozodoievka, followed by a band of schoolboys shouting, "Hurrah for Shimmen-Eli! Hurrah for the milking tailor!"

And everybody roared with laughter.

At this the tailor was deeply hurt. As if it were not enough to have this misfortune happen to him, they made a laughing-stock of him too. So, taking the goat, he went through the town and sounded an alarm among the members of his Guild. How could they stand by and be silent at such an outrage? And he told them the whole story of what had happened to him in Kozodoievka, showed them the goat, and at once they sent for liquor, held a meeting, and decided to go to the rabbi, the elders, and the leading citizens of the community and ask them to come to their aid. Why, who had ever heard of such an outrage? To cheat a poor tailor, take away his last few *rubles,* supposedly sell him a goat and actually palm off the devil alone knew what! And then to play the same trick on him a second time! Such an outrage had never been heard of even in Sodom!

And the delegation came to the rabbi, the elders and the leading men of the town and raised a hue and cry. Why, who had ever heard of such an outrage? To cheat a poor tailor, rob him of his last few *rubles*? And they recounted the story of the tailor and his goat in all its details.

The rabbi, the elders, and the leading men of the town listened to the complaints, and that evening held a meeting at the rabbi's house, where it was decided to write a letter then and there to the rabbi, elders and leading men of Kozodoievka. And this they did, producing a letter in classical Hebrew, written in a style as lofty as the occasion demanded.

And here is the letter, word for word, as it was written:

"To the honorable Rabbi, Elders, Sages, renowned scholars, pillars who uphold and support the entire house of Israel! Joy unto you and joy unto everyone within the sacred community of Kozodoievka! May all that is good come unto you and remain with you. Amen.

"It has come to our attention, worthy Rabbi and Elders, that a great wrong has been committed unto one of our townspeople, the tailor Shimmen-Eli, son of Bendit-Leib, known also as Shimmen-Eli *Shma-Koleinu*, as follows:

"Two of your inhabitants, the *melamed* Chaim-Chana and his spouse Tema-Gittel, did with cunning extort the following sum, six and one-half *rubles* in silver, which they took unto themselves, and wiping their lips said, 'We have done no wrong.' Now, mark you, honorable sirs, such things are not done by Jews! All of us here undersigned are witnesses that this tailor is a poor workingman and has many children whom he supports by the honest toil of his hands. As King David says in the Book of Psalms: 'When thou eatest the

labor of thy hands, happy shalt thou be, and it shall be well
with thee.' And our sages have interpreted it thus: happy
in this world, and well in the next world. Therefore do we
beg you to search out and inquire as to what has been done,
so that your judgment may shine forth like the sun and you
may pass this proper decision: that either the tailor receive
his money back entirely or that he be given the goat that
he had bought, for that one which he brought home with
him is not truly a goat! To this last fact our whole town can
swear.

"Then let there be peace among us. As our sages have said,
'There is nothing so blessed as peace.' Peace unto you, peace
unto the farthest and the nearest, peace unto all Israel. Amen.

"From us, your servants . . ."

And then they all signed their names. First the rabbi himself, then the elders, then the leading citizens, and then, one
after the other, proudly if not always legibly, the entire mem-
bership of the Tailors' Guild.

XI

And it came to pass that night that the moon shone down
on Zolodievka and on all its bleak tumbledown little houses
huddled together without yards, without trees, without fences,
like gravestones in an old cemetery. And though the air was
by no means fresh and the odors of the square and the marketplace were hardly pleasant and the dust was thick everywhere,
nevertheless the people all came out, like roaches from their
cracks, men and women, old people and little children, for
"a breath of fresh air" after the stifling hot day. They sat
on their stoops, talking, gossiping, or simply looking up at
the sky, watching the face of the moon and the myriads of
stars that, if you had eighteen heads, you could not count.

All that night Shimmen-Eli the tailor wandered by himself through the side streets and alleys of the little town with
his goat, hiding from the small mischief-makers who had
followed him all through the day. He thought that when it
was light enough he would start back again toward Kozodoievka. And meanwhile he slipped into Hodel's tavern to
take a drink for his sorrow's sake; unburden his heart, and
seek the sympathetic tavern-keeper's advice in his grievous
plight.

Hodel the tavern-keeper was a widow, a woman with brains,
who knew all the public officials and was a good friend in
need to all the workingmen in town. As a girl she had been
known as a great beauty and had almost married a wealthy
man, an excise collector. The story went that once when he
was passing through Zolodievka the collector had seen her
leading some geese to the *shochet,* and wanted to marry her
at once. But the town gossiped so much that the match fell
through. Later, against her will, she married some poor fellow, an epileptic, and again the tongues of the gossips began
to wag. They said she was still in love with the exciseman,
and they made up this song about her, a song which the women
and maidens still sing to this day in Zolodievka.

It starts like this:

> *The moon was shining.*
> *It was the middle of the night.*
> *Hodel sat at her door.*

And it ends with these words:

> *I love you, my soul,*
> *Without end.*
> *I cannot live without you.*

And it was to this same Hodel that our tailor now poured

out his heart. It was to her that he came for advice. "What shall I do?" he asked. "Tell me. After all, you are not only beautiful but wise. As King David—or who was it?—said in the *Song of Songs:* 'I am black but comely, O ye daughters of Jerusalem.' So tell me what to do."

"What can you do?" answered Hodel, and spat vigorously. "Can't you see it's an evil spirit? What are you keeping it for? Get rid of her. Throw her out. Or the same thing may happen to you that once happened to my Aunt Pearl, may she rest in peace."

"And what happened to her?" asked Shimmen-Eli, frightened.

"This," said Hodel, with a sigh. "My Aunt Pearl was a good honest woman (all of us have been good and honest in our family, though here in this forsaken town—may it burn to the ground—everybody always has the worst to say about everyone). Well, one day my Aunt Pearl was going to market and on the ground in front of her she saw a spool of thread. 'A spool of thread,' she thought, 'comes in handy,' so she bent down and picked it up. The spool jumped in her face and then fell to the ground. She bent down and picked it up again. Again it jumped in her face and again fell down. This happened again and again till at last she spit on it, said, 'Let the devil take it,' and started back home. Once or twice she looked back, and there was the spool of thread rolling after her. Well, she came home frightened to death, fell in a faint, and was sick for almost a whole year afterward. Now, what do you think that was? Tell me. Guess."

"Ah, they're all alike, these women!" said Shimmen-Eli. "Old wives' tales, nonsense, poppycock! If you wanted to listen to what women babbled about, you'd soon be afraid of your own shadow. It is truly written: 'And a voice was given unto them.' Geese, that's what they are! But never

mind. That is life; don't worry. Good night. Good night
to you."

And Shimmen-Eli went on his way.

The night was sprinkled with stars. The moon floated past
clouds that were like tall dark mountains inlaid with silver.
With half a face the moon looked down on the town of
Zolodievka sunk in deep slumber. Some of the people of
the town who were afraid of bedbugs had gone to sleep outdoors, had covered their faces with homespun sheets and were
snoring lustily, dreaming sweet dreams, dreams of profitable
transactions, of considerate landlords, of baskets of food
brought home, dreams of wealth and honor, or of honor alone:
all sorts of dreams. There was not a living creature on the
streets. Not a sound was to be heard. Even the butchers' dogs
who had barked and fought all day, now burrowed themselves between the logs in the back yard, hid their muzzles
in their paws, and slept. From time to time a short bark
escaped one of them when he dreamed of a bone that another
dog was gnawing or of a fly that was buzzing in his ear.
Now and then a beetle flew by, humming like the string of
a bass violin, zh-zh-zh-zh, then fell to the ground and was
silent. Even the town watchman who went around every
night, keeping an eye on the stores and rattling his sticks over
the windows, had this night become drunk, and leaning
against a wall, fell fast asleep. In this silence Shimmen-Eli
was the only one awake, not knowing whether to move or to
stand still or to sit down.

He walked and muttered to himself, "The old woman had
no troubles, so she bought herself a horse . . . Oh, this goat,
this goat! May it break a leg and die! A goat? Yes, a goat.
A little goat. *Chad gadyo, chad gadyo.* One little goat . . ."

He burst out laughing and was frightened by his own
laughter. Passing by the old synagogue renowned for the

spirits of dead men who prayed there every Saturday night
in their shrouds and prayer shawls, he thought he heard a
weird singing as of the wind blowing down a chimney on a
winter night. And quickly turning away he found himself
near the Russian church, from whose steeple a strange bird
whistled shrilly. A terrible fear seized him. He tried to take
heart, to steel himself with a prayer, but the words would
not come.

Then looming before his eyes he saw the forms of friends
long dead. And he remembered the terrifying stories he had
heard in bygone days of devils, spirits, vampires, ghouls,
goblins, of strange creatures that moved on tiny wheels, of
some that walked on their hands, others that looked at you
through a single eye, and spirits that wandered through
eternity in long white shrouds. Shimmen-Eli began to think
that the goat he was leading was really not a goat at all, but
a sprite of some sort that at any moment would stick out its
long, pointed tongue, or flap a pair of wings and utter a
loud cock-a-doodle-doo. He felt his head whirling. He stopped,
loosened the rope that had been tied around his waist, and
urged the goat to leave him. But the goat would not budge.
Shimmen-Eli took a few steps; the goat followed. He turned
to the right; so did the goat. He turned left; the goat did too.

"Shma Yisroel!" screamed Shimmen-Eli, and started to
run as fast as he could. And as he ran he imagined that someone was chasing him and mocking him in a thin, goatlike
voice, but the words were the words of a human: "Blessed
art thou . . . O Lord . . . who quickenest the dead . . ."

XII

When the next day dawned and the men arose to go to the
synagogue, the women to market. and the young girls to

lead the animals to pasture, they found Shimmen-Eli sitting on the ground and near him the goat, wagging his beard and chewing the cud. When they spoke to the tailor he did not answer. He sat like a graven image staring in front of him. Quickly a crowd gathered; people came running from all over town, and a hubbub arose: "Shimmen-Eli . . . goat . . . *Shma-Koleinu* . . . *gilgul* . . . demons . . . spirits . . . werewolves . . ." Rumors flew about, with everybody telling a different story. Someone said he had seen him riding through the night.

"Who rode whom?" asked a man, sticking his head into the circle. "Did Shimmen-Eli ride the goat or did the goat ride Shimmen-Eli?"

The crowd burst out laughing.

"What are you laughing at?" a workingman burst out. "You ought to be ashamed of yourselves! Grown men with beards. Married men with families. Shame on you! Making fun of a poor tailor. Can't you see the man is not himself? He is a sick man. Instead of standing around sharpening your teeth, it would be better if you took him home and called the doctor!"

These words brought the people to their senses, and they stopped laughing at once. Someone ran off for water, others to get Yudel the healer. They took Shimmen-Eli under the arms, led him home and put him to bed. Soon Yudel came running with all his paraphernalia and began to work on him. He rubbed him, blew into his face, applied leeches, tapped his vein and drew a panful of blood.

"The more blood we draw," explained Yudel, "the better it will be, for all illnesses come from within, from the blood itself." And after presenting this bit of medical theory Yudel promised to come again in the evening.

And when Tsippa-Baila-Reiza saw her husband stretched

out on the broken old couch, covered with rags, his eyes
rolled upward, his lips parched, raving in fever, she began
to wring her hands, beat her head against the wall, wailed
and wept as one weeps for the dead.

"Woe is me, wind is me! What will become of me now?
What will become of me and all my children?"

And the children, naked and barefoot, gathered about their
mother and joined her in her lamentations. The older ones
wept silently, hiding their faces; the smaller ones who did not
understand what had happened wailed out loud. And the
youngest of all, a little boy of three, with a pinched yellow
face, stood close to his mother with his tiny crooked legs and
protruding belly and screamed loudest of all. "Ma-ma! I'm
hun-gry!"

All the neighbors came to find out how Shimmen-Eli was,
but the sight of the poor tailor and his family was so heart-
rending that nobody could stay long. Only a few women remained, and stood with tear-stained faces near Tsippa-Baila-
Reiza, their noses red from blowing, their mouths working,
shaking their heads as though to say, "Poor Tsippa-Baila-
Reiza. Nothing can help her now."

Wonder of wonders! For fifty years Shimmen-Eli *Shma-
Koleinu* had lived in Zolodievka in poverty and oppression.
For fifty years he had lain in obscurity. No one spoke of him,
no one knew what sort of man he was. But now that he was
so close to death, the town suddenly became aware of all his
virtues. It suddenly became known that he had been a good
and kind man, generous and charitable; that is to say, he had
forced money out of the rich and divided it among the poor.
He had fought everybody for those poor people, fought
staunchly, and had shared his last bite with others. These
and many other things they told about the poor tailor, as
people tell about a dead man at his funeral. And they all came

to see him from all directions. They did everything they could to save him, to keep him from dying before his time.

XIII

And when the sun had set and night had fallen, the members of the Tailors' Guild came together at Hodel's tavern, ordered whisky, and called a meeting. They argued, shouted, ranted, pounded on the table.

"Why isn't something done? A fine town like Zolodievka— may it burn to the ground! —with so many rich people in it, and not one of them willing to lift a finger! They all live off the sweat of us, and none of them will help us. Who puts all the money into the community fund? We do. Who is skinned alive to support the *shochet*, the bath house, the synagogue? We are! Do we have to stand for everything? Come on, let's go to the rabbi and the elders. Now it's their turn to be useful. They'll have to keep his family alive! Come, let us deal with them!"

And they went to the rabbi with their complaint. In reply, the rabbi read to them the letter that had just been brought by a teamster from Kozodoievka. And this is what it said:

"To the honorable Rabbis, elders, sages and scholars of Zolodievka! May peace reign eternally in your holy community!

"No sooner had we received your letter, which, let us assure you, was as honey in our mouths, than we congregated and carefully studied the matter you referred to. In answer we can say only this, that you have wrongfully accused a townsman of ours. This tailor of yours is a wicked man who with base slander has created a scandal between our two communities and deserves to be punished accordingly. We, the undersigned, are ready under oath to bear witness that with our own eyes we saw the goat give milk. May the goats of all our friends be as bountiful.

"Pay no heed to the accusations of the tailor. Pay no heed to the words of ignorant people who speak falsely.

"Peace be unto you and peace unto all Jews everywhere, now and forever, Amen.

"From your younger brothers who bow in the dust at your feet . . ."

When the rabbi had finished reading this letter, the delegation cried out in anger, "Aha, those Kozodoievka hooligans! They're making fun of us! Let's show them who we are and what our emblem is! Shears and Iron! Let them remember that!"

And at once they called another meeting, sent for more whisky, and it was decided to take this imitation of a goat straight to Kozodoievka, take vengeance on the teacher, wreck his *cheder* and overturn the whole town.

No sooner said than done. They mustered about sixty men for the trip, tailors, shoemakers, carpenters, blacksmiths, butchers, strong young men who enjoyed a fight, each one armed with the tools of his trade: this one with a wooden yardstick, that one with a flatiron, one with a last, another with an axe, some with hammers and cleavers, and others with ordinary household utensils, rolling pins, graters, carving knives . . . And it was decided without further delay that they should march off to Kozodoievka and make war on the town, kill and destroy and lay waste.

"Once for all!" they cried. " 'Let us die with the Philistines!' Let's kill them off and be done with it!"

"But wait," one of them called out. "You are ready for the slaughter, fully armed. But where is the goat?"

"That's right! Where did the demon go?"

"He's been swallowed up."

"Then he's not such a fool. But where could he have gone to?"

"Home to the *melamed*. Can't you understand?"

"He'd be crazy to do that!"

"Where else could he go?"

"What difference does it make? Guess what you want to. The point is, the goat has disappeared!"

XIV

Now let us leave the possessed tailor struggling with the Angel of Death and the workingmen of the town preparing for battle, and let us pass on to the demon himself, that is— the goat.

When the goat became aware of the uproar that had arisen in the town, he thought to himself: what was he going to get out of all this? What was the use of being tied to the tailor's waist and following him wherever he went and starving to death? It was better to run off into the wide world and see what freedom meant. So he made his escape, running off madly across the marketplace, his feet scarcely touching the earth, knocking over men and women, jumping over everything that stood in his way—tables of bread and rolls, baskets of grapes and currants. He leaped over crockery and glassware, scattered and shattered everything in his path. The women screamed, "Who is it? What is it? What happened? A goat, a possessed creature, a demon! Woe is me! Where is he? There, there he is! Catch him! Catch him!"

The men picked themselves up and ran after the goat as fast as they could, and the women, naturally, ran after the men. But in vain. Our goat had tasted the joys of freedom and was gone, never to be seen again.

And the unfortunate tailor? What became of him? And

how did the story end? Reader, don't compel me to tell you.
The end was not a happy one. The story began cheerfully
enough, but it ended like most cheerful stories, very tragically.
And since you know that I am not a gloomy soul who prefers
tears to laughter and likes to point a moral and teach a lesson,
let us part as cheerfully as we can. And I wish that all of you
readers and everybody else in the world may have more op-
portunities to laugh than to cry.

Laughter is healthful. The doctors bid us laugh.

A Yom Kippur Scandal

THAT'S nothing!" called out the man with round eyes, like an ox, who had been sitting all this time in a corner by the window, smoking and listening to our stories of thefts, robberies and expropriations. "I'll tell you a story of a theft that took place in our town, in the synagogue itself, and on *Yom Kippur* at that! It is worth listening to.

"Our town, Kasrilevka—that's where I'm from, you know— is a small town, and a poor one. There is no thievery there. No one steals anything for the simple reason that there is no-body to steal from and nothing worth stealing. And besides, a Jew is not a thief by nature. That is, he may be a thief, but not the sort who will climb through a window or attack you with a knife. He will divert, pervert, subvert and contravert as a matter of course; but he won't pull anything out of your pocket. He won't be caught like a common thief and led through the streets with a yellow placard on his back. Imagine, then, a theft taking place in Kasrilevka, and such a theft at that. Eighteen hundred *rubles* at one crack.

"Here is how it happened. One *Yom Yippur* eve, just before the evening services, a stranger arrived in our town, a salesman of some sort from Lithuania. He left his bag at an inn, and went forth immediately to look for a place of worship, and he came upon the old synagogue. Coming in just before the service began, he found the trustees around the collection plates. *'Sholom aleichem,'* said he. *'Aleichem sholom,'* they answered.

'Where does our guest hail from?' 'From Lithuania.' 'And
your name?' 'Even your grandmother wouldn't know if I told
her.' 'But you have come to our synagogue!' 'Where else should
I go?' 'Then you want to pray here?' 'Can I help myself?
What else can I do?' 'Then put something into the plate.'
'What did you think? That I was not going to pay?'

"To make a long story short, our guest took out three silver
rubles and put them in the plate. Then he put a *ruble* into the
cantor's plate, one into the rabbi's, gave one for the *cheder,*
threw a half into the charity box, and then began to divide
money among the poor who flocked to the door. And in our
town we have so many poor people that if you really wanted
to start giving, you could divide Rothschild's fortune among
them.

"Impressed by his generosity, the men quickly found a place
for him along the east wall. Where did they find room for him
when all the places along the wall are occupied? Don't ask.
Have you ever been at a celebration—a wedding or circumcision—when all the guests are already seated at the table, and
suddenly there is a commotion outside—the rich uncle has arrived? What do you do? You push and shove and squeeze
until a place is made for the rich relative. Squeezing is a Jewish
custom. If no one squeezes us, we squeeze each other."

The man with the eyes that bulged like an ox's paused, looked
at the crowd to see what effect his wit had on us, and went on.

"So our guest went up to his place of honor and called to
the *shammes* to bring him a praying stand. He put on his
tallis and started to pray. He prayed and he prayed, standing on his feet all the time. He never sat down or left his
place all evening long or all the next day. To fast all day
standing on one's feet, without ever sitting down--that only a
Litvak can do!

"But when it was all over, when the final blast of the *shofar* had died down, the Day of Atonement had ended, and Chaim the *melamed,* who had led the evening prayers after *Yom Kippur* from time immemorial, had cleared his throat, and in his tremulous voice had already begun—'*Ma-a-riv a-ro-vim . . .*' suddenly screams were heard. 'Help! Help! Help!' We looked around: the stranger was stretched out on the floor in a dead faint. We poured water on him, revived him, but he fainted again. What was the trouble? Plenty! This Litvak tells us that he had brought with him to Kasrilevka eighteen hundred *rubles.* To leave that much at the inn—think of it, eighteen hundred *rubles*—he had been afraid. Whom could he trust with such a sum of money in a strange town? And yet, to keep it in his pocket on *Yom Kippur* was not exactly proper either. So at last this plan had occurred to him: he had taken the money to the synagogue and slipped it into the praying stand. Only a Litvak could do a thing like that! . . . Now do you see why he had not stepped away from the praying stand for a single minute? And yet during one of the many prayers when we all turn our face to the wall, someone must have stolen the money . . .

"Well, the poor man wept, tore his hair, wrung his hands. What would he do with the money gone? It was not his own money, he said. He was only a clerk. The money was his employer's. He himself was a poor man, with a houseful of children. There was nothing for him to do now but go out and drown himself, or hang himself right here in front of everybody.

"Hearing these words, the crowd stood petrified, forgetting that they had all been fasting since the night before and it was time to go home and eat. It was a disgrace before a stranger, a shame and a scandal in our own eyes. A theft like that— eighteen hundred *rubles*! And where? In the Holy of Holies, in the old synagogue of Kasrilevka. And on what day? On the holiest day of the year, on *Yom Kippur*! Such a thing had never been heard of before.

" '*Shammes,* lock the door!' ordered our Rabbi. We have our own Rabbi in Kasrilevka, Reb Yozifel, a true man of God, a holy man. Not too sharp witted, perhaps, but a good man, a man with no bitterness in him. Sometimes he gets ideas that you would not hit upon if you had eighteen heads on your shoulders . . . When the door was locked, Reb Yozifel turned to the congregation, his face pale as death and his hands trembling, his eyes burning with a strange fire.

"He said, 'Listen to me, my friends, this is an ugly thing, a thing unheard of since the world was created—that here in Kasrilevka there should be a sinner, a renegade to his people, who would have the audacity to take from a stranger, a poor man with a family, a fortune like this. And on what day? On the holiest day of the year, on *Yom Kippur,* and perhaps at the last, most solemn moment—just before the *shofar* was blown! Such a thing has never happened anywhere. I cannot believe it is possible. It simply cannot be. But perhaps—who knows? Man is greedy, and the temptation—especially with a sum like this, eighteen hundred *rubles,* God forbid—is great enough. So if one of us was tempted, if he were fated to commit this evil on a day like this, we must probe the matter thoroughly, strike at the root of this whole affair. Heaven and earth have sworn that the truth must always rise as oil upon the waters. Therefore, my friends, let us search each other now, go through each other's garments, shake out our pockets—all of us from the oldest householder to the *shammes,* not leaving anyone out. Start with me. Search my pockets first.'

"Thus spoke Reb Yozifel, and he was the first to unbind his gabardine and turn his pockets inside out. And following his example all the men loosened their girdles and showed the linings of their pockets, too. They searched each other, they felt and shook one another, until they came to Lazer Yossel, who turned all colors and began to argue that, in the first place, the stranger was a swindler; that his story was the pure fabrication of a Litvak. No one had stolen any money from him. Couldn't they see that it was all a falsehood and a lie?

"The congregation began to clamor and shout. What did he mean by this? All the important men had allowed themselves to be searched, so why should Lazer Yossel escape? There are no privileged characters here. 'Search him! Search him!' the crowd roared.

"Lazer Yossel saw that it was hopeless, and began to plead for mercy with tears in his eyes. He begged them not to search him. He swore by all that was holy that he was as innocent in this as he would want to be of any wrongdoing as long as he lived. Then why didn't he want to be searched? It was a disgrace to him, he said. He begged them to have pity on his youth, not to bring this disgrace down on him. 'Do anything you wish with me,' he said, 'but don't touch my pockets.' How do you like that? Do you suppose we listened to him?

"But wait . . . I forgot to tell you who this Lazer Yossel was. He was not a Kasrilevkite himself. He came from the Devil knows where, at the time of his marriage, to live with his wife's parents. The rich man of our town had dug him up somewhere for his daughter, boasted that he had found a rare nugget, a fitting match for a daughter like his. He knew a thousand pages of *Talmud* by heart, and all of the Bible. He was a master of Hebrew, arithmetic, bookkeeping, algebra, penmanship—in short, everything you could think of. When he arrived in Kasrilevka—this jewel of a young man—everyone came out to gaze at him. What sort of bargain had the rich man picked out? Well, to look at him you could tell nothing. He was a young man, something in trousers. Not bad looking, but with a nose a trifle too long, eyes that burned like two coals, and a sharp tongue. Our leading citizens began to work on him: tried him out on a page of *Gamorah*, a chapter from the Scriptures. a bit of *Rambam*, this, that and the other. He was perfect in everything, the dog! Whenever you went after him, he was at home. Reb Yozifel himself said that he could have been a rabbi in any Jewish congregation. As for world affairs, there is nothing to talk about. We have an authority on such things in our town, Zaidel Reb Shaye's, but he could not hold a candle to Lazer Yossel. And when it came to chess—there was no one like him in all the world! Talk about versatile people . . . Naturally the whole town envied the rich man his find, but some of them felt he was a little too good to be true. He was too clever (and too much of anything is bad!). For a man of his station he was too free and easy, a hail-fellow-well-met, too familiar with all the young folk—boys, girls, and maybe even loose women. There were rumors . . . At the same time he went around alone too much, deep in thought. At the synagogue he came in last, put on his *tallis,* and with his skullcap on askew, thumbed aimlessly through his prayerbook without ever following the services. No one ever saw him doing anything exactly wrong, and yet people murmured that he was not a God-fearing man. Apparently a man cannot be perfect . . .

"And so, when his turn came to be searched and he refused to let them do it, that was all the proof most of the men needed that he was the one who had taken the money. He begged them to let him swear any oath they wished, begged them to chop him, roast him, cut him up—do anything but shake his pockets out. At this point even our Rabbi, Reb Yozifel, although he was a man we had never seen angry, lost his temper and started to shout.

" 'You!' he cried. 'You thus and thus! Do you know what you deserve? You see what all these men have endured. They were able to forget the disgrace and allowed themselves to be searched; but you want to be the only exception! God in heaven! Either confess and hand over the money, or let us see for ourselves what is in your pockets. You are trifling now with the entire Jewish community. Do you know what they can do to you?'

"To make a long story short, the men took hold of this young upstart, threw him down on the floor with force, and began to search him all over, shake out every one of his pockets. And finally they shook out . . . Well, guess what! A couple of well-gnawed chicken bones and a few dozen plum pits still moist from chewing. You can imagine what an impression this made—to discover food in the pockets of our prodigy on this holiest of fast days. Can you imagine the look on the young man's face, and on his father-in-law's? And on that of our poor Rabbi?

"Poor Reb Yozifel! He turned away in shame. He could look no one in the face. On *Yom Kippur,* and in his synagogue . . . As for the rest of us, hungry as we were, we could not stop talking about it all the way home. We rolled with laughter in the streets. Only Reb Yozifel walked home alone, his head bowed, full of grief, unable to look anyone in the eyes, as though the bones had been shaken out of his own pockets."

The story was apparently over. Unconcerned, the man with the round eyes of an ox turned back to the window and resumed smoking.

"Well," we all asked in one voice, "and what about the money?"

"What money?" asked the man innocently, watching the smoke he had exhaled.

"What do you mean—what money? The eighteen hundred *rubles!*"

"Oh," he drawled. "The eighteen hundred. They were gone."

"Gone?"

"Gone forever."

In Haste

For in haste didst thou come forth out of the Land of Egypt
—DEUTERONOMY, 16:3.

TO MY honored, beloved and respected friend, Sholom Aleichem:

I want to begin by informing you that I am still—Bless the Lord—among the living, and that I hope to hear the same from you, Amen. Next I want to tell you that, with God's help, I am now a king; that is, I have come home to Kasrilevka to spend the Passover with my wife and children, my father-in-law and mother-in-law, and with all my loved ones. And at Passover, as we all know, a Jew surrounded by his family is always a king. If only briefly, I hasten to inform you of all this, my dear, true friend. For a detailed account there is no time. It is Passover Eve, and on this day we must all do everything in great haste, standing on one foot. As it is written, "For *in haste* didst thou come forth out of the Land of Egypt."

But what to write of first, I hardly know myself. It seems to me that before anything else I ought to thank you and praise you for the good advice you gave me, to try my hand at matchmaking. Believe me, I shall never, never forget what you have done for me. You led me forth from the Land of Bondage, from the Gehenna of Yehupetz; you freed me from the desolate occupation of a commission salesman, and lifted

me to a noble, respected profession. And for this I am obligated
to praise and exalt you, to bless and adorn your name, as you
well deserve.

It is true that thus far I have not succeeded in negotiating a
single match, but I have made a beginning. Things are
stirring, and once things begin to stir there is always the possibility and the hope that with God's help something may
come of it. Especially in view of the fact that I do not work
alone. I operate in partnership with other matchmakers, the
best matchmakers in the world. As a result of these connections
I now have a reputation of my own. Wherever I come and
introduce myself, Menachem-Mendel from Yehupetz, I am
invited to sit down, I am given tea with preserves, I am treated
like an honored guest. They introduce me to the daughter of
the house, and the daughter shows me what she can do. She
turns to her governess and begins to speak French with her.
Words come pouring like peas out of a sack, and the mother
sits gazing at her daughter proudly, as though to say, "What
do you think of her? She speaks well, doesn't she?"

And listening to these girls, I have picked up some French
myself and I can understand quite a bit of the language. For
instance, if someone says to me, *"Parlez-vous Français?"*
("How are you feeling these days?") I say, *"Merci, bonjour."*
("Not bad, praise the Lord.")

Then, after she has given a demonstration of her French,
they have her sit down at the pianola to play something—
overtures and adagios and finales—so beautiful that it pene-
trates to the very depth of one's soul! In the meantime the
parents ask me to stay for supper and I let them talk me into
it. Why not? . . . At the table they serve me the best portions
of meat and feed me *tzimmes* even on weekdays. Afterwards,
I strike up a conversation with the daughter. "What," I ask,
"is your heart's desire—a lawyer, an engineer, a doctor?"

"Naturally," she says, "a doctor." And once more she starts jabbering in French with the governess, and at this point the mother has an opportunity to display her daughter's handi-work. "Her embroidery and her knitting are a feast to the eye," she says, "and her kindness, her goodness, her con-sideration for others—there is no one like her! And quiet—like a dove. And bright—as the day . . ."

And the father, in his turn, traces his pedigree for me. He tells me what a fine family he comes from, and his wife as well. He tells me who his grandfather was, and his great-grandfather, and all his wife's connections. Every one of them of the finest. Rich people, millionaires, famous and celebrated all over the world. "There is not a single common person in our whole family," he assures me. "And not one pauper," his wife adds. "Not a single workingman," he says. "No tailors and no cobblers," she adds. "You'll find no fakes or frauds among us," he tells me. "Or apostates either, I can assure you," she puts in.

In the doorway, when I'm ready to leave and they wish me a good journey, I sigh and let them know how expensive it is to travel these days. Every step costs money. And if he is not obtuse he knows what I mean, and gives me at least enough for expenses . . .

I tell you, my dear friend, that matchmaking is not at all such a bad profession—especially if God ever intercedes and you actually conclude a match! So far, as I have told you, I have not succeeded in marrying anyone off. I have had no luck. At the start everything looks auspicious. It could hardly be better. It was a match predestined since the Six Days of Creation. But at the last moment everything goes wrong. In this case the youth does not care for the maiden; in the other, the girl thinks the groom is too old. This one has too fine a pedigree; that one does not have enough money. This one wants the moon on a platter; that one doesn't know what he wants. There is plenty of trouble connected with it, and heartaches, and indigestion, I can assure you.

Right now I am on the verge of arranging a couple of matches—naturally with a few partners—which, if the Lord has mercy and they go through, will be something for the whole world to talk about. Both parties come from the wealthiest and finest and oldest families—there is none like them. And the girls are both the greatest beauties. You can't find their equal anywhere. Both are well-educated, gifted, kind, bright, quiet, modest—all the virtues you can think of. And what do I have to offer them? Real merchandise! One—a doctor from Odessa. But he wants no less than thirty thousand *rubles* dowry, and he has a right to it, because according to the practice that he says he has, he should be worth much more. I have another from Byelotzerkiev—a rare find! A bargain at twenty thousand! And another in Yehupetz—only he doesn't want to get married. And a whole flock of young little doctors who are only too anxious to get married.

Besides these I have a pack of lawyers and attorneys and justices at fifteen thousand and ten thousand, and smaller lawyers—young ones just hatched—that you can have for six thousand or five thousand, or even less. On top of that I have a couple of engineers who are already earning a living, and a few engineers still looking for work. And that is not all. I have an assortment of miscellaneous clients, elderly men, relics of past campaigns from Tetrevitz, from Makarevka, from Yampola and from Strishtch, without diplomas, but fine enough specimens, distinguished, skilled, intelligent. In short, there are plenty to pick from. The only trouble is that if the gentleman wants the lady, the lady does not want the gentleman. If the girl is willing, the man is not. Perhaps then you will ask why the man who does not want girl number one will not take num-

ber two, and vice versa? I thought of that myself, but it
doesn't seem to work. Do you know why? Because strangers
are always mixing in. They may be good people. They mean
no harm. But they spoil everything. And meanwhile letters
are flying back and forth. I send telegrams and receive telegrams every day. The whole world rocks and rolls!

And in the midst of it all, Passover gets in the way, like a
bone in the throat, blocking everything. I think it over. My
fortune won't run away from me. The merchandise I deal in
is not so perishable. Why shouldn't I take a few days off and
go to see my family in Kasrilevka? It's been so long since I've
been there. It is not fair to my wife and children to be away
from them so long. It does not look good to others, and it
is even embarrassing to myself. So, to make it short, I have
come home for Passover, and that is where I am writing you
this letter from.

Maybe you will ask, why have I not written to you before
this? Here is the answer. People like us are always worn out,
we never have time. We are always rushing about. We never
rest. I always keep thinking: if not today, then tomorrow.
Soon, soon, with God's help, I'll arrange a worthwhile match,
and then I'll write you all about it in celebration. But as it
happened that all my prospects dragged on and remained
hanging in the air, I kept putting off writing to you till God
should bring me safely home . . .

And now I shall tell you what my homecoming was like.
I'll describe everything just the way you like it. But if my account does not seem rounded out as yours always are, please
excuse me. Each one of us has to tell his story the way he can.

I arrived—that is, the train came into the station—yesterday.
But around here the mud is so deep that it took the wagon
all night to pull through to town. For a time it even looked
as if I might have to spend the Passover on the way some-

where, axle-deep in mud, together with the driver and the horses. You must be familiar with our Kasrilevka mud from the olden times. But ever since they began to talk about paving the roads around here, it seems as if the mud has become thicker and deeper than ever. In fact, people have begun going around without their galoshes, because they were always losing them in the mud. And some women have started a fashion even better than that. They go around without shoes, either. I wonder what they'll think of next!

Well, this morning, when we reached Kasrilevka itself, all the passengers had to get out of the wagon and go the rest of the way by foot. A fine homecoming! I felt my face burning. Acquaintance after acquaintance stopped me on the way, greeted me broadly, shook hands with me knee-deep in the mud—each with his own questions, his own comments. "How goes it with you, Menachem-Mendel?" "What is the latest news on the Yehupetz market?" "Look at the man, will you! In a derby hat and rubber overshoes!"

"Laugh, laugh," I answered, barely able to pull one foot after another out of the mud. "You have the right to laugh! Everywhere else in the world people really need galoshes, but here you can get along without them! Here it's as dry and sandy as in Palestine!"

I barely managed to drag myself home, and here I found a Gehenna. Like the fumes over Gehenna was the thick smoke that rose from the yard and the kitchen, where silverware for the holidays was being boiled, and everything else was being cleaned and scrubbed and scoured. And food, the rich and wonderful Passover food, was being cooked and baked and broiled. The shouting and clamoring of everyone, of mistresses and servants, the commands, the exhortations, the complaints and the threats, were enough to make a person deaf. A small thing—Passover Eve!

The first one to greet me was my mother-in-law, bless her. She is the same as ever, she has not changed in the least. She was in the front yard, standing over a wooden cot, her kerchief tied around her head with two pointed wings sticking out. In one hand she held a can of kerosene, in the other a brush. She was pickling bedbugs. When she saw me, she managed to control her joy. She kept right on with her work, muttering to herself:

"Well, well! You mention the Messiah—and look who comes! Here he is, my bird of Paradise . . . If he doesn't spoil, he'll find his way home. Goats run away, chickens get lost, but men always come back . . . The only place they don't return from is the Other World. Now I know why the cat was washing herself yesterday, and the dog was eating entrails . . . Oh, Sheine-Sheindel, daughter, come here! Welcome your ornament, your jewel, your crown of gold and diamonds! Your holy of holies . . . Quick, take the garbage away!"

At this point my wife runs out, frightened, and sees me. Her welcome is more direct.

"Tfui!" she spat out. "You picked just the right time to come. All year long you roam around that dirty city, lying around in all the attics, engage in every idolatry—and here you come fluttering in on Passover Eve, when we're busy cleaning up and there is no time to say a word to each other. I don't even have the time to put on a clean dress. I look like a fright. And you— fresh from the fine ladies of Yehupetz—may they roast in hell!—who held you in their clutches all year—may they not live through the Passover! Look at him! A plague on him! He doesn't even ask how a person is getting along, how the children are! Soreleh, Feigeleh, Yoseleh, Nechamenu, Moishe-Hershe-leh! Your father has come back! Suddenly remembered you!

May my worst enemies look as beautiful as you look in that derby hat!"

I must tell you the truth, dear friend. I barely recognized the children. And as for them—they didn't know me at all. But though my wife's welcome was not as ardent as I had hoped for, I could see that she was happy, for when I had finished greeting and kissing each of the children, I saw that she had withdrawn to one side and was crying.

But best and friendliest of all was the welcome I received from my father-in-law. He was as happy as if it were his own child he was seeing, or happy like a man who had been locked up in prison all these years and suddenly he sees another prisoner . . . My father-in-law, a distinguished-looking man with fine, dark eyes and a rich beard, had aged noticeably in these past few years, become white as a dove. Quietly he shook hands with me, asked how I was, and with a wink called me into his little alcove, and only when we were there alone did he embrace me.

"Do you know what, Mendel," he said to me with a deep sigh, "I'm growing old. Every year I'm a year older . . . But come, Mendel, sit down. Tell me what's new. You have been all over the world. How are things going on among our people? What is the true story about Dreyfus? What is it people are saying about a new war? What is happening in Palestine? Here we know nothing, we live like cattle . . ."

My father-in-law was getting wound up for a good long talk, but suddenly from outside we heard my mother-in-law's melodious voice:

"Boruch! Boruch!?" (The first Boruch was a shout, the second had a questioning overtone of astonishment in it, as if to say, "Aren't you here yet?")

"Just a minute! Here I come! I'm coming! I'm coming!"

answered my father-in-law, and he bounded from the room. A few times this happened. No sooner had he got started talking, when her voice rang out, "Boruch! Boruch!?" And each time he jumped. "I'm coming! I'm coming!" A little later, after breakfast, after the last few bread crusts found on the premises had been burned and the house itself had been purified for the holidays, and he was given a clean shirt and told that now he could go to the Baths, he became a different man, as though a new soul had been installed in his body. There at least, in the bath house, he thought he would have a chance for a few words. But again he was mistaken, woefully mistaken. As soon as we came in the crowd swarmed about us like bees, like the locusts in a year of famine. They almost ate me up alive. Every one of them wanted me to tell him what was going on in Yehupetz. Was it true, what they had heard about the bad times everywhere, the failures and bankruptcies? Did millionaire Brodsky still have some money? How was the Dreyfus case going to come out? Why didn't they hear about it any more? And how did it happen that England was still messing around with the Boers? These questions and many more they put to me from all sides. They almost pulled me apart. They didn't let me rest. And my father-in-law could not get a word in anywhere.

The same thing happened when we went to buy wine for the *seder*. As soon as we walked down into Yudel Veinshenker's cellar, I was greeted from all sides and had to shake hands with everybody. In the midst of it someone asked for Palestinian wine, and Yudel Veinshenker (much older now, with all his teeth gone) kept shouting that there was no such thing. There never had been and never would be. But one young man who pretended to be more worldly than the others, kept arguing that he had seen it himself in the papers.

"Papers! What papers?" shouted Yudel Veinshenker. "Lies and falsehoods! Some troublemakers must have thought it up! Those Zionists you hear about!"

The young man was stubborn. "As sure as I see you in front of me," he said, "I saw the Palestinian wines mentioned. And what's more, I'll tell you the exact name. Mount Carmel wine. And they sell it in all the shops in Yehupetz."

"In Yehupetz, you say?" several bystanders broke in. "Here is a man straight from Yehupetz. Menachem-Mendel Boruch-Hersh Leah-Dvoshe's! Let's ask Menachem-Mendel. He'll know!"

I tried to speak, but they wouldn't let me. For every word I say they ask me ten questions, and before I'm through with one answer another of them asks me ten more questions. "Why do they call it Mount Carmel wine? Is it from Mount Carmel itself or just from Palestine? How do they bring it from Mount Carmel? How much does it cost? Who makes it? Jewish colonists? Our own colonists? How many colonies do we have now in Palestine? What are their names, and what connection do they have with Baron Rothschild? Oh, Rothschild! How much is he really worth? Who is worth more—Rothschild or the Yehupetzer Brodsky? Why is Rothschild a Zionist and Brodsky not? Is it true, what they say, that Doctor Herzel is buying up Palestine from the Turks for the Zionists?"

"Come," my father-in-law says to me, "they don't let us get in a word anywhere."

And it was only later in the day, while he was grating horseradish outside, that my father-in-law was able to say a few words to me. But only a few words, because every little while we were interrupted by my mother-in-law.

"Boruch! *Boruch!?*"

"Right away! Here I come! Here I come!"

In the meantime the women had finished their work and had dressed themselves in their finest clothes and all their jewelry, like queens. My mother-in-law wore a dark green poplin dress with a flowered silk kerchief on her head. And Sheine-Sheindel had a flowered yellow silk dress with a dark green poplin kerchief on her head. And even I slipped into the alcove and put on my best clothes. Are we not all kings on Passover? And in the meanwhile I took a few sheets of paper and I'm writing you this letter. And once more, dear friend, I beg you to pardon me if I appear to be in a hurry. It's Passover Eve! If all is well and the Lord grants me strength, I shall write to you again in a few days. Then I shall have more time and I shall be able to write at greater length.

From your truest friend,
Menachem-Mendel

P.S. It is not my fate to enjoy anything in this world. There everything was ready, all was serene. The holiday spirit was in the air, and suddenly a misfortune overtook us. A dog stole into the kitchen, no one knows how, and ate up the greens and the chicken neck and the rest of the symbolic trimmings for tonight's *seder*. Suddenly there was an uproar and a tumult. Heavens were splitting open. I was sure murder was being done, or a fire had broken out, or at least someone had been scalded with boiling water. Everybody was yelling at everybody else, and all the cries melted into one uproar. Sheine-Sheindel was yelling at the servant girl; the servant girl was yelling at my father-in-law. "It's all his fault!" she cried. "The master has no brains! He's always leaving the door open! Always!"

But above them all could be heard my mother-in-law.

"Woe is me! Thunder and lightning! When the world calls a man crazy, you may believe it! A fool is worse than a sinner!

How should a person be a prophet and know that he would leave the door open, and suddenly, on Passover Eve, a dog would steal into the kitchen? And of all things to find the chicken bones? It never rains but it pours. I have always said: the dog always gets the best bite of food, and the pudding comes out according to the company (that must mean me!) . . . What can we do now? Boruch! *Boruch?*"

"Here I am! Right away! Here I am!"

I look at my father-in-law and think: "What a woeful lot is yours, poor unfortunate king, and what a woeful thing is thy kingdom."

Once more, be well, And enjoy a *kosher Pesach.*

Yours

M. M.

Eternal Life

IF YOU are willing to listen, I shall tell you the story of how I once took a burden upon myself, a burden which almost, almost ruined my life for me. And why do you think I did it? Simply because I was an inexperienced young man and none too shrewd. So far as that goes, I may be far from clever now, too, because if I were clever, I might have had a little money by now. How does the saying go? If you have money, you are not only clever, but handsome too, and can sing like a nightingale!

Well, there I was, a young man living with my father- and mother-in-law, as was the custom with young married couples in those days. And, as was also the custom in those days, I sat in the synagogue all day studying the *Torah*. Now and then I glanced into secular books too, but that had to be done on the sly so my father- and mother-in-law should not find out; not so much my father-in-law as my mother-in-law, a woman who was the real head of the family. You can really say she wore the pants. She managed all their affairs herself, picked out the husbands for her daughters herself, and herself arranged the entire match. It was she who had picked me out too, she who examined me in the *Torah,* she who brought me to Zvohil from Rademishli. I am from Rademishli, you know—that's where I was born. You must have heard of the town; it was recently in the papers.

So I lived in Zvohil with my mother-in-law, struggled over

the Rambam's *Guide to the Perplexed,* never stepping out of the house, you might say, till the time came when I had to register for military service. Then, as the custom was, I had to bestir myself, go back to Rademishli, straighten out my papers, see what exemption I could claim, and arrange for a passport which I would need if I ever left the district. That, you could say, was my first venture into the outside world. All by myself, to prove that I was now a responsible person, I went forth into the marketplace and hired a sleigh. God sent me a bargain. I found a peasant who was going back to Rademishli with a freshly-painted, broad-backed sleigh with wings at the sides like an eagle. But I had failed to pay attention to the fact that the horse was a white one, and a white horse, my mother-in-law said, was bad luck. "I hope I'm lying," she said, "but this trip will be an unlucky one." "Bite your tongue," burst out my father-in-law, and at once was sorry, because he had to take his punishment right on the spot. But to me he whispered, "Women's nonsense," and I began to pack up for the trip: my *tallis* and *tfillin,* some freshly baked rolls, a few *rubles* for expenses, and three pillows—a pillow to sit on, a pillow to lean against, and a pillow to keep my feet warm. And I was ready to go.

So I said goodbye to everybody, and started on my way to Rademishli. It was late in winter; the hard-packed snow made a perfect road for the sleigh. The horse, though a white one, went as smoothly as a breeze, and my driver turned out to be one of those silent fellows who answers everything either "Uh-huh," meaning "yes," or "Uh-uh" for "no." That's all. You couldn't get another word out of him.

I had left home right after dinner and made myself as comfortable as I could, with a pillow under me, a pillow at my back, and one at my feet. The horse pranced, the driver cluck-clucked, the sleigh slid along, the wind blew, and snowflakes drifted through the air like feathers and covered the wide expanse around us. My heart felt light, my spirits free. After all, it was my first trip alone into God's world. I was all alone, a free man, my own master! I leaned back and spread myself out in the sleigh like a lord. But in winter, no matter how warmly you are dressed, when the frost goes through you, you feel like stopping somewhere to warm yourself and catch your breath before going on again. And I began to dream of a warm inn, a boiling *samovar,* and a fresh pot roast with hot gravy. These dreams made me crave for food. I actually became hungry. I began to ask the driver about an inn, asked if the next one was far away. He answered, "Uh-uh," meaning "no." I asked if it was close, and he answered, "Uh-huh," meaning "yes." "How close?" I asked. But that he would not answer, no matter how hard I tried to make him.

I imagined what it would have been like if this were a Jew driving the sleigh. He would have told me not only where the inn was, but who ran it, what his name was, how many children he had, how much rent he paid, what he got out of it, how long he had been there, who had been there before him—in short, everything. We are a strange people, we Jews.

But there I was, dreaming of a warm inn, seeing a hot *samovar* in front of me, and other good things like that; till God took pity on me, the driver clucked to the horse, turned the sleigh a little aside, and there appeared before us a small gray hut covered with snow, a country inn standing alone in the wide, snow-covered field, like a forsaken, forgotten tombstone.

Driving up to the inn with a flourish, the driver took the horse and sleigh into the barn and I went straight toward the inn itself, opened the door, and stopped dead. Here is what I saw. On the floor in the middle of the room lay a corpse covered with black, with two copper candlesticks holding small candles at its head. All around the body sat small children in ragged clothes beating their heads with their fists and screaming and wailing, "Mo-ther! Mother!" And a tall, thin man with long, thin legs, dressed in a torn summer coat entirely out of season, marched up and down the room with long strides, wringing his hands and saying to himself, "What shall I do? What shall I do? I don't know what to do!"

I understood right away what a happy scene I had come upon. My first thought was to run away. I turned to leave, but the door was slammed shut behind me and my feet felt rooted to the ground. I could not move from the spot. Seeing a stranger, the tall man with the long legs ran up to me, stretched out both arms like a man seeking help.

"What do you think of my misfortune?" he asked, pointing to the weeping children. "Poor little things . . . their mother just died. What shall I do? What shall I do? I don't know what to do!"

"Blessed is He who gives, and He who takes," I said, and started to comfort him with the words one uses on such occasions. But he interrupted me.

"She was as good as dead for the past year, poor thing. It was consumption. She begged for death to come. And now she's dead and here we are, stuck in this forsaken spot. What can I do? Go to the village to find a wagon to take her to town? How can I leave the children here alone in the middle of this field, with night coming on? God in heaven, what shall I do? What shall I do? I don't know what to begin to do!"

With these words the man began to weep, strangely, without tears, as though he were laughing, and a queer sound came from his lips, like a cough. All my strength left me. Who could think of hunger now? Who remembered the cold?

I forgot everything and said to him, "I am driving from Zvohil to Rademishli with a very fine sleigh. If the town you

speak of is not very far from here I can let you take the sleigh
and I'll wait here. If it won't take too long, that is."

"Long may you live!" he cried. "For this good deed you'll
earn eternal life! As I am a Jew, eternal life!" he exclaimed,
and threw his arms around me. "The town is not far away,
only four or five *versts*. It will take no more than an hour and
I'll send the sleigh right back. You are earning eternal life,
I tell you! Eternal life! Children, get up from the ground
and thank this young man. Kiss his hands and his feet! He
is letting me use his sleigh to take your mother to the burial
ground. Eternal life! As sure as I'm a Jew, eternal life!"

This news did not exactly cheer them. When they heard their
father talk about taking their mother away they threw themselves around her again and began to weep louder than ever.
And yet it was good news that a man had been found to do
them this kindness. God himself had sent him there. They
looked at me as at a redeemer, something like Elijah, and I
must tell you the plain truth: I began to see myself as an
extraordinary being. Suddenly in my own eyes I grew in
stature and became what the world calls a hero. I was ready
to lift mountains, turn worlds upside down. There was nothing
that seemed too difficult for me, and these words tore themselves out of my lips:

"I'll tell you what. I'll take her there myself, that is, my
driver and I. I'll save you the trouble of going and leaving
the children behind."

The more I talked the more the little children wept, wept and
looked up at me as at an angel from heaven, and I grew in
my own eyes taller and taller, till I almost reached the sky.
For the moment I forgot I had always been afraid to touch
a dead body, and with my own hands helped to carry the
woman out and lift her into the sleigh. I had to promise the
driver another half-*ruble,* and a drink of whisky on the spot.

At first he scratched the back of his neck and mumbled something in his nose. But after the third drink he softened up and we started on our way, all three of us, the driver and I and the innkeeper's wife, Chava Nechama. That was her name, Chava Nechama, daughter of Raphael Michel. I remember it as if it had been this morning, because all along the way I kept repeating to myself the name that her husband had repeated to me several times. For when the time came to bury her with the proper ceremony, her full name would have to be given. So all the way I repeated to myself, "Chava Nechama, daughter of Raphael Michel. Chava Nechama, daughter of Raphael Michel. Chava Nechama, daughter of Raphael Michel." But while I kept repeating the woman's name, the husband's name escaped me completely. He had told me his name too and assured me that when I came to the town and mentioned the name, the corpse would be taken from me at once and I would be able to go on my way. He was well known there, he said. Year after year he came there for the holidays, contributed money for the synagogue, for the bath house, and everywhere he paid well. He told me more, filled my head with instructions, where I should go, what I should say and do, and every bit of it flew out of my head. You'd think that at least a word of it would have remained. But it didn't. Not a word.

All my thoughts revolved about one thing only, here I was, carrying a dead woman. That alone was enough to make me forget everything, even my own name; for from early childhood I had been mortally afraid of dead bodies. You'd have to pay me a fortune to make me stay alone with a corpse. And now it seemed to me that the glazed, half-open eyes stared at me and the dead, sealed lips would open any minute and a strange voice would be heard as though from a sepulchre, a voice so terrible that merely thinking of it almost threw me into a faint. It is not for nothing that such stories are told of the dead, of people who have fainted out of mere fright, and lost their minds or their powers of speech.

So we rode along, the three of us. I had given the dead woman one of my pillows and had placed her crossways in the sleigh, right at my feet. In order to keep myself from thinking melancholy thoughts I turned away from the body, began to watch the sky and softly to repeat to myself, "Chava Nechama, daughter of Raphael Michel. Chava Nechama, daughter of Raphael Michel," until the name became jumbled in my mind and I found myself saying, "Chava Raphael, daughter of Nechama Michel," and, "Raphael Michel, daughter of Chava Nechama."

I had not been aware that it was getting darker and darker. The wind was blowing stronger all the time and the snow continued to fall until it was so deep that we could not find the road. The sleigh went hither and yon, without direction, and the driver began to grumble at first softly, then louder and more insistently, and I could swear that he was blessing me with a threefold blessing. I asked him, "What is the matter with you?" He spat into the snow and turned upon me with such murderous anger that I shrank back. "Look what you've done!" he cried. "You've been the ruination of me and my horse!" Because of this, because we had taken a dead woman into the sleigh, the horse had strayed from the road, and here we were wandering, and God alone knew how long we would keep on wandering. For night was almost here, and then we would really be lost.

At this good news I was ready to go back to the inn, unload our baggage, forget eternal life. But it was too late, said the driver. We could neither go ahead nor turn back. We were wandering in the middle of the field, the devil alone knew where. The road was snowed under, the sky was black. It was late. The horse was dead tired. May a bad end come to that innkeeper and all the innkeepers of the world! Why hadn't he broken a leg before he had stopped at the inn? Why hadn't he choked on the first glass of whiskey before he had let himself be talked into this folly, and for a miserable half-*ruble* perish here in the wilderness, together with his poor little horse. As for himself, it didn't matter so much. Maybe it was fated that he should come to a bad end, and at this spot. But the poor little horse, what had he done? An innocent animal, to be sacrificed like that?

I could swear that there were tears in his voice. And to make him feel better I told him that I would give him another half-*ruble* and two more glasses of whiskey. At this he became furious and told me plainly that if I didn't keep my mouth shut he would throw our cargo out of the sleigh altogether. And I thought to myself: what would I do if he threw the corpse and me out into the snow? Who knew what a man like that could do when he lost his temper? I had better be quiet, sit in the sleigh buried in pillows and try to keep from falling asleep, because in the first place, how could a person fall asleep with a dead body in front of him? And in the second place, I had heard that in wintertime you mustn't fall asleep outside, because if you did you might fall asleep forever.

But in spite of myself my eyes kept shutting. I would have given anything at that moment for a short nap. And I kept rubbing at my eyes but my eyes would not obey. They kept shutting slowly and opening and shutting again. And the sleigh slid over the soft deep white snow and a strange sweet numbness poured through my limbs and I felt an extraordinary calm descend on me. And I wished that this sweet numbness and calm would last and last. I wished it would last forever. But an unknown force, I don't know where it came from, stood by and prodded me. "Do not sleep. Do not fall asleep." With a great effort I tore my eyes open and the numbness resolved itself into a chill that went through my bones and the calm turned to fear and shrinking and melancholy—may the Lord have mercy on me. I imagined that my corpse was stirring, that it uncovered itself and looked at me with half-shut eyes as though to say, "What did you have against me, young man? Why did you drag me off, a dead woman, the mother of young children, and then fail to bring me to consecrated ground?"

The wind blew. It shrieked with a human voice, whistled right into my ears, confided a horrible secret to me. Terrible thoughts, frightful images followed one another in my mind and it seemed to me that we were all buried under the snow, all of us, the driver, the horse, the dead woman and I. We were all dead, all of us. Only the corpse—isn't it remarkable?— only the dead woman, the innkeeper's wife, was alive!

Suddenly I heard my driver clucking to his horse cheerfully, thanking God, and sighing and crossing himself in the dark. I sat up and looked around. In the distance I saw a gleam of light. The light glimmered, went out, and glimmered again. A house, I thought, and thanked God with all my heart. I turned to the driver. "We must have found the road," I said. "Are we close to town?"

"Uh-huh," said the driver in his usual brief manner, without anger, and I could have thrown my arms around his wide shoulders and kissed him, I was so happy to hear that pleasant brief "Uh-huh" which was more wonderful to me at that moment than the wisest discourse.

"What's your name?" I asked, surprised at myself for not having asked it before.

"Mikita," he answered, in one short word, as was his custom.

"Mikita," I repeated, and the name Mikita took on a strange charm.

He answered, "Uh-huh."

I wished that he would tell me more. I wanted to hear him say something more, at least a few words. Mikita had suddenly become something dear to me, and his horse too, a charming animal! I began a conversation with him about his horse, told him what a fine horse he had. A very fine horse!

To which Mikita answered, "Uh-huh."

"And your sleigh, Mikita, is a fine sleigh too!"

Again he answered, "Uh-huh."

Beyond that he would not say a word.

"Don't you like to talk, Mikita, old fellow?" I asked.

"Uh-huh," he said. And I burst out laughing. I was as happy as though I had found a treasure, or made a wonderful discovery. In a word, I was lucky. I was more than lucky. Do you know what I wanted to do? I wanted to raise my voice and sing. That's a fact. I have always had that habit. When I am feeling good I burst out singing. My wife, bless her, knows this trait of mine, and asks, "What happened now, Noah? How much have you earned today to make you so happy?" To a woman, with her woman's brains, it is possible for a man to be happy only when he has made some money. Why does it happen that women are so much more greedy than men? Who earns the money, we or they? But there! I'm afraid I've gone off on the road to Boiberik again.

Well, with God's help we came to town. It was still very early, long before daybreak. The town was sound asleep. Not a glimmer of light showed anywhere. We barely distinguished a house with a large gate and a besom over the gate, the sign of a guest house or inn. We stopped, climbed down, Mikita and I, and began to pound at the gate with our fists. We pounded and pounded till at last we saw a light in the window. Then we heard someone shuffle up to the gate, and a voice called out, "Who's there?"

"Open, Uncle," I cried, "and you'll earn eternal life."

"Eternal life? Who are you?" came the voice from behind the gate, and the lock began to turn.

"Open the door," I said. "We've brought a corpse with us."

"A what?"

"A corpse."

"What do you mean, a corpse?"

"By a corpse I mean a dead person. A dead woman that we've brought from out in the country."

Inside the gate a silence fell. We heard only the lock being turned again and then the feet shuffling off. The lights went out and we were left standing in the snow. I was so angry that I told the driver to help me, and together we pounded at the window with our fists. And we pounded so heartily that the light went on again and the voice was heard once more, "What do you want? Will you stop bothering me!"

"In God's name," I begged as if pleading with a highwayman for my life, "have pity on me. We have a corpse with us, I tell you."

"What corpse?"

"The innkeeper's wife."

"What innkeeper are you talking about?"

"I've forgotten his name, but hers is Chava Michel, daughter of Chana Raphael, I mean Chana Raphael, daughter of Chava Michel, Chana Chava Chana, I mean . . ."

"Go away, you *shlimazl,* or I'll pour a bucket of water over you!"

And with this, the innkeeper shuffled off again and once more the light went out. There was nothing we could do. It was only an hour or so later, when day was beginning to break that the gate opened a crack and a dark head streaked with white popped out and said to me, "Was it you that banged at the window?"

"Of course! Who do you think?"

"What did you want?"

"I've brought a corpse."

"A corpse? Then take it to the *shammes* of the Burial Society."

"Where does your *shammes* live? What's his name?"

"Yechiel's his name, and he lives at the foot of the hill right near the Baths."

"And where are your Baths?"

"You don't know where the Baths are? You must be a stranger here! Where are you from, young man?"

"Where am I from? From Rademishli. That's where I was born. But right now I'm coming from Zvohil. And I'm bringing a corpse from a village close by. The innkeeper's wife. She died of consumption."

"That's too bad. But what's that got to do with you?"

"Nothing at all. I was driving by and he begged me, the innkeeper, that is. He lives all alone out there in the country with all those small children. There was nowhere to bury her, so when he asked me to earn eternal life, I thought to myself: why not?"

"That doesn't make sense," he said to me. "You'd better see the officers of the Burial Society first."

"And who are your officers? Where do they live?"

"You don't know the officers of our Burial Society? Well, first there's Reb Shepsel, who lives over there beyond the marketplace. Then there is Reb Eleazer-Moishe, who lives right in the middle of the marketplace. And then there is Reb Yossi, he's an officer too, who lives near the old synagogue. But the one you'd better see first is Reb Shepsel. He's the one who runs everything. A hard man, I'm warning you. You won't persuade him so easily."

"Thank you very much," I said. "May you live to tell people

better news than you've told me. And when can I see these men?"

"When do you suppose? In the morning after services."

"Thanks again. But what shall I do until then? At least let me in so I can warm myself. What is this town anyway, another Sodom?"

At this the innkeeper locked the doors again, and once more it was as silent as a tomb. What could we do now? Here we were in the middle of the road with our sleigh, and Mikita fuming, grumbling, scratching his neck, spitting and roaring out his three-dimensional curses. "May that foul innkeeper roast in hell through all eternity, and every other innkeeper with him!" For himself he didn't care. Let the evil spirits take him. But his horse, what did they have against his poor little horse, to torture it, let it starve and freeze like that? An innocent animal being sacrificed. What had it ever done?

I felt disgraced before my driver. What could he be thinking of us? A Jew treating another Jew like this. We who were supposed to be the wise and merciful ones and they, the common, unlearned peasants. Thus I blamed the whole tribe for the discourtesy of one man, as is always our custom.

Well, we waited for daylight to come and the town to begin to show signs of life. And finally it did. Somewhere we heard the grating of a door, the sigh of a bucket. From a few chimneys smoke curled up, and in the distance roosters crowed louder and stronger. Soon the doors all opened and God's creatures appeared, in the image of cows, calves, goats, and also men, women and young girls, wrapped up in shawls, bundled from head to foot like mummies. In short the whole town had come to life as if it were a human being. It awoke, washed, pulled on its clothes, and set out to work: the men to the synagogue to pray and study and say *T'hilim;* the women to the ovens, the calves and the goats; and I to inquire about the officers of

the Burial Society, Reb Shepsel, Reb Eleazer-Moishe, Reb Yossi.
Wherever I asked they put me through a cross-examination.
Which Shepsel? Which Eleazer-Moishe, which Yossi? There
were, they said, several Shepsels, Eleazers and Yossis in town.
And when I told them that I wanted the officers of the Burial
Society, they looked frightened and tried to find out why a
young man should want the officers of the Burial Society so
early in the morning. I didn't let them feel me out long, but
opened my heart to them and told them the whole secret of
the burden I had taken upon myself. You should have seen
what happened then. Do you suppose they rushed to relieve
me of my misfortune? God forbid! They ran out, all right,
every one of them, but it was only to see if there really was a
corpse or if I had invented the whole story. They formed a
ring about us, a ring that kept shifting because of the cold, some
people leaving and others taking their place, looking into the
sleigh, shaking their heads, shrugging their shoulders, and
asking over and over who the corpse was, and where it came
from, who I was, where I had got it, and gave me no help
whatever.

With the greatest of difficulty I managed to find out where
Reb Shepsel lived. I found him with his face turned to the wall,
wrapped in his *tallis* and *tfillin,* praying so ardently, with such
a melodious voice and so much feeling that the walls actually
sang. He cracked his knuckles, rocked back and forth, made
strange movements with his body. I enjoyed it tremendously,
because in the first place I love to listen to such spirited praying, and besides, it gave me a chance to warm my frozen bones.
When Reb Shepsel finally turned his face to me his eyes were
still full of tears and he looked like a man of God, his soul as
far removed from earth as his big fat body was from heaven.
But since he was still in the midst of his prayers and did not
want to interrupt them with secular discourse, he spoke to me

in the holy tongue, that is, in a language that consisted of gestures of the hands, winks of the eye, shrugs and motions of the head and even the nose, with a few Hebrew words thrown in. If you wish, I can relate the conversation to you word by word, and no doubt you will understand which words were his and which were mine.

"*Sholom aleichem,* Reb Shepsel."

"*Aleichem sholom. I-yo. Nu-o.*"

"Thank you. I have been sitting all night."

"*Nu-o? Ma?*"

"I have a request to make of you, Reb Shepsel. You will earn eternal life."

"Eternal life? Good! In what way?"

"I have brought you a corpse."

"Corpse! What corpse?"

"Not far from here there is a country inn. The owner is a poor man whose wife just died of consumption, and she left him with several small children, may God have compassion on them. If I had not taken pity on them, I don't know what the poor innkeeper would have done, alone out there in the middle of the field with the corpse."

"God have mercy on them. Well . . . and did he give you anything for the Burial Society?"

"Where is he going to get the money for that? He's a poor man. Poor as can be, and with a houseful of children. You will earn eternal life, Reb Shepsel."

"Eternal life. Good. Very good! Jews. Poor people . . . ah, yes."

And here he broke in with a series of strange sounds accompanied by so many gestures, winks, blinks, shrugs and motions of the head that I could not begin to understand what he was driving at.

And seeing that I could **not** follow him, he turned his face to the wall in disgust and once more began to pray, but not with the same ardor as before. His voice was lower, but he rocked back and forth faster than ever, till he came to the end, threw off his *tallis* and *tfillin* and fell on me with such fury that you would have thought I had outwitted him in some transaction and ruined him completely.

"Look," he said to me, "our town is such a poor one, with so many paupers of our own for whom shrouds must be provided when they die, and here you come from some strange place with a corpse. They come here from everywhere. Everybody comes here!"

I defended myself as well as I could. I said I was an innocent man trying to do only what was proper with respect to the dead. Suppose a dead body had been found in the street and had to be buried, laid to his eternal rest. "You are," I said, "an honest man, a pious one. You can earn eternal life with this deed."

At this he became even angrier and began to lash out at me, not with blows, but with words.

"Is that so?" he cried. "You are a man who craves eternal life? Then take a walk around our town and see to it that our own people stop dying of hunger and freezing of cold. Then you will earn eternal life. Ah-hah! A young man who deals in eternal life! Go take your merchandise to the ne'er-do-wells. Maybe they will be interested. We have our own duties to perform, our own poor to bury. And if we suddenly began to yearn for this eternal life you talk about we could find our own way to earn it!"

With these words Reb Shepsel showed me out and slammed the door behind me. And I swear to you on my word of honor that from that morning on I have despised all those overly pious people who pray out loud and beat their breasts and bow low and make crazy motions. I have hated those holy ones who talk with God all the time, who pretend to serve Him, and do whatever they want, all in His name! True, you might say that these modern irreligious people nowadays are no better and may even be worse than the old-timers with their false piety. But they're not so revolting. At least they don't pretend to be on speaking terms with God. But there! I'm on the way to Boiberik again.

Well, the president, Reb Shepsel, had driven me off. So what should I do next? Go to the other trustees, of course. But at this point a miracle occurred. I saved myself the trouble of going to them, because they came to me instead. They met me face to face at the door and said:

"Are you the young man we're looking for?"

"And what young man are you looking for?"

"The one who brought a body here. Is that you?"

"Yes, I'm the one. What do you want me for?"

"Come back with us to Reb Shepsel and we'll talk it over."

"Talk it over?" I asked. "What is there to talk over? You take the body from me, let me go on my way—and you'll earn eternal life."

"You don't like the way we do things? Is anyone keeping you here?" they asked. "Go take your body anywhere you want, even to Rademishli, and we'll be grateful to you."

"Thanks for the advice," I told them.

"You're welcome," said they.

So we went back into Reb Shepsel's house and the three trustees began to talk. They argued and quarrelled, called each other names. The other two said Reb Shepsel was stubborn, a hard man to deal with; and Reb Shepsel yelled back at them, shouted, ranted, quoted the law: the town's own poor came first. At this the other two fell on him.

"Is that so? Then you want the young man to take the body back with him?"

"God forbid," I said. "What do you want, I should take the

body back? I barely came here alive, almost got lost on the way. My driver wanted to throw me out of the sleigh in the open field somewhere. I beg you. Have pity on me. Take the corpse off my hands. You'll earn eternal life."

"Eternal life is a fine enough thing," answered one of them, a tall thin man with bony fingers, the one called Eleazer-Moishe. "We'll take the body away from you and bury it, but it will cost you something."

"What do you mean?" I asked. "Here I undertook a responsibility like this, at the risk of my life, almost got lost on the way, and you want money!"

"But you're getting eternal life, aren't you?" said Reb Shepsel with such an ugly leer that I wanted to go after him as he deserved. But I managed to control myself. After all, I was still at their mercy.

"Let's get to work," said the one called Reb Yossi, a small man with a short scraggly beard. "I suppose you know, young man, that you have another problem on your hands. You have no papers, no papers at all."

"What papers?" I asked.

"How do we know whose body it is? Maybe it's not what you said it was," said the tall man with the bony fingers, the one called Eleazer-Moishe.

I stood looking from one to the other, and the tall one with the bony fingers, the one called Eleazer-Moishe, shook his head and pointed at me with his long fingers and said:

"Yes, yes. Maybe you murdered some woman yourself. Maybe it's your own wife that you brought here and made up this story about a country inn, the innkeeper's wife, consumption, small children, eternal life."

I must have looked frightened to death at these words, for the one they called Reb Yossi began to comfort me, telling me that they themselves had nothing against me. They understood very well that I was not a robber or a murderer, but still I was a stranger, and a dead body was not a sack of potatoes. We were dealing with a dead person, a corpse. They had, he explained, a rabbi and a police inspector in their town. A report had to be made out.

"Yes, of course. A report. A report," added the tall one, the one called Eleazer-Moishe, pointing with his finger and looking down at me accusingly as though I had committed some crime. I couldn't say another word. I felt a sweat break out on my forehead and I was ready to faint. I was well aware of the miserable plight I had fallen into. It was a disgrace, a sorrow and a heartache in one. But, I thought to myself, what was the use of starting the whole discussion over again with them? So I took out my purse and said to the three trustees of the Burial Society:

"Listen, my friends, here is the whole story. I see what I have fallen into. It was an evil spirit that made me stop at that country inn to warm myself just when the innkeeper's wife had to go ahead and die, and I had to listen to the poor wretch left with all the children begging me, promising eternal life. And now I have to pay for it. Here is my purse. You'll find about seventy-odd *rubles* in it. Take it and do what you think best. Just leave me enough to get me to Rademishli, and take the body away from me and let me go on my way."

I must have spoken with great feeling for the three trustees looked at each other and would not touch my purse. They told me that their town was not Sodom; they were not robbers. True, the town was a poor one, with more paupers than rich people, but to fall on a strange man and order him to hand over his money, that they would not think of. Whatever I wanted to give of my own free will was all right. To do it without charging at all was impossible. It was a poor town, and there were all the expenses, pallbearers, a shroud, drinks, the cost of the burial lot. But it was not necessary for me to throw my money away. If I started to do that, there would be no end to it.

Well, what more can I tell you? If the innkeeper had had two hundred thousand *rubles,* his wife could not have had a finer funeral. The whole town came to look at the young man who had brought the corpse. They told each other that it was the body of his mother-in-law, a rich woman. (I don't know where they got the mother-in-law story.) At any rate they came to welcome the young man who had brought the rich mother-in-law and was throwing out money right and left. They actually pointed their fingers at me. And as for beggars, they were like the sands of the ocean. In all my life I have never seen so many beggars in one place, not even in front of the synagogue on *Yom Kippur* eve. They pulled at the skirts of my coat, they almost tore me to pieces. How often do they see a young man who throws away money like that? I was lucky that the trustees came to my rescue and kept me from giving away all I had. Especially the tall one with the bony fingers, Eleazer-Moishe, did not step away from me for a moment. He kept pointing at me with his finger and saying, "Young man, do not hand out all your money." But the more he spoke the closer the beggars gathered around me, tearing at my flesh. "It's nothing," yelled the beggars. "It's nothing. When you bury such a rich mother-in-law you can afford to spend a few extra *groschen.* She must have left him enough money. May we have as much!"

"Young man!" yelled one beggar, pulling at my coat, "young man, give the two of us half a *ruble*! At least forty *kopeks.* We were born like this, one lame, the other blind. Give us at least a *gulden, a gulden* for two maimed ones. Surely we deserve a *gulden!*"

"Don't pay attention to him!" shouted another, pushing the

first one aside. "Do you call them cripples? My wife is a real cripple. She can't use her arms or legs, she can't move a limb, and our children are sick too! Give me anything at all and I'll say *kaddish* for your mother-in-law all year—may she rest in paradise!"

Now I can laugh about it. Then it was far from a laughing matter, for the crowd of beggars grew and multiplied about me. In half an hour they flooded the marketplace and it was impossible to proceed with the coffin. The attendants had to use sticks to disperse the mob, and a fight broke out. By that time some peasants began to gather about us too, with their wives and countless children, and at last the news reached the town authorities. The police inspector appeared on horseback with a whip in his hand and with one harsh look about him and a few sharp lashes of the whip sent the mob flying in all directions. He himself dismounted and came up to the coffin to investigate. He started by questioning me, asked who I was, where I had come from, and where I was going. I was paralyzed with fear. I don't know why, but whenever I see an officer of the law I go numb with fear, though I have no real reason to worry. In all my life I have never as much as touched a fly on the wall and I know quite well that a policeman is an ordinary human being, flesh and blood like the rest of us. In fact, I know a Jew who is so friendly with a police officer that they visit each other frequently and when there is a holiday the officer eats fish at my friend's house, and when my friend visits the officer he's treated to hard-boiled eggs. He can't praise the officer highly enough. And yet every time I see a policeman I want to run. It must be something I inherited, because, as you know, I come from a region where pogroms came one after another in the days of Vassilchikov, and I'm descended from the victims of those pogroms. If I wanted to, I could tell you stories enough about those days—but there, I must be well past Boiberik this time.

As I said, the officer began to cross-examine me. He wanted to know who I was, and what I was, and where I was going. How could I tell him the whole story—that I live with my father-in-law in Zvohil and I'm going to Rademishli to get a passport? But the trustees, long may they live, saved me the trouble. Before I could even begin, one of them, the one with the thin beard, called the officer aside and began to talk with him, while the tall one with the bony fingers quickly and in guarded language taught me how to answer the officer.

"Be careful what you say," he whispered. "Tell him the whole truth. You live not far from town and this is your mother-in-law and you brought her here to be buried. Tell him your name and your mother-in-law's too. Your real names, you understand, straight out of the *Hagadah*. And give him the burial fee—don't forget."

And saying this he winked at me and continued, "In the meantime, your driver looks tired and thirsty. We'll take him across the street and give him a chance to rest."

Then the inspector took me into a large building and began to make out some papers. I have no idea at all what nonsense I told him. I said anything and everything that came to my mind and he wrote it all down.

"Your name?"

"Moishe."

"Your father's."

"Itzko."

"Your age?"

"Nineteen."

"Married?"

"Married."

"Children?"

"Of course."

"Your trade?"

"Merchant."

"Who is the dead person?"

"My mother-in-law."

"Her name?"

"Yenta."

"Her father's?"

"Gershon."

"Her age?"

"Forty."

"Cause of death?"

"Fright."

"Fright?"

"Yes, fright."

"What do you mean—fright?" he asked, laying down his pen and lighting a cigarette, looking me over from head to foot. Suddenly my tongue stuck to the roof of my mouth. I thought to myself, if I am inventing a story, I might as well do a good job. So I told him how my mother-in-law had been sitting all alone knitting some socks. She had forgotten that her young son, a boy named Ephraim, was in the room with her. A thirteen-year-old boy, very stupid, something of a clown. He was making shadow figures on the wall and he put his hands up high behind his mother's back, and making a goat's shadow on the wall, opened his mouth and bleated, "Ba-a-a-a." Struck with fright, she fell from her chair and died on the spot.

While I was telling him this story he kept looking at me strangely, not taking his eyes off me. He heard me out till the end, spat on the floor, wiped his red mustaches, and led me out again to the coffin. He removed the black cover, looked at the dead woman's face and shook his head. He looked from

the corpse to me, and from me to the corpse, and then said
to the trustees, "Well, you can go ahead and bury the woman.
As for this young man, I'll have to keep him here until I satisfy
myself that she was really his mother-in-law and that she died
of fright."

You can imagine how I felt when I heard this. I turned aside
—I couldn't help it—and burst out crying like a small child.

"Look here, what are you crying for?" asked the little man
they called Reb Yossi, and comforted me, cheered me up as best
he could. I was innocent, wasn't I? Then what did I have to
be afraid of?

"If you don't eat garlic, they'll never smell it on your breath,"
put in Reb Shepsel with such a smirk that I wanted to give his
fat cheeks a couple of good hard slaps.

God in heaven, what good did it ever do me to make up
this big lie and drag my mother-in-law into it? All I needed
now was to have her find out that I had buried her alive and
spread the news that she had died of fright.

"Don't be afraid," Reb Eleazer broke in, prodding me with
his bony fingers. "God will take care of you. The officer is not
such a bad fellow. Just give him the burial fee I told you about.
He'll understand. He knows that everything you told him is
true."

I cannot tell you any more. I don't even want to remember
what happened to me after that. You understand, of course,
that they took the few *gulden* I had left, put me in jail and I
had to stand trial. But that was child's play compared to what
happened when the news reached my father- and mother-in-law
that their son-in-law was in prison for having brought a dead
woman from somewhere.

Naturally they came at once, identified themselves as my
parents-in-law, and then the excitement really began! On one
side the police went after me. "A fine fellow you are! Now,

if your mother-in-law Yenta, daughter of Gershon, is alive, then who was the dead woman you brought?" On the other side, my mother-in-law, may she live long! "There is only one thing I want to ask you," she kept saying to me. "What did you have against me, to take me and bury me alive?"

Naturally at the trial it turned out that I was innocent, free from all guilt. Of course that cost some money too. Witnesses had to be brought in, the innkeeper and his children, and finally I was set free. But what I went through afterwards, especially from my mother-in-law, that I don't wish my worst enemy to have to go through!

And from that time on, when anybody mentions eternal life, I run away as fast as I can.

Hannukah Money

CAN you guess, children, which is the best of all holidays?
Hannukah, of course.

You don't go to *cheder* for eight days in a row, you eat pancakes every day, spin your *dreidel* to your heart's content, and
from all sides *Hannukah* money comes pouring in. What
holiday could be better than that?

Winter. Outside it's cold, a bitter frost. The windows are
frozen over, decorated with beautiful designs, the sills piled
high with snow. Inside the house it's warm and cheerful.
The silver *Hannukah* lamp stands ready on the table and my
father is walking back and forth, his hands behind his back,
saying the evening prayers. When he is almost through, but
while still praying, he takes out of the chest a waxen candle
(the *shammes*, to light the others with) and starting *Oleinu*,
the last prayer in the regular services, signals to us:

" '*Shehu noteh shomayim . . .*' *Nu! Nu-o!*"

My brother and I don't know what he means. We ask,
"What do you want? A match?"

My father points with his hand toward the kitchen door,
" '*Al-kein n'kaveh l'cho . . .*' *E-o-nu!*"

"What then? A bread knife? Scissors? The mortar and
pestle?"

My father shakes his head. He makes a face at us, comes to
the end of the prayer, and then, able to speak again, says,
"Your mother! Call your mother! I'm ready to light the
candle!"

The two of us, my brother and I, leap for the kitchen, almost falling over each other in our haste.

"Mother! Quick! The *Hannukah* candles!"

"Oh, my goodness! Here I am! *Hannukah* lights!" cries my mother, leaving her work in the kitchen (rendering goose fat, mixing batter for pancakes) and hurries into the parlor with us. And after her comes Braina the cook, a swarthy woman with a round plump face and mustache, her hands always smeared with grease. My mother stands at one side of the room with a pious look on her face, and Braina the cook remains at the door, wipes her hand on her dirty apron, draws her greasy hand over her nose, and leaves a black smear across her face.

My father goes up to the lamp with his lighted candle, bends down and sings in the familiar tune, "Blessed art thou, O Lord . . ." and ends ". . . to kindle the lights of *Hannukah*."

My mother, in her most pious voice, chimes in, "Blessed be He and blessed be His name." And later, "Amen." Braina nods her approval and makes such queer faces that Motel and I are afraid to look at each other.

"These lights we kindle," my father continues, marching up and down the room with an eye on the *Hannukah* lamp. He keeps up this chant till we grow impatient and wish that he would reach his hand into his pocket and take out his purse. We wink at each other, nudge and push each other.

"Motel," I say, "go ask him for *Hannukah* money."

"Why should I ask?"

"Because you're younger. That's why."

"That's why I shouldn't. You go. You're older."

My father is well aware of what we are talking about, but he pretends not to hear. Quietly, without haste, he walks over to the cupboard and begins to count out some money. A cold shiver runs down our backs, our hands shake, our hearts pound. We look up at the ceiling, scratch our earlocks, try to act as if this meant nothing at all to us.

My father coughs.

"H'm . . . Children, come here."

"Huh? What is it?"

"Here is *Hannukah* money for you."

The money in our pockets, we move off, Motel and I, at first slowly, stiffly, like toy soldiers, then faster and faster with a skip and a hop. And before we have reached our room we lose all restraint and turn three somersaults one after the other. Then hopping on one foot we sing:

> "*Einga beinga*
> *Stupa tzeinga*
> *Artze bartze*
> *Gola shwartze*
> *Eimelu reimelu*
> *Beigeli feigeli*
> *Hop!*"

And in our great joy and exuberance we slap our own cheeks twice, so hard that they tingle.

The door opens and in walks Uncle Benny.

"Come here, you rascals. I owe you some *Hannukah* money."

Uncle Benny puts his hand into his vest pocket, takes out two silver *gulden,* and gives us each one.

II

Nobody in the world would ever guess that our father and Uncle Benny are brothers. My father is tall and thin; my uncle is short and fat. My father is dark, my uncle is fair. My father is gloomy and silent, my uncle jolly and talkative.

As different as day and night, summer and winter. And yet they are blood brothers.

My father takes a large sheet of paper ruled off into squares, black and white, and asks us to bring him a handful of dry beans from the kitchen, dark ones and white ones. They are going to play checkers.

(Once a miracle happened, and this is our celebration.)

Mother is in the kitchen rendering goose fat and frying pancakes. My brother and I are spinning our *dreidel*. My father and Uncle Benny sit down and play checkers.

"One thing I'll have to ask you," my father says. "Once you've made a move it's a move. You can't keep changing your mind."

"A move is a move," my uncle agrees, and makes a move.

"A move is a move," repeats my father and jumps my uncle's bean.

"That's right," says Uncle Benny, "a move is a move," and jumps twice.

The longer they play the more absorbed they become. They chew their beards, beat time under the table with their feet, and together they hum one song:

"Oh, what shall I do? What shall I do? What shall I do?" sings my father, chewing an end of his beard. "If I move here," he chants, as one does over the *Gamorah,* "then he'll move there. Maybe I'd better move . . . over here."

"Over here . . . over here," echoes Uncle Benny in the same tone.

"Why should I worry?" my father hums again. "If he should take this *one* then I'll take those *two.* On the other hand, maybe he thinks he can take three . . ."

"Take three . . . take three . . . take three . . ." Uncle Benny helps him out.

"Ah, you're no good, Benny. You're no good at all," sings my father and makes a move.

"You're worse than no good, my brother," sings Uncle Benny and pushes a bean forward, then snatches it back.

"You can't do that, Benny!" my father cries. "You said a move was a move!" And he catches Uncle Benny's hand.

"No!" Uncle Benny insists. "If I haven't finished I can still move."

"No!" my father declares just as emphatically. "We decided on that before we started. Remember. You can't change your mind."

"I can't?" asks Uncle Benny. "How many times did you change yours?"

"I?" says my father indignantly. "See! That's why I hate to play with you, Benny!"

"Who is forcing you to play with me?"

At this point my mother comes in from the kitchen, her face flaming from the heat.

"Already? Fighting already?" she asks. "Over a few beans?"

Behind her comes Braina with a large platter of steaming pancakes. We all move toward the table. My brother Motel and I, who only a moment ago had been fighting like cat and dog, make up quickly, become friends again, and go after the pancakes with the greatest gusto.

III

In bed that night I lie awake and think: how much would I be worth if all my uncles and aunts and other relatives gave me *Hannukah* money? First of all there is Uncle Moishe-Aaron, my mother's brother, stingy but rich. Then Uncle Itzy and Aunt Dveira, with whom my father and mother have not been on speaking terms for years and years. Then Uncle Beinish and Aunt Yenta. And how about our sister Ida and her husband Sholom-Zeidel? And all the other relatives?

"Motel, are you asleep?"

"Yes. What do you want?"

"How much *Hannukah* money do you think Uncle Moishe-Aaron will give us?"

"How should I know? I'm not a prophet."

A minute later: "Motel, are you sleeping?"

"Yes. What now?"

"Do you think anyone else in the whole world has as many uncles and aunts as we have?"

"Maybe yes . . . and maybe no."

Two minutes later: "Motel, are you asleep?"

"Of course."

"If you're asleep, how can you talk to me?"

"You keep bothering me so I have to answer."

Three minutes later: "Motel, are you awake?"

This time he answers with a snore. I sit up in bed, take out my father's present, smooth it out, examine it. A whole *ruble.*

"Think of it," I say to myself. "A piece of paper, and what can't you buy with it! Toys, knives, canes, purses, nuts and candy, raisins, figs. Everything."

I hide the *ruble* under my pillow and say my prayers. A little later Braina comes in from the kitchen with a platter full of *rubles* . . . She isn't walking, she's floating in the air, chanting, "These lights we kindle . . ." And Motel begins to swallow *rubles* as if they were pancakes.

"Motel!" I scream with all my might. "God help you, Motel! What are you doing? Eating money?"

I sit up with a start . . . spit three times. It was a dream. And I fall asleep again.

IV

The next morning after we have said our prayers and eaten breakfast, our mother puts on our fur-lined jackets and bundles us up in warm shawls and we start off for our *Hannukah* money. First of all, naturally, we stop off at Uncle Moishe-Aaron's.

Our Uncle Moishe-Aaron is a sickly man. He has trouble with his bowels. Whenever we come we find him at the wash bowl after having come in from the back yard, washing and drying his hands with the appropriate prayer.

"Good morning, Uncle Moishe-Aaron!" we cry out together, my brother and I. Our Aunt Pessil, a tiny woman with one black eyebrow and one white one, comes forward to meet us. She takes off our coats, unwinds our shawls, and proceeds to blow our noses into her apron.

"Blow!" says Aunt Pessil. "Blow hard. Don't be afraid. Again! Again! That's the way!"

And Uncle Moishe-Aaron, a little man with a moth-eaten mustache and ears stuffed with cotton, dressed in his old ragged fur-lined jacket and with his quilted skullcap on his head, stands at the water bowl, wiping his hands, wrinkling his face, blinking at us with his eyes, while he groans out his prayer.

My brother and I sit down uneasily. We are always miserable and frightened in this house. Aunt Pessil sits opposite us, her arms folded across her chest, and puts us through her usual examination.

"How is your father?"

"All right."

"And your mother?"

"All right."

"Have they killed any geese yet?"

"Oh, yes."

"Did they have much fat?"

"Quite a lot."

"Did your mother make pancakes yet?"

"Yes."

"Has Uncle Benny come yet?"

"Yes."

"Did they play checkers?"

"Yes."

And so on and so on . . .

Aunt Pessil blows our noses again and turns to Uncle Moishe-Aaron.

"Moishe-Aaron, we ought to give the children some *Hannukah* money."

Uncle Moishe-Aaron doesn't hear. He keeps on drying his hands, and comes to the end of his prayer with a drawn-out groan.

Aunt Pessil repeats: "Moishe-Aaron! The children! *Hannukah* money."

"Huh? What?" says Uncle Moishe-Aaron, and shifts the cotton from one ear to the other.

"The children. *Hannukah* money!" Aunt Pessil shouts right into his ear.

"Oh, my bowels, my bowels," groans Uncle Moishe-Aaron (that's the way he always talks), holding his belly with both hands. "Did you say *Hannukah* money? What do children need money for? What will you do with it, huh? Spend it? Squander it? How much did your father give you? Huh?"

"He gave me a *ruble*," I say, "and him a half."

"A *ruble*! Hm . . . Some people spoil their children, ruin them. What will you do with the *ruble*, huh? Change it? Huh? No! Don't change it. Do you hear what I say? Don't change it. Or do you want to change it? Huh?"

"What does it matter to you whether they change it or don't change it?" breaks in Aunt Pessil. "Give them what they have coming and let them go on their way."

Uncle Moishe-Aaron shuffles off to his room and begins to search through all the chests and drawers, finds a coin here, a coin there, and mutters to himself:

"Hm . . . How they spoil their children. Ruin them. Simply ruin them."

And coming back, he pushes a few hard coins into our hands. Once more (for the last time) Aunt Pessil blows our noses, puts on our coats, wraps the shawls around us, and we go on our way. We run over the white frozen crunchy snow, counting the money that Uncle Moishe-Aaron has given us. Our hands are frozen, red and stiff. The coins are copper, large and heavy, very old six-*kopek* pieces, strange, old-fashioned three-*kopek* pieces rubbed smooth and thin, *groschens* that we've never seen before, thick and green with age. It's hard for us, in fact impossible, to figure out how much *Hannukah* money Uncle Moishe-Aaron has given us.

V

Our second stop for *Hannukah* money is at Uncle Itzy's and Aunt Dveira's, with whom my parents have not been on speaking terms for many years. Why they don't speak to each other I don't know, but I do know that they never speak, although they go to the same synagogue and sit next to each other on the same bench. And at the holidays when it comes to auctioning off the various honors, they always try to outbid each other. A fierce battle takes place each time. The whole congregation takes sides, helps them to bid, eggs them on.

The *shammes,* who acts as auctioneer, stands on the platform, working hard. His skullcap is off to one side, his prayer-shawl keeps slipping off his shoulders.

"Eighteen *gulden* for *Shi-shi!*

"Twenty *gulden* for *Shi-shi!*"

The bidding gets hotter and hotter. My father and Uncle Itzy are bent over their Bibles, from all appearances unaware of what is going on. But every time one of them bids the other one raises it.

The congregation enjoys the spectacle and helps along. "Thirty . . . thirty-five . . . thirty-seven and a half . . ." But the battle is between my father and Uncle Itzy, and they continue the bidding until one or the other has to give up.

And yet whenever there is a celebration in the family, a birth, a circumcision, a *Bar Mitzvah,* an engagement party, a wedding or a divorce, the feud is forgotten. We all attend, exchange gifts, make merry, drink together and dance together like the best of friends.

"Good morning, Uncle Itzy! Good morning, Aunt Dveira!" we cry out together, my brother Motel and I, and they receive us like honored guests.

"Did you come all this way just to see us, or was there something else on your mind?" Uncle Itzy asks and pinches our cheeks. He opens his purse and gives us our *Hannukah* money, a new silver twenty-*kopek* piece to me and another one to my brother. And from there we go straight to Uncle Beinish's.

VI

If you want a picture of complete chaos, go to our Uncle Beinish's house. No matter when you come you find a perfect bedlam. They have a house full of children, half-naked, dirty, unkempt, unwashed, always bruised, usually scratched, often bloodied and with black eyes. One of the children may be laughing, another crying; one singing, another shrieking; one humming, another whistling; this one has put on his father's coat with the sleeves rolled up, and that one is riding a broomstick; this one is drinking milk from a pitcher, that one is cracking nuts, another is walking about with a herring's head in his hand, and still another is sucking on a stick of candy while from his nose two runnels flow down toward his mouth. Aunt Yenta must be strong as an ox to put up with this crew. She curses them, pinches them, shakes them all day long. She isn't particular. Whichever one comes within reach gets a slap or a shove or a prod in the side.

An ordinary slap by itself is not worth mentioning. "I hope you choke; I hope you die; why doesn't someone kidnap you!" These are the lesser curses. And words like "the plague" and "cholera" and "violent death" are uttered casually, without anger, as one might say "Good evening" or "Good Sabbath." The house becomes quiet only when Uncle Beinish comes home. But since Uncle Beinish is a busy man who spends all his time at the store, coming home only for meals, their house is a perpetual Gehenna.

When we come in we find little Ezriel riding on his older brother Getzi's back, with Froike and Mendel whipping Getzi on, one with the sleeve of an old jacket, the other with the cover of a prayer book. Chaim'l, who has found the windpipe of a slaughtered goose somewhere, is blowing at it until he is blue in the face, and succeeds in producing an eerie sound like the squeal of a stuck pig. Zeinvilleh is playing a tune on a comb and David, a small boy of about four, has put his shoes on his hands and beats time with them. Sender'l rushes by carrying a kitten by the scruff of the neck. The kitten's tongue hangs out, its eyes are shut, its feet hang limply. You can almost hear it say, "See how I suffer here; they torture me, they make life unbearable." In another corner Esther, the oldest girl, is trying to comb and braid her little sister Haska's hair, but since the hair is curly and has not been combed for a long time, the child stands shrieking at the top of her voice and Esther keeps slapping her to make her stop. The only quiet one is Pinny, a tiny boy with crooked legs, his shirt tail pinned up behind him. The only trouble with him is that wherever he goes he leaves a trail behind him.

But none of this disturbs Aunt Yenta in the least. It does not prevent her from sitting calmly at the table drinking chicory, with an infant at her breast and an older child on her knee. Between sips of chicory she cuddles the baby at her breast and digs her elbow into the child on her knee. "Look at you eat, you pig! May the worms eat you! Esther, Rochel, Haska, where the devil are you? Quick, wipe his nose! Bring me a saucer, quick! Here I am, drinking without a saucer! Mendel, don't make so much noise! I'll give you such a crack that you'll turn over three times! Oh, my heart, my soul, my comfort. What, murderers, you want more food? All you do all day is eat, eat, eat! Why don't you choke!"

When they catch sight of the two of us the children fall on us like locusts, grabbing us by our hands, our feet, some leaping at our heads. Chaim'l blows the windpipe right into my ear. David, still wearing his shoes on his hands, throws his arms around us. Pinny, with the shirt tail pinned behind him, gets hold of one of my legs and wraps himself about it like a little snake. A confusion of sounds and voices surrounds us, deafens our ears.

"May you scream with a toothache!" shouts Aunt Yenta from the other room. "A person can get deaf here! They're devils, not children! May your souls burn forever and ever!"

And in the midst of all this noise and confusion Uncle Beinish comes in with his *tallis* and *tfillin,* apparently on his way from the synagogue, and at once everything becomes quiet. The children vanish.

"Good morning, Uncle Beinish!" we cry out together, my brother Motel and I.

"What are you doing here, you *shkotzim*?" asks Uncle Beinish. "Ah, *Hannukah* money!" And he gives us each a ten-*kopek* piece.

The children peek at us from their corners with bright little eyes like mice, wink and signal with their hands, make strange faces at us, try hard to make us laugh. But with great effort we control ourselves, take the money, and run off as fast as we can from this living Gehenna.

VII

The next place we go to for *Hannukah* money is our sister Ida's. Since she was a child Ida has always been a lugubrious creature. No matter what silly little thing happened, she could always be counted on to burst out crying. She was always shedding tears over her own or other people's troubles. But when she became engaged to Sholom-Zeidel, that was when she really cried! Perhaps you think it was because the young man didn't please her? God forbid! She had never even seen the man! No, she wept because a bride is supposed to weep before her wedding. When the tailors brought her trousseau she wept all night long. Later, when her girl friends came for their last party together she ran off to her room every few minutes to weep into her pillows. But she was really at her best on her wedding day! That day she didn't stop crying for a minute.

But the climax came at the veiling, when Menashe Fiddele, the fiddler, led her to the dais and Reb Boruch B'dachun climbed up on the table, folded his arms over his ample stomach, lowered his head as though he were bemoaning the dead, and began, in a mournful tone that could move a stone to tears, the following song:

> *Dearest Bride, dearest bride!*
> *Weep all you please;*
> *Your tears are becoming,*
> *They need not cease.*
>
> *Weeping is ordained*
> *For brides to be.*
> *And soon you will stand*
> *Under the canopy.*
>
> *For you must learn*
> *That now your life*
> *Is full of sadness,*
> *Woe and strife;*
>
> *That man is not made*
> *Of iron or stone.*
> *He is only a being*
> *Of flesh and bone;*
>
> *That sinners are lashed*
> *In the depths of hell,*
> *And they scream and howl*
> *And lament as well.*
>
> *Then learn to practice virtue*
> *And humility.*
> *Weep, maiden, weep,*
> *Let your tears run free."*

And so on and so on without end.

The women who stood around her, helping to undo her

beautiful long braids, could not control themselves. They gave themselves up to their lamentations wholeheartedly, made the oddest faces, wiped their eyes and blew their noses. And poor Ida wept loudest of all. She wailed and moaned and blubbered so hard that she fainted three times and they barely revived her in time for the ceremony.

But our brother-in-law, on the other hand, was as merry as our sister Ida was sad. If anything, Sholom-Zeidel was too merry, a practical joker, a clown, a zany, who fastened himself to you like a leech and got under your skin. He was always teasing us, my brother and me, pinching our ears and filliping our noses. That gave him his greatest pleasure. The first year they were married there were times when for days Motel and I went around with swollen noses, stinging ears. So when we heard that the young couple was leaving our home to set up their own establishment we were really overjoyed. But for the rest of the family the day they moved was a day of mourning. Ida wept, poured buckets of tears, and my mother, watching her, wept also. Sholom-Zeidel, who was supposed to be doing the packing, skipped back and forth, stole up behind us cunningly, and pinched our ears or filliped our noses. And when he bade us farewell he had the impudence to tell us not to wait to be invited but to come as often as we liked. We swore to each other on our honor, my brother and I, never to set foot in his house as long as we lived.

But a person forgets all things, even a pinched ear. How can you keep from going to your own married sister for *Hannukah* money?

When we come into the house, Sholom-Zeidel greets us heartily.

"Well, well! Look who's here! I'm glad you came. I've been waiting. I have some *Hannukah* money for you!"

And Sholom-Zeidel takes out his purse and hands each

one of us several shiny silver coins. And before we can even
count how many he has given us, his hand flies out, pinch,
fillip go his fingers, and once more our ears and noses feel
the sharp sting.

"Leave them alone! Haven't you tortured them enough?"
our sister Ida begs him with tears in her eyes, and calling us
aside, fills our pockets with cake, nuts and figs, and gives us
Hannukah money besides.

We make our escape as quickly as we can and hurry home.

VIII

"Well, Motel," I say, "let's get down to business. Let's figure
out how much money we've collected. But I'll tell you what.
You wait. First let me count mine and then you'll count
yours."

And I begin to count. A *ruble* and three twenty-*kopek*
pieces, four *gulden*, five *grivnye*, six *piatekas* . . . how much
is that altogether? It must be a *ruble* and three twenties and
four *gulden* and five *grivnye* and six *piatekas* . . .

My brother Motel won't wait until I am through, and
he gets busy with his own finances. He moves each coin from
one hand to the other and counts.

"A twenty and a twenty are two twenties, and one more is
three. And two *gulden* is three twenties and two *gulden* and
a *grivnye* and another *grivnye* and one more—that makes
two twenties and three *gulden,* I mean three *gulden* and two
twenties . . . What am I talking about? I'll have to start all
over again from the beginning."

And he starts all over from the beginning. We count and
we count and we can't get the total. We figure and we figure
and we can't get it straight. When we get to Uncle Moishe-

Aaron's old *piatekas,* huge sixes, smoothly rubbed threes and swollen *groschens* we get so mixed up that we don't know where in the world we are. We try to exchange these coins with our mother, our father, with Braina the cook, but it doesn't work. Nobody wants to have anything to do with them.

"What sort of *piatekas* are those? Who palmed them off on you?"

We are ashamed to tell, and we keep quiet.

"Do you know what," says my brother Motel, "let's throw them into the oven, or outside in the snow, when no one is looking."

"What a smart boy you are!" I tell him. "It would be better to give them to a beggar."

But just to spite us no one comes to our door. We wait and we wait and not a single one appears. We can't get rid of Uncle Moishe-Aaron's present.

Tit for Tat

ONCE I was a rabbiner. A rabbiner, not a rabbi. That is, I was called rabbi—but a rabbi of the crown.

To old-country Jews I don't have to explain what a rabbi of the crown is. They know the breed. What are his great responsibilities? He fills out birth certificates, officiates at circumcisions, performs marriages, grants divorces. He gets his share from the living and the dead. In the synagogue he has a place of honor, and when the congregation rises, he is the first to stand. On legal holidays he appears in a stovepipe hat and holds forth in his best Russian: *"Gospoda Prihozhane!"* To take it for granted that among our people a rabbiner is well loved—let's not say any more. Say rather that we put up with him, as we do a government inspector or a deputy sheriff. And yet he is chosen from among the people, that is, every three years a proclamation is sent us: *"Na Osnavania Predpisania . . ."* Or, as we would say: "Your Lord, the Governor, orders you to come together in the synagogue, poor little Jews, and pick out a rabbiner for yourselves . . ."

Then the campaign begins. Candidates, hot discussions, brandy, and maybe even a bribe or two. After which come charges and countercharges, the elections are annulled, and we are ordered to hold new elections. Again the proclamations: *"Na Osnavania Predpisania . . ."* Again candidates, discussions, party organizations, brandy, a bribe or two . . . That was the life!

Well, there I was—a rabbiner in a small town in the province of Poltava. But I was anxious to be a modern one. I wanted to serve the public. So I dropped the formalities of my position and began to mingle with the people—as we say: to stick my head into the community pot. I got busy with the *Talmud Torah,* the charity fund, interpreted a law, settled disputes or just gave plain advice.

The love of settling disputes, helping people out, or advising them, I inherited from my father and my uncles. They— may they rest in peace—also enjoyed being bothered all the time with other people's business. There are two kinds of people in the world: those that you can't bother at all, and others whom you can bother all the time. You can climb right on their heads—naturally not in one jump, but gradually. First you climb into their laps, then on to their shoulders, then their heads—and after that you can jump up and down on their heads and stamp on their hearts with your heavy boots— as long as you want to.

I was that kind, and without boasting I can tell you that I had plenty of ardent followers and plain hangers on who weren't ashamed to come every day and fill my head with their clamoring and sit around till late at night. They never refused a glass of tea, or cigarettes. Newspapers and books they took without asking. In short, I was a regular fellow.

Well, there came a day . . . The door opened, and in walked the very foremost men of the town, the sparkling best, the very cream of the city. Four householders—men of affairs— you could almost say: real men of substance. And who were these men? Three of them were the *Troika*—that was what we called them in our town because they were together all the time—partners in whatever business any one of them was in. They always fought, they were always suspicious of each other, and watched everything the others did, and still they never

separated—working always on this principle: if the business
is a good one and there is profit to be made, why shouldn't I
have a lick at the bone too? And on the other hand, if it should
end in disaster—you'll be buried along with me, and lie with
me deep in the earth. And what does God do? He brings
together the three partners with a fourth one. They operate
together a little less than a year and end up in a brawl. That
is why they're here.

What had happened? "Since God created thieves, swindlers
and crooks, you never saw a thief, swindler or crook like this
one." That is the way the three old partners described the fourth
one to me. And he, the fourth, said the same about them.
Exactly the same, word for word. And who was this fourth
one? He was a quiet little man, a little innocent-looking fellow, with thick, dark eyebrows under which a pair of shrewd,
ironic, little eyes watched everything you did. Everyone
called him Nachman Lekach.

His real name was Nachman Noss'n, but everybody called
him Nachman Lekach, because as you know, *Noss'n* is the
Hebrew for "he gave," and *Lekach* means "he took," and in
all the time we knew him, no one had ever seen him give anything to anyone—while at taking no one was better.

Where were we? Oh, yes . . . So they came to the rabbiner
with the complaints, to see if he could find a way of straighten-
ing out their tangled accounts. "Whatever you decide, Rabbi,
and whatever you decree, and whatever you say, will be final."

That is how the three old partners said it, and the fourth,
Reb Nachman, nodded with that innocent look on his face
to indicate that he too left it all up to me: "For the reason,"
his eyes said, "that I know that I have done no wrong." And
he sat down in a corner, folded his arms across his chest like
an old woman, fixed his shrewd, ironic, little eyes on me, and
waited to see what his partners would have to say. And when

they had all laid out their complaints and charges, presented all their evidence, said all they had to say, he got up, patted down his thick eyebrows, and not looking at the others at all, only at me, with those deep, deep, shrewd little eyes of his, he proceeded to demolish their claims and charges—so completely, that it looked as if they were the thieves, swindlers and crooks—the three partners of his—and he, Nachman Lekach, was a man of virtue and piety, the little chicken that is slaughtered before *Yom Kippur* to atone for our sins—a sacrificial lamb. "And every word that you heard them say is a complete lie, it never was and never could be. It's simply out of the question." And he proved with evidence, arguments and supporting data that everything he said was true and holy, as if Moses himself had said it.

All the time he was talking, the others, the *Troika,* could hardly sit in their chairs. Every moment one or another of them jumped up, clutched his head—or his heart: "Of all things! How can a man talk like that! Such lies and falsehoods!" It was almost impossible to calm them down, to keep them from tearing at the fourth one's beard. As for me—the rabbiner—it was hard, very hard to crawl out from this horrible tangle, because by now it was clear that I had a fine band to deal with, all four of them swindlers, thieves and crooks, and informers to boot, and all four of them deserving a severe punishment. But what? At last this idea occurred to me, and I said to them:

"Are you ready, my friends? I am prepared to hand down my decision. My mind is made up. But I won't disclose what I have to say until each of you has deposited twenty-five *rubles*— to prove that you will act upon the decision I am about to hand down."

"With the greatest of pleasure," the three spoke out at once, and Nachman Lekach nodded his head, and all four reached into their pockets, and each one counted out his twenty-five on the table. I gathered up the money, locked it up in a drawer, and then I gave them my decision in these words:

"Having heard the complaints and the arguments of both parties, and having examined your accounts and studied your evidence, I find according to my understanding and deep conviction, that all four of you are in the wrong, and not only in the wrong, but that it is a shame and a scandal for Jewish people to conduct themselves in such a manner—to falsify accounts, perjure yourselves and even act as informers. Therefore I have decided that since we have a *Talmud Torah* in our town with many children who have neither clothes nor shoes, and whose parents have nothing with which to pay their tuition, and since there has been no help at all from you gentlemen (to get a few pennies from you one has to reach down into your very gizzards) therefore it is my decision that this hundred *rubles* of yours shall go to the *Talmud Torah,* and as for you, gentlemen, you can go home, in good health, and thanks for your contribution. The poor children will now have some shoes and socks and shirts and pants, and I'm sure they'll pray to God for you and your children. Amen."

Having heard the sentence, the three old partners—the *Troika*—looked from one to the other—flushed, unable to speak. A decision like this they had not anticipated. The only one who could say a word was Reb Nachman Lekach. He got up, patted down his thick eyebrows, held out a hand, and looking at me with his ironic little eyes, said this:

"I thank you, Rabbi Rabbiner, in behalf of all four of us, for the wise decision which you have just made known. Such a judgment could have been made by no one since King Solomon himself. There is only one thing that you forgot to say, Rabbi Rabbiner, and that is: what is your fee for this wise and just decision?"

"I beg your pardon," I tell him. "You've come to the wrong address. I am not one of those rabbiners who tax the living and the dead." That is the way I answered him, like a real gentleman. And this was his reply:

"If that's the case, then you are not only a sage and a Rabbi among men, you're an honest man besides. So, if you would care to listen, I'd like to tell you a story. Say that we will pay you for your pains at least with a story."

"Good enough. Even with two stories."

"In that case, sit down, Rabbi Rabbiner, and let us have your cigarette case. I'll tell you an interesting story, a true one, too, something that happened to me. What happened to others I don't like to talk about."

And we lit our cigarettes, sat down around the table, and Reb Nachman spread out his thick eyebrows, and looking at me with his shrewd, smiling, little eyes, he slowly began to tell his true story of what had once happened to him himself.

All this happened to me a long time ago. I was still a young man and I was living not far from here, in a village near the railroad. I traded in this and that, I had a small tavern, made a living. A Rothschild I didn't become, but bread we had, and in time there were about ten Jewish families living close by— because, as you know, if one of us makes a living, others come around. They think you're shoveling up gold . . . But that isn't the point. What I was getting at was that right in the midst of the busy season one year, when things were moving and traffic was heavy, my wife had to go and have a baby— our boy—our first son. What do you say to that? "Congratulations! Congratulations everybody!" But that isn't all. You have to have a *bris,* the circumcision. I dropped everything, went into town, bought all the good things I could find, and came back with the *Mohel* with all his instruments, and for

good measure I also brought the *shammes* of the synagogue.
I thought that with these two holy men and myself and the
neighbors we'd have the ten men that we needed, with one
to spare. But what does God do? He has one of my neighbors
get sick—he is sick in bed and can't come to the *bris,* you
can't carry him. And another has to pack up and go off to the
city. He can't wait another day! And here I am without the
ten men. Go do something. Here it is—Friday! Of all days,
my wife has to pick Friday to have the *bris*—the day before
the Sabbath. The *Mohel* is frantic—he has to go back right
away. The *shammes* is actually in tears. "What did you ever
drag us off here for?" they both want to know. And what
can I do?

All I can think of is to run off to the railroad station. Who
knows—so many people come through every day—maybe
God will send some one. And that's just what happened. I
came running up to the station—the agent has just called out
that a train is about to leave. I look around—a little roly-poly
man carrying a huge traveling bag comes flying by, all sweating and out of breath, straight toward the lunch counter. He
looks over the dishes—what is there a good Jew can take in a
country railroad station? A piece of herring—an egg. Poor
fellow—you could see his mouth was watering. I grab him
by the sleeve. "Uncle, are you looking for something to eat?"
I ask him, and the look he gives me says: "How did you know
that?" I keep on talking: "May you live to be a hundred—
God himself must have sent you." He still doesn't understand,
so I proceed: "Do you want to earn the blessings of eternity—
and at the same time eat a beef roast that will melt in your
mouth, with a fresh, white loaf right out of the oven?" He
still looks at me as if I'm crazy. "Who are you? What do you
want?"

So I tell him the whole story—what a misfortune had over-

taken us: here we are, all ready for the *bris,* the *Mohel* is waiting, the food is ready—and such food!—and we need a tenth
man! "What's that got to do with me?" he asks, and I tell
him: "What's that got to do with you? Why—everything
depends on you—you're the tenth man! I beg you—come
with me. You will earn all the rewards of heaven—and have
a delicious dinner in the bargain!" "Are you crazy," he asks
me, "or are you just out of your head? My train is leaving in
a few minutes, and it's Friday afternoon—almost sundown.
Do you know what that means? In a few more hours the
Sabbath will catch up with me, and I'll be stranded." "So
what!" I tell him. "So you'll take the next train. And in the
meantime you'll earn eternal life—and taste a soup, with fresh
dumplings, that only my wife can make . . ."

Well, why make the story long? I had my way. The roast
and the hot soup with fresh dumplings did their work. You
could see my customer licking his lips. So I grab the traveling
bag and I lead him home, and we go through with the *bris.*
It was a real pleasure! You could smell the roast all over the
house, it had so much garlic in it. A roast like that, with fresh
warm twist, is a delicacy from heaven. And when you consider
that we had some fresh dill pickles, and a bottle of beer, and
some cognac before the meal and cherry cider after the meal—
you can imagine the state our guest was in! His cheeks shone
and his forehead glistened. But what then? Before we knew
it the afternoon was gone. My guest jumps up, he looks around,
sees what time it is, and almost has a stroke! He reaches for
his traveling bag: "Where is it?" I say to him, "What's your
hurry? In the first place, do you think we'll let you run off
like that—before the Sabbath? And in the second place—who
are you to leave on a journey an hour or two before the Sabbath? And if you're going to get caught out in the country
somewhere, you might just as w'll stay here with us."

He groans and he sighs. How could I do a thing like that to him—keep him so late? What did I have against him? Why hadn't I reminded him earlier? He doesn't stop bothering me. So I say to him: "In the first place, did I have to tell you that it was Friday afternoon? Didn't you know it yourself? And in the second place, how do you know—maybe it's the way God wanted it? Maybe He wanted you to stay here for the Sabbath so you could taste some of my wife's fish? I can guarantee you, that as long as you've eaten fish, you haven't eaten fish like my wife's fish—not even in a dream!" Well, that ended the argument. We said our evening prayers, had a glass of wine, and my wife brings the fish to the table. My guest's nostrils swell out, a new light shines in his eyes and he goes after that fish as if he hadn't eaten a thing all day. He can't get over it. He praises it to the skies. He fills a glass with brandy and drinks a toast to the fish. And then comes the soup, a specially rich Sabbath soup with noodles. And he likes that, too, and the *tzimmes* also, and the meat that goes with the *tzimmes,* a nice, fat piece of brisket. I'm telling you, he just sat there licking his fingers! When we're finishing the last course he turns to me: "Do you know what I'll tell you? Now that it's all over, I'm really glad that I stayed over for *Shabbes.* It's been a long time since I've enjoyed a Sabbath as I've enjoyed this one." "If that's how you feel, I'm happy," I tell him. "But wait. This is only a sample. Wait till tomorrow. Then you'll see what my wife can do."

And so it was. The next day, after services, we sit down at the table. Well, you should have seen the spread. First the appetizers: crisp wafers and chopped herring, and onions and chicken fat, with radishes and chopped liver and eggs and *gribbenes.* And after that the cold fish and the meat from yesterday's *tzimmes,* and then the jellied neat's foot, or *fisnoga* as you call it, with thin slices of garlic, and after that the

potato *cholent* with the *kugel* that had been in the oven all
night—and you know what that smells like when you take
it out of the oven and take the cover off the pot. And what
it tastes like. Our visitor could not find words to praise it. So
I tell him: "This is still nothing. Wait until you have tasted
our borsht tonight, then you'll know what good food is." At
that he laughs out loud—a friendly laugh, it is true—and
says to me: "Yes, but how far do you think I'll be from here
by the time your borsht is ready?" So I laugh even louder than
he does, and say: "You can forget that right now! Do you
think you'll be going off tonight?"

And so it was. As soon as the lights were lit and we had a
glass of wine to start off the new week, my friend begins to
pack his things again. So I call out to him: "Are you crazy?
Do you think we'll let you go off, the Lord knows where, at
night? And besides, where's your train?" "What?" he yells
at me. "No train? Why, you're murdering me! You know I
have to leave!" But I say, "May this be the greatest misfortune
in your life. Your train will come, if all is well, around dawn
tomorrow. In the meantime I hope your appetite and digestion
are good, because I can smell the borsht already! All I ask," I
say, "is just tell me the truth. Tell me if you've ever touched a
borsht like this before. But I want the absolute truth!" What's
the use of talking—he had to admit it: never before in all
his life had he tasted a borsht like this. Never. He even started
to ask how you made the borsht, what you put into it, and
how long you cooked it. Everything. And I say: "Don't worry
about that! Here, taste this wine and tell me what you think
of *it*. After all, you're an expert. But the truth! Remember—
nothing but the truth! Because if there is anything I hate, it's
flattery . . ."

So we took a glass, and then another glass, and we went to
bed. And what do you think happened? My traveler overslept,

and missed the early morning train. When he wakes up he boil over! He jumps on me like a murderer. Wasn't it up to me, out of fairness and decency, to wake him up in time? Because of me he's going to have to take a loss, a heavy loss—he doesn't even know himself how heavy. It was all my fault. I ruined him. I! . . . So I let him talk. I listen, quietly, and when he's all through, I say: "Tell me yourself, aren't you a queer sort of person? In the first place, what's your hurry? What are you rushing for? How long is a person's life altogether? Does he have to spoil that little with rushing and hurrying? And in the second place, have you forgotten that today is the third day since the *bris*? Doesn't that mean a thing to you? Where we come from, on the third day we're in the habit of putting on a feast better than the one at the *bris* itself. The third day— it's something to celebrate! You're not going to spoil the celebration, are you?"

What can he do? He can't control himself any more, and he starts laughing—a hysterical laugh. "What good does it do to talk?" he says. "You're a real leech!" "Just as you say," I tell him, "but after all, you're a visitor, aren't you?"

At the dinner table, after we've had a drink or two, I call out to him: "Look," I say, "it may not be proper—after all, we're Jews—to talk about milk and such things while we're eating meat, but I'd like to know your honest opinion: what do you think of *kreplach* with cheese?" He looks at me with distrust. "How did we get around to that?" he asks. "Just like this," I explain to him. "I'd like to have you try the cheese *kreplach* that my wife makes—because tonight, you see, we're going to have a dairy supper . . ." This is too much for him, and he comes right back at me with, "Not this time! You're try- ing to keep me here another day, I can see that. But you can't do it. It isn't right! It isn't right!" And from the way he fusses and fumes it's easy to see that I won't have to coax him too long, or fight with him either, because what is he but a man with an appetite, who has only one philosophy, which he practices at the table? So I say this to him: "I give you my word of honor, and if that isn't enough, I'll give you my hand as well—here, shake—that tomorrow I'll wake you up in time for the earliest train. I promise it, even if the world turns upside down. If I don't, may I—you know what!" At this he softens and says to me: "Remember, we're shaking hands on that!" And I: "A promise is a promise." And my wife makes a dairy supper—how can I describe it to you? With such *kreplach* that my traveler has to admit that it was all true: he has a wife too, and she makes *kreplach* too, but how can you compare hers with these? It's like night to day!

And I kept my word, because a promise is a promise. I woke him when it was still dark, and started the samovar. He finished packing and began to say goodbye to me and the rest of the household in a very handsome, friendly style. You could see he was a gentleman. But I interrupt him: "We'll say goodbye a little later. First, we have to settle up." "What do you mean—settle up?" "Settle up," I say, "means to add up the figures. That's what I'm going to do now. I'll add them up, let you know what it comes to, and you will be so kind as to pay me."

His face flames red. "Pay you?" he shouts. "Pay you for what?" "For what?" I repeat. "You want to know for what? For everything. The food, the drink, the lodging." This time he becomes white—not red—and he says to me: "I don't understand you at all. You came and invited me to the *bris.* You stopped me at the train. You took my bag away from me. You promised me eternal life." "That's right," I interrupt him. "That's right. But what's one thing got to do with the other? When you came to the *bris* you earned your reward in heaven. But food and drink and lodging—do I have to give you these things for nothing? After all, you're a businessman, aren't you? You should understand that fish costs money, and that the wine you drank was the very best, and the beer, too, and the cherry cider. And you remember how you praised the *tzimmes* and the puddings and the borsht. You remember how you licked your fingers. And the cheese *kreplach* smelled pretty good to you, too. Now, I'm glad you enjoyed these things; I don't begrudge you that in the least. But certainly you wouldn't expect that just because you earned a reward in heaven, and enjoyed yourself in the bargain, that *I* should pay for it?" My traveling friend was really sweating; he looked as if he'd have a stroke. He began to throw himself around, yell, scream, call for help. "This is Sodom!" he cried. "Worse than Sodom! It's the worst outrage the world has ever heard of! How much do you want?" Calmly I took a piece of paper and a pencil and began to add it up. I itemized everything, I gave him an inventory of everything he ate, of every hour he spent in my place. All in all it added up to something like thirty-odd *rubles* and some *kopeks*—I don't remember it exactly.

When he saw the total, my good man went green and yellow, his hands shook, and his eyes almost popped out, and again he let out a yell, louder than before. "What did I fall into—a nest of thieves? Isn't there a single human being here? Is there a God anywhere?" So I say to him, "Look, sir, do you know what? Do you know what you're yelling about? Do you have to eat your heart out? Here is my suggestion: let's ride into town together—it's not far from here—and we'll find some people—there's a rabbiner there—let's ask the rabbi. And we'll abide by what he says." When he heard me talk like that, he quieted down a little. And—don't worry—we hired a horse and wagon, climbed in, and rode off to town, the two of us, and went straight to the rabbi.

When we got to the rabbi's house, we found him just finishing his morning prayers. He folded up his prayer shawl and
put his philacteries away. "Good morning," we said to him,
and he: "What's the news today?" The news? My friend
tears loose and lets him have the whole story—everything
from A to Z. He doesn't leave a word out. He tells how he
stopped at the station, and so on and so on, and when he's
through he whips out the bill I had given him and hands
it to the rabbi. And when the rabbi had heard everything,
he says: "Having heard one side I should now like to hear
the other." And turning to me, he asks, "What do you have
to say to all that?" I answer: "Everything he says is true. There's
not a word I can add. Only one thing I'd like to have him
tell you—on his word of honor: did he eat the fish, and did
he drink the beer and cognac and the cider, and did he smack
his lips over the borsht that my wife made?" At this the man
becomes almost frantic, he jumps and he thrashes about like an
apoplectic. The rabbi begs him not to boil like that, not to
be so angry, because anger is a grave sin. And he asks him
again about the fish and the borsht and the *kreplach*, and if it
was true that he had drunk not only the wine, but beer and
cognac and cider as well. Then the rabbi puts on his spectacles,
looks the bill over from top to bottom, checks every line, and
finds it correct! Thirty-odd *rubles* and some *kopeks,* and he
makes his judgment brief: he tells the man to pay the whole
thing, and for the wagon back and forth, and a judgment
fee for the rabbi himself . . .

The man stumbles out of the rabbi's house looking as if
he'd been in a steam bath too long, takes out his purse, pulls
out two twenty-fives and snaps at me: "Give me the change."
"What change?" I ask, and he says: "For the thirty you
charged me—for that bill you gave me." "Bill? What bill?
What thirty are you talking about? What do you think I am,

a highwayman? Do you expect me to take money from you?
I see a man at the railroad station, a total stranger; I take his
bag away from him, and drag him off almost by force to our
own *bris,* and spend a wonderful *Shabbes* with him. So am
I going to charge him for the favor he did me, and for the
pleasure I had?" Now he looks at me as if I really am crazy,
and says: "Then why did you carry on like this? Why did you
drag me to the rabbi?" "Why this? Why that?" I say to him.
"You're a queer sort of person, you are! I wanted to show
you what kind of man our rabbi was, that's all . . ."

When he finished the story, my litigant, Reb Nachman
Lekach, got up with a flourish, and the other three partners
followed him. They buttoned their coats and prepared to
leave. But I held them off. I passed the cigarettes around again,
and said to the story-teller:

"So you told me a story about a rabbi. Now maybe you'll
be so kind as to let me tell you a story—also about a rabbi,
but a much shorter story than the one you told."

And without waiting for a yes or no, I started right in, and
made it brief:

This happened, I began, not so long ago, and in a large city,
on *Yom Kippur* eve. A stranger falls into the town—a businessman, a traveler, who goes here and there, everywhere,
sells merchandise, collects money . . . On this day he comes
into the city, walks up and down in front of the synagogue,
holding his sides with both hands, asks everybody he sees
where he can find the rabbi. "What do you want the rabbi
for?" people ask. "What business is that of yours?" he wants to
know. So they don't tell him. And he asks one man, he asks
another: "Can you tell where the rabbi lives?" "What do you
want the rabbi for?" "What do you care?" This one and

that one, till finally he gets the answer, finds the rabbi's house, goes in, still holding his sides with both hands. He calls the rabbi aside, shuts the door, and says, "Rabbi, this is my story. I am a traveling man, and I have money with me, quite a pile. It's not my money. It belongs to my clients—first to God and then to my clients. It's *Yom Kippur* eve. I can't carry money with me on *Yom Kippur,* and I'm afraid to leave it at my lodgings. A sum like that! So do me a favor—take it, put it away in your strong box till tomorrow night, after *Yom Kippur.*"

And without waiting, the man unbuttons his vest and draws out one pack after another, crisp and clean, the real red, crackling, hundred *ruble* notes!

Seeing how much there was, the rabbi said to him: "I beg your pardon. You don't know me, you don't know who I am." "What do you mean, I don't know who you are? You're a rabbi, aren't you?" "Yes, I'm a rabbi. But I don't know *you* —who you are or what you are." They bargain back and forth. The traveler: "You're a rabbi." The rabbi: "I don't know who you are." And time does not stand still. It's almost *Yom Kippur*! Finally the rabbi agrees to take the money. The only thing is, who should be the witnesses? You can't trust just anyone in a matter like that.

So the rabbi sends for the leading townspeople, the very cream, rich and respectable citizens, and says to them: "This is what I called you for. This man has money with him, a tidy sum, not his own, but first God's and then his clients'. He wants me to keep it for him till after *Yom Kippur.* Therefore I want you to be witnesses, to see how much he leaves with me, so that later—you understand?" And the rabbi took the trouble to count it all over three times before the eyes of the townspeople, wrapped the notes in a kerchief, sealed the kerchief with wax, and stamped his initials on the seal. He passed this from one man to the other, saying, "Now look. Here is my signature, and remember, you're the witnesses." The kerchief with the money in it he handed over to his wife, had her lock it in a chest, and hide the keys where no one could find them. And he himself, the rabbi, went to *shul,* and prayed and fasted as it was ordained, lived through *Yom Kippur,* came home, had a bite to eat, looked up, and there was the traveler. "Good evening, Rabbi." "Good evening. Sit down. What can I do for you?" "Nothing. I came for my package." "What package?" "The money." "What money?" "The money I left with you to keep for me." "You gave *me* money to keep for you? When was that?"

The traveler laughs out loud. He thinks the rabbi is joking with him. The rabbi asks: "What are you laughing at?" And the man says: "It's the first time I met a rabbi who liked to play tricks." At this the rabbi is insulted. No one, he pointed out, had ever called him a trickster before. "Tell me, my good man, what do you want here?"

When he heard these words, the stranger felt his heart stop. "Why, Rabbi, in the name of all that's holy, do you want to kill me? Didn't I give you all my money? That is, not mine, but first God's and then my clients'? I'll remind you, you wrapped it in a kerchief, sealed it with wax, locked it in your wife's chest, hid the key where no one could find it. And here is better proof: there were witnesses, the leading citizens of the city!" And he goes ahead and calls them all off by name. In the midst of it a cold sweat breaks out on his forehead, he feels faint, and asks for a glass of water.

The rabbi sends the *shammes* off to the men the traveler had named—the leading citizens, the flower of the community. They come running from all directions. "What's the matter? What's happened?" "A misfortune. A plot! A millstone around our necks! He insists that he brought a pile of money to me yesterday, to keep over *Yom Kippur,* and that you were witnesses to the act."

The householders look at each other, as if to say: "Here is where we get a nice bone to lick!" And they fall on the traveler: how could he do a thing like that? He ought to be ashamed of himself! Thinking up an ugly plot like that against their rabbi!

When he saw what was happening, his arms and legs went limp, he just about fainted. But the rabbi got up, went to the chest, took out the kerchief and handed it to him.

"What's the matter with you! Here! Here is your money! Take it and count it, see if it's right, here in front of your witnesses. The seal, as you see, is untouched. The wax is whole, just as it ought to be."

The traveler felt as if a new soul had been installed in his body. His hands trembled and tears stood in his eyes.

"Why did you have to do it, Rabbi? Why did you have to play this trick on me? A trick like this."

"I just wanted to show you—the kind—of—leading citizens—we have in our town."

A Daughter's Grave

"YOU'RE on your way to the Fair, and we're coming home from the Fair. I have done my weeping already, and you're still going to weep . . . So let me make room for you. Here, move a little closer. You'll be more comfortable."

"There, that's good!"

Thus spoke two passengers sitting behind me in the train. That is, one of them spoke, and the other threw in a word like an echo, from time to time.

"We were both there together, my old woman and I," said the first. "There she is over there, sleeping on the floor. Poor thing, she's all worn out. She's done enough weeping for all of us, there at the cemetery. She fell face down on the grave—and you couldn't drag her away! I begged her, 'Isn't that enough? Your tears won't bring her back to life again!' Did she listen to me? But what do you expect? Such a tragedy! An only daughter. A treasure. Gifted and beautiful and clever. A high school graduate . . . It's two years now since she died. Maybe you think it was consumption? Not at all! She was strong and healthy. She did it herself—took her own life . . ."

"Is that a fact!"

From their conversation I understood the kind of Fair they were talking about. I recalled that it was September, the season of mourning, dear to the hearts of Jews. All over the Pale, during those weeks before *Rosh Hashono,* Jews travel from one town to another, paying their respects to the remains of mothers and fathers, sisters and brothers, children and other relatives. Bereaved mothers, orphaned daughters, lonely sisters and just unfortunate women throw themselves on the dear hallowed graves, shed a few tears, pour out their grief, ease their tortured souls . . .

I can tell you: this isn't the first year I've been a traveling man, but I can't remember when we've had such a good crop of mourners as this September. The railroads, bless the Lord, will make money. The carriages are packed. They are full of long-faced men and women with swollen red eyes and shiny noses. Some are on the way *to* the Fair, and others are coming home *from* the Fair . . . Outside you can smell early autumn. In your heart you feel autumn. And you're longing, you're longing for home . . .

I can't help but overhear the rest of the conversation.

"Maybe you think it was one of today's tragedies? Black smocks, red flags, Siberia? Heaven forbid! That much, at least, God has spared me. I saw to that! After all, I had a reason to. An only daughter. Such a gifted girl. So beautiful and clever. And a high school graduate!

"I did everything I could. I watched where she went and whom she talked with, and what she said and what books she read. 'Daughter, darling,' I said. 'If you want to read books, go right ahead! But I have to know,' I said, 'what you're reading.' It's true I don't know too much about such things, but I have a certain intuition, an inner feeling. Me—all I have to do is look into a book—even if it's in French—and I can tell you right away what it smacks of!"

"Imagine that!"

"I didn't want my child to play with fire. I was afraid . . . But don't think I resorted to trickery or force. On the contrary, I was gentle. All I did was remind her of a proverb. 'Daughter, darling,' I said. 'Let the wheel turn as it will. Neither you nor I can stop it . . .' That's the way I talked to her. And what did she say? Not a thing! An angel. Quiet as a dove! . . . And what does God do? The bad times pass. We live through all the troubles . . . Revolutions! Constitutions! Black smocks, red flags, shorn hair, bombs and the devil knows what else! All these things are gone. Although before those times passed, you can understand, I almost lost my wits. After all, didn't I have a right to? There was plenty to be afraid of. An only child. Gifted and beautiful. A high school graduate!"

"So! What happened?"

"To make a long story short . . . Praise the Lord! We lived through those terrible times. Now, with God's help, we could start thinking about marrying her off. A dowry? That's the least of my worries. Let the Lord only send the right man along! And the merry-go-round began. Matches, matchmakers, prospects, suitors! And my daughter shows no interest. You think maybe she doesn't want to get married? Who knows? . . . What then? I'll tell you. I began to look, to check up, and I find something. She's been reading a book—in secret! And not alone. Three of them were reading it together. She, and a friend of hers, our cantor's daughter—a smart girl, too, a high school graduate—and a third. Who is that? A nobody. A good-for-nothing, with a round face full of pimples and weak eyes without lashes, and gold-rimmed glasses to make him look still handsomer. A repulsive creature. And on top of it all, persistent. You couldn't get rid of him. He crawled after them—like a worm! Why do I call him a worm? I'll explain it to you. There are all kinds of people in the world. Some are oxen. Some are horses. Some are dogs. There are some who are pigs. And this one was a worm. Now do you understand?"

"Of course!"

"How did this worm ever find his way into my house?

Through the cantor's daughter. He's a cousin of hers. He was studying to become a druggist—or a lawyer—or a dentist—the devil alone knows what! All I know is that to me he was the Angel of Death. I didn't like him from the very beginning. I even said so to my wife. But she said to me, 'What foolish notions you have!' Still, I keep an eye on them. I keep my ears open, and I'm not at all pleased with the way the three of them are always reading together, and the way they talk together, getting all wrought up and feverish . . .

"So I say to her one time, 'Daughter, darling, what's this book the three of you are so worked up about?'

" 'Nothing,' she says. 'It's just a book.'

" 'I see it's a book,' I tell her, 'but what kind of a book?'

" 'And if I told you,' says she, 'would you know?'

" 'Why shouldn't I know?' says I. And she laughs and tells me, 'It isn't what you're afraid of. It's just an ordinary book. It's name is *Sanni*. A novel by Archie Bashe's.'

" 'Archie Bashe's?' I say to her. 'Why, that was a blind teacher we had in this town. He died a long time ago.'

"Again she laughs, and I say to myself, 'Ah-ha, my daughter! You laugh, and your poor father is bleeding inwardly!' Here is what I thought: the old troubles were beginning again . . . And do you think I didn't get hold of that book and read it myself?"

"My goodness! Really!"

"Not exactly myself . . . But I got somebody to read it for me. A young man who works for me, a clerk in my shop. A very smart young fellow. Reads Russian like a professor . . . So one evening I sneaked the book away from my daughter's room, gave it to this clerk of mine, and said, 'Here, Berel, take it and read it through. And tomorrow you'll tell me what it's all about.' I barely lived through that night. The next morning, as soon as he came to work, I grabbed hold of him. '*Nu,*

Berel,' I said. 'What about the book?' And he says, 'What a book!' And his eyes are about ready to pop out of his head. 'All night long,' he tells me, 'I couldn't sleep. I couldn't tear myself away!'

" 'Is that so?' I ask. 'Well, then, tell me more! Let me in on it too!' And my Berel tells me a story . . . How can I describe it to you? It just made no sense. Listen to this:

"It's about a big, strong Russian named Sanni who was always drinking whiskey and eating sour pickles! And he had a sister whose name was Lida, and she was madly in love with a doctor, but she had an affair with an army officer and became pregnant. And there was a student named Yura who was head-over-heels in love with a girl, a school teacher, named Krasavitza. And this girl went out for a boat ride one evening—do you think she went with her boy friend? Not at all! She went out with that drunkard, Sanni!

" 'Is that all?' I asked.

" 'Wait a minute,' he tells me. 'That isn't all. There's another teacher too, a man named Ivan, and one day he goes with this drunkard to watch some naked girls bathing . . .'

" 'Come, come,' I say. 'What does it all lead up to? What's the point of it?'

" 'The point of it is this,' he tells me. 'This drunkard, Sanni, has a habit—he brays like a stallion and one time he comes home to his own sister Lida and he . . .'

" 'Go to the devil!' I tell him. 'That's enough about that drunkard. Tell me what happens! What is it all about? How does it end?'

" 'Oh,' he says, 'it ends like this. The army officer shoots himself, and the student shoots himself too, and Krasavitza takes poison, and a Jew—there's a Jew in the book too, Solo-veitchik, hangs himself.'

"I lose my patience. 'Go!' I say. 'Go hang yourself together with him!' And he says, 'Why do you talk to me like that? Is it my fault?' And I say, 'No, not yours. I mean this Archie Bashe's.' That's what I tell Berel, but in my mind I'm thinking of that repulsive young fellow, the devil take him! And do you suppose one day I didn't catch him alone and take him to one side . . ."

"You did!"

"Of course! And I said to him, 'Look here! Where on earth did you ever pick up that trash?'

" 'What trash?' says he, flashing his gold-rimmed glasses at me.

" 'This story of Archie Bashie's,' I say, 'with that drunkard in it—Sanni.'

" 'Sanni,' he tells me seriously, 'is not a drunkard.'

" 'What else is he?' I want to know.

" 'Sanni,' he tells me, 'is a Hero!'

" 'And what makes him a Hero?' I ask. 'The fact that he drinks brandy out of a tea glass, eats sour pickles, and brays like a stallion?'

"The young fellow becomes furious. He takes off his glasses and looks at me with his red-rimmed eyes. 'You've heard the tune, Uncle,' he says to me, 'but you don't know the words. Sanni,' he says, pointing his finger up in the air, 'Sanni is a Man of Nature—a Free Man! He says what he means and does what he wants!' And he goes on and on, he doesn't stop. Freedom, and love, and again freedom, and once more love . . . And he puffs out his small pigeon's chest, makes gestures with his hands, and rants like a visiting preacher.

"I stand there looking at him, and think to myself, 'Heavenly Father, what is this repulsive thing talking about? How would it be if I took him by the collar and threw him out of doors so hard he would have to stop and pick up all his teeth?' But then I think it over: still, would it be better if he talked about bombs? Well, go be smart and foresee that there are things worse than bombs, and on account of trash like that I would lose my child, my only one, the apple of my eye, and that my wife would very nearly go out of her head, and that I myself out of shame and agony would have to give up my business and sell my home and go to live in another town! But I am getting ahead of myself. Let me tell you exactly how it came about and what started it.

"It started during the agrarian riots. When these riots started we naturally feared that it would end in another pogrom, as such things always do, and we lived in a state of terror. But if the Lord wishes, miracles happen, and from evil good comes out. How so? From the provincial capital authorities sent down a platoon of soldiers, and it became quiet and peaceful again. And besides, because of the soldiers, the whole town came to life, business flourished. For what can be better for any small town than a company of soldiers with doctors and officers and corporals and commanders and I don't know what else they call them?"

"Why, naturally!"

"But go be smart and foresee that the cantor's daughter would fall in love with an officer and declare that she was willing to be converted in order to marry him? You can imagine what went on in our town! But don't worry. The cantor's daughter was *not* converted and she did *not* marry the officer; because as soon as the agrarian riots ended the troops were sent back where they came from, and in his great hurry the officer even forgot to say goodbye to his beloved . . . But the girl did not forget. And woe to her parents! You can imagine what they went through. The whole town seethed. Everywhere, from every mouth: 'The cantor's daughter, the cantor's daughter.' Evil tongues were busy. Someone sent a midwife to the girl. Someone else asked the cantor what they were going to name

the child. Though actually it was very possible that the whole
story was a lie. You know what damage a few long tongues
can do in a small town!"

"How well I know!"

"Oh, what a pitiful sight they were! I mean the cantor and
his wife . . . We could hardly stand it. Because after all—were
they to blame? But at the same time I warned my daughter,
once for all, no matter how friendly they had been before, from
that day on she must have nothing to do with the cantor's
daughter. And with me—when I say something, there is nothing more to be said. She may be an only daughter, but a father
has to be respected! How was I to know that my daughter
would keep on seeing her in secret? But when did I find that
out? When it was too late. When it was all over . . ."

Suddenly behind my back I heard someone cough and sigh
in her sleep, and the man who was telling the story became
silent. He waited a few minutes and then continued in a lower
tone than before.

"It was the midnight services a week before *Rosh Hashono.*
I remember it as if it happened yesterday. You should have seen
our poor cantor as he led the services. It was pitiful to hear him.
His sobbing was real, his groans were genuine. It was enough
to melt a stone. And nobody knew what he was living through
the way I did. These modern children! You can pity their
parents . . . Well, the very next morning, I came home early
from the synagogue, had a bite to eat, took my keys and went
to the marketplace. I opened my shop and waited for Berel to
come. I waited a half-hour. I waited an hour. No clerk, no
Berel. At last I look up and there he is. 'Berel, why so late?'
And he tells me, 'I was at the cantor's.' 'Why all of a sudden
at the cantor's?' And he tells me, 'Why, haven't you heard what
happened to Haika?' 'What happened to Haika?' I ask. 'Why,
she poisoned herself . . .'"

"Think of that!"

"As soon as I heard that I ran straight home. My first thought was: what would Etka say? (That was my daughter, you know.) I come into the house and ask my wife, 'Where is Etka?' 'Etka is still in bed. Why, what's the matter?' 'What's the matter?' I say, 'Why, Haika just took poison.' When she heard this my wife threw her hands over her head and began to weep and wail. 'What's the matter?' I ask. 'Why,' she says, 'only last night Etka was with her. They went walking together —for about two hours!' 'Etka—with Haika?' I say. 'What are you talking about? How could that happen?' 'Oh,' she moaned. 'Don't ask me. I had to let her do it. She begged me not to tell you that she saw her every day. Something terrible has happened! I know it! I hope it's not true!' And with these words my wife runs into Etka's room and falls down on the floor in a faint. I come after her, run to the bed, screaming, 'Etka!' Etka? Did I say Etka? There is no Etka . . ."

"No Etka?"

"She was dead. Face down across the bed—dead. On her table was a bottle, and near it a note, in Yiddish, in her own hand. She used to write the most beautiful Yiddish; it was a pleasure to read it. 'My dear, faithful parents,' she had written. 'Forgive me for having caused you this grief and shame. Forgive me. Forgive me. We promised each other that we'd do it—Haika and I. On the same day, at the same hour, by the same means; because without each other we could not live. I know,' she wrote, 'dear parents, that I am committing a great wrong. I fought with myself for a long time, but it had to be. There is only one thing I ask of you, my dear ones, and that is that you bury me together with Haika, in a grave next to hers. Be well, and forget—forget that you ever had a daughter Etka . . .'

"Can you imagine that! To expect us to forget that we ever had a daugter Etka!"

Behind my back I heard a shuffle, the sound of steps, a sigh, and then a woman's voice, stifled and still sleepy:

"Avrom! Avrom!"

"Yes, Gitka—what is it? Did you sleep? Maybe you want some tea . . . Just a minute, we're coming to a station. I'll get some hot water. Where is the teakettle? Where is the tea and sugar?"

The Miracle of Hashono Rabo

THE miracle of *Hashono Rabo*—that was what we called
the train wreck that almost took place on *Hashono Rabo,*
the day when our judgment is sealed in Heaven, and our
fate decided. And it happened right in my home town of
Heissin. That is, not in the town itself, but a few stations
away, at a place called Sobolivka.

You who have ridden on the train in our region know
what the service on the Straggler Special is like. When it
reaches a station and stops, it forgets when to start again.
According to the timetable, it has a definite schedule. For
instance, at Zatkovitz it says that the train is supposed to
stop exactly an hour and fifty-eight minutes; and at Sobolivka,
the place I am now telling you about, not a second more
than an hour and thirty-two minutes. But take my word for
it, no matter where it stops—whether at Zatkovitz or at Sobolivka, it stands at least two, and sometimes more than three
hours. It depends on how long the switching and fueling
take, and what switching and fueling mean to a train like
the Straggler Special, I don't have to tell you.

First of all the locomotive has to be uncoupled, and then
the train crew—the conductor, the engineer and the fireman—
sit down together with the stationmaster, the guard and the
telegraph operator, and drink beer—one bottle after another.

And while these important operations, or maneuvers, are
going on, what do the passengers do? You have seen what

228

they do. They go crazy with boredom. Some yawn; some find themselves a corner and take a nap; and some walk back and forth on the platform, their hands clasped behind their backs, idly humming a tune.

On the day that I am telling you about, while the Straggler was waiting in the station of Sobolivka, a man was seen standing nearby, his hands clasped behind his back, watching. He was not a passenger, simply an inquisitive onlooker, a resident of Sobolivka. And what was a Sobolivka householder doing there? Nothing! It was *Hashono Rabo*—a half holiday; the man had been at the synagogue already, had eaten already, and as it was a half holiday and there was nothing for him to do at home, he took his walking stick and went out for a walk to the station, to meet the train.

Meeting the train, as you know, is an old custom in our part of the country. When the train is due, everyone who is not otherwise occupied, rushes off to the station. Maybe they'll see somebody there. See whom? See what? A man from Teplik? An old woman from Obodivka? A priest from Golovonievska? In Sobolivka that's great excitement—and you go. And especially since in those days the train was still a novelty, there was always something new to see, something strange to hear. Anyway, on that special *Hashono Rabo,* when the fate of all of us had been sealed already, as I told you before, there stood the train at the station, uncoupled and waiting; and watching it with a mild curiosity, in a half-holiday mood, stood a householder of Sobolivka with a stick under his arm.

Well, you may say, what of that? What if a resident of Sobolivka stands and looks at an uncoupled locomotive? Let him stand and look! But no. It had to happen that on this day, among the waiting passengers, was a priest from Golovonievska, a village not far from Heissin. Having nothing to do, the priest walked back and forth on the same platform, his hands also clasped behind his back, and he also stopped to look at the locomotive. Seeing nothing unusual, he turned to the Sobolivker and said, "Tell me, Yudko, what is there to stare at?"

The man answered crossly, "What do you mean—Yudko? My name is not Yudko. My name is Berko."

So the priest said, "Let it be Berko. Well, tell me then, Berko, what are you looking at so seriously?"

Without taking his eyes from the locomotive, the man answered, "I am standing here beholding the wonders of God. Think—a simple thing like that. You turn one screw this way, another screw that way, and this strange and terrifying machine moves off."

"How do you know that?" the priest asks him. "How do you know that if you turn one screw this way, another the other way, the machine will start?"

Answers the man from Sobolivka, "If I didn't know, would I have said so?"

Says the priest, "What do you know? How to eat potato pudding? But this is not a pudding."

At this the man becomes angry (the people of Sobolivka are famous for their tempers), and he says, "Well then, my Father, maybe you'd care to climb up into the locomotive with me and have me show you what makes these things move and what makes them stop?"

This did not sound so good to the priest. What was this little man trying to say? Was he going to tell *him* the principle whereby a locomotive moved or stood still? So he answered him sharply, "Go, Hershko. Climb up then."

As sharply the other corrected him, "My name is not Hershko. My name is Berko."

"All right," said the priest. "Let it be Berko. So climb up, Berko."

"What do you mean—climb up? Why should I climb up?
You can go first, Father."

"You're the teacher this time—not I," says the priest, with
some bitterness. "So lead the way."

They argued, they bickered; the debate became heated, but
in the end they both climbed up, and the Sobolivka householder began to instruct the priest in the workings of modern
machinery. Slowly he turned one handle, slowly, he turned
another, and before they could say a single word, they were
horrified to find that the locomotive had begun to move.
And away it went!

Now this is the best time, I think, to leave the two good men
to themselves in the roaring locomotive, while we pause and
consider who is this man of Sobolivka who was so bold and
so brave that he dared to climb together with the priest into
the locomotive . . .

Berel Essigmacher—that was the name of the man I'm
telling you about. And why did they call him Essigmacher?
Because his business was that of making vinegar—*essig* in
Yiddish—the very best vinegar in our corner of the world.
The business he had inherited from his father, but he himself
had invented a machine—so he says—that gave the vinegar
its distinctive and superior quality. If he only had the time, he
could make enough vinegar to provide for the needs of three
whole provinces. But why should he? He didn't have to. He
wasn't that greedy. That's the kind of man this Essigmacher
was.

He had studied nowhere, and yet he could do the most
delicate work you could imagine, and he understood the
workings of all kinds of engines. How did this happen? Well,
all you had to remember, he explained, was that the manu-
facture of vinegar had much in common with that of whiskey.
Both were made in a distillery; and a still had almost the

same machinery as a locomotive. A still whistled, and so did a locomotive. What difference was there? The important thing—so said Berel himself and showed you what he meant with his hands—the important thing was the power that came from the heat. You started, he explained, by heating the boiler, and the boiler heated the water. The water turned to steam, the steam pushed a rod, and the rod turned the wheels. If you wanted to turn it right, you twisted the lever right, if you wanted to turn it left, you twisted it left. It was as plain as the nose on your face.

And now, having introduced you to this man of Sobolivka, I have at the same time no doubt answered many of the questions you had in mind. So we might as well go back to the wreck of the Straggler Special.

You can imagine the horror and dismay of the passengers when they saw the locomotive go off by itself, no one knew by what strange power. And besides that, the confusion that overwhelmed the crew itself. The first thing they did was to jump up and chase after the engine as if they thought they could catch up with it. But it did not take them long to realize that they were wasting their strength; and as if to tease them, the locomotive suddenly proved that it could develop speed. In fact it flew like mad. It was the first time that anyone had ever seen it move so fast. There was nothing to do but turn back, and this they did. And then, together with the guard and station master, they sat down and drew up a complete and detailed report; after which they sent off telegrams to every station along the line: BEWARE RUNAWAY LOCOMOTIVE. TAKE ACTION. WIRE REPLY.

What a panic this telegram created you can well imagine. What does this mean: Beware runaway locomotive? How does a locomotive run away? And what was this: Take action? What action could they take—besides sending telegrams?

And so once more telegrams began to fly back and forth, forth and back, from one end of the line to the other. The instruments clicked and clattered as if they were possessed. Every station wired every other station, and the frightful news spread fast, till every town and every hamlet knew all the tragic details. In our town, for instance, in Heissin, we knew the exact number of people killed and injured. So violent a death! Such innocent victims! And when did it happen? On what day? Exactly on *Hashono Rabo,* when the tickets of our fate are made out, inscribed and sealed high up in Heaven! Apparently Heaven wanted it thus . . .

That is what people said in Heissin and all the nearby towns, and it is impossible to describe the agony and the suffering that we all endured. But how did that compare with the suffering of the poor passengers themselves, who were stranded in the station at Sobolivka without a locomotive, like sheep without a shepherd? What could they do? It was *Hashono Rabo.* Where could they go? Celebrate the holiday in a strange town? And they all huddled together in a corner and began to discuss their plight and to speculate about what had happened to the Fugitive, as they had now named the vanished locomotive. Who knew what might happen to a *shlimazl* like that? Just think of it—a monster like that careening down the track! How could it keep from colliding somewhere along the way with its sister train creeping from Heissin through Zatkovitz on its way to Sobolivka? What would happen to the passengers in the other train? In their imagination they saw the collision—a frightful catastrophe with all its gory details. They saw it before their eyes—overturned carriages, shattered wheels, severed heads, broken legs and arms, battered satchels and suitcases spattered with blood! And suddenly—another telegram! A telegram from Zatkovitz. And what did it say? Here it is:

THIS INSTANT LOCOMOTIVE FLEW PAST ZATKOVITZ WITH BLINDING
SPEED CARRYING TWO PASSENGERS ONE A PRIEST. BOTH WAVED THEIR
HANDS POINTED. CAN'T SAY WHAT THEY MEANT. NOW ON WAY TO
HEISSIN.

What do you think of that? Two men in a runaway locomotive—and one of them a priest? Where were they going—
and why—and who could the other man be? Asking here
and there they finally found out that it was a resident of Sobolivka. But who? Did anyone know? What a question! Of
course they knew! Berel Essigmacher of Sobolivka! How did
they know? How does anyone ever know? They knew! Some
neighbors of his swore they had seen him and the priest from
a distance standing together near the unhitched locomotive,
gesturing with their hands. What did that mean? Why should
a vinegar maker be standing with a priest near a locomotive,
gesturing with his hands?

The talking and the shouting went on so long that soon the
story reached Sobolivka, and though the town is only a short
distance from the tracks, still by the time the story was relayed
from one person to another it had been altered so much, assumed so many different forms, that by the time it reached
Berel's home the story was so fantastic that Berel's wife fainted
at least ten times and they had to bring a doctor. And all
Sobolivka came pouring into the station. The place became
so crowded, the noise so deafening, that the stationmaster
instructed the guard to clear the platform.

If so, what are we doing there? Let's be off and see what
happened to our friend the vinegar maker and the priest on
the Fugitive, the runaway locomotive.

It is very easy to talk about seeing what happened in the
runaway locomotive, but we'll have to take Mr. Essigmacher's
word for it. The stories he tells about his adventure are so

remarkable that if only half of them were true, it would be enough! And from what I know of him he doesn't seem to be the sort of person who makes up stories.

At first—this is Essigmacher's version—when the locomotive began to move, he scarcely knew what was happening. Not that he was alarmed; he was simply upset by the fact that the locomotive would not behave as it should. According to logic, he said, it should have stopped dead at the second turn of the lever. Instead, it went faster than ever, as if ten thousand evil spirits were pushing it down the tracks. It flew with such speed that the telegraph poles shimmered and flickered in front of his eyes like the spots you see when you're dizzy. A little later, when he came back to his senses, he remembered that a locomotive had brakes that could slow it down or stop it altogether. There should be brakes somewhere—hand brakes —air brakes—a wheel that you gave a good turn and it came pressing down on the rims of the wheels and they stopped turning . . . How could he ever have forgotten a simple thing like that! And he made a leap for the wheel, was going to give it a turn, when suddenly someone grabbed him by the arm and yelled, "Stop!"

Who was it? The priest, pale as a sheet. "What are you trying to do?" he asked. "Nothing," said Berel, "I'm just trying to stop the engine." "May God help you," cries the priest, "if you ever touch anything on that machine again! If you do, I'll pick you up by the collar and throw you out of here so fast that you'll forget your name was ever Moshko!" "Not Moshko," Berel corrects him. "My name is Berko." And he tries to explain what is meant by a wheel that's called a brake. But the priest won't let him. He was a stubborn man!

"You've turned enough things here already, and look where your turning got us! If you touch that wheel, I'll touch *you*! You'll wish you'd broken your neck before you ever saw me!"

"But, Father!" pleaded Berel. "Don't you think that my life means as much to me as yours does to you?"

"Your life!" snorted the priest bitterly. "What good is your life? A dog like you . . ."

At this Berel became angry and he turned upon the priest with a fury that will not soon be forgotten. "In the first place," he pointed out, "even if I were a dog you ought to feel sorry for me. According to our law even a dog mustn't be harmed. It's a living thing. And in the second place, in the eyes of the Almighty, in what way is my life any less important than any other life? Are we not alike? Do we not all have the same pedigree? Are we not all descended from the same man— Adam? And are all of us not going to the same identical place —the rich, black earth? And thirdly, Father, look at the difference between you and me. I am doing everything I can to make the locomotive stop, that is, I have the welfare of both of us in mind; while you are ready to throw me out of here, that is, to murder a human being!"

That and many other fine things he told him. There in the flying locomotive he delivered a sermon complete with quotations and examples, until the poor, helpless priest was ready to collapse. And in the midst of the lofty discourse the station of Zatkovitz suddenly came into view, with the stationmaster and the guard straining themselves at the edge of the platform. Berel and the priest tried to signal to them; they yelled and waved their arms, but nobody knew what they were trying to say. The station flew past, and the locomotive was on its way to the next town—Heissin. As they went farther on, the priest became more friendly, but on one thing he still insisted. Berel must not touch the machine. But he did say this much:

"Tell me, Leibko . . ."

"My name," corrected Berel, "is not Leibko. It's Berko."

"All right," said the priest, "let it be Berko. Tell me, Berko, would you be willing to jump off this locomotive together with me?"

"What for?" asked Berel. "Just to get ourselves killed?"

To this the priest answered, "We're going to get killed anyway."

Said Berel, "Where was that decided? What proof do you have? If God wants to—Oh, Father, what He can do!"

Says the priest, "What do you think He'll do?"

Says Berel, "That depends on Him. Listen, Father, I'll tell you something. Today we Jews have a sort of holiday—*Hashono Rabo*. Today up in Heaven, every human being, every living thing, gets a certificate that's signed and sealed, a certificate of life or death. So, Father, if God marked me down for death, there's nothing I can do. What difference does it make to me if I'm killed jumping off the locomotive or standing *in* the locomotive? As a matter of fact, I can be walking along the street, and can't I slip and get killed? But on the other hand, if it was inscribed that I should go on living, then why should I jump?"

This is the way the vinegar maker of Sobolivka tells the story, and he swears that every word is true. He does not remember how it happened or when he first became aware that something had happened. It was somewhere close to Heissin; they could see the chimney on the station. Berel looked at the priest and the priest looked at Berel. What was this? The locomotive was slowing down. Little by little its speed decreased. Soon it was barely crawling. Now it paused, then moved a few feet farther, then thought it over and stopped completely.

What had happened? He suddenly remembered: the fire must have gone out. And when the fire in a locomotive goes out, the water stops boiling, and when the water stops boiling —well, you don't have to be a vinegar maker in Sobolivka to know that the wheels stop turning. And that's all there is to it. And naturally, being Berel, he turned to the priest right then and there. "Well, Father, what did I tell you?" he said. "If God Almighty had not decided this morning in Heaven that I should go on living here on earth, who knows how much longer the fire might have continued to burn, and how much farther we might have gone by now?"

The priest said nothing. He stood where he was, with his head down, silent. What was there to say? But later, when it came time to part, he came up to Berel and held out his hand. "Goodbye, Itzko," he said. And Berel answered, "My name is not Itzko. It's Berko."

"Let it be Berko," said the priest. "I never knew you were such a . . ." And that was the last he heard. For rolling up the skirts of his cassock, the priest had started off with long strides back to his home in Golovonievska.

Berel himself went on to Heissin and there he had a real holiday. Like the good Jew that he was, he offered up thanks for his deliverance, and then he told his story from start to finish to everyone he saw, each time with new incidents and new miracles.

And everybody wanted the vinegar maker of Sobolivka to come home with him, spend the night with him, and tell him in person the story of the Miracle of *Hashono Rabo*.

And what a celebration we had that night! What a *Simchas Torah* that was! What a *Simchas Torah*!

You Mustn't Weep—It's Yom-Tev

I AM willing to bet any amount you want that no one in the world was as happy at the coming of Spring as were the two of us—I, the cantor Peisi's son, Motel, and the neighbor's calf, Meni. (It was I who had given him that name.) Both of us together had crept out of our narrow winter quarters to greet the first day of spring, both of us together had felt the warm rays of the sun and together we had smelled the fresh odors of the newly sprouted grass. I, Motel, the cantor's son, came out of a cold, damp cellar that smelled of sour dough and medicine and Meni, the neighbor's calf, was let out of even the worse stench of a small, filthy shed with flimsy walls through whose chinks the snow sifted in winter and the rain beat in summer.

Having escaped into God's free world, the two of us, Meni and I, began to show our unbounded joy, each in his own way. I, Motel, the cantor's son, lifted up both my arms above my head, opened my mouth, and drew in as much of the fresh warm air as my lungs could contain. And I felt as though I were growing in height, as though I were drawn up there into the blue sky where the fleecy clouds drifted, up there where the birds dipped and rose and were lost to view. And from my overfilled breast there escaped a song that was even lovelier than the songs my father used to lead in the synagogue during holidays, a song without words, without notes, without motif— more like the song of a waterfall or the waves of the ocean—a

239

sort of *Song of Songs,* a hymn of praise: "O Father," I sang,
"O Heavenly Father . . ."

Meni, the neighbor's calf, showed his joy quite differently.
First of all, he buried his black, wet muzzle in the dirt, poked
at the earth three or four times with his forepaws, lifted up his
tail, reared himself up and let out a loud ma-a-a-a. This sounded
so funny to me that I had to burst out laughing and to mimic
the ma-a-a-a. The calf apparently was pleased by this for it
was not long before he repeated it all once more with the same
intonation and the same leap. Naturally I did it over again,
in every detail. This was repeated, several times—I leaped, the
calf leaped; the calf let out his ma-a-a-a. I let out a ma-a-a-a.
Who knows how long this might have gone on if it hadn't been
for my brother Elihu who came up from behind and slapped
me sharply across the neck.

"What's the matter with you! A boy like you, almost nine
years old, dancing with a calf! Into the house, you good-for-
nothing. You'll get it from father."

Nonsense! My father won't do anything to me. My father is
sick. He hasn't led the prayers in the synagogue since the
Autumn Festivals. All night long I hear him coughing, and
every day the doctor comes to the house. The doctor is a large,
heavy-set man with a black mustache and laughing eyes—a
cheerful man. He has only one name for me—*Pupik.* Whenever he sees me he pokes me in the belly. He keeps telling my
mother not to stuff me with potatoes, and for the patient he
prescribes bouillon and milk, milk and bouillon. My mother
listens to him quietly and when he is gone she hides her face
in her apron and her shoulders shake. Then she wipes her
eyes, calls my brother Elihu aside and they whisper in low
voices. What they are talking about I do not know, but they
seem to be quarreling. My mother wants to send Elihu some-

where and he won't go. He says to her, "Rather than go to
them for help I'd kill myself. I'd sooner die."

"Bite your tongue," says my mother in a low voice, gritting
her teeth and looking as if she wanted to slap him. But soon
she calms down and pleads with him: "What can I do, my son?
You see how ill he is. We must do something for him."

"Then sell something," says my brother, looking out of the
corners of his eyes at the glass cabinet. My mother follows his
glance, wipes her eyes again and sighs, "What can I sell? My
soul? There is nothing left. Or shall I sell the empty cabinet?"

"Well, why not?" says my brother.

"Murderer!" cries out my mother. "How did I ever get such
murderers for children?"

My mother fumes and rages, cries her heart out, then wipes
her eyes and forgives him. The same thing also happened with
the books, with the silver collar on my father's *tallis,* with the
two gilded goblets, with my mother's silk dress, and all the
other things which were sold one by one, each to a different
buyer . . .

The books were sold to Michal, the baggage-man, a man
with a thin beard which he was constantly scratching. My poor
brother had to go to him three times before he brought him to
the house. My mother, relieved and happy to see him at last,
put her finger across her lips to show him that he must speak
softly so my father shouldn't hear. Michal understood, raised
his eyes to the shelf, scratched his beard and said to her, "Well,
show us, what have you got up there."

My mother beckoned to me to climb up on the table and
take down the books. I didn't have to be told twice. I jumped
up so eagerly that I sprawled over the table and my brother,
snapping at me to stop jumping like a crazy fool, pushed me
aside. He climbed up on the table himself and handed the

books down to Michal who scratched his beard with one hand, while with the other he leafed through the books and found fault with each one. This one had a poor binding, that one had a worn back, another was simply worthless. And after he had looked through half of them, examined all the bindings, felt all the backs, he scratched his beard again:

"If it was a complete set of *Mishnayos,* I might consider buying it . . ."

My mother turned pale, and my brother on the contrary became red as fire. He leaped angrily at the baggage-man, "Why didn't you tell us in the beginning that all you wanted to buy were *Mishnayos?* What did you have to come here and take up our time for?"

"Be quiet!" my mother begged him, and a hoarse voice was heard from the next room where my father lay.

"Who is there?"

"Nobody," my mother said and pushing my brother Elihu into my father's room, began to bargain with Michal herself and finally sold him the books, apparently for very little, because when my brother came back again and asked her how much, she pushed him aside, saying, "It's none of your business." And Michal snatched up the books quickly, shoved them into his bag and disappeared.

Of all the things in the house that we sold none gave me as much pleasure as the glass cabinet.

It is true that when they ripped the silver collar off my father's *tallis,* it was a treat, too. First of all there was the bargaining with Yosel the goldsmith, a pale man with a red birthmark on his face. Three times he went away, but in the end he won out, and he sat down crosslegged near the window with my father's *tallis,* took out a small knife with a yellow, bone handle, bent his middle finger and began to rip the collar

with such skill that I envied him! And yet you should have
seen how my mother carried on. She cried and cried and cried.
Even my brother Elihu, who has been confirmed already and
is practically a man, ready to be married, turned toward the
door and pretended to be blowing his nose.

"What's going on there?" called my father from the sick-
room.

"Nothing," my mother answered, wiping her eyes, and her
lower lip and the whole lower part of her face trembled so
that it was all I could do to keep from laughing.

But how does that compare with the taking away of the glass
cabinet?

First of all, how could anybody take it away? I had always
taken it for granted that the cabinet was built into the wall,
so how could it be moved? And if it was, where would my
mother keep the bread and the dishes and the pewter spoons
and forks (our two silver spoons and one silver fork, had been
sold long ago). And where would we keep the *matzos* at Passover? These thoughts went through my head while Nachman
the carpenter was measuring the cabinet with the big red
thumbnail of his dirty right hand. He kept insisting that the
cabinet wouldn't go through the door. "Here," he said, "is
the width of the cabinet, and here is the width of the door—
it will never go through here."

"Then how did it ever get in?" asked my brother Elihu.

"Don't ask me," answered Nachman angrily. "Go ask the
cabinet. How should I know how it got in?"

For one moment I was really afraid for the cabinet. That
is, I was afraid it would remain at our house. But it wasn't
long before Nachman returned with his two tall sons, both of
them also carpenters, and they took hold of the cabinet as
easily as the devil took hold of the *melamed*. First came Nachman, then the two sons, and behind them came I. The father

directed them; "Kopel, this way. Mendel, to the right. Kopel, don't rush. Mendel, wait . . ." I imitated the gestures of all three, but my mother and brother refused to have anything to do with it. They stood looking at the empty wall, now covered with cobwebs, and wept . . . A regular circus. Always crying. Suddenly we heard a loud crash. Right in the doorway the glass had shattered. The carpenter and his sons began to roar at each other, and curse, each blaming the other for the broken glass. "Graceful as a lead bird!" "Bears' feet." "The devil take you." "Go break your head in hell."

"What's going on there?" a weak voice called from the sick-room.

"Nothing," my mother answered, wiping her eyes.

But these experiences were as nothing compared with the selling of my brother's couch and my cot. My brother's couch was once the sofa we all sat on, but after Elihu became engaged he began to sleep on it, and I inherited his old cot. Long ago when times were good and my father was still well and conducted services in the butchers' synagogue with his choir of four, the sofa still had springs. Now the springs belonged to me. I did all sorts of tricks with them; cut my hands and almost poked my eyes out. One day I put them around my neck and nearly choked to death. Finally, my brother spanked me and threw the springs up into the attic.

It was old Hannah who bought the couch and the cot from us. Before she paid her deposit my mother wouldn't let her look under the covers.

"You can buy what you see in front of you. There is nothing more to look at." But after she had finished bargaining and had given my mother a deposit she went up to the couch and the cot, lifted up the bedclothes, looked slowly into every corner, and spat violently. My mother resented her spitting and was ready to return the money, but my brother Elihu interfered:

"Once you've bought it, it's final."

That night we put the bedclothes on the floor and my brother and I spread ourselves out like lords, covered ourselves with one blanket (his blanket had already been sold) and I was pleased to hear my brother say that sleeping on the floor wasn't so bad. I waited till he had said his prayers and gone to sleep and then I began to roll around on the floor, over and over again. There was plenty of room, praise the Lord. It was like a field, a field in paradise . . .

"What can we do now?" said my mother one morning, as she looked around with a deep frown at the four empty walls. My brother and I followed her glance. Then looking at me with pity in his eyes my brother said sternly:

"Go outside, Motel. We have something to talk about."

I ran out, skipping on one foot. Naturally I went straight to the neighbor's calf. In the last few months Meni had grown into a handsome calf, with a lovely black muzzle, and brown eyes full of understanding. It was always looking for something to eat and liked to have its throat scratched.

"Again. So you're playing with that calf again? You can't stay away from your dear friend?"

It was my brother Elihu speaking, this time without anger, without curses. And taking my hand he led me to Hirsch-Ber the cantor. There, at Hirsch-Ber's, he told me I would be well off. First of all I would have enough to eat. At home things were bad, he said. Our father was very ill; we had to do everything we could for him. And we were doing everything we could. And he unbuttoned his coat and showed me his vest underneath.

"This is where I used to wear my watch," he said. "A gift

from my father-in-law and I sold it. If he ever found out—I don't know what he'd do. The world would turn upside down.

"Well, here we are," my brother said, in a friendly tone. Hirsch-Ber the cantor was a good musician. That is, he couldn't sing himself, he had no voice at all, poor fellow (so said my father) but he understood music. He had fifteen boys in his choir and he was a terribly mean master. That much I knew. He listened to me sing one or two pieces with all the frills and flourishes, then patted my head and told my brother that my soprano wasn't bad. Not only wasn't it bad, my brother insisted, but it was excellent. Elihu bargained with him, took a payment, and told me I was going to stay here for a while. He told me to obey Hirsch-Ber and not to get homesick.

It was easy for him to say, "Don't get homesick." But how could I keep from being homesick in the summer time when the sun shone, the sky was clear as crystal, and even the mud had already dried up? In front of our house there was a pile of logs, not ours, but Yossi, the *nogid's*. He was planning to build a dwelling and since he had nowhere to keep the logs he kept them in front of our house. God bless Yossi, the *nogid*, for that. Out of his logs I made myself a fortress. In this fortress I was happy, Meni the calf was happy, we ruled alone here. So how could I keep from being homesick?

I have been at Hirsch-Ber's for three weeks already and I have hardly done any singing at all. I have another job—I take care of his Dobtzie. Dobtzie is a deformed child, a hunchback. She is not quite two, but I have to hold her all the time and she is heavy. It's all I can do to lift her. Dobtzie is fond of me. She puts her thin arms about me and clutches me with her thin fingers. She calls me Kiko—I do not know why. But she loves me. She won't let me sleep at night. "Kiko ki." That means that she wants me to rock her. Dobtzie adores me. When I am eating she tears the food out of my hands. "Kiko pi." That means, "Give it to me." How I long for home. The food is not so wonderful here, either. It's a holiday—*Shevuos* eve. I wish I could go outside and see the heavens split open, as they do on *Shevuos,* but Dobtzie won't let me. Dobtzie loves me too much to let me out of her sight. "Kiko ki." She wants me to stay and rock her. I rock and I rock until I fall asleep. In my sleep a visitor comes to me—Meni, the neighbor's calf. He looks at me with his big eyes, like a human being's and says, "Come." And we both run, downhill to the river. I roll up my pants. Hop! I am in the river. I swim and Meni swims after me. It's lovely on the other side. There is no cantor, no Dobtzie, no sick father. I wake. It was all a dream. Oh, if I could only run away, run away. But how can I run away? Where could I run? Home, of course.

Hirsch-Ber is up already. He tells me to dress quickly and go with him to the synagogue. There is a big morning ahead of us. There are some special pieces to sing today. When we get there I see my brother Elihu. What is he doing here? He usually goes to the butchers' synagogue, where our father is cantor. What does this mean? My brother goes up and talks something over with Hirsch-Ber, who does not seem to be well-pleased. Finally he says, "But remember, bring him back right after dinner."

"Come along," my brother says to me, "you're going home to see father." And we start to go off together, Elihu walking sedately, and I skipping along.

"What's your hurry?" says my brother, holding me back. He apparently wants to talk to me.

"You know father is sick. He's very, very sick. God knows what will become of him. We have to save him, but have nothing left and no one wants to help. Mother absolutely won't let

him go to the hospital. She will sooner die than let him go
there. Here she comes. Be quiet."

With outstretched arms my mother comes to meet me. She
falls on my neck and I feel a tear not my own fall on my cheek.
My brother Elihu goes inside to my father, and my mother and
I remain standing outside. A group of women gather about
us—our neighbor's wife, Fat Pessie, and her daughter Mindel
and her daughter-in-law Pearl and several others.

"Oh! A guest for *Shevuos*," they say. "May you enjoy his
company!"

My mother lowers her tear-swollen eyes. "A guest?" she
says. "The child has only come to see his sick father." And then
turning to Pessie she adds in a whisper, "A town full of people,
but does anyone care? Twenty-three years in one synagogue;
he ruined his health. I might still be able to save nim, but I
have nothing to do it with. We've sold everything, even the
pillows. Sent the child out to a cantor. Everything for him.
Everything to help him . . ."

While my mother talks I keep turning my head this way and
that.

"What are you looking for?" my mother asks.

"What do you suppose?" says Pessie. "He must be looking
for the calf." And she turns to me with a strangely pleasant
tone in her voice.

"Ah, little one, the calf is gone. We had to sell it to the
butcher. What else could we do? It's enough to feed one
animal without having two to worry about."

So the calf had become just a mouth to feed!

A strange woman, Pessie. She sticks her nose into everything.
She wants to know what we're going to have for dinner.

"Why do you ask?" my mother wants to know.

"Just like that," says Pessie, carelessly, and lifting up her
shawl pushes into my mother's hands a bowl of thick cream.
My mother shoves it back with both hands.

"For heaven's sake, Pessie, what are you doing? What do you think we are? Beggars? Don't you know us better than that?"

"It's because I do know you," Pessie defends herself. "I'm not giving you anything, just lending it to you. Our cow has been good to us lately. We've had more than we can use. You'll return it some day."

The women talk and I keep thinking of the pile of logs, and my playmate the calf whom I won't see any more. If I weren't ashamed I'd burst out crying.

"If your father asks how you're getting along," my mother tells me, "say, 'God be thanked.' "

My brother explains this further:

"Don't complain about anything to him. Don't tell him any of your childish stories. Just say, 'God be thanked.' Understand?" And with these words my brother Elihu took me into the sick room to see my father. The table was crowded with jars and bottles and boxes of pills. The air smelled like a druggist's shop. The window was tightly closed. In honor of *Shevuos* the room had been decorated with greens. The floor was covered with sweet-smelling grass. My brother had done it all.

When my father saw me come in he beckoned to me with a long, thin finger. My brother pushed me forward. I could hardly recognize my father. His face was like chalk. His gray hairs shone on his head, each hair singly as if pasted on. His dark eyes were sunken deep into his head. His teeth looked artificial. His neck was so thin that it could barely support his head. He made strange movements with his lips, like a tired swimmer trying to breathe. As I approached the bed he placed his hot, bony fingers on my face, and twisted his mouth into a wan smile that was like the smile of death.

Just then my mother came into the room, followed by the jolly doctor with the big, black mustache. He greeted me like an old friend, poked me in the belly and said cheerfully to my father.

"So you have a guest for *Shevuos*! May you enjoy his company!"

"Thank you," said my mother and beckoned to the doctor to examine the patient and prescribe something for him. The doctor threw the window open and began to scold my brother for keeping it shut. "I've told you a thousand times that a window likes to be kept open."

My brother Elihu pointed at my mother. It was her fault. She wouldn't let him open the window because she was afraid my father would catch cold. My mother motioned to the doctor to hurry and examine the patient, give him something. The doctor calmly took out his big gold watch. I could see my brother staring at it. The doctor saw it, too.

"Do you want to know what time it is? I have four minutes to half past eleven. What do you have?"

"My watch has stopped," said my brother, turning red from the tip of his nose to the backs of his ears.

My mother was becoming restless. She wanted the doctor to hurry up and give something for the patient. But the doctor was in no hurry. He asked my mother all sorts of trivial questions. When was my brother getting married? What did Hirsch-Ber think of my singing? I ought to have a good voice, because a voice is inherited. My mother answered him patiently. Suddenly the doctor turned his chair around and faced my father and took the dry, feverish hand in his.

"Well, cantor," he said, "how were the Services this *Shevuos*?"

"God be praised," answered my father, with the smile of a ghost.

"That's good. And the coughing? Are you coughing less? Are you sleeping better?" asked the doctor, bending closer.

"No," said my father, barely catching his breath. "On the contrary, I cough as much as ever. I sleep very little. But God be praised. It's *Shevuos*—a holy day. We received the Commandments this day. And we have a guest—a guest for *Shevuos* . . ."

Everyone's eyes were turned on the "guest," and the guest looked down on the floor. His thoughts were elsewhere. They were outdoors with the logs where reeds and stickers grew, with the neighbor's calf that had been like a dear human friend, and now had been sold to the butcher. They were down by the river that tumbled downhill—far from the sick room that smelled like a drugstore.

The bowl of cream that our neighbor Pessie had lent to us was very useful. My brother and I made a feast out of it, both of us dipping chunks of fresh white bread into the chilled sour cream, and finding it very good.

"The only trouble with it is that there isn't enough . . ." said my brother. He was being unusually friendly that day. He didn't even make me go back to Hirsch-Ber right away. He let me play at home a while instead.

"After all, you're a guest here today," he said, and told me I could go outside and play on the logs for a while. But he warned me not to climb too much and tear my best pair of pants. My best pair of pants! That was a good joke. You should have seen those pants. But let's not talk about them . . . Let's talk about Yossi the *nogid's* logs instead. Yossi the *nogid* thought the logs belonged to him. That's what he thought! Really they were my logs. I made a palace out of them and a vineyard. I was a prince. The prince walked proudly in his vineyard, tore up a reed and marched back and forth with it. Everyone envied me. Even the *nogid's* son, Hennich with the

squinting eye, begrudged me my good fortune. He went by
in his shiny new clothes, pointed at my pants and laughed and
squinted his eye and shouted:

"Watch out, you'll be losing something."

"Better run along," I said, "before I call my brother Elihu."

All the little boys were afraid of my brother Elihu. Hennich
with his squinting eyes moved off and I was again alone, once
more a prince in his vineyard. What a pity that Meni couldn't
be here with me. He had been sold to the butcher, said Pessie.
Why? To be slaughtered? Was he born for this—to be
slaughtered? For what end is a calf ever born, and for what end
a human being?

Suddenly I hear a terrible screaming and wailing from our
house. I recognize my mother's voice. I look up. People are
running in and out of the house. I continue to lie stretched
out on a log. I feel good. But what's this? Here comes Yossi
the *nogid*. Yossi is the president of the butchers' synagogue
where my father has been cantor for twenty-three years. Yossi
was once a butcher himself, but he now deals in cattle and furs,
and is a rich man, a very, very rich man.

Yossi is waving his arms, shouting angrily at my mother:

"Why wasn't I told that Peisi the cantor was so sick? Why
was everybody so quiet about it?"

"Did you want me to shout?" says my mother, weeping. "The
whole town saw how I struggled, how I tried to save him. And
he wanted to be saved, too . . ."

My mother was unable to say any more. She wrung her
hands and threw her head back. My brother caught her in his
arms.

"Mother, why do you have to explain to him? Mother, don't
forget this is *yom-tev*—it's *Shevuos*! You mustn't weep!
Mother!"

But Yossi continues to shout. "The whole town? Who is the

town? You should have come to me! I'll take care of everything. The funeral, the attendants, the shroud, everything! I'll
pay for it all. And if something has to be done for the children,
come to me, too, don't be ashamed to come."

But that comforted my mother not at all. She kept on weeping and wailing and fainting in my brother's arms. And my
brother, who was almost in tears himself, kept reminding her,
"Today is *yom-tev,* mother! It's *Shevuos,* you mustn't cry,
mother."

And then at once it all became clear to me. My heart shrank.
I felt lost. I wanted to burst out crying, and I didn't know
for whom. I was so sorry for my mother, I couldn't bear to
see her cry like that.

And I left my palace and my vineyard and I came up to her
from behind and cried in the same tone as my brother.

"Mother! Today is *yom-tev.* It's *Shevuos,* mother! You
mustn't weep!"

I'm Lucky—I'm an Orphan

NEVER before in my life have I been the privileged character I am now. What is the reason for this?

As you know, my father, Peisi the cantor, died the first day of *Shevuos,* and I was left an orphan.

The first day after *Shevuos* my brother and I began to say *kaddish,* the prayer for the dead. It was my brother Elihu who taught me how to say it. My brother Elihu is a devoted brother, but a poor teacher. He is quick tempered and he beats me. Taking the prayer book in his hand, that first day after *Shevuos,* he sat down with me and began to teach me the words: *"Yisgadal v'yiskadash shmei rabo."* He expected me to know it by heart right away. He repeated it with me one time after another from beginning to end and then told me to say it by myself. I tried, but it didn't work.

The first few lines weren't bad, but after that I always got stuck. Every time this happened he prodded me with his elbow, and said my mind must be elsewhere (how did he guess?), that I must be thinking about the calf (how could he know?). But he didn't give up. He repeated it with me once more. I started out like a flash, but again, after a few lines, I got stuck. The words wouldn't come. So he grabbed me by the ear and shouted, "If father could only get up from his grave now and see what a stupid child he had . . . !"

"Then I wouldn't have to be saying *kaddish* for him!" I said, promptly.

For this I caught a juicy slap on the cheek. Hearing the noise my mother cried out, "God be with you! What are you doing? Whom are you slapping? Have you forgotten that the child is an orphan?"

I sleep with my mother now in the bed my father had slept in—the only piece of furniture left in the house. She lets me have most of the blanket.

"Cover yourself," she says to me, "and go to sleep, my poor little child. You might as well try to sleep; I have no food to give you."

I cover myself with the blanket, but I can't fall asleep. I keep repeating the words of *kaddish* to myself.

I don't go to *cheder* these days. I am not learning anything these days. I don't even pray, I don't sing in the choir.

I'm lucky. I'm an orphan.

Congratulate me. I know the whole *kaddish* by heart now—every bit of it. In the synagogue I stand on a bench and rattle it off without a pause. I have a good singing voice—inherited from my father—a real soprano. All the boys stand around me and envy me. The women weep. Some of the men even give me a *kopek*. Yossi the *nogid's* son, Hennich with the squinting eye (who is by nature very jealous), stands in front of me and sticks out his tongue. He is eager—he is anxious—he is dying —to make me laugh. But just to spite him I won't laugh. One time Aaron the *shammes* caught him at it, and grabbing him by the ear, led him to the door. Served him right!

Since I have to say *kaddish* in the morning and at night, I don't stay with Hirsch-Ber any more, and I don't have to carry Dobtzie around all the time. I am a free man. I spend all day at the river, either fishing or bathing. I have figured out for myself a good way to catch fish. If you like, I'll teach it to you.

You take off your shirt, tie your sleeves into knots, and walk slowly through the water up to your neck. You have to keep going a long, long time. When you feel the shirt growing heavy it's a sign that it is full. Then you come out as quickly as you can, and shake out the weeds and mud, and look carefully inside. Tangled in the weeds you will sometimes find a few little tadpoles. These you can throw back; it's a pity to let them die. In the thick mud you may find a leech. These are worth money: for ten you can get three *groschen,* a *kopek* and a half. But it isn't easy work . . . For fish there is no use even looking. At one time there may have been fish in the river, but now there are none. I don't care. I'd be glad enough just to find leeches, but you don't even always find those. This summer I didn't catch a single one.

How my brother Elihu found out that I have been going fishing I don't know. When he did find out he almost pulled my ear off. It was lucky that Fat Pessie, our neighbor, saw him do it. One's own mother couldn't take up for her child any better.

"Is that the way to treat an orphan?" she cried.

My brother Elihu is ashamed and lets go my ear. Everybody takes up for me these days.

I'm lucky. I'm an orphan.

Our neighbor, Fat Pessie, must have fallen in love with me. She goes after my mother and won't stop bothering her. She wants me to go and live at her house.

"Why should it bother you?" she asks. "I have twelve at the table already, so he'll be one more." She almost got my mother to consent that time, but my brother Elihu spoke up.

"Who will keep an eye on him and see that he goes to say *kaddish?*"

"I'll see that he goes," said Pessie. "There, does that satisfy you?"

Pessie is not a rich woman. Her husband is a bookbinder; his name is Moishe. He is known as a very skilled workman, but being skilled is not enough. You need luck besides. That is what Pessie tells my mother. My mother goes her one better. She says that even to be unlucky, to be a *shlimazl*, you have to have luck. As an example she points at me. Here I am, an orphan—and everybody wants me! There are some people who are willing to keep me for good, but my mother says that as long as she is alive she won't give me up. And she bursts out crying. Later she asks my brother's advice.

"What do you think? Should we let him stay at Pessie's?"

My brother is almost a grown man now. If he weren't, would my mother be asking his advice? With his hand he strokes his chin, as though he had a beard already. He likes to talk like a grown man.

"Let him go. So long as he doesn't become a *sheigetz*."

And it is agreed that I should live at Pessie's for the time being, provided that I don't become a *sheigetz*. What do they call being a *sheigetz*? To tie a piece of paper to the cat's tail so she'll chase it around and around—that is being a *sheigetz*. Rattling a stick along the fence around the priest's house and making a lot of noise—that is being a *sheigetz*. Pulling the cork out of the water carrier's tank so that half the water runs out—that is being a *sheigetz*.

"It's your luck that you're an orphan!" cries Leibke the water carrier. "If you weren't, I'd break every bone in your body! You can believe me, too!"

I believe him all right, but I also know that he won't touch me. For I am an orphan.

I'm lucky. I'm an orphan.

Our neighbor Pessie told a big lie. She said she feeds twelve at her table, but according to my reckoning I am the fourteenth. She must have forgotten their blind Uncle Boruch. Maybe she didn't count him because he is so old and has no teeth to chew with. I won't argue about that. It is true that he can't chew, but he still knows how to swallow. He swallows like a goose, and grabs all the food he can reach. Everybody grabs there. I grab too, and for that they jump on me. Under the table each one kicks me. The one who kicks the hardest is Vashti. Vashti is a terror. His name is really Hershel, but they call him Vashti. Everyone in this house has a nickname.

You can be sure that there is a reason for each name. Pinny is called "Barrel" because he is round and fat. Haym is rough and shaggy so they call him "Buffalo." Mendel has a pointed nose so they call him "Sharpnose." Feitel is called "Petelili" because he stammers. Berel is never satisfied with one slice of bread smeared with chickenfat; he always says, "Give me more!" In short, everyone in this house has a nickname. Even the cat—poor innocent creature. What harm did she ever do anyone? And yet she has a nickname too. They call her "Feiga-Leah the *shammeste*." Do you want to know why? Because she is fat and Feiga-Leah, the wife of the *shammes,* is also fat. You can't imagine how many times every one of them has been beaten for calling the cat by a human name. But beatings have no effect. Once they have given someone a nickname, the name sticks.

I have a nickname too. Guess what it is . . . "Motel with the Lips." They don't like my lips. They say that when I eat I always smack my lips. I would like to see a person who can eat without smacking his lips! I am not one of those proud people whose feelings are easily hurt, but this nickname I simply can't stand. And just because I can't stand it they keep on teasing me and calling me by it all the time. Nothing can make them stop. First I was "Motel with the Lips," then "The Lips," and finally just "Lippy."

"Lippy, where have you been?"

"Lippy, wipe your nose."

It annoys me and then it hurts me so that I start crying. Seeing me, their father, Pessie's husband, Moishe the bookbinder, asks, "Why are you crying?"

I answer, "Why shouldn't I cry? My name is Motel and they call me Lippy."

He asks who called me that, and I say Vashti.

He was going to beat Vashti and Vashti said it wasn't he, it was Barrel. And Barrel said it was Buffalo.

And so it went. One blamed another and the other blamed a third. It was like a circle without an end. At last their father made up his mind. He laid them down one by one and gave each one a good whipping with the cover of a prayerbook.

"You rascals!" he cried. "I'll show you how to make fun of an orphan! The devil take every one of you!"

And so it goes. Everybody comes to my defense. Everybody takes up for me.

I'm lucky. I'm an orphan.

Dreyfus in Kasrilevka

I DOUBT if the Dreyfus case made such a stir anywhere as it did in Kasrilevka.

Paris, they say, seethed like a boiling vat. The papers carried streamers, generals shot themselves, and small boys ran like mad in the streets, threw their caps in the air, and shouted wildly, "Long live Dreyfus!" or "Long live Esterhazy!" Meanwhile the Jews were insulted and beaten, as always. But the anguish and pain that Kasrilevka underwent, Paris will not experience till Judgment Day.

How did Kasrilevka get wind of the Dreyfus case? Well, how did it find out about the war between the English and the Boers, or what went on in China? What do they have to do with China? Tea they got from Wisotzky in Moscow. In Kasrilevka they do not wear the light summer material that comes from China and is called pongee. That is not for their purses. They are lucky if they have a pair of trousers and an undershirt, and they sweat just as well, especially if the summer is a hot one.

So how did Kasrilevka learn about the Dreyfus case? From Zeidel.

Zeidel, Reb Shaye's son, was the only person in town who subscribed to a newspaper, and all the news of the world they learned from him, or rather through him. He read and they interpreted. He spoke and they supplied the commentary. He told what he read in the paper, but they turned it around to suit themselves, because they understood better than he did.

One day Zeidel came to the synagogue and told how in Paris a certain Jewish captain named Dreyfus had been imprisoned for turning over certain government papers to the enemy. This went into one ear and out of the other. Someone remarked in passing, "What won't a Jew do to make a living?"

And another added spitefully, "A Jew has no business climbing so high, interfering with kings and their affairs."

Later when Zeidel came to them and told them a fresh tale, that the whole thing was a plot, that the Jewish Captain Dreyfus was innocent and that it was an intrigue of certain officers who were themselves involved, then the town became interested in the case. At once Dreyfus became a Kasrilevkite. When two people came together, he was the third.

"Have you heard?"

"I've heard."

"Sent away for good."

"A life sentence."

"For nothing at all."

"A false accusation."

Later when Zeidel came to them and told them that there was a possibility that the case might be tried again, that there were some good people who undertook to show the world that the whole thing had been a plot, Kasrilevka began to rock indeed. First of all, Dreyfus was one of *ours*. Secondly, how could such an ugly thing happen in Paris? It didn't do any credit to the French. Arguments broke out everywhere; bets were made. Some said the case would be tried again, others said it would not. Once the decision had been made, it was final. All was lost.

As the case went on, they got tired of waiting for Zeidel to appear in the synagogue with the news; they began to go to his house. Then they could not wait that long, and they began to go along with him to the postoffice for his paper. There they read, digested the news, discussed, shouted, gesticulated, all together and in their loudest voices. More than once the postmaster had to let them know in gentle terms that the postoffice was not the synagogue. "This is not your synagogue, you Jews. This is not *kahal shermaki.*"

They heard him the way Haman hears the *grager* on *Purim*. He shouted, and they continued to read the paper and discuss Dreyfus.

They talked not only of Dreyfus. New people were always coming into the case. First Esterhazy, then Picquart, then General Mercies, Pellieux Gonse . . .

There were two people whom Kasrilevka came to love and revere. These were Emile Zola and Labori. For Zola each one would gladly have died. If Zola had come to Kasrilevka the whole town would have come out to greet him, they would have borne him aloft on their shoulders.

"What do you think of his letters?"

"Pearls. Diamonds. Rubies."

They also thought highly of Labori. The crowd delighted in him, praised him to the skies, and, as we say, licked their fingers over his speeches. Although no one in Kasrilevka had ever heard him, they were sure he must know how to make a fine speech.

I doubt if Dreyfus' relatives in Paris awaited his return from the Island as anxiously as the Jews of Kasrilevka. They traveled with him over the sea, felt themselves rocking on the waves. A gale arose and tossed the ship up and down, up and down, like a stick of wood. "Lord of Eternity," they prayed in their hearts, "be merciful and bring him safely to the place of the trial. Open the eyes of the judges, clear their brains, so they may find the guilty one and the whole world may know of our innocence. Amen. *Selah.*"

The day when the good news came that Dreyfus had arrived was celebrated like a holiday in Kasrilevka. If they had not been ashamed to do so, they would have closed their shops.

"Have you heard?"

"Thank the Lord."

"Ah, I would have liked to have been there when he met his wife."

"And I would have liked to see the children when they were told, 'Your father has arrived.' "

And the women, when they heard the news, hid their faces in their aprons and pretended to blow their noses so no one could see they were crying. Poor as Kasrilevka was, there was not a person there who would not have given his very last penny to take one look at the arrival.

As the trial began, a great excitement took hold of the town. They tore not only the paper to pieces, but Zeidel himself. They choked on their food, they did not sleep nights. They waited for the next day, the next and the next.

Suddenly there arose a hubbub, a tumult. That was when the lawyer, Labori, was shot. All Kasrilevka was beside itself.

"Why? For what? Such an outrage! Without cause! Worse than in Sodom!"

That shot was fired at their heads. The bullet was lodged in their breasts, just as if the assassin had shot at Kasrilevka itself.

"God in Heaven," they prayed, "reveal thy wonders. Thou knowest how if thou wishest. Perform a miracle, that Labori might live."

And God performed the miracle. Labori lived.

When the last day of the trial came, the Kasrilevkites shook as with a fever. They wished they could fall asleep for twenty-four hours and not wake up till Dreyfus was declared a free man.

But as if in spite, not a single one of them slept a wink that night. They rolled all night from side to side, waged war with the bedbugs, and waited for day to come.

At the first sign of dawn they rushed to the postoffice. The outer gates were still closed. Little by little a crowd gathered outside and the street was filled with people. Men walked up and down, yawning, stretching, pulling their earlocks and praying under their breath.

When Yadama the janitor opened the gates they poured in after him. Yadama grew furious. He would show them who was master here, and pushed and shoved till they were all out in the street again. There they waited for Zeidel to come. And at last he came.

When Zeidel opened the paper and read the news aloud, there arose such an outcry, such a clamor, such a roar that the heavens could have split open. Their outcry was not against the judges who gave the wrong verdict, not at the generals who swore falsely, not at the French who showed themselves up so badly. The outcry was against Zeidel.

"It cannot be!" Kasrilevka shouted with one voice. "Such a verdict is impossible! Heaven and earth swore that the truth must prevail. What kind of lies are you telling us?"

"Fools!" shouted Zeidel, and thrust the paper into their faces. "Look! See what the paper says!"

"Paper! Paper!" shouted Kasrilevka. "And if you stood with one foot in heaven and the other on earth, would we believe you?"

"Such a thing must not be. It must never be! Never! Never!"

And—who was right?

The Convoy

THAT was what they called the new Government Inspector who had recently come to Teplik. To be accurate, his real name was Agamemnon Afonagenovitch, but the Jews of Teplik, who love to tamper with names, changed his for two reasons: first, because Haman Ivanovitch was shorter and easier to say. Just try, for instance, to roll your tongue around in your mouth and say, A-ga-mem-non A-fo-na-ge-no-vitch! That is the first reason. And the second is that since Teplik was founded, no one remembers ever having heard of an Inspector so much like the Haman of Scriptures as this Haman Ivanovitch Plisetsky of whom we speak.

In Teplik they have had all kinds of Inspectors—good ones, bad ones, those who take bribes eagerly and those who would not touch a *kopek*—except possibly as a New Year gift, which doesn't count, or a birthday present, which you could hardly refuse. All of us have birthdays, and everywhere a birthday is celebrated as a holiday. It has been that way since the dawn of history, since Pharaoh was king of Egypt, as we read in *Genesis*. Pharaoh, when his birthday came, ordered a feast for all his slaves, set his cupbearer free from prison, and hanged his baker on a tree, as Joseph had foretold in interpreting the dreams three days before.

But let us go back to this other tyrant, this Haman we have been talking about. When he arrived in Teplik, the first thing he did was to start cleaning up the town. And when I say

265

cleaning, I mean just that. The horse thieves of Teplik, renowned throughout the world, were smoked out in a month
or two. Even if you needed one for an exhibit you couldn't
find one. If there was any person he had any reason to suspect, he did not wait or hesitate, but packed him off by convoy
to the prison at Heissin. Let them reckon with him there.

After the thieves and petty pilferers, he turned his attention
to the streets of the town and to the Jews. He issued the order
that from that day on, the streets must all be kept clean. No
one must empty rubbish into the streets, pour slops out of
the front door, or do anything else unseemly. And the Jews,
he declared, must not open their shops before noon on Sunday,
teachers must not hold classes without a special permit, and
to make it complete, he forbade the *eirev,* the zone of exemption. As you recall, on the Sabbath we must not carry anything
on our persons, not even a handkerchief. In our own house
we could, and in our yard also, but in the city at large not a
thing. So every Friday afternoon we used to make a fence
around the entire Jewish settlement. A fence? You could
call it that, though it consisted of no more than a strong piece
of cord that ran from tree to tree around the entire village.
This we called an *eirev,* and it made all the village one's own
yard, and people could carry whatever they needed without fear
of committing a sin.

But now Haman said that the *eirev* had to go. The Jews
could get along without their telegraph, without these wires
strung all around the town. Even in the synagogue itself,
when some of the men had a fight over this or that honor and
slapped each other in the face, he liked to interfere. That's the
kind of tyrant he was!

Well, he had his way. The stores were closed Sunday till
noon. And if not right on the dot—if some of them opened

a minute or two earlier—he pretended not to notice. For what choice did he have? He did as much as he could. But to be a watchman at every Jewish shop, to catch anyone who opened the door just an inch—that was not humanly possible.

But the *eirev,* the zone of exemption, gave him trouble at first. Every Friday afternoon the cord was strung up all around the town, and Saturday morning he had it torn down. But the next week a new *eirev* appeared, and the week after that another one. This happened several weeks in succession. No matter how much his spies watched, they could not find the culprit, until he condescended to go himself, hide behind a hedge and spend the whole night watching. Finally toward daybreak he caught Peisi, the *shammes'* son, in the very act of stretching the cord. Without ceremony he grabbed Peisi by the left ear and dragged him off to jail and locked him up for the whole day. From that day on Teplik had to get along without an *eirev.* And still people carried their handkerchiefs and watches around on the Sabbath—with no apparent consequences.

Not so simple was the war he waged against the teachers. They made life wretched for him. Here he arrested a teacher with twenty pupils and closed his *cheder,* and there he discovered him with the same pupils in another street. He closed up this *cheder* too, swore out a warrant; looked around—and there was the same man, high up in the women's balcony of the synagogue with the same twenty pupils shouting at the tops of their voices. A curse on these Jewish children, you couldn't drive them away from their studies! "For heaven's sake, if you have to go up there with those pupils of yours, stay there and be damned! But don't make so much noise! Don't force me to listen to you!"

That is how Plisetsky appealed to the teacher, and he swore that if he ever caught him again he would banish him from

Teplik within twenty-four hours. The teacher heard him out
with the greatest respect and discontinued his classes in the
women's balcony. But the next day he started again in a
cellar not far away, and went on teaching with the very same
ear-splitting chant as before—that familiar, deafening chant
without which the study of Hebrew apparently has no more
flavor than the cold puddings that wealthy people in the big
cities eat these days.

Haman Ivanovitch battled with these teachers so long, till
with a final curse he shut his eyes and pretended not to know
that they were there.

II. THE *NOGID* OF TEPLIK, SHOLOM-BER TEPLIKER OF TEPLIK

Since most of the inhabitants of Teplik were Jews, the new
Inspector had to spend the greater part of his time dealing
with Jews, and in a short time he became acquainted with
most of them, knew them by name, learned all their secrets,
spoke to them in a half-Yiddish, half-Russian language of
his own, and became quite intimate with many of them—almost like one of the family.

The richer townspeople, the leading citizens—the soup ladles,
as we call them, because they are always stirring the community pot—in their turn, when they saw how friendly he
was, began to win their way into his good favor—first, with
a piece of Sabbath fish ("Jew fish," he called it), a glass of
Passover brandy ("Jew brandy"), and a few pieces of *matzo*
("Jew *matzo*"). And afterward, with a fawning smile, they
moved on to the next stage—of slipping something into his
hand. But his response to this gesture was so unexpected and
sharp that they learned something that they remembered forever after, and they passed it on to their children and grandchildren: "Never bribe a man—until you know who he is and
what he is."

"If you're trying to bribe me," cried Haman, "it must mean that you've committed some crime. Here, take him and put him away!"

The words, "Take him and put him away!" were always at the tip of his tongue. They meant several different things: to throw a person in jail for a day or two; to put him away for several weeks; or even to send him off to Heissin, where the prison was, by convoy. And once he had given this order, nothing more could be done about it. Not all the kings of east or west could help. That's the kind of a man he was! And yet so inconsistent was he that if some penniless wretch fell into his hands, this tyrant reached into his own pocket and gave the fellow a *ruble* or two, and said to him in his mixture of Russian and Yiddish:

"Here is a loan to help you on your way."

But considerate as he was of poor people, so intolerant was he of the rich. And especially if the rich man was from Teplik. And most especially the *nogid* of Teplik, Sholom-Ber Tepliker of Teplik. Him he could not tolerate at all, and for a long, long time he tried to catch the man at some misdemeanor, without success, till God came to his aid and he had him in his hands. This is how it happened.

This Sholom-Ber Tepliker of Teplik, in addition to being a man of wealth, was as stubborn and proud a creature as you would ever find. If he ever decided to do something, nothing could stop him. It would be easier to pick up all of Teplik and move it somewhere else than to make him change his mind. Thus when Haman Ivanovitch decreed that no one was to throw rubbish or slops out into the street, Sholom-Ber Tepliker of Teplik asked this question, "Whose business is that? It's my rubbish and my slops, and I can do with it as I wish!"

"But, Reb Sholom-Ber," people tried to tell him, "if this Haman ever catches you, there'll be trouble!"

"Don't worry," said Sholom-Ber. He was a man who did not like to waste his words.

"But, Reb Sholom-Ber, he'll serve a warrant."

"Let him serve seventy-seven warrants!"

"But, Reb Sholom-Ber, what if someone should slip in front of your house and break a leg?"

"Let that Haman break a leg!" cried Sholom-Ber, and ordered his servant girl to throw as much rubbish in front of the house as she wanted to.

So Plisetsky came to him with the police and served papers on him, and Sholom-Ber protested vociferously, and told them all what he thought of them, as only a *nogid* can. Plisetsky told him to shut his mouth, and in the course of giving this advice threw in a few words like, "the nerve of the Jew," and "dirty Jewish mouth," and a few other pleasant remarks of the same general type. At this Sholom-Ber became angry and let it be known before all those present that the Inspector was a second Haman, in fact he was Haman himself, the very same one they told about in the Bible. All this was added as an extra clause to the complaint, and between one thing and another, the leading citizen of Teplik, Sholom-Ber himself, was sentenced to two weeks in the district jail. And all the prayers and all the vows and all the pledges to the Almighty could not help him!

It is to be understood that all of Teplik rocked at the news. Imagine it! Two weeks behind bars for Teplik's Sholom-Ber! And the whole town came to see him being led off to jail. They say that not even a babe was left in its cradle. Everybody who could see was there to watch him. And as they led him through the marketplace to the town jail, Sholom-Ber Tepliker of Teplik lowered his eyes for the first time in his life. And his wife, Stissi-Pearl, for very shame, hid herself in her house. And everybody else in town stood along the road watching the spectacle and saying nothing, although deep in their hearts many of them were glad.

In the first place, he had it coming. Just because he was rich was no reason for a man to be so insolent. And in the second place he was disliked by everyone because in spite of his haughty manner he was a low and petty creature and his wife, Stissi-Pearl, begrudged a person a dry crust of bread, though, as everybody in Teplik knew well enough, their very gizzards were stuffed with gold and they had no one to spend it on—not even a child.

"If I had their money," every Tepliker was in the habit of saying, "if I only had half as much, or a third as much, the town would get more pleasure out of it than it does now . . ." And that might very well have been so, but since in all of Teplik there was no one else who had any money at all, there was no one who got any pleasure out of it—neither the town itself, nor Sholom-Ber, nor his wife Stissi-Pearl. Though it may be that the latter two did get some joy out of it. It all depends what you call joy. If you measured it by the position one held in the community, then Sholom-Ber had it. Wherever he was, whether in the synagogue or at a public gathering or a celebration, he had the place of honor. It was always the others who came up to him to wish him a good Sabbath, a good morning, or greet him at the holidays. When Sholom-Ber spoke, the others listened in silence, and whatever he said was a thing of wisdom. And more than that—every year, at *Simchas-Torah,* it was at his home that the whole town gathered. Sholom-Ber sat like a king and asked everyone who came to take some brandy, and Stissi-Pearl his wife watched every glass. There were other occasions also during the year, which, if you were a Tepliker, would have some meaning, but if you were not, would have none at all. And besides all this, there was the simple fact that Sholom-Ber was convinced that he was the only one who was anything at all. Only he, and no one else.

In Teplik there was only one Sholom-Ber Tepliker. In Teplik there was only one like that. There was no other . . .

III. A CHEERFUL PAUPER

In Teplik, if there had been no meddlers and informers, that is, if there had been no people who paid attention to what everybody else was doing, ninety-nine out of every hundred transgressions would have gone unpunished, and Teplik would have had as many sinners as Sodom itself. But since the people of Teplik have a way of keeping very well informed of the activities of their neighbors, every time they see anything that looks wrong, or hear anything, or smell anything, or even imagine anything that might not be just right, they make a note of it and see to it that the information reaches the proper authorities in the proper manner. And Plisetsky could boast that he did not ever have to hire any spies. The householders of Teplik were competent enough spies themselves.

After an introduction like this, you will not be surprised to hear that one bright morning the police surrounded the hut of Berel the Redhead with the crooked leg, just as he was sitting on the ground, the skirts of his gabardine rolled up around his waist, pouring from a large jug into small bottles the raisin wine that he sold to his neighbors for sacramental purposes. With great absorption he pressed each cork in and pounded it down. Plisetsky opened the door quietly, observed the red-haired Berel at his work, remaining standing a few minutes on the threshold, and beckoned to his assistants. When Berel raised his eyes and saw Haman Ivanovitch standing over him, he got up from the ground, came up to the Inspector with his strange limp, and looked him right in the eye as though to say, "Are you going to punish me for this? Go ahead, punish me! What can you take away from me? The hole in my pocket?"

How did it happen that Berel was so bold? Because he had nothing to be afraid of. True, he had made wine out of raisins, poured it into small bottles and sold it to his acquaintances for the Sabbath, and in that way earned his livelihood. But what a wine it was, and what a livelihood! The wine was no wine; the livelihood no livelihood. And yet both served their purpose. Every Friday night a benediction had to be made over wine, so this was wine. And it kept him occupied, gave him something to live on—not much, but enough, as he said, for a thin gruel to dip his hard crust into. And that was better than nothing. Think of how many people there are in Teplik who have no work at all and earn nothing at all and have nothing at all! Really nothing! Absolutely nothing at all!

And it was these very men, who did nothing and earned nothing and had nothing, who were most envious of Berel the Redhead, who had the reputation among them of living like a mogul. Was there not a rumor current that he had fish and meat every Sabbath, and certainly white bread? And did he not send his children to *cheder*? And didn't he clothe them, and have a goat of his own? And all from these raisins that he shook up and made into wine! So they sat down and wrote a letter to Plisetsky with all the necessary information. And this is how it read:

"Whereas we have always been concerned with the public welfare, and whereas the public welfare is threatened by all illegal transactions, and whereas Berel the Redhead, hereafter referred to by his legal name of Berko Krivak, has for so many years dealt in wine without a permit, and whereas the aforementioned Berko Krivak manufactures this wine with his own hands, also without a permit, therefore . . ." And so on and so on and so on . . .

The pride of a pauper is nothing to sneer at. The poorer a man is, the prouder he is—prouder than some of the richest people in the world. I once knew a pauper who met another on the street.

"How can you compare yourself to me, you idiot!" said the first. "You still have a pair of boots and a torn old overcoat, and I don't have these things even in my dreams!"

This was said in such a tone of boastfulness that if Roth-schild himself had been standing there, he would have lost confidence in himself.

In the meantime, returning to our story, Haman Ivano-vitch stood contemplating Berel's apartments, which consisted of three rooms, or to be more accurate, of two small alcoves and a kitchen, and each of these rooms was filled with beds and the beds were full of children. The children were half-dressed and half-naked, that is, they were dressed from the neck to the navel, and from there down they were naked. To this half-naked audience the Inspector was a rare sight, the like of which they had never seen. Without hesitation the children jumped out of bed, quietly stole up to the dazzling figure and stared up at him, examined his gold buttons and felt the scabbard at his side. And while they drank in all the de-tails of his attire, this conversation took place above their heads:

Plisetsky: According to what they wrote about you, you must be making a lot of money.

Berel: It could have been a little worse. It could have been a lot better.

Plisetsky: Then why are your children naked and bare-foot?

Berel: They grow better that way.

Plisetsky: And what do you do with your money?

Berel: I do as the *Talmud* advises us.

Plisetsky: The *Talmud*? And what does that say?

Berel: It tells us to divide our money three ways. One third is to be put away; one third is to be kept in cash, and the rest in merchandise.

Plisetsky: I see you're in good spirits.

Berel: What do I have to worry about? What do I need and what do I have? But tell me, my Lord and Master, what is it that my good neighbors said about me, and what is it that I can expect as a result of this visit of yours?

Plisetsky: If you want to know so much you'll be old and gray in a hurry. But first show me all your chests and drawers. I have to search your home. Maybe in addition to the wine I'll find other good things too.

Berel: With the greatest pleasure. Only this: if you discover any gold or silver or government bonds, let's divide it, half for me and half for you.

Plisetsky: You're a little too cheerful—like some people before their death.

Berel: It may be so. No one knows what tomorrow will bring. As the *Talmud* says, "Repent for your sins a day before you die." And as we never know when the Angel of Death might grab us by the neck, so . . .

At this point Plisetsky interrupted him, called in the police and told them to take him to jail. When he heard the word "jail," Berel felt a chill pass through him, and a wailing arose among the children as if a corpse were being carried out.

Naturally in Teplik it did not take long for the news to get around, and from all sides people came crowding to see another Jew being led off to prison—no one knew why. That is, why he was being led was no secret. How could a thing like that be kept a secret in Teplik? Especially when they saw Haman Ivanovitch carrying a small bottle of wine, the kind they

knew Berel made without a license. The only thing they did
not know was what would come of it. A fine—or prison?
They tried to figure out which. And yet they had much more
sympathy for this pauper than for Sholom-Ber the *nogid*.
But they could do nothing to help him, except sigh as he walked
past.

IV. ANOTHER TRANSGRESSOR

That same day Haman Ivanovitch went after the Jews of
Teplik in one more way. He arrested another Jew, one who,
quite obviously, had not committed any crime. This is how
it happened:

There was a young man in town, a boy you might call him,
named Hennich. This Hennich had an older brother, David-
Leib, who was to be called up for military service that year,
and David-Leib claimed exemption because Hennich was
not yet eighteen years old and thus was technically dependent
on him. That was as the law provided. The papers were all
made out and filed with the authorities in Heissin. But filing
papers was not enough. They also had to produce the brother
in person so that the authorities could see for themselves how
old he was. The order came to Plisetsky, and when Plisetsky
was ordered to produce, he produced. He sent the constable
and had Hennich brought to him at the station.

Hennich, you could see at a glance, was not a very gifted
youth. His complexion was pasty, almost lifeless; he had a
cataract in one eye, and his head shook with some nervous dis-
order. In addition to this, his fright at being picked up by the
constable was such that it gave a touch of madness to his appearance, and the impression he made on the Inspector was not
a very good one.

"Are you Hennich Tellerlecker?" Plisetsky asked, grabbing hold of him and looking him over from head to foot.

"I am Hennich Tellerlecker," answered the boy, and then realizing that he was there on account of his brother, he blurted out, "And I'm not eighteen yet! I swear I'm not!"

"So I see," said Plisetsky. "Only seventeen and a half—not counting Sundays and Holidays." And he looked at Hennich so fiercely that the poor lad went hot and cold all over, his heart sank, and he said to himself, "It's all up. David-Leib is gone from us . . ." But he still wanted to do something for his brother, and suddenly he became bold and cried out, "I swear that I am not more than seventeen and a month. Not a day more. If I am lying I hope I may never come home again. Maybe I look older, but I am not! We are all like that in our family. By fifteen our beards start growing . . ."

Plisetsky looked at him, shook his head and smiled, as though to say, "That's all you need besides the cataract and that complexion of yours—a handsome beard." And then he told his deputy to put him away until he could examine the papers more carefully. And Hennich was put away.

So a third citizen of Teplik took up his residence that day in the town jail.

He was greeted at once by Berel. "Look who's here! And what was it you did now, my little bird, and who was it that told them you had done it?"

Sholom-Ber was more reserved. From his corner he looked the lad over coldly, as if he were a thief who had just been caught stealing. And Hennich looked back like a half-wit, with his mouth open, at the sight of the town's *nogid* in the same cell with him, and he began to babble, without knowing what he was saying.

"I don't know what I did. I don't know anything. It's

on account of David-Leib. If I'm more than eighteen . . ."

Berel interrupted him. "What are you flapping your mouth for? Say something! Make sense!"

"I am telling you about my brother . . ." And suddenly he turned upon Berel with these words: "Tell me! How do I look to you?"

"How do you look? You look like a wild man!" Berel answered with a laugh and looked at Sholom-Ber to see if he was laughing too. But the *nogid* was not laughing at all. He was looking at the wretched Hennich shaking in his rags and tatters, wondering why things like that had to go on living in this world.

"No," said Hennich, looking at the rich man with his good eye and at Berel with the other. "That isn't what I meant. What I mean is, how old do I look?"

"Oh, how old? Well, I'd say about twenty-two or so—or a trifle more . . ."

In his great sorrow and anger Hennich let out a shriek and turned on Berel:

"Are you crazy? What are you talking about? David-Leib was just twenty and he is almost three years older than me. So what are you talking about?"

And he looked so mournful and woebegone that Sholom-Ber himself became interested and asked him:

"There are two of you then—two brothers—is that it?"

"Two brothers and our old mother. And a sister of thirteen who is out doing housework. And a younger brother apprenticed to a shopkeeper. And two smaller girls and a little boy in *Talmud Torah*. And all of us depend on him, on David-Leib—all of us. If they send him away we'll have to get sacks and go begging. House to house. What else can we do?"

And he told the whole story as well as he could—not too clearly, not too consecutively, but always insisting that he was not yet eighteen in spite of the beard and in spite of what everybody said. And he turned aside with a cough, wiping his nose and his eyes.

"It's a pity, the poor fellow," said the *nogid* in spite of himself.

"A *shlimazl,*" added Berel with a half-smile. "And his brother, in some ways, is not much better. He'd make as good a soldier as I would." And he stuck out his lame leg and looked at it from all sides.

V. THE CONVOY STARTS

Until the day that we now come to, and until the last minute, Sholom-Ber Tepliker of Teplik did not believe that he would be compelled to go with the convoy to Heissin. All the time that he waited he busied himself, writing letters to the proper people, using what influence he had to free himself. But Plisetsky was busy too and his influence was greater, and he saw to it that our fine citizen of Teplik took that trip to Heissin with the convoy—and on foot!

"I'll see to it that you go," Haman Ivanovitch said to him in half-Russian, half-Yiddish, "with your own feet." And to make it worse, the day was bright and hot, a midsummer day. No one could escape the heat, it was like a furnace, a lime-kiln. Shopkeepers closed their shops, workers left their tools, teachers their schools, and they all went to see the *nogid* being led away. And the people of Teplik, seeing him standing with lowered head, said to each other, "Let that be a lesson to us." But in their hearts they rejoiced. They were having their revenge. Pity they had only for Berel the Redhead and for Hennich.

For Sholom-Ber's journey his wife had sent a large basket with fresh white loaves, roast duck and other good things

Berel's wife and all their children came to bid Berel farewell, bringing a small loaf of bread, boiled fish and potatoes and a bunch of fresh garlic. Only Hennich had no food at all to take along, but some strangers in the crowd collected enough to buy him a dark loaf, a couple of small salted fish, and onions. And all these delicacies were handed over to the guard, who took them willingly, promising that every bit of it would be safe in his hands. And then Haman Ivanovitch appeared on his porch and told the guard to start moving. The guard moved, and the prisoners with him, and after them all of Teplik.

The convoy consisted of one Lavre, the guard, a hairy crea-ture with a fur jacket that he wore winter and summer, a tall fur hat, and a long knotty staff with a large wooden knob at one end and a sharp iron point at the other. The roast duck and the salt fish under one arm, the bread and garlic under the other, his report for the district officials stuck in his bosom, he started off quickly with his wards, much more quickly than you would have imagined. That was because our prisoners wanted to get rid of their followers, and when the older people had dropped away, they begged the guard to chase the little children back. They had kept them company out beyond the town, beyond the mill, and showed no signs of weariness. Lavre raised his staff with the iron point and the youngsters disappeared like frightened birds, and the prisoners remained alone in the open fields. They did not have to hurry any more, they began to take shorter steps and slower ones, and one of them suggested to the guard that it might be well to sit down for a while on the fresh green grass and take a little rest.

The guard was not such an evil man, and it did not take long to convince him. In fact, it is hard to say who was more eager to stop. He too was willing to rest and to sample the baskets he had been carrying, and to see what those odors were

that had been tickling his nostrils all the way. He had already
broken off a few twists of one of the large white loaves and
found them to his liking. He had tasted one of the fishes too
and found that with garlic it was not at all bad. Walking behind the prisoners, he was able to taste this and that without
their knowledge, until Sholom-Ber happened to look around
and caught him pinching his large white loaf and nibbling at
what he had pinched off.

"Our protector," he said to the others guardedly, "has good
active jaws."

"Pray that he doesn't choke," said Berel, cheerfully. "Now
that you mention it, my own appetite is not so bad either.
What do you say, Hennich, are you beginning to feel a little
weak inside too?"

Hennich moistened his lips and said in his own strange
manner:

"Very hungry, no. But a little something to chew, maybe.
If I had something."

"I have everything," said Sholom-Ber with a quick glance
back at their guard.

"Everything?" wondered Berel. "Without a glass of brandy
you can never say everything." And to make sure that the
guard caught the full meaning, he said it over, in Russian:
"Isn't it true, Lavre, that a meal without brandy is like eating
without teeth?"

"True . . . very true . . ." the guard answered earnestly.

And they juggled their words so long, till they all understood and agreed that as it was not very far from where they
were to Granov, at most a couple of *versts,* one of the prisoners
—naturally Hennich, the youngest—should dash off for a
bottle of brandy; and the other two prisoners, Sholom-Ber
Tepliker of Teplik and Berel the Redhead, guaranteed that he
would not try to escape. And when they had sent him off, the

others sat down on the grass in the middle of the field, under a tree on a hillock, the prisoners talking with each other in low tones, and the guard sitting near them but looking with both eyes up the road to Granov.

VI. HE REMINDS HIM OF OLD WRONGS

If I were a painter or a photographer I would have taken a picture of this group, the three figures sitting there in the middle of the field on the hillock under a wild pear tree with small green leaves and those small, hard pears that no one can eat and that no one ever knows what to do with.

Between Lavre, the guard, with the tall fur cap, on one side, and Berel the Redhead with the crooked leg and the red, freckled face on the other, our Sholom-Ber Tepliker of Teplik, with the small eyes and the thin beard, with his black, satin gabardine and with his black, silk hat, looked like a man of state among two common fellows. A man like that usually knows how to conduct himself. He may act like anybody else, like a plain and modest man, and yet he is not just like anybody else. Other people talk about the things that *he* wants to talk about, and when *he* talks, others listen, and when others talk, he has the right to interrupt.

"What do you think of this heat?" he said to Berel with a sigh and a glance in all directions. And he rolled his sleeves up to the elbows and fanned himself with his silk hat.

"It's not at all cold," answered Berel, following the rich man's glance.

"I hope it doesn't rain," the other went on, with a look up at the sky.

Berel looked up too. "It would be a pity," he agreed, "with all of us dressed up like this."

"Not a bad fellow, this guard of ours," continued Sholom-

Ber, with his eyes on a long, empty wagon that a pair of large oxen were pulling up the road, with a little boy on the driver's seat dangling a whip above their ears.

"Our guard?" echoed Berel. "He's a gentleman compared with those good neighbors of mine who ran to the police with the news that a poor hardworking man was selling a few bottles of raisin wine. It wasn't even anything new. It's been going on for years . . ."

"What do you think," interrupted the *nogid* again, with his eyes on the road that led to Granov. "What do you think? He couldn't have lost his way, could he? I mean, made tracks? That boy—what's his name?"

"Him?" said Berel. "Why should he do a thing like that? What did he ever do that was wrong? He's no more a criminal than I am."

"Speaking of that," said Sholom-Ber, "what do you think they'll do to you?" He was sitting now with his eyes closed, meditatively chewing at a blade of grass.

"For what? For that raisin wine? They won't hang me, that much I know. But beyond that—" he shrugged his shoulders, "let them do what they want. What can they take away from me? The holes in my pockets? And if they want me to sit a while, I'll sit. But what I want to know is what will they do with *you*? You're somebody! You have money, position, property . . .

"I'll tell you the truth, Reb Sholom-Ber. Don't be offended. But if I were you I'd never have given them a chance to throw me into jail like this; for a little thing like that, a bit of rubbish, a pan of dirty water! In the first place, I would not have been so stubborn, especially with the police. In the second, if I were you, I wouldn't have let them march me off this way. Teplik itself should never have allowed it, letting its *nogid* be sent to jail by convoy, like a common nobody, a penniless lout."

At another time Berel would have paid dearly for talking like this to Sholom-Ber. He would certainly have been sent flying head first. But now on his way by convoy to Heissin, Sholom-Ber was not a privileged character. Now a person could say anything he wanted to him. And Berel the Redhead got even with him as well as he could, smoothly, without ever losing his temper. He edged up close to Sholom-Ber with his crooked leg, so close that the rich man had to move away a little, and he spoke to him like this:

"Do you know, Reb Sholom-Ber, how long we have known each other? It's been a long, long time. I remember when you were a brat no taller than that" (Berel held his hand down close to the ground). "You must be about my age, at the most a year older, or two, and you ought to remember me from those days because my grandfather and your father were—don't be afraid, I was not going to say relatives, although they were that too, forty-second cousins once removed on my mother's side. What I was going to say was that we sat close to each other in the synagogue, your father along the east wall and my grandfather in the opposite row so that when we all stood facing east I had your back right in my face. I still remember your father's shiny silk coat and his broad shoulders and the silver stripes on his *tallis;* and my grandfather, Reb Naftali the vintner—you must remember him—used to pull his own yellow *tallis* over his head and pinch me every time I looked up from my prayerbook. Because apparently I was just as anxious to be praying as you were . . . When we were supposed to be standing motionless you were always looking down at your new boots that squeaked. And how I used to envy you, always with new boots while mine were always old, always patched. I could never get good boots on account of my foot. And that was not the only trouble I had on account of that foot. It was hard for me to walk, but that too was nothing.

What was worse was being called Limpy and being mimicked. And worst of all was the way you did it, Reb Sholom-Ber—don't be offended! You and others like you, from the richer families, spoiled little brats . . ."

"I?" cried the *nogid* with a start, and then he remembered that it was true, they used to mimic Berel, make fun of the way he jumped on one foot.

"And making fun of me would not have been so bad either, but what was even worse than that was that you never let me play with the rest of you. You chased me away with sticks and stepped with your heels on my ailing foot, right on my toes, and pretended it had been an accident. Stepped on them to make me scream, so I screamed, and you laughed and held your sides . . ."

"Now, *that* you simply made up!" the *nogid* called out, his face red with shame, and he remembered how spoiled he had been as a child. He had been able to do anything that he wanted to.

"No, I'm not making it up. It was true and I'll prove it to you. I told my grandfather and he went and told your father, and your father would not believe it. He scolded my grandfather, swore that his child was a well-behaved boy who wouldn't have a thing to do with paupers' children. How do you like that? Paupers' children! From that time on I knew what I was—a pauper's child. But I did not know what it meant and I asked my grandfather, and he told me. He taught me what it meant to be a poor man's child, and what it was to be a rich man's. But I still could not understand why a rich man's child could step on the toes of a poor man's child, and the poor man's child could do nothing about it. So I asked my grandfather that too, and he explained it to me this way: that a rich man is not a poor man and a poor man is not a rich man. In short, the rich were rich and the poor were poor. And still that did not make sense, so I looked into his eyes, maybe there I could find an explanation that his words could not give me. But all I saw was something like a dark cloud pass over his face, and the wrinkles on his forehead. And that was all . . . And I must admit there is nothing I can do about it. Ever since that time I have had nothing but scorn for the rich and the children of the rich, and most of all I have scorned and hated you . . ."

"Me?"

"You. Yes, you! You were just a child then, no larger than a grasshopper. We were both children. But even later, when we were older, when we were *Bar-Mitzvah,* young men already, you always turned away from me, as if you didn't know me. You were afraid that I might greet you, and you might have to answer me. You begrudged me even that, apparently. It was not worth your time . . ."

The *nogid* of Teplik, Sholom-Ber Tepliker, squirmed and made a weak gesture with his hands. "That couldn't have been," he said without conviction, and at the same time he admitted to himself that it was possible. He remembered that his father was always reminding him that he was not like other children, that the others were not his equal.

"Don't be offended, Reb Sholom-Ber. Foolish little things are never forgotten. When I was married the first time (you were married a short time earlier) I sent you an invitation, but you did not even acknowledge it."

"I swear I don't remember that."

"How should you remember? I bet you don't remember this either, that when my wife died, I sent my Uncle Yossi (my grandfather was dead already by that time) to tell you that I was alone with two small children, forlorn and helpless. Your answer was that you were a man who did not meddle in public affairs."

"Did *I* say that? Oh, no! Your uncle must have told you a lie."

"That may be so. Maybe *you're* right. All I know is that you did nothing to help me that time, or later either, when my house burned down and I was left as naked as when I was born. Or later yet, that time we met at Heissin at the inn, if you remember, during the Fair. You had come, if I remember correctly, to buy some horses or a cow, or maybe to sell some grain."

The rich man rubbed his forehead, like a man trying to remember something, something that eluded him. And he wondered why he should have forgotten and the other had not. And he did not like it that Berel the Redhead, who in Teplik would not have dared say two superfluous words to him, should point out all his shortcomings and remind him of all his past misdeeds. He did not like it at all, and he was on the point of saying so when Hennich arrived from Granov with the bottle of brandy, all out of breath from running, afraid that someone might catch him with the bottle and have him arrested . . .

And the three transgressors sat down to their feast, beginning with a drop of brandy. They offered the guard a glass too, and he did not refuse. But they could see that the drink did not appeal to him. He made a face, wiped his thick mustache with his sleeve, and cursed forsaken Granov and its fiery brandy.

"May seven devils take it! It's too bitter!" he swore, and he lifted up his hand as if he were taking an oath that as long as he lived he would never take another drop. And yet, when they had finished the fish and were about to attack the roast duck, they prevailed upon him to try another sip. It was hard work, but they succeeded, and he agreed to try it again, and when they urged him to finish the glass because they wanted him to take another, he agreed to that too.

When they had finished eating, the four of them lay down

under the pear tree for a little while, not to take a nap—that they did not even have in mind—but simply to look up at the deep blue heavens and watch the tiny white clouds that passed by overhead and disintegrated and then disappeared like smoke, and the ravens that swept and turned and at the same time appeared motionless.

Lying on the ground after eating, and looking up at the sky, is an excellent way of overcoming sleeplessness. The first to prove this was the guard himself, who almost at once let out a snore like a frightened horse. And shortly afterward was heard the only slightly more modest accompaniment that issued from the capable though less consistent nostrils of the boy Hennich. He did well while he tried, but he awoke too often, sat up too frequently to babble something that was on his mind:

"So tired . . . ran four versts . . . afraid, afraid he'd catch me . . . the Inspector . . ."

The only ones who did not sleep were the rich man, Sholom-Ber Tepliker of Teplik, and Berel the winemaker. Sholom-Ber was worrying. He wanted to know what it was that had happened that time in Heissin at the Fair, what it was he had refused to do. And Berel did him a favor and told him the whole story in these words.

VII. A TRIVIAL INCIDENT IS NOT FORGOTTEN

"Don't be offended," Berel began. "A trivial incident is never forgotten. I came to Heissin not for the Fair. My oxen were still in pasture and my ships were still at sea. Then why did I have to come to Heissin at that very time? I came to look over a boy whom the *shadchan* had found for my older daughter, by my first wife. I had finally decided to marry her off. She was still young, poor child, but her stepmother kept nagging me. She wanted her out of the house. And what could

I do? I asked what good it would do her. Who would help her cook and bake and scrub the smaller children's heads, and whom would she be able to curse and pull around by the hair? But try to convince a woman! So we decided to marry her off.

"That's easy to say. But how? What with? With your five fingers? There isn't much that people in our class can do, but clothes at least we have to get. Do I mean fine clothes? No. But even a cotton dress and some shoes and stockings cost money. And you have to get a few nightgowns, a couple of pillows, a bedspread, maybe a blanket. That's not counting the dowry, and how can a person give less than a hundred *rubles*? And here I was, with less than a hundred *kopeks*.

"And as if to tease me, Moishe-Aaron, the matchmaker, keeps swamping me with letters, one letter after another, saying that he had found a young man in Heissin, just the right boy for my daughter, one boy in a hundred, one in a million. I'd never find another one like him. And whose boy is it? Yankel the carpenter's, a poor man's child, but a very gifted one, advanced in his studies, a good penman—everything! And he played the fiddle like the devil himself!

"So I wrote to Moishe-Aaron and told him that first of all I was in no hurry to consider a match, and in the second place I had to know how much dowry he expected, because maybe it was not for my purse at all. And in the third place, why didn't Yankel come here first, at least to take a look at the girl. So he answers me at once—Moishe-Aaron, that is—and tells me that my first point, that I was not interested in a match, was nonsense, because he knew and everybody else knew that a daughter is not a son, and it's never too soon to marry her off. And as for what I had said about a dowry, that was foolish of me. Were we talking about an ox or a cow that we should start bargaining? These were his very words. And as for coming to look at my daughter, that was not necessary, either.

Yankel knew all about her already. A neighbor of his from Heissin had been in my house and had seen the girl and he could not begin to praise her highly enough.

"At any rate—a letter here, a letter there—I took my feet in my hands, as the saying is, and went off to Heissin. And when I saw the boy I felt as if I had never seen anyone like him in my life before. His face was like that of a prince, his brain a prime minister's. When he spoke, every word was a jewel. And when he played the fiddle you could forget every musician who ever lived! I was in love with him myself and I swore that no matter what happened I would have him for my daughter. But go do something when your pocket's empty! If I only had a hundred *rubles*! Or even part of it to give as a deposit! The boy himself did not care about a dowry. Give it to him or don't give it to him, it was all the same. But the carpenter, the devil take him, was stubborn and you couldn't budge him. If a grand duchess herself wanted to marry his son she'd have to pay a dowry before she could lead him to the canopy.

"I turned to the *shadchan*. 'Reb Moishe-Aaron,' I said, 'do something. Say something.' 'What can I say?' he asked. 'Do something quick. It looks bad. You'll never get anywhere with this stubborn ox. Only yesterday I almost hit him over the head with his plane.' Did you ever hear anything like that? Yet there was the boy before my eyes. I couldn't drive him out. I simply had to have him for my daughter. I'd die if I didn't have him!

"In the meantime, I looked around at the inn, and whom did I see? Reb Sholom-Ber Tepliker! God alone, I told myself, could have brought him there. And I wasn't shy. I went right up and greeted you, like an old friend. I was so happy to see you! Why? Because, I thought to myself, you would surely ask me what I was doing here in Heissin, and I would tell you that I was here for a match. And you would say, 'With whom?' And I would say, 'With Yankel the carpenter.' And you would say, 'How much dowry are you giving?' And I would say, 'Ah, that's the whole problem! The carpenter says that I'll have to lay down a hundred, and all I have is a fig.' And then you would say . . .

"But what happened really? You didn't ask me a thing. So without your asking, I told you that I had come not for the Fair, but to arrange a match for my daughter. Why did I do that? Because I thought that then you would have to ask with whom, and then I could say, 'With Yankel the carpenter.' And then you would say, 'What dowry are you giving?' And I'd say . . . But you know already what I was going to say, and yet what happened? Not the trace of a question!

"So I decided to tell you without being asked. I told you whom the match was with, and I praised the boy to the skies, as I could do in all truthfulness. Well . . . I did all the talking. You didn't say a word. My story made no impression, as if it went through one ear and out through the other. So I said to myself, why should I be a diplomat? The time had come to say it directly—tear the tooth out by the root! And what did you do then? You refused me outright. And scolded me besides."

"I scolded you? What did I say?"

"Do you want me to tell you? Ah, trivial things are never forgotten. And so I remember. You asked me what right did I have to bother you, what right did I have to expect you to go throwing out a hundred *rubles* at a time . . ."

"But did you tell me what you needed the money for?"

"Did I tell you? Don't you remember? And this was your answer: 'What makes you so anxious to marry off your daughter to a millionaire?' And when I told you how well the boy played the fiddle, you said to me, 'It's lucky he plays the fiddle. What if it was the trumpet?' Here I was, suffering anguish, desperate for help, and you made fun of me, practiced your jokes on me . . . Apparently you were feeling good that day."

Reb Sholom-Ber Tepliker of Teplik listened to the whole story, sweated, said nothing. What had really happened that day he did not remember, but there had been something to do with a hundred *rubles*. That much he remembered. And he was ashamed of himself, ashamed to think that he had once refused a small thing like that which would have meant so much to this man and his family. The story itself now interested him too, and he asked: "Well, how did the match turn out?"

"There wasn't any."

"What do you mean—there wasn't any?"

"The carpenter wouldn't have anything more to do with me. The devil take him!"

"And your daughter? The girl?"

"My daughter? I buried her long ago. I killed her and buried her myself. You don't believe me? Well, what could I do? Could I make a dowry with my own hands? . . . A year went by, two years went by. There is no such thing, you know, as a Jewish convent. And the stepmother continued to nag. So I married the child off to a bookbinder as penniless as myself. A good man, an honest one, but sickly, tubercular. He struggled along a few years and then he died, leaving me this inheritance —three little children. Yes, I was the one to inherit them, because my daughter had caught his disease and she died too, a year later. Do you see? So now I have not only children from my own two marriages, but three little orphans besides. But such children! You won't find their equal in the richest families. 'Grandpa, where are you going?' they asked when Haman had me taken away. 'To Heissin,' I told them. 'When I come back I'll bring you all some chocolate.' And do you think they didn't know that I was telling them a lie? You should have seen them stand around me, like little lambs, without a sound, but with tears in their eyes. You can imagine what they looked like—if I tell you that Haman Ivanovitch himself reached into his pocket and gave them a *gulden* to buy sweets with."

VIII. WHICH PERTAINS TO HENNICH AND HIS FAMILY

Berel the Redhead had nothing more to say. After a pause he stood up, straightened his ailing leg, and limping over to Hennich snapped his finger across the lad's nose.

"Look here!" he said. "Haven't you slept long enough already?"

Hennich awoke with a start, wiped his eyes, and seeing the *nogid* looking at him, picked himself up quickly and began to babble:

"I didn't begin to sleep! I was thinking about poor David-Leib. They say more than eighteen. And what will happen to the poor children?"

"Listen to him talk!" said Berel to Sholom-Ber. "A real *schlimazl!* I was telling you just now about my bad luck, but compared to him I'm a rich man, a millionaire! And a man of influence, too . . . I'm the man who got David-Leib the job that he supports the family with. Eight mouths!"

"Nine you can say," Hennich corrected him. "Two brothers and an old mother. A sister of thirteen who does house work. And a younger brother in a shop. And two smaller girls. And a boy in *cheder,* a younger one. And where am I?"

"You? You are as good as buried!" Berel told him. "What are you now, and what will you ever be?" And turning to Sholom-Ber he said, "Now his brother David-Leib compared to him is a prime minister. A genius he's not; but he's not a fool, either. He's honest. The whole family is honest; they wouldn't steal a *beigel* from anyone. But David-Leib is both honest *and* capable.

"Well, one day he came to me with this story. In Heissin a sugar refinery had just been built that was owned by Reb Zalmen Rademishler, and Reb Zalmen Rademishler belonged to the Sadagora *chassidim*. Now I belong to the Sadagora *chassidim* too, and David-Leib's father—may he rest in peace—was also one of them. So he wanted me to go to see Reb Zalmen and ask him if he would find work somewhere in his refinery for him. 'What kind of work would you want?' I asked, and he told me, 'Anything at all, so long as it's work.' 'Idiot,' I said, 'tell me what you can do.' And he said, 'I can do anything. I know arithmetic and bookkeeping. I can write and I can copy.' 'Where did you learn all that?' I asked him. 'By myself,' he said, and took a piece of paper out of his pocket for me to show Reb Zalmen what his handwriting was like.

"Well, he bothered me so much that in order to get rid of him I put on my shoes and again went to Heissin, on foot. And when I came to Reb Zalmen's refinery they wouldn't let me in. What's the matter? And they tell me this. If I came just to visit Reb Zalmen, he did not have time to see me. And if I had some business to do, I should go into the office. I said to myself, 'Bah! I don't like this at all!' What kind of talk was this—no time—business—office? We Sadagora *chassidim* don't believe in such tricks. 'Go,' I said, 'tell Reb Zalmen that I, Berel the Redhead from Teplik, am here to see him about something important, and *not* on business, and I *can't* wait, because I have no time either!' So they tell me that Reb Zalmen is at his prayers, he just started a little while ago. 'If so,' I said, 'that's different.' But at the same time, was that an excuse? Couldn't he see me anyway? But the answer to that is that he was a rich man and people had to show respect for him. If I were rich, the whole world would respect me too.

"So I sat down and waited. I waited an hour and two and three, right by the door. All around me was rush and bustle. People came and went, this one in, that one out. It was getting late. Someone came past me with a tray and a *samovar* and food that I'd never even seen before. So I said to myself, 'This I don't like either!' And I decided: why be formal? So I opened the door and in I went. 'How do you do, Reb Zal-men,' I said. 'How do you do,' said he, 'and where are you from?' 'From Teplik,' I answer him. 'Didn't you recognize me? I'm Berel. I was in Sadagora together with you once, to see our Rabbi.' 'Maybe so,' he said, 'but I didn't remember you and I still don't know you. My eyesight is not so good any more, not good at all. I went to all the doctors around here and then I went to Mendelstam, and he gave me black glasses to wear and told me not to read or write and keep away from sunlight.' 'Oh-ho,' I said to myself, 'you're telling me a story I heard from my grandmother!' And then to him, 'Listen to me, Reb Zalmen. This is what I came for. You remember Benny from Teplik, don't you?' And he said, 'Which Benny?' 'Benny Tellerlecker,' I tell him. 'No,' he says, 'this is the first time I've heard the name—Tellerlecker.' 'That,' I said, 'won't help you. You knew him well enough. We all drank wine together in Sadagora and danced together on the Rabbi's table, and more than once embraced each other, you and he and I, and now he's in Eternity—may he intercede for us there.'

"When he heard his, Reb Zalmen became another man altogether. These rich men must be very much afraid of death. 'What do you want?' he asks, 'what do you want of me?' 'What should I want?' I say, 'I want to fulfill my promise to the dead. A few hours before he died, this same Benny Tellerlecker called me and a few other friends together and told us that he had gone to see you a couple of times here in Heissin, wanted to talk with you about something, but had not been allowed to come in. He was a quiet little man, you remember, and he never liked intrigue or politics; so when he saw that he was not wanted he turned around and went back home again. But now, that he was about to begin another journey, and a longer one, from which no one ever returns, he wanted to bid farewell to each of us separately, and through each of us he sent his regards first to the Rabbi of our order, and then to you. And he asked me to give this message to you: he leaves everything he has to you—that is, he leaves his whole family to you, and he knows that you will never abandon them.'

" 'What can I do for them?' said he, reaching into his pocket. 'Ah-ha,' thought I, 'a donation. Never!' And I said, 'What I want you to do is to take his eldest son, David-Leib, and give him work, a job.' When a rich man hears the word *job* he has a stroke. 'Where can I get him a job? Where can I find work for him? Every job is taken.' 'That story,' I said, 'you can tell someone else, not me! I don't want to hear any excuses from you. You have to find a job for Benny's son. He knows arithmetic and bookkeeping, he can copy and write. So please be so kind now and call for a glass of brandy and a bite to eat, because I'm starved. I've had nothing in my mouth all day.'

"Well, why should I drag out the story? We Sadagora *chassidim* are simple people. Reb Zalmen promised me that he would take the boy, so when I came home I sent David-Leib back to Heissin. For a while he lay around, waiting. Reb Zalmen told him that he would have to talk it over with his son first, his son Reb Yossil, and Reb Yossil was not in town. Later, when Reb Yossil returned, Reb Zalmen was out of town. But at last they had to take him in, and today he is their chief executioner."

"Cashier," corrected Hennich, and explained to them what a cashier was. "He has to do with money. He takes it and he gives it out."

"Thanks for making it clear," said Berel. "Otherwise we would never have known."

And he went over to the guard, pulled him by the sleeve, and woke him up.

"Hey, Lavre, what's the matter with you? It's time to sober up."

And Lavre obeyed him. Slowly he got up from the ground, slowly he looked up at the sky to see where the sun was, then he picked up his staff, lined up and counted his three wards, and together they continued their journey.

IX. THE *NOGID* REPENTS

The sun was close to setting, the heat had begun to abate, and the convoy was near the outskirts of Granov, the first scheduled stop on their journey, when the three prisoners stopped near a windmill, turned their faces toward the east, and began their evening prayers. Lavre stood a little to one side leaning against his staff, his cap pushed back, and looked with curiosity at the Jews nodding and swaying and once or twice beating their breasts.

Of the three, it was Reb Sholom-Ber Tepliker of Teplik who prayed with the greatest feeling. That evening he was not satisfied with merely touching his breast twice, he really beat it. "Forgive us, Our Father, for we have sinned; pardon us, Our King, for we have transgressed." With all his heart he regretted his past behavior, the things he had done and the things he had neglected to do. And he compared himself to this tattered creature, Berel the Redhead, and he was ashamed of himself. Berel, who had hardly enough to keep himself alive, had not hesitated to go a long distance on foot in someone else's behalf, to force his way into a rich man's presence, humble himself in order to do someone else a favor. And he, Sholom-Ber Tepliker of Teplik, had been unwilling even to hear about someone else's troubles; he had been cold, cold as ice. And he was sorry that he had acted that way, and most of all he was sorry for the way he had treated Berel in connection with the match he had tried to arrange for his young daughter, in Heissin, at the time of the Fair.

He felt now that he owed something to Berel the Redhead for the share he might have had in the killing of his daughter. For if he had listened to Berel's request, if he had shown a trace of pity, a trace of love for a poor man, his daughter might still be alive and happy. And Sholom-Ber felt that if he could still right at least a small part of the wrong, he would feel much better. But he did not know how to do it. And as he went on with his prayers his whole life passed in review before his eyes, almost for the first time. And he could not understand how he had ever been so satisfied with himself, and had thought that he had done his duty if only he said his prayers every day and dropped an occasional three-*kopek* piece in the charity box.

The Tepliker *nogid*, Sholom-Ber Tepliker of Teplik, remembered how he had bargained for every *groschen* that had to be torn from him by force. He had given the Holy Scrolls to the synagogue for his own glory, but he had refused a small loan to the scribe who had made the scrolls. And he burned with shame. He felt that until that day his soul had been asleep, that his heart had lain under a weight somewhere, with ice around it. And he wanted to do something for Berel, and he did not know how.

He had lived fifty-six years, more than three-quarters of the seventy he hoped to live, and all his life had been one long war to add one *groschen* to another. To whom would he leave it all? He had no children, and his kinsmen all hated him. And he remembered things he had long forgotten, and a cold chill gripped his heart. He promised that from now on, at least, in his old age, he would be more considerate of his fellow men.

Having finished their prayers, our convoy resumed its journey. Berel limped along, joking with Hennich, and the *nogid* walked alone, deep in thought. He walked faster and faster, without looking to left or right, without knowing that he was getting ahead of the others.

"What's your hurry, Reb Sholom-Ber?" the redhead called to him. "I can't keep up with you."

"Is it hard for you to walk, Reb Berel?" the *nogid* asked. "Here, give me your hand and we'll go together. And when we come home again, with the Lord's help, I want you to come to me, both of you. There is something I have to tell you."

Berel could not understand. What did he have to tell them? And why at his home? Why not now, where they were? And why had he suddenly become so humble?

Hennich did not even try to understand. All he said was, "If only the Lord has mercy. If only David-Leib is saved."

"Don't worry," said Sholom-Ber. "Even if he goes, I'll take care of all of you. I'll take care of everybody."

When the convoy entered Granov the sun had already set, all but a bright golden strip along the horizon. They were greeted with music, a chorus of the croaking of frogs mingled with the bleating of sheep and goats being led home for the night in a cloud of dust. And that was their good fortune.

In the cloud of dust the people did not see *who* was being led through their town! Otherwise the good people of Granov might have welcomed them with the same respect and escorted them beyond the town with the same parade with which they were greeted and escorted at Michaelovka and Mitchulka and Krasnopilka and Zdakovitz and all the other points along the way between Teplik and Heissin.

The Fiddle

TODAY I'll play you something on the fiddle.

I don't know how you feel, but as for me, there is nothing more wonderful than to be able to play a fiddle. As far back as I can remember my heart has gone out to the fiddle. In fact, I loved everything about music. Whenever there was a wedding in our town I was the first one on hand to greet the musicians. I would steal up behind the bass violin, pluck a string—boom!—and run off. Boom—and run off again. For doing this I once caught the devil from Berel Bass. Berel Bass, a fierce-looking man with a flat nose and a sharp eye, pretended not to see me as I stole up behind his bass violin. But just as I was stretching my hand out to pull at the string he caught me by the ear and led me to the door with a great show of courtesy.

"Don't forget to kiss the *mazuza* on your way out," he said.

But that experience taught me nothing. I couldn't stay away from musicians. I was in love with every one of them, from Shaike Fiddele, with his fine black beard and slim white fingers to round-shouldered Getzie Peikler with the big bald spot that reached down to his ears. Many a time when they chased me away, I hid myself under a bench and listened to them playing. From under the bench I watched Shaike's nimble fingers dancing over the strings and listened to the sweet tones that he so skillfully drew out of his little fiddle.

After that I would go around for days in a trance with Shaike and his fiddle constantly before my eyes and moving

301

through my dreams at night. Pretending that I was Shaike, I would crook my left arm, move my fingers, and draw the right arm across as though I held a bow. All this while I threw my head to one side and dreamily shut my eyes. Just like Shaike. Exactly like him.

When the rabbi caught me—this was in *cheder*—drumming my fingers in the air, throwing my head back and rolling my eyes, he gave me a loud smack. "You rascal, you are supposed to be learning something, and here you are—fooling around—catching flies!"

I vowed to myself, "Let the world come to an end, I must have a fiddle. No matter what it cost, I must have one." But how do you make a fiddle? Naturally, of cedarwood. It is easy to say—cedarwood. But where do you get this wood that is supposed to grow only in the Holy Land? So what does God do? He gives me this idea: we had an old sofa at our house, an inheritance from my grandfather, Reb Anshel, over which my two uncles and my father had quarreled for a long time. My uncle Ben argued that he was the oldest son, therefore the sofa was his. Uncle Sender argued that he was the youngest, therefore the sofa belonged to him. My father admitted that he, being only a son-in-law, had no claim to the sofa, but since his wife, my mother, was my grandfather's only daughter, the sofa rightfully belonged to her. All this time the sofa remained at our house. But my two aunts, Aunt Itke and Aunt Zlatke, entered the feud. They carried their bickerings back and forth between them. The sofa this, the sofa that. Your sofa, my sofa. The whole town rocked with it. Meanwhile, the sofa remained our sofa.

This sofa of which I speak had a wooden frame with a thin veneer which was loose and puffed out in several places. Now this veneer, which was loose in spots, was the real cedarwood that fiddles are made of. That was what I had heard in *cheder*. The sofa had one drawback which was really a virtue. When you sat down on it you couldn't get up, because it sloped—there was a bulge on one end and a depression in the middle. This meant that no one wanted to sit on it. So it was put away in a corner and was pensioned off.

But now I began to cast an eye at this sofa. I had already arranged for a bow a long time ago. I had a friend, Yudel the teamster's Shimeleh, and he promised me as many hairs as I would need from the tail of his father's horse. And a piece of resin, to rub the bow with, I had all my own. I hated to rely on miracles. I got it in a trade with another friend of mine— Maier, Lippe-Sarah's boy—for a small piece of steel from my mother's old crinoline that had been lying up in the attic. Later, out of this piece of steel, Maier made himself a knife sharpened at both ends, and I was even ready to trade back with him, but he wouldn't think of it. He shouted at me:

"You think you're smart! You and your father, too! Here I go and work for three nights, sharpening and sharpening, and cut all my fingers, and you come around and want it back again!"

Well, I had everything. There was only one thing to do—to pick off enough of the cedar veneer from the sofa. And for that I chose a very good time—when my mother was out shopping and my father lay down for his afternoon nap. I crept into the corner with a big nail and began clawing away with real energy. In his sleep my father heard someone burrowing, and apparently thought it was a mouse. He began to hiss: "Shhh, shhhhh." I didn't move, I didn't breathe.

My father turned over on his other side and when I heard that he was snoring again I went back to my work. Suddenly I looked up—there stood my father, watching me with a puzzled look. At first he didn't seem to know what was going on, but when he saw the gouged-out sofa he dragged me out by the ear and shook me till I rattled. I thought I was going to faint.

"God help you—what are you doing to the child?" my mother screamed from the threshold.

"Your pride and joy! He's driving me into my grave!" gasped my father, pale as the white-washed wall, as he clasped at his heart and went into a coughing spell.

"Why do you eat yourself up like that?" asked my mother. "You're sick enough without that. Just take a look at yourself, just look!"

The desire to play the fiddle grew as I grew. The older I grew, the more anxious I was to be able to play, and as if in spite I had to listen to music every day. Just about halfway between home and *cheder* there was a small sod-covered shack, and whenever you passed that shack you heard all sorts of sounds, the strains of all kinds of instruments, and especially the sound of a fiddle. It was the home of a musician, Naftaltzi Bezborodka, a Jew with a shortened coat, with clipped earlocks and with a starched collar. His nose was large and looked almost as if it were pasted on, his lips were thick, his teeth black, his face was pockmarked and without the trace of a beard. And that was why they called him Bezborodka, the beardless one. His wife was a crone who was known as Mother Eve, and they had at least a dozen and a half children—tattered, half-naked, barefoot, and every one of them, from the oldest to the youngest, played on some instrument—this one the fiddle, that one the cello, the other the bass, one the trumpet, another the flute, the bassoon, the harp, the cymbal, the balalaika, the drum. Some of them could whistle the most complicated melody with their lips, or through their teeth, on glass tumblers or pots, or on pieces of wood. They were magicians—or devils of some sort!

With this family I became acquainted in a most unexpected way. I was standing under their window one day, drinking in the music, when one of the boys caught sight of me and came out. He was Pinny, the flutist, a boy about fifteen, but barefoot like the rest.

"What do you think of the music?" he asked.

"I wish I could play that well in ten years," I told him.

"You can," he said, and explained that for two *rubles* a month his father would teach me to play. Or, if I wanted, he himself would teach me.

"What instrument would you like to play?" he asked. "The fiddle?"

"The fiddle," I said.

"The fiddle," he repeated. "Could you pay a *ruble* and a half a month—or are you as penniless as I am?"

"I can pay," I told him. "But there is one thing. Neither my father nor my mother nor my rabbi must know a thing about it."

"God forbid!" he exclaimed. "Why should anyone find out?" He moved up closer to me and whispered, "Have you got a cigar butt—or a cigarette?" I shook my head. "No? You don't smoke? Well, then, lend me a few *groschen* so I can buy some cigarettes. But don't tell anybody. My father doesn't know that I smoke, and if my mother found out she'd take the money away and buy some bread."

He took the money and said in a friendly voice, "Come on in. You'll get nothing done standing out here."

With great fear, my heart pounding and my legs trembling, I crossed the threshold of this small paradise.

My new friend Pinny introduced me to his father. "This is Sholom—Nochem-Vevik's. A rich man's son . . . He wants to learn to play the fiddle."

Naftaltzi Bezborodka pulled at his earlock, straightened his collar, and buttoned up his coat. Then he began a long and detailed lecture on the subject of music in general and fiddle-playing in particular. He gave me to understand that the fiddle was the best and finest of all instruments—there was no instrument that ranked higher. Else why is the fiddle the chief instrument in an orchestra, and not the trombone or the flute? Because the fiddle is the mother of all instruments . . .

Thus Naftaltzi spoke, accompanying his words with motions of his hands and large nose. I stood gaping at him, swallowing every word that came out.

"The fiddle," Naftaltzi continued, apparently pleased with his lecture, "the fiddle, you understand, is an instrument that is older than all other instruments. The first fiddler in the world was Tubal Cain or Methuselah, I am not sure which. You may know, you study such things in *cheder*. The second fiddler was King David. The third, a man named Paganini, also a Jew. The best fiddlers have always been Jews. I can name you a dozen. Not to mention myself . . . They say I don't play badly, but how can I compare myself to Paganini? Paganini, we are told, sold his soul to the devil for a fiddle. He never would play for the great of the world—the kings and the princes —no matter how much they gave him. He preferred to play for the common people in the taverns and the villages, or even in the woods for the beasts and birds. Ah, what a fiddler Paganini was!"

Suddenly he turned around: "Fellow artists—to your instruments!"

Thus Naftaltzi called out to his band of children, who gathered about him immediately, each with his own instrument. Naftaltzi himself struck the table with his bow, threw a sharp look at each child separately and at all of them at once, and the concert began. They went at it with such fury that I was almost knocked off my feet. Each one tried to outdo the other, but loudest of all played a little boy named Chemeleh, a thin child with a running nose and bare spindly legs. Chemeleh played a strange instrument—some sort of a sack—and when he blew, it gave out an unearthly shriek, like a cat when its tail is stepped on. With his bare foot Chemeleh marked time and all the while watched me out of his small impish eyes and winked at me as if to say, "I am doing well, ain't I?" . . . But hardest of all worked Naftaltzi himself. He both played and conducted, working with his hands, his feet, his nose, his eyes, his whole body; and if anyone made a mistake, he gritted his teeth and yelled out:

"*Forte,* you fool! *Forte, fortissimo!* Count, stupid—count! One, two, three! One, two, three!"

I arranged with Naftaltzi Bezborodka to take three lessons a week, an hour and a half each time, for two *rubles* a month. I begged him over and over to keep this a secret, or I would get into trouble. He gave me his word of honor that he would breathe it to no one.

"We are people," he said gravely, adjusting his collar, "of small means, but when it comes to honor and integrity, we have more than the richest of the rich. By the way—can you spare me a few *groschen*?"

I pulled a *ruble* out of my pocket. Naftaltzi took it from me like a professor—very refined—with the tips of his fingers. Then he called Mother Eve, and hardly looking at her, said, "Here, get something for dinner."

Mother Eve took the money from him with both hands and every one of her fingers, inspected it carefully, and said, "What shall I buy?"

"Anything you want," he said with a show of indifference.

"Get a few rolls—two or three herring—a sausage. And don't forget—an onion, some vinegar and oil—and, maybe, a bottle of brandy . . ."

When the food was laid out on the table the crowd fell on it with such gusto as after a fast. Watching them made me so ravenous that when they asked me to join them I couldn't refuse. And I don't know when I enjoyed any food as much as I did that meal.

When we were through, Bezborodka winked at the crowd, signaled for them to reach for their instruments, and I was treated to another concert, this time an "original composition." This they played with such verve and spirit that my ears rang and my head swam and I left the house drunk with Naftaltzi Bezborodka's "composition."

All that day in *cheder* the rabbi, the boys and the books all danced before my eyes and the music rang incessantly in my ears. At night I dreamed of Paganini riding the devil. He hit me over the head with his fiddle. I woke screaming, my head splitting, and I began to babble—I don't know what. Later my older sister Pessel told me that I was out of my head. What I said made no sense—crazy words like "composition," "Paganini," "the devil" . . . Another thing my sister told me was that while I was sick someone came to ask about me— somebody from Naftaltzi the musician—a barefoot boy. He was chased away and told never to come back.

"What did that fiddler's boy want from you?" my sister nagged, but I held my tongue.

"I don't know. I don't know a thing. What are you talking about?"

"How does it look?" my mother said. "You are a grown boy already—we are trying to arrange a match for you—and you pick yourself friends like these. Barefoot fiddlers! What

have you got to do with musicians anyway? What did Naftaltzi's boy want of you?"

"Which Naftaltzi?" I asked innocently. "What musicians?"

"Look at him!" my father broke in. "He doesn't know a
thing. Poor little fellow! At your age I was engaged a long
time already, and you are still playing games with children.
Get dressed and go to *cheder*. And if you meet Hershel Beltax
on the way and he asks what was the matter with you, tell
him you had a fever. Do you hear what I said? A fever."

I didn't begin to understand. What did I have to do with
Hershel Beltax? And why did I have to tell him about a
fever? In a few weeks my question was answered.

Hershel Beltax (he was called that because he and his father
and his grandfather had all worked for the tax collector)
was a man with a round little belly, a short red beard, small
moist eyes and a broad white forehead—the mark of a wise
man. He had the reputation in town of being an intelligent man,
accomplished and learned—up to a certain point—in the *Torah*.
He was a fine writer—that is, he had a clear handwriting.
It was said that at one time his writings were known all over
the countryside. And besides that he had money and a daughter,
an only daughter, with red hair and moist eyes—the exact
image of him. Her name was Esther, she was called by a nickname—Flesterl. She was timid and delicate, and terribly
afraid of us schoolboys because we teased her all the time.
When we met her we sang this song:

> *Esther, Flester,*
> *Where is your sister?*

What was so terrible about that? Nothing, it seemed to

me, and yet when Esther heard it she covered her ears and ran off crying. She would hide in her room and not go out on the street for days.

But that was a long time ago when she was a child. Now she was a grown girl with long red braids and went about dressed in the latest fashion. My mother was very fond of her. "Gentle as a dove," she used to say. Sometimes on Saturday Esther used to come to visit my sister and when she saw me she would turn even redder than she was and drop her eyes. And my sister would call me over and start asking me questions—and watch us both to see how we acted.

One day—into the *cheder* walked my father with Hershel Beltax, and behind them trailed Reb Sholom-Shachne, the matchmaker, a man with a curly black beard, a man with six fingers, as people used to say. Seeing such guests, the rabbi, Reb Zorach, grabbed his coat and put on his hat in such a hurry that one of his earlocks was caught behind his ear, and his skullcap stuck out from under his hat, and his cheeks began to flame. We could see that something unusual was about to happen. Lately Reb Sholom-Shachne the matchmaker had been coming to the *cheder* frequently and each time he came he called the rabbi out of the room and there through the doorway we could see them whispering together, shrugging their shoulders, gesturing with their hands—ending up with a sigh.

"Well, it's the same old story. If it's to be, it will be. Regardless."

Now when these guests came in, the rabbi, Reb Zorach, was so confused he didn't know what to do or where to seat them. He grabbed hold of a low bench on which his wife used to salt the meat, and carried it around the room with him, till he finally put it down and sat on it himself. But

he quickly jumped up and said to his guests, "Here is a bench.
Won't you sit down?"

"That's all right, Reb Zorach," said my father. "We just
came in for a minute. We'd like to hear my son recite something—out of the Bible." And he inclined his head toward
Hershel Beltax.

"Surely, why not?" said the rabbi, and picking up the Bible
he handed it to Hershel Beltax, with a look that said, "Here—
do what you can with it."

Hershel Beltax took the Bible like a man who knew what
he was doing, bent his head sideways, shut one eye, shuffled
the pages and handed it to me open at the first paragraph of
the *Song of Songs*.

"The *Song of Songs?*" said Reb Zorach with a smile, as
though to say, "You couldn't find something harder?" "The
Song of Songs," says Hershel Beltax, "is not as easy as you think.
One has to understand it."

"That's not a lie," said Reb Sholom-Shachne, the matchmaker, with a laugh.

The rabbi beckons to me. I walk up to the table, and
begin to chant in a loud voice, with a fine rhythm:

"The *Song of Songs!* A song above all other songs. Other
songs have been sung by a prophet, but this song was sung
by a prophet who was the son of a prophet. Other songs have
been sung by a sage, but this was sung by a sage who was the
son of a sage. Other songs have been sung by a king. This
was sung by a king who was the son of a king."

While I sang I watched my examiners and saw on the face of
each of them a different expression. On my father's face I
saw great pride and joy. On the rabbi's face was fear lest I
make a mistake. His lips silently repeated each word. Hershel
Beltax sat with his head bent sideways, his beard between his

lips, one eye shut, and the other raised aloft, listening with a very knowing look. Reb Sholom-Shachne the matchmaker did not take his eyes off Hershel Beltax the whole time. He sat with his body bent forward, swaying back and forth along with me, interrupting me with a sound that was part exclamation, part laugh, part a cough, pointing his fingers at me:

"When I said he knew it I really meant he knew it."

A few weeks later plates were broken, and I became engaged to Hershel Beltax's daughter, Flesterl.

Sometimes it happens that a person ages more in one day than in ten years. When I became engaged I suddenly felt grown up—seemingly the same boy and yet not the same. From the smallest boy to the rabbi himself they all treated me with respect. After all, I was a young man engaged to be married—and I had a watch! No longer did my father scold me—and as for whippings—that was out of the question. How could you whip a young man who wore a gold watch? It would be a shame and a disgrace. Once a boy named Eli who, like me, was engaged to be married, received a whipping in *cheder* because he was caught skating on the ice with some peasant boys. The whole town talked about it, and when his fiancée learned of the scandal she cried so long that her parents broke the engagement. And the young man, Eli, was so heartbroken and so ashamed that he wanted to throw himself into the river. Fortunately, the water was frozen over . . .

Such a calamity befell me, too, but not over a whipping, and not over skating on ice, but over a fiddle. And here is the story:

In our tavern we had a frequent guest, Tchetchek, the bandleader, whom we called Colonel. He was a strapping fellow, tall, with a large, round beard and sinister eyebrows. His speech was a mixture of several languages, and when he spoke

he moved his eyebrows up and down. When he lowered his
eyebrows his face became black as night, and when he raised
them, his face glowed like the sun, because under those thick
eyebrows were a pair of eyes that were bright blue and full
of laughter. He wore a uniform with gold buttons and that
was why we called him Colonel. He came to our tavern frequently—not because he was a heavy drinker, but because my
father used to make a raisin wine—"the best—and rarest—
Hungarian wine" that Tchetchek could hardly praise enough.
He would put his enormous hand on my father's thin shoulder
and roar in his queer mixed language:

"Herr Kellermeister, you have the best Hungarian wine
in the world. There is no such wine even in Budapest, *pred-
bozhe.*"

Tchetchek was very friendly with me. He praised me
for my stories and liked to ask questions like: "Who was
Adam? Who was Isaac? Who was Joseph?"

"You mean—*Yosef?*" I would say.

"I mean Joseph."

"*Yosef,*" I corrected him again.

"To us he is Joseph, to you he is *Yosef,*" he would say and
pinch my cheek. "Joseph or *Yosef, Yosef* or Joseph, it's all the
same, all equal—*wszystko yedno.*"

But when I became engaged Tchetchek's attitude also
changed. Instead of treating me like a child he began to talk
to me as to an equal, to tell me stories of the army and of
musicians. (The Colonel had wonderful stories to tell but
no one had time to listen except me.) Once, when he was
talking about music, I questioned him, "What instrument
does the Colonel play?"

"All instruments," he said, and raised his eyebrows.

"The fiddle too?" I asked, and his face became in my eyes
the face of an angel.

"Come to my house some day," he said, "and I will play for you."

"I can only come on the Sabbath. But please, Colonel, no one must know." "*Przed bohem,*" he said fervently and raised his eyebrows.

Tchetchek lived far off beyond the town in a small white cottage with small windows and brightly painted shutters, surrounded by a garden full of bright, yellow sunflowers that carried themselves as proudly as lilies or roses. They bent their heads a little, swayed in the breeze and beckoned to me, "Come to us, young man, come to us. Here is space, here is freedom, here it is bright and fresh, warm and cheerful." And after the stench and heat and dust of the town, the noise and turmoil of the crowded *cheder,* I was glad to come, for here was space and freedom, here it was bright and fresh, warm and cheerful. I felt like running, leaping, yelling, singing, or like throwing myself on the ground with my face deep in the fragrant grass. But that is not for you, Jewish children. Yellow sunflowers, green grass, fresh air, the clean earth, the clear sky, these are not for you . . .

When I came to the gate the first time, I was met by a shaggy, black dog with fiery, red eyes, who jumped at me with such force that I was almost knocked over. Luckily he was tied to a rope. When Tchetchek heard me yell he came running out of the house, without his uniform on, and told the dog to be quiet. Then he took me by the hand and led me up to the black dog. He told me not to be afraid. "Here, pat him—he won't hurt you." And taking my hand he passed it over the dog's fur, calling him odd names in a kindly voice. The dog dropped his tail, licked himself all over and gave me a look that said, "Lucky for you my master is standing here, or you would be leaving without a hand."

Having recovered from my fright, I entered the house with the Colonel and there I was struck dumb: all the walls were covered with guns, and on the floor lay a skin with the head of a lion—or maybe a leopard—with fierce teeth. The lion didn't bother me so much—he was dead. But those guns— all those guns! I didn't enjoy the fresh plums and juicy apples with which my host treated me. I couldn't keep my eyes away from the walls. But later, when Tchetchek took out of its red case a small round fiddle with an odd belly, spread over it his large round beard and placed on it his huge powerful hand and passed the bow over it a few times, and the first melody poured out, I forgot in one instant the black dog, the fierce lion and the loaded guns. I saw only Tchetchek's spreading beard, his overhanging eyebrows, I saw only a round fiddle with an odd belly, and fingers which danced over the strings with such speed that it was hard to imagine where so many fingers came from.

Then Tchetchek himself disappeared—with his spreading beard, his thick eyebrows, and his wonderful fingers—and I saw nothing in front of me. I only heard a singing, a sighing, a weeping, a sobbing, a talking, a roaring—all sorts of strange sounds that I had never heard in my life before. Sounds sweet as honey, smooth as oil, kept pouring without end straight into my heart, and my soul soared far far away into another world, into a paradise of pure sound.

"Would you like some tea?" calls out Tchetchek, putting down the fiddle and slapping me on the back.

I felt as though I had fallen from the seventh heaven down to earth again.

After that I visited Tchetchek every Saturday to listen to his playing. I went straight to the house, not afraid of anyone, and I even became so familiar with the black dog that he would wag his tail when he saw me, and try to lick my hand. But I wouldn't allow that. "Let's be friends at a distance," I said.

At home no one knew where I spent my Saturdays. No one stopped me. After all, I was not a child any more.

And they wouldn't have known until now if a fresh calamity had not occurred—a great calamity which I shall now describe.

Who should care if a young fellow takes a Sabbath walk by himself a short distance out of town? Whose business is it? Apparently there are people who care, and one such person was Ephraim Klotz, a busybody who knew what was cooking in every pot. He made it his business to know. This man watched me closely, followed me, found out where I was going, and later swore with many pious oaths that he had seen me at the Colonel's house eating pork and smoking cigarettes on the Sabbath.

Every Saturday when I was on my way to Tchetchek's I would meet him on the bridge, walking along in a sleeveless, patched, summer coat that reached to his ankles. He walked with his arms folded behind him, his overcoat flapping, humming to himself in a thin voice.

"A good Sabbath," I would say to him.

"Good Sabbath," he would reply. "Where is the young man going?"

"Just for a walk," I said.

"For a walk? Alone?" he repeated, with a meaningful smile . . .

One afternoon when I was sitting with Tchetchek and drinking tea, we heard the dog barking and tearing at his rope. Looking out of the window, I thought I saw someone small and dark with short legs running out of sight. From his way of running I could swear it was Ephraim Klotz.

That night, when I got home, I saw Ephraim Klotz sitting at the table. He was talking with great animation and laugh-

ing his odd little laugh that sounded like dried peas pouring out
of a dish. Seeing me, he fell silent and began to drum with
his short fingers on the table. Opposite him sat my father,
his face pale, twisting his beard and tearing hairs out one by one
—a sign that he was angry.

"Where are you coming from?" asked my father, with a
glance at Ephraim Klotz.

"Where should I be coming from?" I said.

"Where have you been all day?" said my father.

"Where should I be all day? In *shul*."

"What did you do there all day?"

"What should I be doing there? Studying . . ."

"What were you studying?" said my father.

"What should I be studying? The *Gamorah* . . ."

"Which *Gamorah*?" said my father.

At this point Ephraim Klotz laughed his shrill laugh and my
father could stand it no more. He rose from his seat and leaning
over, gave me two resounding, fiery slaps in the face. My
mother heard the commotion from the next room and came
running in . . .

"Nochem," she cried, "God be with you! What are you
doing? The boy is engaged to be married. Suppose his father-
in-law hears of this?"

My mother was right. My future father-in-law heard the
whole story. Ephraim repeated it to him himself. It was too
good to keep.

The next day the engagement was broken and I was a privileged person no more. My father was so upset that he became
ill and stayed in bed for days. He would not let me come near
him, no matter how much my mother pleaded for me.

"The shame of it," he said. "The disgrace. That is worst of
all."

"Forget about it," my mother begged. "God will send us

another match. Our lives won't be ruined by this. Perhaps it was not his lot."

Among those who came to visit my father while he was ill was the bandmaster. When my father saw him, he took off his skullcap, sat up in bed, and extending an emaciated hand, said to him:

"Ah, Colonel, Colonel . . ."

More he could not say because his voice became choked with tears and he was seized with a fit of coughing. This was the first time in my life that I had seen my father cry. My heart ached and my soul went out to him. I stood staring out of the window, swallowing tears. How I regretted the trouble I had caused!

Silently I swore to myself never, never to disobey my father again, never to cause him such grief, never in this world.

No more fiddles.

The Day before Yom Kippur

(Sketches of Disappearing Types)

I. NOAH-WOLF THE BUTCHER

IF THE day before *Yom Kippur* were three times as long as it is, it would not be long enough for Noah-Wolf the butcher to finish his work in time for the evening services.

And this is his work: he has to apologize to a townful of people for his year's misdeeds. He has to go to all the customers who buy meat from him, all the neighbors who live in the same street with him or have their shops near his, or sit close to him in the butchers' synagogue.

There is not a person in our town with whom Noah-Wolf has not had an argument at one time or another. Not that Noah-Wolf is such an evil person, but he undoubtedly has, as he himself says, an ugly temper. He simply has to fight with people.

If you come into his shop for some meat, you are met with a pailful of cold water. And he cannot even tell you why.

A housewife comes in: "Reb Noah-Wolf, do you have any fresh meat today?"

And he answers: "How should I have fresh meat? If you want rotten meat, you can get it."

Or: "Noah-Wolf, give me a good portion."

"I'll give you just the kind of portion you deserve."

Or this: "What kind of carcass are you giving me, Noah-Wolf! Look at it!"

"What does a carcass like you know about carcasses?"

That is how Noah-Wolf treats his customers, the house-wives themselves. So how would you expect him to treat the servant girls? When one of them has to go to his shop, she curses her fate. She knows what a greeting she can expect. Either he will slap her across the face with a beef tongue, or he'll fit her marketbasket over her head, or he'll simply chase her out.

"Get out of here! Go to some other shop! There are enough butchers without me!"

Nevertheless one thing has nothing to do with another. Noah-Wolf the butcher may be stubborn and eccentric, and yet his customers won't go anywhere else, because they know that he is the most honorable butcher in town. They know that his scale is true and that he keeps his word. If he tells you that the meat was slaughtered yesterday, you know that it is so. And if he promises you some sweetbreads, or a piece of lung, or a neat's foot for Saturday, you can sleep in peace. The lung or the foot is as good as yours. Furthermore, he will never connive with your servant girl to rob you behind your back. And he won't combine with other butchers to raise their prices. That is why the servant girls slander him, and the other butchers would like to drown him in a spoonful of water. He sticks in their throats like a bone. He is a stubborn man. If he makes up his mind on anything, he's like an ox being dragged to slaughter. You can't make him budge.

And he even looks like an ox. He is tall and broad and red-faced, and his hands are enormous. When he raises his cleaver to split a side of meat he does it as ferociously as if the ox or cow had committed some crime and had been condemned to be chopped to pieces by him in person.

"That man is a murderer!" they say in our town, and there are grown people who are actually afraid of him.

But if all year long he gets under your skin, he changes with the coming of the New Year. Then you would hardly recognize him. He becomes someone else, pious, God-fearing, virtuous, and sees omens in everything. He stops fighting with the other butchers, becomes soft as butter toward his customers, is considerate to the servant girls, becomes so unctuous you could almost spread him over a boil. Even when he chops his meat now he does it differently, not murderously as before, but gently, mercifully. A different Noah-Wolf altogether.

The day before *Yom Kippur* he locks up very early (he had said his morning prayers when most of us were still asleep), puts on his holiday gabardine, and goes from house to house, to all his customers and neighbors, friends and acquaintances, to offer his apologies, to ask for pardon for the year's misdeeds.

"Good *yom-tev*," he says. "If anything I have said offended you, I want to apologize, and wish you a happy New Year."

And they say to him: "The same to you, Noah-Wolf. May God pardon us all."

And they invite him to sit down and they treat him to a piece of holiday torte.

II. EZRIEL THE FISHERMAN

Since the world was created, you have never seen as ill-tempered a creature as Ezriel the fisherman.

An ill-tempered man with angry eyes, thick eyebrows, bristling mustache, and a beard that looks as if it has been pasted on. And he wears a quilted jacket summer and winter, with the fringes of his *tallis-ḳot'n* sticking out underneath. And he smells of raw fish a mile away.

All week long you don't see him at all. But before every Sabbath and every holiday he appears in the marketplace with his wagon piled high with fish. On top of the wagon sits a girl with pockmarked face, watching the fish. And his wife, Maita, a heavy, swollen woman, stands alongside the wagon with a stick and watches the fish.

"Fish—fish—fresh and quivering! Women! Fish for Sabbath!"

That is the way Ezriel the fisherman announces his wares across the marketplace, in his loud, familiar chant, and he never takes an eye off the women who have already crowded around his wagon and laid siege to it from all sides, clutching the fish by the heads, peering under the gills, poking at the eyes or prodding at the bellies to see if the fish is fresh. These liberties Ezriel hates and despises like something un-*ḳosher*, and he chases the women away.

"Away from here! You've pawed over them long enough already!"

This he hurls at them in a quick undertone, and then, once more to the world at large, in his loud, clear chant:

"Fish—fish—fresh and quivering! Women! Fish for Sabbath!"

Every woman, whether a housewife or a servant girl, is treated alike by Ezriel the fisherman. He watches her like a hawk. He does not suspect anyone of being a thief, but he knows that when it comes to fish, you can never tell. The richest, most honorable, most charitable woman is frequently torn by the desire to make off with a good, fresh fish if no one is looking. "Fish," he says, "is a temptation that is hard for a woman to resist."

Every year at least one scandal takes place around Ezriel's

wagon. He slaps some woman across the face with a wet
and shiny pickerel. From all directions men and women come
running up; there is noise and confusion. The crowd puts in
a word for the woman, gives her advice, tells her to file a
complaint with the Justice of the Peace, or have Ezriel dragged
off to the rabbi. But since the pain is moral rather than physical,
it soon wears off, and the whole affair comes to nothing.

Most of the women know him already. They would think
no more of edging too close to his fish than to the gold and
precious stones under a king's guard.

"How much are your rubies and emeralds today?" a woman
may ask, standing with her basket at some distance and
pointing with her little finger at the wagon.

"I deal in fish, not rubies!" Ezriel answers proudly, without even condescending to give the woman a glance with his
angry eyes. And once more he lets out his call to the world
at large:

"Fish—fish—fresh and quivering! Women! Fish!"

"An apoplectic man!" the women say of him. They would
much rather not have anything to do with him, but that is
impossible. There is not another fisherman in town, so what
can one do? Lie down on the ground and die? Or live through
the Sabbath without fish? But that is even worse than dying,
for if a woman dies she knows she is dead: it's all over. But
if she comes home without fish for Saturday, then she has her
husband's wrath to contend with. And that is worse than
dying.

"I wish something terrible would happen to him!"

That is what the women say when *Yom Kippur* eve comes
around and they rush off to the marketplace with their
baskets, afraid that they might be too late, because the day
before *Yom Kippur* Ezriel is in the habit of getting up so early
that God himself is still in bed. And when other people are

just getting ready for their morning prayers, Ezriel is through
with everything and is all dressed up for the holiday. His
heavy, quilted jacket has been put away and he wears the
coarse, shiny, black gabardine that is seen only on the Sabbath and high holidays, but which nevertheless is saturated
through and through with the odor of raw fish.

Ezriel begins his fast earlier than anyone. Earlier than anyone he comes to the synagogue that afternoon, takes his
place close to the back wall, covers his head with his prayer
shawl, and stands without rest for twenty-four hours. He
won't sit down even for a minute. He prays quietly, so that no
one can hear a word. He weeps a great deal, but no one can
ever see a tear.

But that is in the evening. Before that, all day long, he goes
around the town to his customers, bringing his apologies, asking their pardon.

"If anything I have said to you during the year offended
you, I want to apologize, and wish you a happy New Year."

And they say to him:

"The same to you, Reb Ezriel. May God pardon us all."

And they invite him to sit down and they treat him to a
piece of holiday torte.

III. GETZI THE GOVERNOR

Getzi the Governor—that is what we always called the
shammes, the sexton, of the old synagogue.

Everywhere, in all the synagogues of the world, a *shammes*
may be a *shammes.* But Getzi, the *shammes* of our old synagogue, is more like a member of the board of governors than
a *shammes.* Did I say a member of the board? He acts like
the president of the board!

Getzi does not permit any secular business in the synagogue. He says that a synagogue is a place of worship. If you want to talk business you can go to the marketplace. If you want to discuss politics there is a bath house. Under no conditions will he let you talk during an intermission or a recess. Getzi is a man who shows no respect for anyone. You can be the holder of a pew by the eastern wall, you can have seventeen silver stripes on your *tallis,* he won't debase himself before you. You can be the richest person in town, Reb Joshua Hershel himself, if you say a single word out loud, you hear his hand come pounding down on the table, and a cry of "Qui-et!" so loud that you are almost deafened.

Or try to take one of the sacred tomes from the synagogue bookshelf, and forget to bring it back in time! You'll be put in your place soon enough.

Or if on the Sabbath you pledge a half pound of candles for the synagogue, or eighteen *kopeks* for the poor fund, and then forget to give it! You might as well go bankrupt, or leave everything behind and rush off to America!

Or try to send Getzi on an errand that has nothing to do with the synagogue. This is what you'll hear: "Do *you* have feet? Then go yourself!"

That's the kind of man Getzi is.

The only ones who dare to be impudent with Getzi are the small fry. Inquisitive youngsters, small boys barely learning their alphabet, mischief makers, pranksters of all kinds, these make life miserable for him. The things they do to him would make anyone shudder. They turn over the prayer stands when no one is looking, they let water out of the washbowl, tie knots in the towels, let tallow drip on all the holy books, and tear *Yekum Purkon* out of all the prayer books, so that no matter which one you open the prayer is missing.

These little troublemakers shortened Getzi's life, they taught him the terrors of Gehenna. He kept constant watch; maybe he would catch one of them in the act. And when he caught one, he evened accounts for everything the whole band had ever done. To emerge from his grasp with only a light bruise, a black eye, or an ear that was only partly pulled off, that was luck indeed. Getzi hated drawn-out affairs, worthless investigations and formal trials. No matter whom he caught, a rich man's child or an orphan in rags, it made no difference.

Getzi knows all about slapping. When you feel his hand you behold your grandfather in Paradise. A powerful man, from a family known for its strength, although to look at him you would have hesitated to give two broken *kopeks* for him. Lean, dried up, skin and bones. But his sidelocks were thick and black, and he himself was dark as a Tartar, with fierce, black eyes, hollow cheeks, a crooked nose, and black drooping mustache. All these things taken together made him look either as if he was about to sneeze but was trying not to, or as if he had something to tell you but was keeping it to himself, or simply as if he were an ill-tempered, evil man.

The most evil man in town, was what a lot of people called him. A worm-eaten, spiteful creature who knew no master and did whatever he pleased. If he wanted to open the synagogue, he opened it. If he wanted to shut it, he shut it. When winter came, you had to get down and beg him to start the fire. But when he did make up his mind to start it, you thought you were in a steam bath.

Let some wandering pauper beg with his last breath to be allowed to spend the night in the synagogue. "A synagogue is not a poorhouse," says Getzi, and drives the poor man out without a trace of pity.

And when the High Holidays come around, Getzi rules in the synagogue with a strong and ruthless hand. If he has conceived a dislike for you, you will never get his permission

to let your son or son-in-law sit where you would like to
have him. You can resign yourself to this: he will sit where
Getzi wants him to. And if you go up to the trustees with your
complaint, you'll get this answer: "Go to the governor."

And you know that what they mean is Getzi the *shammes*.
To his face you will call him Getzi, but behind his back he is
the Governor.

It's like that all the time. During *Succos,* if Getzi does not
bring the *esrog* to you on time and you complain, he says:
"You can wait a minute, can't you? I waited longer for you!"

So once more you bring your charges to the trustees. But
this is the only answer you get:

"What can a person do with a governor?"

All year long it's the same. Getzi provides the materials
for all the holidays, candles for *Hannukah,* noisemakers for
Purim, matzo for Passover, and greens for *Shevuos.* Getzi
runs the whole town, rules over it like a king. Like a king?
Like a conqueror! All of us have to endure it. The only time
when people dare to talk is on the Sabbath or a holiday, at
dusk, when we sit and wait in the gathering darkness for
the evening services. Then we can say something. For a few
minutes we do not have to be afraid of the *shammes,* we can
talk freely and openly. And no matter what we talk about,
we come finally to the Getzi captivity, which seems worse
to us than the Babylonian captivity we have heard about. We
ask each other, "How long? Till when? How long will this
captivity last?" And that is as far as we go. What else can
we do? We Jews have suffered under so many evil kings
and governors!

But there is one day of the year when Governor Getzi sus-
pends his tyranny. Not a whole day, but a half day, really
only a few hours. That is the day before *Yom Kippur,* right
after the morning prayers, and before people start coming

for the high services, when Getzi once more becomes king. But during those few hours he forgets that he is *shammes,* forgets he is governor. He is dressed in his holiday best, and he runs from house to house, stops everywhere, with these words:

"If anything I have said to you at any time offended you, forgive me. And may you have a happy New Year."

And he gets this reluctant answer: "You too, you too."

And they invite him to sit down and they give him a piece of holiday torte.

Three Little Heads

I OFFER you a present for *Shevuos,* a picture of three little heads, three wonderfully fine heads of three poor, tattered, barefoot Jewish children. All three little heads are dark, with curly hair and eyes big and luminous that stare at you with wonder and always seem to ask the question: "Why?" You look back at them with wonder and a feeling of guilt as if somehow you are to blame for their having been created, three more superfluous creatures on the face of the earth.

The three little heads—Avremchik, Moisechik and Dvorka —are two brothers and their little sister. Avremchik and Moisechik—that was what their father, Peiseh the boxmaker, called them, in the Russian manner. If he hadn't been afraid of what his wife would say, and if he weren't such a bitterly poor man, he'd have changed his own name too, from Peiseh the boxmaker to Piotr Pereplotchik. But since he was afraid of his wife, and since he was as poor as he could be, he remained, for the time being, Peiseh the boxmaker, till the time should some day come, the happy time when everything would be different, as Bebel said and as Karl Marx said, and as all good and wise men say. But until that lucky time arrived, he would have to stand from morning till dark, cutting cardboard and pasting boxes and containers.

So Peiseh the boxmaker stands on his feet all day and cuts cardboard and puts together boxes, and sings songs, some of the old ones and some new ones, some Jewish songs and some not a bit Jewish—many of them not a bit Jewish—happy sad songs with a sad happy tune.

"Will you ever stop singing those outlandish songs? You must have fallen in love with them! Since you have come to the big city you are not a Jew any more."

The three—Avremchik, Moisechik and Dvorka—were born and grew up in the same place, between the wall and the oven in a single crowded room. Every day the three saw the same things before them: their jolly father who cut the cardboard, pasted boxes and sang songs; and their worried, exhausted mother, who cooked and baked, swept and scrubbed and was never finished. Both were always at work, the mother at the oven, the father at his boxes. Who would ever need so many boxes? What would they do with all these boxes? The whole world must be full of boxes. That's how it seemed to the three little heads, and they waited for their father to get so many boxes ready that he would have to pile them on his head, and fill both arms with them—maybe a hundred thousand boxes —and then go out with them. Later he came back without any boxes—with no boxes at all, but with a little money for their mother, and with oddly shaped buns, *beigel* and candy for the children.

How good their father was to them, how wonderfully good! Their mother was good too, but she was the one to scold them. Rushing between washtub and oven, she pushed them out of her way, gave their hands a slap, boxed an ear. She did not want them to upset things playing house. She did not want Avremchik to cut up the scraps of cardboard that fell from his father's work table, or Moisechik to steal paste from the pot, or Dvorka to make mud cakes. Their mother always wanted them to sit quietly and sedately. Their mother forgot that young heads worked all the time, that young spirits tore themselves, pulled with all their might, strained toward—toward what?

Toward the outdoors, toward the light, toward the window—
the window . . .

One window—that's all there was. One small window. The
three little heads try to reach the one small window—and
what can they see there? A wall, a high, broad, gray damp
wall, always damp, always dripping, even in summer. Does the
sun ever come in here at all? Of course the sun comes in—
sometimes. That is, not the sun itself, but a glimmering reflection of the sun. And when that happens it is a time for rejoicing. The three little heads crowd against the small window,
look up, way up, and glimpse a long, narrow, blue strip, like
a long blue ribbon.

"There, do you see that, children? That's the sky!"

That is Avremchik speaking. Avremchik knows. Avremchik
goes to *cheder*. He is already studying the alphabet. The *cheder*
is not so far—two houses away, or rather, two doors away. Oh,
what stories Avremchik tells about *cheder*! Avremchik says
that he himself saw, on his word of honor, a huge brick
building covered with small windowpanes from top to bottom.
He swears that he saw with his own eyes, on his word of honor,
a chimney, a tall chimney reaching to the sky, with smoke pouring out of it, and machines that run by themselves without
anybody operating them, and carts that move without horses.
And other such fabulous tales Avremchik brings back from his
trips to *cheder,* and swears, as his mother swears, on his word
of honor. And Moisechik and Dvorka listen to him and sigh
with envy, because Avremchik knows everything—everything.

For instance, Avremchik knows that a tree grows. Of course
he himself has never seen a tree grow any more than they have
—there are no trees on their street—but he knows (he heard it
in *cheder*) that trees bear fruit. And that is why when you
eat fruit you say, "Blessed art thou, O Lord our God, King of
the universe, who createst the fruit of the tree." Avremchik

knows (what doesn't he know?) that potatoes, for instance, or cucumbers, or onions or garlic grow on the ground. And that is why for these things you say, "Blessed art thou, O Lord our God, King of the universe, who createst the fruit of the earth." Avremchik knows everything! But he doesn't know how or in what manner these things grow either. For on their street there is no field, no garden, there are no trees, there's not a blade of grass—not one! On their street there are only tall buildings, gray walls, high chimneys pouring smoke, and every building is covered with windowpanes, thousands of little windowpanes, and inside the buildings are machines that run by themselves, and carts that move without horses. And aside from that there is nothing, nothing.

Even a bird is rarely seen. Sometimes a sparrow blunders into the neighborhood and the sparrow is as gray as the walls themselves. It pecks once or twice at the cobblestones, rises and flies away. And chickens, ducks, geese? Once in a great while they have a quarter of a chicken for Saturday, chicken with a pale scrawny leg. How many legs does a chicken have? Obviously four. Just like a horse. That is Avremchick's opinion, and Avremchik knows everything.

Sometimes their mother comes from market bringing a chicken's head with glazed filmy eyes. "It's dead," says the older Avremchik, and the three little heads look at each other with large dark eyes and sigh. Born and brought up in the great city, in the large buildings, in crowded quarters, the three children never had a chance to see anything alive—a hen, a cow, or any other creature except a cat. They have their own cat, a live one, a large cat, gray as the tall gray damp walls. The cat is their one joy. They play with it whenever they can. They tie a kerchief around its head and call it Auntie, and laugh uproariously.

But then their mother catches them at it and goes after them, slaps one's hands, boxes another's ears, sends them back to their place behind the oven. The oldest, Avremchik, begins to talk and the younger ones listen, look up wide-eyed at their older brother, and listen. Avremchik says that their mother is right. He says that you're not supposed to play with a cat, because a cat is an unclean thing, an evil spirit. Avremchik knows everything, everything. Is there anything in the world that he doesn't know?

Avremchik knows everything. He knows that there is a land, a land far away, far, far away, that is called America. There in America they have many friends and relatives. There in America Jews have a better life and a happier one. Next year, or the year after, if all is well and someone sends them tickets from over there, they plan to go to America too. Without tickets you can't go, because there is an ocean you have to cross, and storms come up and toss the ship about. Avremchik knows everything.

Everything . . . Even what goes on in the next world. For instance, he knows that in the next world there is a Paradise —for Jews, of course. In that Paradise you'll find the most brilliant trees with all kinds of fruit, rivers flowing with all good things. Diamonds and precious stones are scattered over the streets; all you have to do is bend down and fill your pockets with them. And pious Jews sit day and night studying the holy books and enjoying the divine presence.

Avremchik tells them all these things, and the children's eyes sparkle and they envy their brother, who knows every-thing—even what happens in heaven. Avremchik swears that twice a year—one night of *Succos* and one night of *Shevuos*—the skies split open. Of course he has never seen the skies split open, because where they live you can't see the sky. But some of his schoolmates saw it happen. They swore that they saw it. And they wouldn't swear to a lie, would they? That would be a sin. And to prove that the skies really split open, Avremchik runs to his mother and pulls her skirts.

"Mama, isn't it true that this *Shevuos* at midnight the heavens will split open? Isn't it true?"

"Split open? My head is splitting open!" cries their mother, pulling herself away from his grasp.

And getting only this answer from their mother, Avremchik waits for their father to come home. Their father has gone to market with a stack of boxes.

"Children, what do you think he's going to bring us today?"

And the children begin to guess. They count on their fingers—everything that could possibly be at the market, everything that the eye could see and the heart could long for—all those oddly shaped buns and the *beigel* and the candy. But none of them guessed right, and I am afraid that none of you will guess it either. This time Peiseh the boxmaker brought neither buns nor *beigel* nor candy. He brought grasses, a bagful of grasses, strange, long, green, sweetsmelling grasses.

And the three little heads, Avremchik, Moisechik and Dvorka, surrounded their father.

"Oh, what is it? What did you bring? What is it?"

"Greens. Can't you see?"

"What do you mean—greens?"

"Greens for the holidays. It's *Shevuos* tonight. All Jews need greens for *Shevuos*."

"Where do you get them?"

"Where do you get them? M-m-m . . . You buy them at the market."

And saying this, he scatters the green, fragrant grasses over the freshly swept floor. He keeps some of it in his hands and fingers it and sniffs at it joyfully.

"Isn't it wonderful?"

"Wonderful for you!" says their mother. "A wonderful litter. Something new for the children to mess with."

That's how their mother takes it, as she goes on with her work, always worried, always burdened, just the opposite of their father.

And the three little heads look at their mother, look at their father, look at each other. And when their parents' backs are turned for a moment, they throw themselves on the floor, bury their heads in the fragrant grasses, fondle and kiss the rough blades that are called greens, and that Jews must have for their holidays, and that you buy at the market.

Everything can be found at the market, even greens. Their father brings them everything. There are so many things that Jews must have, and they get them. Even greens . . . Even greens . . .

A Country Passover

LET the winds blow. Let the storms rage. Let the world turn upside down. An old oak that has been standing since the beginning of time, whose roots have sunk deep into the earth, cares nothing about winds. He pays no heed to storms . . .

This old oak is not a symbol. It is a living person named Nachman Verebivker of Verebivka. He is tall and broad shouldered, a giant of a man. The whole town envies him his strength, and at the same time pokes fun at him. "How do you do?" they greet him. "How is your health today?" Nachman knows they are making fun of his height, so he bends his shoulders to make himself look smaller, a little less like a peasant. But it doesn't help. God has made him big.

Nachman is an old settler in Verebivka. The peasants who call him "Our Lachman" consider him a pretty good fellow, a man of intelligence, with whom they like to talk things over once in a while. They come to ask him what to do about their grain. "Lachman" has an almanac, so he ought to know if grain will be high or low this year. Sometimes they discuss affairs of the world. "Lachman" goes to town occasionally, he sees people, he knows what goes on outside of their village.

It is impossible to imagine Verebivka without Nachman Verebivker. Not only did his father Feitel Verebivker live and die there, but also his grandfather, Aryah, may he rest in peace. Aryah, a wise man and one who liked to play with words,

used to boast that the town was named Verebivka because
Aryah Verebivker lived there. Actually he had lived there long
before the town was ever known by that name. And do you
think he said this only to be talking? He was not that kind
of a man. What he was referring to was the decrees against
the Jews. Even in those days they spoke of driving the Jews out
of the villages; and not only talked but actually drove them.
All of them were driven out, that is, all but old Aryah Verebivker. It is said that the governor himself could do nothing
about it, for Aryah proved that according to law he could not be
forced out of Verebivka. He had lived there too long for that
. . . Oh, those men of old!

Naturally if one is such an exception as to be permitted to
live in Verebivka, one has a right to feel secure, and can
laugh at the whole world. Why does a man have to worry about
decrees, proclamations or statutes? Why does he have to pay
attention to the stories that the peasant Kurachka, his neighbor,
is always bringing from the district office? Kurachka was a
short, heavy-set man who wore a short, heavy jacket and tall
boots and a large watch on a silver chain, like a landed pro-
prietor. He was clerk in the district office and knew everyone's
troubles. In addition he read all the choice newspapers that
printed inflammatory stories against the Jews.

By nature Kurachka was not such a bad fellow. He was a
neighbor of Nachman's and supposedly a good friend. When
Kurachka had a toothache, "Lachman" gave him a remedy for
it. When Kurachka's wife was having a baby, "Lachman's"
wife acted as midwife. But for some time now, since he had
started reading those choice newspapers, Kurachka had become a changed man. The spirit of Esau had entered into
him. He was always coming with another piece of news:
a new governor had been appointed, a new proclamation had

been issued, a new decree had been announced about the Jews. And hearing this, the Jew Nachman felt heavy-hearted. A chill went through him, but he never let on that he was disturbed. He heard him out with a smile and showed him the palm of his hand, as though to say, "When hair grows on this hand, then I'll begin to worry."

Let governors change, let ministers issue proclamations. What did Nachman Verebivker of Verebivka care about that?

The living that Nachman Verebivker made was a fairly good one, though it did not compare to that of former years. When his grandfather Aryah was alive, times had been different. Ah, those times! Then all Verebivka, you might say, belonged to them. They owned a tavern, a store, a mill, a granary. They had everything they wanted. But that was long ago. Now they had lost all these things. No tavern, no store, no granary. Nothing, simply nothing. But if that was so, you ask, then why did he remain in Verebivka? Well, then, where else could he go? Should he go dig a hole for himself? If he sold his home he would not be a Verebivker any more. He would become an outcast, a stranger. This way, at least, he had a place he could call his own, a roof over his head, a home of his own. And behind his house he had a garden. His wife and daughters worked the garden themselves and all summer they had greens to eat and then potatoes for the whole winter and into spring. But you can't live on potatoes alone. You have to have bread, too, and bread there was none. So Nachman would take his stick and go through the countryside looking for something to buy. He never came back empty-handed. Whatever God sent his way he bought—some scrap metal, a basket of millet, an old sack, a hide. The hide he would stretch, air out, and take to Avrom-Eli the tanner in town. And from all these great transactions he either made a *ruble* or lost a *ruble*. That's what happens in business. *"Kupetz kak streletz,"* Nachman would say in Russian: "A businessman is like a hunter," and Avrom-Eli the tanner, a man with a bluish nose, and fingers that looked as though they had been dipped in ink, laughed at him for being so coarsened by country living that even his jokes were now of peasant origin.

Nachman agreed. He had become coarse. It was lucky that his grandfather could not see him now. What a man he had been! Also a giant of a man, but learned as well. He knew his prayers and all the Psalms by heart. Those men of old! And he, Nachman—what did he know? He could barely read his prayers; but that at least was something. His children would not know that much . . .

When he looked at his children, growing up big and burly like himself, and unable to read or write, also like himself, he grew sick at heart. And most of all was he saddened by the sight of his youngest child, his baby, a boy named Feitel, after his father, Feitel Verebivker. A fine, promising little boy, different from the others, smaller in build, more gentle and refined in appearance. A true child of Israel. And what a brain! Just one time, for the fun of it, they had shown him the letter *aleph* and the letter *beis* in a prayer book, and he never forgot which was which. And a child like that had to grow up in a village among calves and pigs, with Kurachka's son Pedka as his playmate. Feitel and Pedka rode a broomstick together, pretending it was a horse. Together they chased cats, dug caves, amused themselves as small children will. When Nachman saw his favorite child playing with the peasant boy, his heart was heavy within him.

Pedka was an alert child, too, the same age as Feitel, with a bright winning face and flaxen hair. They liked to be together and would do anything in the world for each other. All winter

long they remained indoors, close to the oven, but they longed
for each other and often stood by the window each hoping to see
the other. But now the winter, the long dark winter, was past.
The snow was gone. The sun shone. The wind had dried the
earth. The grass sprouted. And down below the hill the brook
gurgled once more. The little calf spread its nostrils and took
a deep breath. The rooster shut an eye and stood lost in thought.
Everything was coming to life again everywhere. Everything
was growing, rejoicing. It was Passover Eve. Neither Pedka
nor Feitel could be kept at home any longer. They burst out
into God's green world, took each other by the hand, and
raced toward the hill which beckoned to them both, "Come,
children, come." They leaped up toward the sunlight, which
greeted them both, "Come children, come." And when they
grew tired of running and leaping they sat down on God's
earth which knew neither Jew nor Gentile, but invited them
both, equally : "Come to me, children, come . . ."

There was so much to talk about after not having seen
each other all winter. Feitel boasted to his friend that he knew
almost the whole alphabet by heart. And Pedka boasted about
his new whip. Then Feitel said that they were having their
Passover Feast that very night. They had baked *matzos* for
the whole eight days and they had wine too. "Do you remember, Pedka, that *matzo* I brought you last year?" *"Matza?"*
said Pedka, and over his fair face there spread a broad smile,
as he remembered. "Would you like to taste some *matzo* now,
Pedka, fresh *matzo?*" What a question to ask. Would he like
some *matzo!* "Then let's go there," said Feitel, pointing to
the green hill that beckoned to them. They climbed up the
hill and stood enchanted, looking between their outspread
fingers at the rays of the sun, and then threw themselves on
the earth, still damp but already fragrant with the coming

growth. Feitel reached inside his shirt and pulled out a fresh round white *matzo* punctured with rows of tiny holes. He broke the *matzo* in half and divided it with his friend, "Well, what do you think about it?" he asked. But what could Pedka say with his mouth full of matzo that crackled between his teeth and melted on his tongue like snow? One more minute and the *matzo* was gone.

"Do you have any more?" asked Pedka, looking with his gray eyes into Feitel's shirt, and licking his lips like a cat that had swallowed the butter. "Would you like some more?" said Feitel, laughing and chewing his last crumbs, and looking at his friend out of mischievous black eyes. What a question! Would Pedka like more? "Then wait a while," said Feitel, "next year you'll get some more!" At this promise they both burst out laughing, and then without any signal, as if they had arranged it before, they threw themselves on the ground and rolled down hill faster and faster like two balls . . .

On the other side of the hill they stood up and watched the foaming brook, which ran off to the left, and they themselves ran to the right farther and farther across the fields which were not yet green but gave promise of becoming green soon. They could not smell the grass itself yet, but there was an odor in the air of coming grass. They walked on and on without words, as though in a dream, over the soft, sweet-smelling earth under the kindly sun. They seemed to be flying rather than walking, flying together with the birds that soared overhead, dipping and rising in the open sky which God had created for all living creatures.

Now they had come to the mill—the mill that belonged to the village mayor. Once it had belonged to Nachman Verebivker, but now it belonged to the mayor, a shrewd and rich man. He had tricked Nachman out of the mill and also a store

he had once owned in the village. Usually at this time of the
year the mill was turning, but now it stood still. There was
no wind. Strange to have no wind in the early spring. For
the boys this was a piece of good luck. Now they could examine the mill. There was plenty to see. They looked closely at
the stones, the wheels, and finally sat down and began to talk,
one of those conversations that has no beginning and no end.
Feitel told Pedka all the wonders of the city, where his father
had taken him once. He had gone to market, had seen stores,
not one store as in Verebivka, but many stores. Then in the
evening they had gone to the synagogue, because it was the
anniversary of his grandfather's death. "Do you understand,
Pedka, or don't you?"

Perhaps Pedka understood, but he wasn't listening. Suddenly
he dove in with a story of his own. He told Feitel how last
year he had seen a bird's nest high up in a tree, how he had
tried to climb the tree but couldn't, how he tried to reach
it with a stick, but it was too high and finally how he had
started to throw stones at the nest, and kept on throwing
them until he knocked down two small bleeding birds.

"Were they dead?" asked Feitel, incredulous, frightened.

"But they were so small," Pedka defended himself.

"But you killed them?"

"They had no feathers yet, they were nothing but tiny birds
with yellow bills and round little bellies."

"But you killed them. You killed them."

It was quite late when the two young comrades saw by the
sun that it was time to go home. Feitel had forgotten all about
the holiday that night and he suddenly remembered that his
mother still had to wash his head and put new clothes on
him. He jumped up, with Pedka after him, and together they
started for home, running and leaping with the same joy and

eagerness with which they had started out hours ago. And so
that neither one should be left behind they took each other
by the hand like true comrades and began to run toward the
village as fast as they could. And when they arrived this is
what they saw.

Nachman Verebivker's house was surrounded by all the
people of the village. Kurachka, the clerk; Aponas, the
mayor; the constable; the inspector; the sheriff—all the officials
were there. Everybody was talking at once. Nachman and his
wife stood in the middle of the crowd explaining, defending
themselves, making all sorts of motions with their hands.
Nachman stood with his shoulders bent, trying to make himself less conspicuous, wiping the sweat from his brow. Near
by stood the older children with frightened faces. Suddenly the
whole picture changed. Someone pointed at the two boys and
the whole crowd—the clerk, the mayor, the police officers, all
stood open-mouthed. Only Nachman looked over the crowd,
straightened his broad shoulders, cried out, "Well?" and burst
out laughing. His wife clapped her hands together and burst
out crying.

The mayor, the constable, the inspector, the sheriff all stepped
out of the crowd and turned to the boys.

"Where were you all this time, you . . . you . . ."

"Where were we? We were at the mill, that's where we
were."

Both boys, Feitel and Pedka, got what they had coming and
neither understood why. Feitel's father gave him a good beating so that he'd know better next time. But what should he
know next time? And apparently out of pity his mother
took him away from his father, gave him a few cuffs of her
own and quickly began to wash his head for the holiday. Then
she put on his new pants, his only new clothes for Passover,

and as she did so she sighed. Why did she sigh? Feitel could
not understand. But a little later he heard her say to his father.
"Ah, if *Pesach* were only over already. I hope it goes by without trouble. For my part it could have gone by before it started."
Feitel racked his brain but he could not understand why she
wanted the holiday to be over before it had started. He couldn't
understand his father's whipping or his mother's cuffs. What
kind of Passover Eve was this?

Pedka understood as little as Feitel did. First of all his
father Kurachka had grabbed him by the hair, swung him
around savagely and given him a resounding slap for good
measure. Pedka accepted the slaps like a philosopher. He was
accustomed to them. A little later he heard his mother talking
with the other peasant women. Such queer stories they told!
There was one about a child who had been lured into a cellar
by some Jews on the eve of Passover. They kept him there
a day and a night and were just about to begin torturing him
when people heard the screams of the child, came running
from all directions, and rescued him. His body had already
been pierced on four sides in the sign of the cross. The woman
who told the story was a heavy, red-faced, blustering creature
in a wide headdress. The other women in their brightly colored
kerchiefs, stood around her in a circle, listening to the story,
shaking their heads and crossing themselves. "Poor child,
they said, "Poor little thing." And some of the women looked
at him—at Pedka. And Pedka couldn't understand why they
looked at him so strangely and what the story had to do with
him and with Feitel. He could not understand why his father
Kurachka had pulled him by the hair and slapped him in the
bargain. He didn't enjoy hair pullings and slaps, but they
didn't bother him too much. What did bother him was the
reason for these things. Why—on this day of all days? Why?

"Well?" Feitel heard his father say joyfully to his mother the morning after Passover, as though some great good fortune had come to him. "You were afraid, just like a woman. Our Passover is gone, their Passover is gone, and nothing has happened."

"God be thanked," his mother answered, and still Feitel did not understand what his mother had been afraid of. And why they were so happy that Passover was gone. Wouldn't it have been much better if it had lasted and lasted? That afternoon when Feitel met Pedka outdoors he blurted everything out. He told how they had celebrated Passover and what good things they had to eat, and he described what all the good Passover dishes tasted like, and how sweet the wine was that they had drunk. Pedka listened solemnly, then looked inside Feitel's blouse. He was still dreaming about the *matzo* he had tasted the other day. Suddenly a shrill voice was heard calling, "Hvedka—H-vedka!"

That was Pedka's mother calling him for dinner. But he was in no hurry. This time he wouldn't have his hair pulled. In the first place they were not at the mill. And in the second place it was "after Passover." After Passover they did not have to be afraid of the Jews. And he lay on the grass on his stomach with his flaxen head between his hands and opposite him lay Feitel also on his stomach with his dark head between his hands. The sky was blue, the sun was warm and a soft breeze played about their heads. The calf stood nearby and so did the rooster with all his wives. And the two young heads, the fair one and the dark one, were propped up facing each other and the boys talked and talked and talked . . .

Nachman was not at home. Early in the morning with his stick in his hand he had gone out over the countryside looking for something to buy. He stopped at every house. He greeted each peasant with a friendly good morning, calling each one by name, and talked about everything under the sun except what had happened the day before Passover and the terror that had lasted all through Passover. And before leaving he touched the peasant's wagon. "Do you have something you don't need, neighbor?"

"Nothing, Lachman."

"Some metal, millet, anything at all? A skin maybe?"

"Believe me, Lachman, I don't have a thing. Times are hard."

"Hard? You must have drunk everything up. A holiday like that."

"I—drink—on a holiday? These are hard times, I tell you."

The peasant sighed and Nachman sighed with him. Then they talked about other things so that it wouldn't look as if he had come to buy anything.

From this peasant's house he went to that of another and then to a third, till at last he found something, so that he shouldn't have to come home empty-handed.

Nachman Verebivker, loaded down and sweating, hurried home with his long strides and thought of only one thing: how much could he earn, how much could he lose . . .

He had completely forgotten the Passover incident. He had completely forgotten the Passover terror. And Kurachka and his governors and his decrees had fled his mind. He had forgotten about them completely.

Let the winds blow. Let the storms rage. Let the world turn upside down. An old oak that has been standing since the beginning of time whose roots are sunk deep in the earth cares nothing about winds. He pays no heed to storms . . .

The Lottery Ticket

BENYOMCHIK—that boy of mine—is a regular lottery ticket."

That is the way Yisroel, the *shammes* at the old synagogue, described his young son, Benjamin, who was known in our town as a promising lad when he was still a pupil in Yarachmiel-Moishe's *cheder*. Yarachmiel-Moishe could not praise him highly enough.

"Your youngster," he said to Yisroel the *shammes* one morning in the synagogue, "is one of the best boys I have. He is a hard worker—a very hard worker. And the understanding he has! The memory! Oh-ho!"

The "Oh-ho" Yarachmiel-Moisne sang out with such enthusiasm that Yisroel the *shammes* glowed with pride.

"May God grant you health and fortune for these words," Yisroel said to the teacher and helped him put away his *tallis* and *tfillin*. This he did out of gratitude for the teacher's praise of his son. For the lessons the boy received Yisroel paid the same amount that all the other parents did—two *rubles* a quarter besides the usual presents at *Hannukah* and *Purim,* although Yisroel supported his own family on little more than the *Hannukah* and *Purim* gifts that others gave him.

Afterwards, when Benyomchik had gone through all of Yarachmiel-Moishe's classes, Yisroel the *shammes* wanted very much to send him to Eli-Maier, the *Gamorah* teacher, but Eli-Maier would not take him. In the first place, his school was

347

already full. In the second place, Yisroel could not begin to pay what the well-to-do householders did. So Benyomchik did what many other boys do. If they have nothing to pay with, they study by themselves. That's what we have a large synagogue for, with a lot of bookstands, and candle-ends salvaged from memorials for the dead, and books—all the books one needs: Bibles, the tracts and commentaries, and whatnot. If a person only wants to, he can study anywhere, even in an attic. Do you know how many great people, scholars of renown, grew up among us that way, bent over tiny candle-ends in the synagogue? And how many more we might have had by now—holy men of genius, *Talmudists* and *Kabalists*—we cannot even guess.

But something happened: in the last forty or fifty years a ray of wordly light has stolen into our corner of the earth and has reached even into our very synagogues, even there where the impoverished lads sat with their tomes. There you found them secretly snatching their first taste of secular food, some rhetoric as an appetizer, then swallowing—or choking over—a Russian grammar, with maybe a few chapters of a novel for dessert. From studies like these, naturally, no *Talmudic* scholars or famous rabbis emerged. Instead, Jewish youths wandered off into the world and were ruined, became doctors, lawyers, writers of prose and verse, teachers—and plain non-believers. Not a single rabbi who was worth anything. That is, there were a number of rabbis. But what kind? Crown rabbis wished onto us by the czar, whether we wanted them or not. As if he had said, "Here is a loaded bomb; hold on to it." But let us proceed . . .

Benyomchik did not study in the synagogue all alone. He had two companions, penniless boys like himself, and that was how the trouble started. One man by himself cannot do wrong as easily as he can with others. It was always that way.

Look at Adam. So long as he walked in the Garden alone, all was still and heavenly. But as soon as Mother Eve appeared, all was changed. She talked him into eating of the fruit of the Tree of Knowledge, and who knows what more she would not have done if they had not been driven out in time?

It was the same with Benjamin. If Benjamin had sat alone in the synagogue, all would have been well. But he studied together with these comrades, boys as naked and barefoot, as hungry and thirsty as himself; and together they longed for the large, bright world, the world of wisdom and knowledge. They sat at the table, bent over the yellowed pages, but their thoughts were far away, among the great of the earth, among the learned ones, the fortunate ones. It pulled and dragged at them like a magnet—this outside world. So was it strange that one Saturday night three boys left their study table in the synagogue—Itzik, Yossil and Benyomchik—and disappeared? They were hunted everywhere, all over town, in every corner and hole, but they were gone without a trace. Well, the other two lads, Itzik and Yossil, were waifs, orphans without father or mother. Whom did they run away from? But Benyomchik! Yisroel the *shammes* turned the town upside down, searched everywhere, and calmed down only on the following day, when a letter came from the three boys, asking everybody not to worry; they were, bless the Lord, safe and sound. They had become aware (that is how they wrote) that here in the synagogue there was no future for them, and therefore they had gone off to attend a seminary, a *yeshiva,* in Vilna or Volozhin or Mir. They had cleverly listed all three seminaries so that no one should know where to go and look for them.

But all that was unnecessary. No one ran after them. The town itself was in fact happy about it. In the first place, it meant that there would be two or three fewer people to keep alive—you could not let them starve to death. And in the second place, it was such a fine thing to see poor boys who wanted to become educated. If all the others in the town could only have done it, they would have gone off somewhere too, rather than stay here and struggle for a living.

Whatever happened to the two other lads—Itzik and Yossil—no one knows, but after about six months Yisroel the *shammes* got a letter from Benyomchik—not from Volozhin, not from Vilna and not from Mir, but from another large city. He told them not to worry because at last he was on the right path, some day he would amount to something—if only, with the help of God, he succeeded in passing his examinations to enter the *gymnasium.* He wanted to prepare himself for the study of medicine and when he became a doctor he would be able to make a good living and could then support his father and mother in their old age. His father would not have to work so hard any more, being a *shammes,* and his mother a *shammeste.*

"And there is one thing, my dear and loyal parents," he wrote, "that you must never worry about. A person can have all the education there is and still remember his debt to God. I want you to know that I pray every day, that I use the *tfillin,* and wash before meals and say grace before and after I eat—that is, when there is something to eat. Usually we eat every other day, sometimes a piece of dry bread alone and sometimes dry bread with salt water. And when there is nothing at all, we suck a piece of sugar. Sugar is a remedy for hunger, it drives away the appetite. But there is something besides food, and that we have in plenty! Don't forget: we have four grammar texts to go through, and geography and history, and how many other things! Mathematics we won't even talk about. That is too simple. When we were still home we used to study algebra in the synagogue, and the rhetoric books we devoured in those days help us now when we have compositions to write. There is only one thing wrong: we have so far not been able to correct our accent altogether. But that will be done in time. So don't worry; everything will turn out all right. The important thing is not to become discouraged. We must have faith in the Eternal."

When Yisroel the *shammes* received this letter he went at once to Yarachmiel-Moishe the *melamed,* an old colleague, an honest man and a confidant.

"Do me a favor," he said. "Read this letter through and answer it. I could have written to him myself, but I am sure you can do it better."

Yarachmiel-Moishe the *melamed* knew very well that the *shammes* was telling a big lie, but you can't make it appear that you know. So he took out his glasses and put them on his nose—a strange pair of glasses, held together by a piece of wire and two pieces of string; lenses there were none—one frame was covered with a circular piece of tin and the other was empty, just a hole.

Yisroel could not resist asking, "What good are these glasses, Rabbi? Can you see anything with them?"

"They're better than nothing, and besides, I'm used to them," Yarachmiel-Moishe answered, and held the letter off at a distance, one eye (the one behind the tin) closed; and with the other he read like water going over a dam, in a loud clear voice, stopping every so often to look at Yisroel as if to say, "How is that for reading?" And Yisroel stood by, his head a little to one side, beaming with joy, as if to say, "And the letter itself—how is that for writing?"

And when Yarachmiel-Moishe took off his glasses and gave him the letter back again, Yisroel asked, "Well, Rabbi, what do you think of it?"

"What can I tell you? It's good. It's very good. He says

that he prays every day, with his *tfillin* too. May it be no worse in the future."

"What I meant was that he is growing up. My Benyomchik is becoming something," said Yisroel. At the tip of his tongue were other words but he was afraid to use them—words like *"gymnasium," "examinations,"* and finally "doctor" itself. So he said, "I'm wondering what to think about it. You said that he was studying to be a—doctor? What do you think of that? What is your opinion, Rabbi? You're a man of experience."

Yarachmiel-Moishe knows that he is a man of experience, but what can he say? Naturally, if it were up to him, he would not have let him study in the *gymnasium*. What does a man like Yisroel want to have a son in the *gymnasium* for? And studying to be a doctor! But he wants advice . . .

Yarachmiel-Moishe looks with glazed eyes at the wall and sighs. The *shammes* understands what the sigh means; he feels a little like that himself, he is not too well pleased with the *gymnasium*. If it were only a *yeshiva* . . . And yet, there was the other side too: his son, Benyomchik—a doctor!

"But, Rabbi, he says he is not forgetting. He prays every day. He is still one of us."

And then, after another pause: "Rabbi, I asked you to do me a favor. Won't you answer the letter? And another thing, Rabbi. You know our town. People love to talk. So I want to ask you: keep it to yourself. You understand?"

"I understand. Of course I understand," said Yarachmiel-Moishe, and once more saddling his nose with the strange glasses, he took a piece of paper, pen and ink, dipped the pen into the ink, and waited for the *shammes* to tell him what to write.

"Tell him this," says the *shammes,* and dictates:

"To my beloved son, Benjamin. To begin with I want to

tell you that we are all, bless the Lord, in the best of health, and may we hear no worse from you now or in the future, Amen. And secondly, tell him that Simma, my wife, and I send our friendliest greetings and ask him to write to us frequently, let us know how he is getting along, and tell him that we wish him all the luck in the world and that he should succeed in his work, and tell him not to worry. God is our father. The main thing is that he should take care of himself, in his health and in his habits and in his prayers: he should remember that he is a Jew. That is the main thing, and tell him that I am sending him a *ruble, a ruble* I'm sending him" (here the *shammes* feels through all his pockets) "and tell him that I would have sent more if I had it, but right now conditions are very bad. I am not earning a thing; no one is dying and no one is getting married and no one is having children. And what else do I make a penny from? I don't remember when there has been a wedding, not one since Reb Hersh married off his youngest daughter. That is, a few weddings there have been, but I am speaking of *real* weddings, weddings worth mentioning . . ."

"Sh-h . . . don't rush like that," says the teacher. "You're pounding away like a post horse. I can't catch up to you . . . Mmmmmm. Well. What next?"

"And tell him further . . . that there is nothing to say. And tell him that I send him my friendliest regards, and Simma, his mother, sends her friendliest regards, and all his sisters too, Pessil and Sossil and Brochele. And remind him to be sure to remember that he is a Jew, not to forget the synagogue. That is the main thing. And when you're through, I'll sign my name to it."

When the teacher had written all this down, Yisroel the *shammes* rolled up his sleeve, took the pen carefully with two fingers and prepared himself for the delicate operation. He spelled out his own name carefully—Y-i-s-r-o-e-l—and the name of his father—N-a-f-t-o-l-i—and the family name—R-i-t-e-l-m-a-n. And while he wrote, his tongue moved from side to side, following his fingers from right to left and from left to right.

It is to be understood that it did not take long for people all over town to learn the secret, that Yisroel the *shammes'* young son was studying, or getting ready to study, to be a doctor. And this did not hurt Yisroel in the least, though there were some people who teased him:

"So you're going to have a doctor in the family—going around bareheaded? With brass buttons, maybe, like a state official? How will that look, Yisroel? I mean for you—like a hen that hatches ducklings . . ."

Yisroel the *shammes* let them talk, and himself said nothing. But deep in his heart he thought: "Laugh, laugh at my Benyomchik! He's still my lottery ticket!"

One day—it was Passover eve—Simma the *shammeste* and her three daughters, Pessil, Sossil and Brochele, were cleaning up for the holiday, when the door opened, and in came a striking young man in a coat with white buttons and an odd-looking cap on his head. He fell on Simma's neck and then on the three girls, hugging and kissing and squeezing them.

The young man was Benjamin.

Simma was so happy she burst out crying. And Yisroel hurried in, frightened and out of breath. He shouted at his wife, "Stop crying, will you! Look how upset she is! Do you know what you're crying about?"

But when he himself had looked the boy over and seen how much he had grown and changed, he almost began to cry too. But a man does not do such things.

"When did you get here?" he asked his son. "Turn around,

let me see what you look like from the back. What kind of suit is that? Take off your coat—why don't you take off your coat?"

And when Benjamin took off his coat and stood there in his blue uniform with silver buttons—his cheeks rosy and his eyes shining—he charmed not only the rest of the family, but everyone who saw him. "What do you think of Yisroel-the-*shammes'* son?" they said. "How he has grown! What a fine looking boy he is!" And Mintzi, the neighbor's daughter, a girl of nineteen with black eyes and a heavy black braid tied with a red ribbon that suited her so well, came in to see if Simma had an extra pot that she could borrow, although she knew very well that in all her life Simma had never had an extra pot. But it gave her a chance to see Benjamin close up, to glance at him with her lively black eyes and to toss her head with the thick black braid and the bright red ribbon—it gave her a chance to turn around and run off, and a little later to come back again under another pretext, until Benjamin's three sisters looked at each other as if to say: "How do you like the way she runs in and out?"

In the meantime Benjamin called his mother aside. "Here is something for *Pesach*," he said, and pushed some money into her hand. Poor Simma! She had never held so much money before in all her life! And for the girls he had presents and presents—ribbons and combs and mirrors and trinkets without number! And for his mother a silk shawl, a yellow one with red and blue flowers. And once more Simma the *shammeste* burst out crying.

And Yisroel asked with a laugh, "What's all this? How did you ever get so much money, my boy?"

"Why shouldn't I have money?" asks Benjamin, proudly. "I'm earning money now, bless the Lord. Eight *rubles* a month. I'm a tutor. I have a few children to teach and I get paid for it. I'm in the fifth class at the *gymnasium*. There are eight classes altogether, so in three more years I'll be through. And then—the university, to study medicine."

Benjamin talks and talks, and they all stand around him. They can't take their eyes off him, and they think, "Can that really be Benjamin? That barefoot Benyomchik who used to spend all his time in the synagogue, studying? Eight *rubles* a month . . . eight classes . . . a silk shawl . . . the university . . . doctor . . .

The Lord alone knows if anyone else had such a happy Passover, such a cheerful *seder,* that year. And I am not talking about the wine, or the brandy, or the fish, or the dumplings, or the pudding. I am speaking now of the *Hagadah,* the Passover ceremonial, that Yisroel and Benjamin both chanted, one louder than the other. It was wonderful to listen to! When they came to *"Rabbi Eleazer omer, minayin shekol mako umako,"* and the men both began to sway with a new vigor and struck up a louder tone, Simma, who had been sitting all the time with her eyes on Benjamin, suddenly began to pucker up her lips as if to cry, and the three sisters, Pessil and Sossil and Brochele, seeing her, could control themselves no longer and began to laugh; and seeing them, the others began to laugh too, even Simma herself . . . Ah, what a Passover that was! You can well imagine!

The next morning, the first day of Passover, when Benjamin came to the synagogue, everybody gaped at the boy in the student's uniform with the silver buttons as if he were a strange animal from the jungle. The smallest boys, full of mischief, crowded around him and pointed at him with their fingers and laughed right in his face. But Benjamin stood all the time with his small prayerbook in his hand and prayed. And when he was called up to the *Torah* (Reb Monish, the *gabai,* arranged it in order to please Yisroel) and

Benjamin recited the benediction in a loud clear tone with an accent and an emphasis that one saved for the holidays, the whole synagogue was agog with wonder: "What do you think about Yisroel's young scholar?"

And when they were all ready to leave the synagogue, the rich man of the village, Reb Hersh, turned to the *shammes*. "Yisroel," Reb Hersh said broadly, as a rich man does when he speaks to one of the lesser creatures, looking a little to one side and clearing his throat and nose in a double cough, "Yisroel, ah-h, come here, hm-m, with that young man of yours. Let me—hm-m—take a look at him."

Hearing that Reb Hersh wanted to talk to Yisroel-the-*shammes'* "young scholar" the crowd gathered around to hear what the rich man would say and what the other would answer. Benjamin approached Reb Hersh as if he were an equal, not at all self-consciously, greeted him like an acquaintance of old, and Reb Hersh looked him over from head to foot, not quite knowing how to start. Should he address him in the respectful plural—a child like that? That would be showing too much respect for the son of the *shammes*. And yet, to use the singular, to say *du,* as you might say, "Hey, there . . ."—maybe that would not be right either. After all, he was a *gymnasium* student with silver buttons, he looked almost like a young prince . . . So at last he spoke to him neither one way nor the other, but vaguely and impersonally: "How are things? When did the visitor come? When is he going back?"

Benjamin put his right foot forward. With one hand he toyed with a button at his chest, with the other he stroked his upper lip. And he answered every question—confidently, without any shame or hesitation. Reb Hersh liked it—and yet he did not like it. "Not a foolish lad at all, but he doesn't know his place." And he became involved in a broad discussion about his school: "How many classes are there? What is the significance of eight classes? Why not nine? And what is the difference between one class and another?"

And Benjamin thought: "He looks so important, and yet he is such an ox!" And he gave him to understand what the difference was between one class and another. Reb Hersh did not like this at all, having a child explaining things to him, and making it sound so simple that it needed no explanation. He said, "Why, everybody knows that. But what is the sense of having eight classes instead of nine?"

"Simply because if there were nine classes, you would say: Why should there be nine and not ten?"

At this the crowd begins to laugh, that is, everybody laughs except Reb Hersh. He thinks: "A tramp—that's all he is." And with his double cough he says, "Hm-m. It's time to go home. Hm-m . . ."

If you did not see Yisroel the *shammes* then, standing a little to one side, looking from one to the other and swallowing each word of Benjamin's, you have never seen a happy and fortunate man. He was waiting for Reb Hersh to stop questioning his son so he could take him home, where the women were waiting anxiously. On the table, the fresh crisp *matzos* were also waiting, and in the oven a delicious Passover borsht was simmering, and hot *kneidlach* with chicken fat, and maybe even a potato pudding! And at last when Reb Hersh had coughed his double cough again and gone off with a few of his close friends, Yisroel the *shammes* invited his one and only good friend and confidant, Yarachmiel-Moishe the teacher, to come along with them, as the others had gone with Reb Hersh, for a glass of wine. And when they arrived he poured out for the old teacher a glass of genuine raisin wine, and Simma brought in such wonderful *chremzlach* that it would have been hard even for an epicure to tell if there was more honey in them or more chicken fat, because they were so sugary and so rich that they stuck to the gums and ran down his beard. Yarachmiel-Moishe, a quiet man, who rarely said a word, now at the first glass of genuine raisin wine found his head whirling round and his tongue running loose and wild. He called Benjamin over to him, and put him through a quick but thorough examination of the Scriptures and commentaries that he had once studied in his *cheder*.

Benjamin remembered not only the Scriptures, but the commentaries as well, so thoroughly that Yisroel the *shammes'* heart almost burst with pleasure. He followed the teacher out through the door. "What do you think of him?" he asked.

"A perfect vessel—a saint!" answered Yarachmiel-Moishe, puckering his lips and shaking his head.

"But a Jew all the same? He hasn't forgotten that?" said the *shammes,* and watched the teacher's eyes for the answer.

"With God's help," said the teacher.

"A lottery ticket! A lottery ticket! Do you agree with me?"

At this Yarachmiel-Moishe tossed his head—it was hard to tell if it was a nod or a shake—blinked his eyes and made a gesture with his hands that meant that he thought the boy either was, or was not, a lottery ticket.

"A good day!" he cried, and once more kissed the *mazuza.* "May God keep us alive and well another year, and may we come to each other in joy—for your daughters' weddings and then your son's—and may the Jews have some relief from all their troubles, may there be good news for all of us, it's time that God had mercy on us, improved our lot, lightened our load . . . And may all things be good everywhere, and cheer in every heart. And—ah . . ."

Yarachmiel-Moishe himself did not know what more he wanted. It seemed as if he had already poured out everything that was on his mind. He stood with his tongue out, unable to say one thing or another . . . Yet how can a man go away like this, without a word of farewell of any kind? Fortunately he remembered one more thing:

"And may—may the Messiah come soon!"

"Amen!" answers Yisroel the *shammes,* and in his heart he thinks: First let my Benjamin graduate as a doctor. And *then* let the Messiah come.

As cheerful and bright as everything was at Yisroel the *shammes'* when Benjamin arrived, so was it dark and gloomy when he went away again.

And the three years passed, the three years before Benjamin could enter the university. It was not an easy time. Yisroel the *shammes* experienced one trouble after another at home, and his son Benjamin over there in the city. Many a night Yisroel could not fall asleep here, and Benjamin his son there. Yisroel could not sleep because he kept thinking of the difficult time Benjamin had, of all the hard work he had to do. And Benjamin could not sleep because he was getting ready for his examinations.

"If God helps me and I pass my examinations," Benjamin wrote home, "I'll come to see you again, my dear and faithful ones, and be with you all summer to rest my bones."

And Yisroel the *shammes* waited for the good news of the examination as a pious Jew waits for the Messiah.

At last summer came, but Benjamin did not. His letters began to come less and less often, and as time went on they became shorter and more gloomy. All he ever said was that on such and such a day he would have to take this or that examination.

"The next examination," wrote Benjamin in his last letter, "is my Day of Judgment, because if I get less than a ninety-four I shall not be able to get in, and if I can't get in now I shall have to stay over another year. And who knows what will happen next year? Maybe next year it will be even worse. What will I do then? What will happen to me? Why did I ever have to work so hard, wear myself out like this? Study so hard, starve day after day, freeze in unheated rooms and spend so many sleepless nights? I am not the only one to ask these questions. There are many others like me—Jewish boys—who stayed over from last year and can't get in because their average is not quite high enough. I don't know what I shall do . . ."

Yisroel the *shammes* went around in a daze. He could not understand why Benjamin's letters suddenly should have become so melancholy. He asked Yarachmiel-Moishe to write to Benjamin and ask him what he meant by "average" and "ninety-four." In short, he asked Benjamin to write and explain everything, and not to worry, but rely on the Eternal One who could do everything. And the main thing still was that he should remember he was a Jew, and if the Lord willed, all would be well . . .

But this letter was never answered, and neither were all the others that Yisroel sent later. But he kept writing and writing, until at last, ashamed to come again to Yarachmiel-Moishe, he gave up writing.

"What can be the matter?" Simma asked her husband. "There has been no letter for such a long time."

And she got an answer: "What do you expect? Is that all he has to do? Write letters? Wait a little. Let him finish his examinations, whatever they are, and then he'll write!"

But Yisroel himself went around with a heavy heart and low spirits. He could not find a place to turn. What went through his head during those days, may no other father ever know. And his dreams every night were frightful and horrible, with black canopies, black candles, everything black . . .

Have you ever heard of Lemel the *starosta?* Or is this the first time you have heard his name? In addition to being the *starosta,* the mayor, a man of substance and influence, what in plain Yiddish we refer to as a soup-ladle, right here in town, he was also a power of some sort in the provincial capital, knew all the important people, dealt with them, was intimate with them. Whenever he comes to the capital, he says, he never knows where to go first. Everybody wants to drag him off to himself. *"Pan* Lemel!" shout the Poles. *"Gospodin* Lemel!" plead the Russians. *"Reb* Lemel, you're ours!" say the Jews. He simply does not know what to do! And every time that he comes back from the capital he has news to oring, something startling to talk about for the next three months. A sensational bankruptcy, a terrible fire, a murder to make your hair stand on end. And although Lemel's bankruptcies took place too often, his fires and murders almost every week, it never occurred to anyone to contradict him. They knew he could not help it—he liked to talk, to tell stories, and if necessary, to make them up himself.

So you can imagine what a time our *starosta* had when an envelope came to his office from the provincial capital with a document instructing him to remove from the rolls of the Jewish community the name of Benjamin, son of Yisroel Ritelman, because of the fact that he had assumed another faith.

As soon as Lemel the *starosta* finished reading the message he forgot all his work and ran out into the street with the paper, stopped everyone he saw, whispered the secret into each one's ear, and soon had the story spread all over town.

No doubt you have heard of the halcyon days. The skies are clear, there is no breeze, not a drop of rain, everything is quiet, serene. The people are asleep, the town itself looks dead. Suddenly, no one knows how or where, something explodes, like a bomb from the sky, like an earthquake. The people awaken, start to run. They run this way and that. "What is it? Where? What happened?"

The story of Yisroel-the-*shammes*' son was like that bomb. It tore the town to pieces and woke up everybody. They were all as upset and excited as if this had to do with their own health or livelihood, as if this were the only thing they had to worry about. Some dropped their work, others left the table with their food untouched and went off to the marketplace to see what was going on. Around Reb Hersh's house there stood a whole ring of people, and Reb Hersh himself stood by the porch in a gabardine and skullcap, surrounded by his kinsmen, intimate friends, acquaintances, total strangers—men who catered to him, scraped and bowed and showed their respect for the man who might be able to do them a favor some time. Reb Hersh held forth and his followers echoed:

"Of course! Naturally! That's right, Reb Hersh!"

And Reb Hersh went on:

"A *shammes,* a ne'er-do-well, a pauper—and he wants to be better than anyone else! He has a son, so what does he have to become? A doctor. Nothing less. And if he became a *shammes* like his father, or, heaven spare us, a teacher, what would happen then? I'd like to hear what our *shammes* has to say now. Or maybe he doesn't know yet. I don't see him anywhere around? Where can he be?"

Where was he? There were some in the crowd who did not hesitate to hurry off to the synagogue to look for him. And some even went to his home, but they could not find him anywhere.

And the truth is that Yisroel knew nothing about it. At that moment, when all the town was in an uproar, Yisroel was sitting with his one and only good friend and confidant, Yarachmiel-Moishe the teacher. In the same mail that brought the document to the town hall there was a large envelope for Yisroel himself, and it was from his son. It was the longest letter that had ever come from Benjamin. With great difficulty he had read through a couple of pages, but had understood little more than a word here and there. So he took it to Yarachmiel-Moishe.

"It's here!" he shouted from the doorway, with joy.

"A letter from your son?"

"And what a letter! It's like a cushion!"

When he heard these words, Yarachmiel-Moishe told his pupils to take a rest, and he himself put on the glasses we had seen before, and began to read the letter in a loud, clear voice, almost a chant. At the start all was well, but soon he began to halt and stutter, as if he were walking over pointed rocks. He came upon hard, strange words he had never seen before. He had to set his glasses straight, he held the letter up to the window, shrugged his shoulders, chewed his words, muttered, "Hm-m . . . What language is this? Nation . . . emancipation . . . quota . . . he's beginning to use strange words, that son of yours . . ."

Yisroel sat at the end of the table, holding his head in his hands, and looked only at Yarachmiel-Moishe, listened to every word, tried to catch the meaning—and made nothing of it. He could not begin to understand why suddenly Benjamin should have to defend himself, try to justify himself, insist with so many oaths that he was the same person as before, that what he had done was out of greater love and greater loyalty . . . Yisroel could not understand why he should be any different now, and why he should ask his forgiveness.

What was there to forgive? "But it could not have been other-wise," he wrote. "I have struggled so long with myself. I know the pain I am giving you, but the fight I have carried on since childhood for an education, my need, my desire for learning has become so great, so strong, that I *finally yielded*."

"What? What was that? Read it again, read it once more. What did he say?"

Yarachmiel-Moishe adjusted his glasses to read it again, but just then the door was pushed open and in came Bassya-Hinda, the teacher's wife, a tall gaunt woman with a sallow face, carrying a large market basket. In the basket were all sorts of good things—potatoes and onions, two black radishes, a small piece of beef-lung that she had barely managed to coax from the butcher, because there are always customers by the hundred who want beef-lung. Women fight over it as men do over the greatest honors at the synagogue, and the reason is this: it costs so little and there are no bones in it, and if you cook it with potatoes and onions and a lot of pepper and it simmers long enough, it tastes quite well . . .

Coming in and seeing the *shammes* sitting with her husband and reading something, Bassya-Hinda took a quick glance to see if the poor *shammes* knew already. But she could not tell from their faces, so she put the basket down, and while she wiped her face with her hand, winked at her husband.

" 'Chmiel-Moishe, come here," she said, and he, seeing that she wanted to say something to him, took off his glasses and excused himself for a minute. And there on the other side of the doorway, this conversation took place between husband and wife:

She: Does he know?

He: Who?

She: The *shlimazl*.

He: Which *shlimazl*?

She: The *shammes.*
He: Know what?
She: About his son.
He: Which son?
She: Benjamin.
He: What about him?
She: The whole town is full of it.
He: Full of what?
She: His son.
He: But what about?
She: Oh, you make me tired!

The Lord knows how long this conversation would have dragged on, if at this point the *shammes* himself had not forced his way into the room and in a frightened voice, asked, "What—what are you saying? What did you say Benjamin did? What?"

Bassya-Hinda did not know what to do now. Why should she be the one to tell him? Better send him straight to Lemel the *starosta,* let him take care of it himself.

"Nothing," she said, wiping her face again. "What do I know? They say a paper came in. I don't know—something about your son."

"What kind of paper?"

"Something. In the town hall."

"Who has it—the paper?"

"The *starosta.*"

"What is it about?"

"Your Benjamin. Something."

"What's the matter with Benjamin?" he asked, this time angrily. "What happened to him?"

"I should know? Ask me! Go over there, go to Lemel. He's somewhere in the marketplace. He has the paper."

Paper . . . Lemel . . . the town hall . . . Benjamin . . .

what did all this mean? Yisroel felt his cheeks grow hot and
he heard a whistling in his ears. He pulled down his cap, bent
over double, and stumbled out . . .

There are people who love to watch a person in agony, who
stare at him when he weeps, look after him when he follows
a corpse at a funeral, stand by when he wrings his hands.
I do not care for such scenes. Say what you will, I don't like
mournful pictures. My muse does not wear a black veil on her
face. My muse is a poor—but cheerful one . . .

Where did Yisroel run? Whom did he see? What did he
hear? What did he say? Do not ask, it will give you no joy
to know. What will you have gained, for instance, when you
have learned that there were people who finally lived to
have revenge on Yisroel the *shammes,* who had gone around
so long showing off his lottery ticket?

"He had it coming," said Reb Hersh, with his peculiar
double-cough, and stroked his paunch comfortably. "It should
be a lesson for people. A pauper should be careful how he
jumps in your face. A doctor he had to have . . ."

Others, it is true, had pity on the *shammes,* "poor fellow"—
and you know what that means. My grandfather Minda had
a saying, "Look out for people who pity you, and God protect
you from those who call you 'poor fellow.'"

So I won't tell you what Yisroel did or whom he saw, but
it was dusk when he turned in at his cottage, looking like
a ghost. Entering without a word, he sat down on the ground,
took off his boots, tore his shirt at the heart as one does for
the dead, and prepared to sit in mourning for an hour, as one
does at a time like that. Simma did the same, and so did the
three sisters. Together they sat on the ground, moaning and
weeping for the one they had lost.

Later, when Yarachmiel-Moishe the teacher came to offer

condolence, this is what he found: Yisroel sitting with his head thrown forward between his knees, Simma with her hands covering her face and Pessil, Sossil and Brochele sitting with red swollen eyes, each one looking with expressionless face into a separate corner, as if in their shame and pain they could not face each other openly.

He came into the house quietly without a greeting of any kind, as one does in a house of mourning, and slowly lowering himself to the edge of a bench at one side of the room, sighed. That was all. He didn't say a word. A little later, another sigh, and again silence; and later still a sigh again. It was only after a while that he looked around and decided that it was not right to sit there and not say a word, he ought to say something to comfort them. But what was there to say? When a family is in mourning because a person has died, you can come to sit with them for a while, and say, "The Lord giveth and the Lord taketh away." Or, "Man is, after all, like a fly." Or, "Death—that is something none of us can escape." Or, "Vanity of vanities, all of us will die." Or other such sayings that cannot make one especially happy, but are still a comfort. If a person says something, gets it off his chest, he feels a trifle better. But what can one say at a time like this, when it is a living person they are mourning for? Yarachmiel-Moishe turned a little on his bench with a shy cough, wanted to say something, but the words would not come. He tried a few different times, till finally he started again and it worked. And now he was unable to stop, he did not know where or how to end it.

"Ah, well, it's the same story as always. What can you call it—a trial from heaven, from the Lord. For everything is from Him; without Him nothing is done, nothing occurs, not a finger here on earth is lifted. He is a real Master, let

us agree on that. Oh, what a Master! And we obey Him—
how we obey Him! . . . So it was decreed that this had
to happen, exactly as it happened. And here is the proof: that
if it did not have to happen this way, it would not have happened. But it did happen, so it must have been ordained.
If He had wanted something else to happen, it would have
happened the other way. It would have . . ."

Yarachmiel-Moishe began to feel that he did not know
what he was saying, so he paused, took a pinch of snuff, lowered his head to one side, and heaved a deep sigh. He told
himself that it was time to go, but talking about going is an
easy matter. How are you going to do it, though, if you
are glued to the bench? There is no visit that is worse than
one to a house of mourning. You are supposed to leave without a word of parting, without a sign or a look. But how
can you do it? Yarachmiel-Moishe sat waiting for a miracle
to happen. If only they would doze off a little so he could
leave while they slept. Or if something happened outside, a
riot, a fire—anything—so he could escape in the excitement.
He sat looking around at the ceiling, at the four walls, and
then he said to himself: "It is time to think about going.
The children will turn the *cheder* upside down . . ."

When the hour was up, Yisroel and his family rose from
the floor, quietly, without talking, put on their shoes and
crawled off each to his own corner, to his own work. Yisroel
rushed through his late-afternoon prayers and hurried off
to the synagogue to be in time for evening services. After
all, he was the *shammes,* his time was not his own. He had
to be where he was needed. Work—that was the only remedy,
the means of chasing all worries away, of forgetting all
troubles . . .

In the synagogue a few busybodies came up to him.

"What do you hear from your lottery ticket? How is your son getting along?"

"A son? Have I got a son?" answered Yisroel with a bitter little smile.

And seeing the bitterness and the ache in the smile, the meddlers retreated. All they had to do was look at his face and they did not want to talk to him any more about his son.

What happened afterward? What became of Benjamin? Did he write any more letters? And what did he write? And did his father answer him? And if he answered, what did he say? Don't press me with questions. I shall not say a word. I'll tell you only that as far as Yisroel was concerned, there was no Benjamin any more anywhere. Benjamin was dead. In the lottery, Yisroel had drawn a blank.

Cnards

NOWADAYS a game of cards is an everyday affair.
Where don't we play cards nowadays? *When* don't
we play cards? And *who* doesn't play cards nowadays?

There was a time, if you know what I mean, when we used
to play cards only once a year—at *Hannukah*.

That is, if you want the whole truth, people used to get
together for a game in those days too—a real game, a hot game!
But where? In a secret chamber, behind locked doors.

In winter, in *cheder,* between the late-afternoon and evening
prayers, when the rabbi was at the synagogue warming himself
by the stove and we were left alone; or in summer, in a dark
corner of the stable, near a thin crack in the wall; or at other
times of the year when we bribed Getzel, the *shammes,* and
locked ourselves up in the synagogue, high up in the women's
balcony, turned a lectern face down for a table, and dealt out
a hand of *Starshy Kozir* or Thirty-one or Turtle-myrtle.

One day Riva-Leah, the *gabai's* wife, of blessed memory (she
has gone to her rest these many years) found a strange object in
her lectern and almost fainted dead away. Who could have
planted a thing like that—in her lectern?

Aghast, she ran out of the synagogue into the street, shouting
at the top of her voice:

"Help, fellow Jews! Help! A misfortune has come to pass!
A calamity! A plot! Come with me and I'll show you!"

What was the calamity and what kind of a plot? You

couldn't get any answer from Riva-Leah. Only this: "Come, come with me and I'll show you!"

And before long she had drawn around her a fine assemblage, consisting of the rabbi, the *shochet,* a few of the elders, and the cantor, together with a liberal sprinkling of our secular aristocracy.

Naturally, when the rest of the people saw Riva-Leah proceeding up the street followed by the rabbi, the *shochet,* a few of the elders and the cantor and so many of our leading citizens, they joined the procession too. And then the women and boys, and the little children, torn by curiosity, fell in behind, and together they marched into the synagogue. At the head, came Riva-Leah, and behind her, the townspeople.

You can imagine what a terror gripped the town. People thought—it must be something serious. Either someone had left a foundling, or some poor wretch had been found hanging from the rafters, or, God forbid, someone had been murdered.

Worried and frightened, they clattered up to the women's balcony—Riva-Leah first, followed by the rabbi, the *shochet,* the cantor, with the rest of the town after them.

"Where—where is it?" the crowd asked Riva-Leah, and listened for the cry of the foundling and looked for the hanging body or the trail of blood leading to the corpse that some unknown enemy had left there to bring trouble on our town.

And then imagine how astounded they all were when, instead of a foundling or a bleeding corpse, they found this strange and ominous object in Riva-Leah's lectern: a picture of a bearded man—obviously a Russian Orthodox priest—with an odd black cross at his side. And not just one priest, but two priests and two crosses, one priest upright, and the other one standing on his head . . .

They all bent down and peered into Riva-Leah's lectern: first the rabbi, then the *shammes,* then the *shochet* and the elders

and the cantor; then the leading citizens; then the common
people. They looked and drew away. For to touch the thing
with their hands—for that no one was bold enough. That is,
no one except one man, Velvel Ramshevitch, the cantor's son-
in-law.

When Velvel Ramshevitch looked and saw what it was his
face lit up, and then with a laugh, he cried, "It's nothing!
What's there to get excited about? It's just the king of clubs!"

"And what is the king of clubs?"

"A card. A card—that you play with."

"How did it get here?" they wanted to know. "In the lectern of Riva-Leah, the *gabai's* wife, in the women's balcony
of the synagogue? That's one thing. And the other is, how
does it happen that you, the cantor's son-in-law, know what
a card is, and that it's called the king of clubs? And that it's
a game that people play?"

At this our Velvel realized that he had fallen into a trap.
And he turned every color imaginable and began to babble and
to bleat, make sounds like a sheep or a goat, sounds that no one
could understand, no human being, at any rate . . .

But that is not the story I started to tell. It is only an introduction to our tale about cnards. I merely wanted to show
you what a forbidden thing cards used to be and how carefully
we had to hide our knowledge of them.

There was only one lucky week in the year when we could
play cards freely and openly.

That was the week of *Hannukah.*

And freely and openly we gathered that week at Velvel
Ramshevitch's house. He was a free soul even then: he had
shaved his beard and sidelocks, smoked on Saturdays on his
front porch where all could see, and ate pork sausage—even on
fast days! And he dared anyone to criticize him.

And his wife, Chayela, the cantor's daughter, imitating him, threw away the wig that all respectable married women wore in those days and went about in her own yellow hair; sprinkled powder over her pockmarked face and spent all her time with a gay young crowd, laughing and making merry—showing everybody her large, stained teeth.

The Chapel—that was what we all called Ramshevitch's house—was open to all the young people in town. There we could read a newspaper or a secular book, there we could smoke a cigarette on the Sabbath, nibble at sausage on fast days, and—most important of all—play a game of cards.

They both loved a good game of cards, and if anything she loved it even more than he did. She could hardly keep away from the table. It was even rumored that they made their living that way, for it was obvious that she was always winning. No matter who dealt she always had trumps. She beat everybody. There was nothing we could do about it.

As you remember, in those days many young men were supported by their fathers-in-law while they themselves went on with their holy studies. And in our town, because of this same Chayela with the blond hair and pockmarked face, more than one such son-in-law gambled away his entire dowry and his wife's pearls, and even drove his father-in-law into bankruptcy.

With one such son-in-law, in fact, she once played through a whole winter, and before she was through with him he had divorced his wife, a wonderful girl, a beauty, and come to live with the Ramshevitches. No use telling you what a scandal it made in our town. Everybody was horrified.

But that is still not the story of cnards that I started to tell. It is only the introduction to the scene of the story which took place in the Chapel I have mentioned—the Ramshevitch home —on the first night of *Hannukah*.

As I was saying, it was the first night of *Hannukah*. We were all sitting in the Chapel, playing our favorite Jewish card game, a real *kosher* game of Okeh.

And we played, as usual, in shifts. One group finished a game and the next group sat down to play. It was that way all the time. One group played in the morning, another in the afternoon, and a third at night. And one of the Ramshevitches played with each group. Either he—or she—or both. At night, if he was sleeping, she played; and if she was asleep, then he played. And sometimes it happened that one night passed, and two nights, and three nights, and neither of them slept. They both played. Except for a half-hour or so when one of them dropped out between games and took a nap.

That was something all of us learned to do. Whenever we got too tired to play, we found something to lean against and dozed off.

It was the same with eating. On the table there was always a bottle and a small glass, herring and sausage. And when you were hungry you took a few minutes off and ate.

Naturally, you understand, we paid for all this. At each game part of the winnings were taken out for "the maid," though in the Chapel there never had been a maid. The Ramshevitches did not need a maid. There was no cooking to do, no beds to make—and no house to clean. There was no time for these things. So what did they need a maid for? Nevertheless with every hand the few cents were put aside and all of us knew that this went for rent and heat, for new decks of cards, and for food. Human beings must eat. And this I can say: there was as much to eat and drink as any of us ever wished for.

And it was the same with cigarettes. Whole boxes full of cigarettes. And whoever wanted to reached for one. And the Ramshevitches smoked more than anybody; and she smoked more than he did. I cannot imagine Chayela Ramshevitch without a cigarette in her mouth. Add to this the powdered pockmarked face and the uncombed blond hair, with the tired, puffy eyes. And the rooms thick with smoke, and the noise and the tumult. Think of all these together and you can picture to yourself what the Chapel looked like at *Hannukah,* when we could play cards openly and freely and we did not have to hide ourselves, or worry about being seen by any of the good people of the town.

That day—I am now coming to the story of the cnards—I was on the third shift. That is, I was one of the group that sat down to play in the evening, when the second candle was lit, and didn't get up until it was time for the third candle the next evening.

It was not the host—Velvel Ramshevitch—who lit the *Hannukah* candles that evening, but one of the guests, an elegant specimen—Eli Rafalski, one of those sons-in-law I mentioned earlier, who loved a card game more than almost anything else in the world, but who, nevertheless, had not strayed from the path in matters of Godliness. That was one thing you could say about the Ramshevitches: they didn't ask you what you were. You could be as pious as you wanted to be: so long as you had something in your pocket, and you played Okeh, and there was room at the table for another hand, you were welcome to sit down with us and were an honored guest! May my enemies have as many plagues and I as many lucky years as the number of times we played with people five nights and five days in succession, and then broke up without ever knowing who they were or what they were or where they had come from. A game of cards is not a marriage contract. You can play a very good game without knowing your opponent or his pedigree.

Well, there we were, sitting around the table, so absorbed in our work that we did not notice that two strangers had come

in, men so unusual and odd in appearance that when we heard
their "Good evening," and looked up at them, we were struck
motionless and dumb.

Perhaps you want to know what they looked like to have
frightened us so? I'll describe them to you as well as I can, and
briefly.

One of them was a tall man—long and thin—in a long, black
silken coat; earlocks—long and narrow, curly, reaching almost
to his belt; a fur cap on his head; and a long beard and a pair
of whiskers so thick and black that if you had met this man
on a dark night on a deserted road, you'd want to say your
prayers.

The other was just the opposite: short and round, also with
earlocks and with a strange beard and whiskers, but not quite
as overgrown as the other. In one hand he held a lantern and
in the other a kerchief full of money.

Noticing the effect they had on us, the tall, thin one with
the curly earlocks smiled at us gently through his whiskers,
and repeated, "Good evening, my dear people. We have come
here to greet you in honor of *Hannukah*."

And as he spoke he looked around at the *Hannukah* candles
at the far end of the room, then at the table with the cards, and
heaved a deep sigh. His companion, the short, round one,
sighed also. Both of them sought with their eyes for a place to
sit down.

Luckily the host, Ramshevitch, remembered that it was his
duty to be polite, so he got up from the table and shook hands
with the newcomers and asked them to sit down. And the rest
of us followed suit, each one separately, some of us shaking
hands with them and others just nodding from a distance.

The two sat down, looked at each other again, and gave
another deep sigh. And once more the host remembered his
manners.

"What's your name?" he asked, as one always should. "Where are you from? Have you been here long? Where are you going to?"

It was the tall, thin one who answered, in a tone as sweet as honey. Speaking slowly, one word at a time and with a delicate sweet smile that came out of his thick and frightful whiskers (he did not even seem to be talking to us, but looked rather as if he were deep in prayer, in humble communion with the Lord), he said:

"My dear friends, I am the grandchild of the *Bal-Shem-Tov,* the founder of Chassidism. I have but one duty, to wander about the world and collect money for the *yeshivas,* the holy seminaries, both here and in the Holy Land of our fathers."

And he sighed again. "And this is my companion who goes with me everywhere and who guards the contributions." With his eyes he indicated the fat one, and this time both of them sighed deeply. "We have devoted our whole life to the *yeshivas,* in order that God's Law may not be forgotten.

"And so, my friends," he continued, with another sigh, "give us a contribution—whatever you are able. One," he said, nodding his head as if in prayer, "can give more, and another can give less."

And his companion, rolling his eyes aloft, added, "And all who give more, will receive more from Heaven."

And he laid his kerchief full of money on the table with a clang. A corner came open and we could see the glint of silver and gold.

Money, they say, attracts money. Seeing all the money already in the kerchief, we had no choice but to add more from our own pockets, and as we did it each one of us thought (I am sure of it): "Ah, if I had the money in that kerchief! What couldn't I do with it . . ."

Our hostess, Chayela Ramshevitch, could not conceal her

excitement. Her eyes fairly blazed. We were all aware of it, even the *Bal-Shem-Tov's* grandchild and his companion, who was in no apparent hurry to remove the kerchief from her sight. The two continued to sit there with their eyes on the cards scattered around the table, and we could see that this was the first time in their lives that either one of them had seen such a thing.

At last the *Bal-Shem-Tov's* grandchild raised his eyes. "I hope I am not disturbing you, but I'd like to ask a question," he said in his unctuous voice and with his soft, sweet smile, pointing with an extended little finger at one card after another. "What sort of thing is this—on the table here?"

"Why, cards," answered our host and hostess together, with a glance at us that seemed to say, "So there are still people on earth so uncivilized that they don't even know what cards are!"

The *Bal-Shem-Tov's* grandchild shut an eye, wrinkled up his nose and forehead, turned his face toward his companion, and with an unearthly sigh, repeated: "Cnards?"

And his companion, with a sigh of his own, repeated after him, "Cnards."

"No, that's wrong," Chayela Ramshevitch undertook to correct them, without once taking her eyes off the kerchief full of money. "Not cnards—cards!"

Naturally they did not say a word to her, nor did they turn their soft, smiling, clever eyes upon her. They were holy men, and such men, you understand, never glance at a female.

But turning to their host, Velvel himself, the *Bal-Shem-Tov's* grandchild said, "I don't want to disturb you, but tell me— what are these things—these cnards? What are they good for? That is, what do you do with them?"

"You play with them," answered Ramshevitch. "Don't you know? When *Hannukah* comes, people play cards."

Again the *Bal-Shem-Tov's* grandchild shut an eye, and turning his face slowly toward his companion, said:

"When *Hannukah* comes—they play cnards."

"Imagine that," echoed his companion.

"But what does that mean?" asked the *Bal-Shem-Tov's* grandchild, slowly, unctuously. "How does one play with these—cnards? And why? What for?"

"For money," answered Ramshevitch, looking from us to the kerchief on the table.

Apparently this answer sounded wild and meaningless to both of them, for they turned upon each other with such a strange, bewildered expression that all of us burst out laughing.

But our hostess come to their defense. "What is there to laugh at?" she demanded, and lit a cigarette to hide her own laughter. And Ramshevitch helped her out by explaining to them briefly and clearly the meaning and the use of cards; concluding with the observation that cards were both a diversion and a vocation. In short, you could say that cards were a trade. A trade like any other.

And saying this, Velvel the cantor's son-in-law picked up the cards again with a quick glance at all of us to see if we were ready, and to show the meddlers that we were busy and that time was short. Let them stop bothering us; it was time for them to get up and be on their way.

But that was apparently not their intention. On the contrary, they edged still closer to the table and stared at our host who was now shuffling the cards. Their eyes grew large as though they were expecting something to pop out at any minute.

"I hope I am not disturbing you," said the *Bal-Shem-Tov's* grandchild again in his unctuous tone and with his fine sweet smile . . .

"Do you want to watch us play?" Ramshevitch interrupted. "Then go ahead and watch. You can't do us any harm. Well, children! Let's get to work! Time doesn't stand still! Whose deal is it now?"

And the interrupted work was resumed with a new vigor, a new warmth, with skill and cunning; as they say in society, with *éclat*.

And the visitors looked on, listened to every word we said, and studied our hands. And every time that one of us cautiously looked at our covered card, our two guests bent and turned and twisted until they could see the card too, and made such strange faces that it was all we could do to keep from splitting with laughter. It was lucky we were all so absorbed in the game that nothing less than an earthquake could have disturbed us.

I am afraid that I was the only one who really kept an eye on them. From time to time I looked up and I began to think that to them we must look even stranger than they did to us. We and not they were peculiar, involved in a strange pursuit, speaking a wild language and conducting ourselves in general like savages: sitting bareheaded, inhaling smoke, exchanging little squares of paper, throwing money into a plate, and talking to each other in a language that might have been Turkish or Greek. For who could understand the meaning of *pass, deuce, pair, flush, jack, queen, king, ace,* and other such words that belong to the language of cards?

I can swear to you that we had forgotten all about the two holy men in our midst, when suddenly a pale white hand came slapping down on the deck of cards, and we heard these words:

"There! Now we understand it! We've caught on to it! It's a temptation, I tell you! A terrible temptation! The work of the devil himself and all the evil spirits! Do us a favor, please! Give us some too! Oh, what a diabolic invention! I hope the Lord will pardon us. Man is sinful. I beg you, give us some! We want to feel the taste of these cnards too!"

It was the *Bal-Shem-Tov's* grandchild who said this. He said it in such a trembling voice, with such fire and feeling, almost with tears in his eyes, that it almost tore our hearts out. And to our sympathy was added the sight of the kerchief full of gold and silver . . . Each one of us, I am afraid, would have liked the kerchief and what was in it to become his personal property. You should have seen our Chayela Ramshevitch. Her eyes were aflame and her cheeks were flushed, and she said to her husband and to the rest of us:

"They are asking us a favor. Why shouldn't we let them? After all, it's *Hannukah*." And her eyes were on the kerchief with the money which the *Bal-Shem-Tov's* grandchild had now drawn close to him, and from which with trembling fingers he was taking out coin after coin, one for himself and one for his companion, making two even piles of silver, one for each of them. At the same time he murmured to himself apologetically:

"Never mind! We have a great and powerful God! If we win, the *yeshivas* will have more money. And if we should lose, then the Lord will pardon us. He is long-suffering, as Jeremiah so truthfully said."

Thus he spoke, with a glance aloft, and his companion followed him, also with an upward glance and with these holy words:

"Long-suffering and full of kindness and truth."

All of this happened so suddenly, so unexpectedly, that not one of us had time even to be surprised. It seemed as natural as could be. And in addition I must confess that our minds were playing with the kerchief of money and our eyes were fixed on the two piles of silver.

There was only one thing left to decide: which of us should drop out. With two new players added, the question now was, which of us should make room for them. You understand, of course, that none of us was anxious to retire when the rare opportunity presented itself of playing with the grandchild of so holy a man as the *Bal-Shem-Tov,* especially when he had been so thoughtful as to have brought with him a kerchief full of money. And the argument began.

"You go take a rest." "No, you." "Why should I?" "You look tired."

The first to be sacrificed on the altar of hospitality was the pampered son-in-law I have already told you about, Eli Rafalski, the one who a little earlier in the evening had lit the *Hannukah* candles for us. And it was our hostess, Chayela Ramshevitch, who decided that. She insisted that it was time for him to go home. It was late, his wife's parents would complain; they might even create a scandal, and it would get them all into trouble.

That was her excuse, but all of us knew the truth. Eli had lost all he had and no one wanted to let him have any more. In the midst of a game no one loans out money.

That took care of one. For the second we drew lots. And then we went to work. Little by little the two fresh even stacks of silver disappeared, the kerchief became lighter and lighter, while in front of each of us now appeared the funds once destined for the *yeshivas* of all the world. Soon the kerchief was almost empty and it began to look as if the *Bal-Shem-Tov's* grandchild would be lucky if he still had his gabardine to go away in. We were beginning to wonder what would happen if we took their last *kopek* away. What would the town say? What would the whole world say?

But all of you who play the game know the mysterious

quality that cards possess. One minute you're flat on the ground, ready to be carried out in a blanket, and suddenly your luck changes—you don't know yourself how it happened! That's just what happened to our visitors. They began to win hand after hand, especially when the *Bal-Shem-Tov's* grandchild began to deal.

"They are possessed by the devil. Let me have them," he said, taking the cards and beginning to deal them out, at first clumsily and inaccurately, with trembling, inexperienced hands, and eyes that followed each card until it landed. Looking at him we could not suppress our laughter. But as time went on he began to do it faster and faster until the cards sped from his hands in an endless stream. And everything went his way. No matter what cards you had, he had better ones. If you had three jacks, he had three queens. If you had kings, he had aces. If you had aces, he had a flush. And if you became frightened and dropped out with an unpromising pair, he had nothing at all! Until, with a start, he pushed his chair back, sprang to his feet, and stretched himself.

"*Raboisa!*" he cried, gathering up his winnings and stuffing them not into the kerchief but into his own pockets. And then with a glance aloft he sighed, and his companion followed him with the same upward glance and the same sigh, and finished the quotation from the Passover services which the other had started:

"*Masters, the time has come to say the morning prayers!*"

Stunned and sleepy, hungry and depressed, sulking as losers always do, we remained sitting a while, unable to move. Then gradually one by one we got up and went to the table for a drink and a bite to eat. That is, all except our two guests, who were ready to take their leave, and coming to the doorway did not forget to kiss the *mazuza*.

But suddenly our host, Velvel Ramshevitch, jumped in front of them, and spreading our his arms, blocked their way with these words:

"Oh, no! You can't go away from here without taking a bite to eat!"

Velvel could not have imagined a vengeance more complete. Our poor guests stood as though trapped, looking at each other as if we were forcing them to empty their pockets of all their winnings. The first to recover his speech was the *Bal-Shem-Tov's* grandchild, who addressed us once more with his unctuous tone and his sweet little smile:

"We thank you wholeheartedly for your kindness. Hospitality to wayfarers is, according to our Law, one of the greatest of all acts of virtue. But you must not forget that my companion and I are careful about what meat we allow to touch our lips. No doubt it's *kosher,* but . . ."

That was too much for us. "Oh, so you can't eat our food!" we cried. "You're afraid it isn't *kosher* enough for you, but our cards were *kosher* enough? To take our money away was proper enough? No, we won't let you get away with that! You tasted our hospitality at the card table; now you must taste some sausage too!"

Crestfallen, they looked at each other. Then the *Bal-Shem-Tov's* grandchild let out a deep sigh, almost a groan, and said to us. "Just as you say, my friends. After all, we are in a Jewish home, and we must never be suspicions of our own people. And what if the food, heaven forbid, is not as *kosher* as it might be? Our Lord is a great and mighty One . . ."

And murmuring a prayer that none of us could make out, he turned humbly toward the table were our hostess was preparing sardines, herring and sausages. Picking up a glass he turned to us. "Your health, my friends. I drink your health," he said, and lifted the glass and barely moistened his lips.

Then, with a trembling hand he took a bite of herring, and then a thin slice of sausage. His companion followed him, and together they struggled with their food, almost choking on it. And only when they were through did Velvel take his full revenge. Without a trace of pity, he addressed them in these words:

"Do you know what you have just eaten? It was not Jewish food at all. Do you know what kind of sausage that was? Do you know what it was made of? Gentlemen, you have just been eating real, genuine . . ."

Before he could finish the sentence our two visitors clutched their heads in terror, opened their mouths wide as if to spit everything out, and then with a bitter groan sprang for the door and swept out of the house like a cyclone.

Our vengeance was so complete that we almost forgot how much we had lost that night, forgot the depths to which we had sunk, and looking at each other we laughed and laughed and laughed. We thought we would never stop laughing, but we did—and suddenly too—when from the table where we had been playing we heard a shriek that was barely human.

"Quick! Quick! Come here! Oh, may lightning strike me! I can't bear it!"

It was Chayela Ramshevitch. We had not even noticed that as soon as she had finished eating she had gone back to the table to clean things up. First, as always, she gathered up the cards we had played with; they could still be sold or traded for new decks. And in sorting out the cards she had noticed something strange. There were too many aces—far too many. Six or seven to the deck.

We grabbed up the rest of the cards and discovered not only aces but a wealth of everything else as well: kings and queens and jacks, in fact everything! And many of them! Well, we didn't go home to rest as we had planned. Instead, we made a pilgrimage. We went to every synagogue in town, visited every chapel and prayer house. We looked everywhere, searched everywhere, asked everywhere. But no one had seen the *Bal-Shem-Tov's* grandchild and his companion. No one had even heard of them.

Unsuccessful, dejected, we decided to try the railroad station. There we searched everywhere. We went through the station itself, through every carriage in the waiting train. Not a sign of the grandchild or his companion. The earth must have swallowed them both!

It was after the third bell had rung, the last whistle had blown, that we heard a familiar voice from one of the carriages.

"Cnards!"

We sprang toward the carriage from which the word had come. From an open window of a second-class carriage, two strange men were watching us with interest and amusement. One was tall and thin, the other short and fat. Both were clean-shaven, both wore short tailored jackets and derby hats. And yet they were familiar. Not so much the faces as the eyes— soft, smiling, shrewd little eyes.

The first to recognize them was the pampered son-in-law, Eli Rafalski. As soon as he saw their smiling faces he pointed straight at them:

"There they are!" he cried. "There they are! The two cnard players—as sure as my name is Rafalski!"

But the train was already moving. The wheels had just begun to turn. And slowly passing us by, the two men looked at us once more with their soft, smiling shrewd eyes. And for Eli Rafalski, who had been so acute as to recognize them, they had a special farewell.

Together they raised their thumbs to their noses, and made a broad arc with their outstretched fingers.

Glossary*

Al-ḳein n'Kvach l'cho (*Al-ḳen ne Kave lecho*): The beginning of the second part of the prayer *Alenu:* "Therefore we hope . . ."

Bar Mitzvah: A thirteen-year-old Jewish boy who is confirmed; the confirmation ceremony itself.

beigel (*bagel*): Hard circular roll with hole in the center like a doughnut.

blintzes: Cheese or *ḳasha* rolled in thin dough and fried.

bris: Circumcision ceremony.

Bubi-Kama (*Baba Kama*): "First Gate," a Talmudic treatise on compensation for damages.

chad gadyo (*Had Gadya*): "One Kid," an Aramaic nursery song sung at the conclusion of the *Seder* home service on Passover.

Chassidim: Plural of *chassid;* members of a mythical sect founded in the middle of the 18th Century by Rabbi *Bal-Shem.*

cheder: Old-style orthodox Hebrew school.

cholent: Potted meat and vegetables cooked on Friday and simmered overnight for Sabbath eating.

chremzlach: Fried *matzo* pancakes, usually served with jelly or sprinkled with powdered sugar.

datcha: Summer cottage in the country.

dreidel (from the German *drehen,* "to turn"): A small top, spun with the fingers, and played with by children on *Hannuḳah* in East European countries.

dybbuḳ (same as *gilgul*): A soul condemned to wander for a time in this world. To escape the perpetual torments from evil spirits it seeks refuge in the body of a pious man or woman over whom the demons have no power.

eirev (*erub*): The law limiting the movements of the pious and the carrying of objects on the Sabbath, hence also the rope used to define the area of free movement.

---

* Many of the spellings of Hebrew words used in these stories are rendered phonetically as they occurred in popular usage. In such cases, throughout the glossary, the correct transliterated spelling is given in parentheses.

esrog (*ethrog*): A large sweet-smelling citrus-fruit of the lemon family waved together with palm, myrtle and willow branches in the synagogue procession during the Feast of Tabernacles.

fisnoga: Comical combination of the Yiddish *fis* (feet) and the Russian *noga* (feet).

gabai: Synagogue treasurer.

Gamorah (*Gemara*): The Aramaic name for the *Talmud,* i.e. to learn. (See *Talmud*).

gilgul (see *dybbuk*).

gospoda (Russian): Term of address, "Gentlemen!"

gragar: A noisemaking toy used by Jewish children during the *Purim* festival; a rasping chatterbox.

gribbenes: Small crisp pieces left from rendered poultry fat, eaten as a delicacy.

grivnye: Silver coin worth ten *kopeks.*

groschen: Small German silver coin whose old value was about two cents.

gulden: An Austrian silver florin worth about forty-eight cents.

Hagadah: The book containing the Passover home service, consisting in large part of the narrative of the Jewish exodus from Egypt.

hamantash: A triangular pocket of dough filled with poppyseed or prunes and eaten on *Purim.*

Hannukah (*Channukah*): Described variously as "The Festival of Lights," "The Feast of Dedication," and "The Feast of the Maccabees." It is celebrated for eight days from the 25th day of *Kislev* (December). It was instituted by Judas Maccabeus and the elders of Israel in 165 B.C. to commemorate the rout of the invader Antiochus Ephinanes, and the purification of the Temple sanctuary.

haroses: A mixture of nuts and apples to symbolize the clay which the children of Israel worked into bricks as slaves in Egypt. Eaten at the *Seder* services on Passover.

Hashono Rabo (*Hoshana Rabbah*): The seventh day of *Succoth* (Feast of Booths).

Kabala (*Cabala*): Called "the hidden wisdom," mystical, esoteric knowledge that, beginning with the 13th Century, arose in opposition to the rationalism of the *Talmud.*

kaddish: The mourner's prayer recited in synagogue twice daily for one year by the immediate male relatives, above thirteen years, of the deceased.

kasha: Groats.

Kazatsky (*Kazatske*): A lively Russian dance.

kneidlach: Balls of boiled matzo meal cooked in chicken soup.

knishes: Potato or *kasha* dumpling, fried or baked.

kopek: A small copper coin; there are 100 *kopeks* in a *ruble.*

kosher: Food that is permitted to be eaten and prepared according to the Jewish dietary laws.

kreplach: Small pockets of dough filled with chopped meat, usually boiled and eaten with chicken soup.

kugel: Noodle or bread suet pudding, frequently cooked with raisins.

mah nishtano: Literally, "What is the difference?" The first words in the opening "Four Questions" of the Passover *Hagadah,* traditionally asked by the youngest child in the household at the *Seder* service. (See *Seder*).

matzos: Unleavened bread eaten exclusively during Passover to recall the Jewish Exodus from Egypt.

mazl-tov: Good luck!

mazuza (*mezuzah*): Small rectangular piece of parchment inscribed with the passages Deut. VI. 4-9 and XI. 13-21, and written in 22 lines. The parchment is rolled up and inserted in a wooden or metal case and nailed in a slanting position to the right-hand doorpost of every orthodox Jewish residence as a talisman against evil.

Megila (*Megillah*): Literally, "a roll," referring to the *Book of Esther* which is read aloud in the synagogue on *Purim.*

Medresh (*Midrash*): A body of exegetical literature, devotional and ethical in character, which attempts to illuminate the literal text of the Bible with its inner meanings. The *Midrash* is constantly cited by pious and learned Jews in Scriptural and Talmudic disputation.

melamed: Old style orthodox Hebrew teacher.

Mishnayos (The *Mishna*): A compilation of oral laws and Rabbinic teachings, edited by Judah ha-Nasi in the early 3rd Century A.D., which forms the text of the *Talmud.* It is obligatory for pious Jews to study it constantly.

Mohel: The religious functionary who performs circumcisions.

nogid: A rich man, the leading secular citizen of a community.

nu: Exclamatory question, i.e. "Well? So what?"

Oleinu (*Alenu*): Literally, "it is our duty," the last prayer in the daily Jewish liturgy.

Pesach: Passover, the festival commemorating the liberation of the

Jews from their bondage in Egypt. It lasts seven days, beginning with the 15th of *Nisan* (March-April).

Perek: A chapter of the *Talmud.*

piatekas: Five-*kopek* piece.

Pupik: Navel; a term of teasing endearment.

Purim: Festival of Lots, celebrating the deliverance of the Jews from Haman's plot to exterminate them, as recounted in the *Book of Esther.* It is celebrated on the 14th and 15th of *Adar,* the 12th Jewish lunar month (March).

Rabbiner: A crown rabbi, chosen by election at the requirement of the Czar, to be an official functionary. Generally unpopular in old Russia.

Raboisi (*Raboisai*): Respectful Hebrew term of address used in Talmudic disputation, saying grace after meals, etc. Literally, "my masters."

Rambam: Popular name for Rabbi Moses ben Maimon (Maimonides) eminent, Spanish-Jewish philosopher and physician (1135-1204).

Reb: Mister.

Rosh Hashono (*Rosh Hashanah*): The Jewish New Year, celebrated on the 1st of *Tishri* (in September), is the most solemn day next to *Yom Kippur* (Day of of Atonement).

Rov: Rabbi.

schnorrer: A shameless beggar.

seder: The home service performed on the first two nights of Passover (see *Hagadah*).

Shabbes: Sabbath (Saturday).

shadchan: Marriage-broker.

Shahu notch shomayem (bastardized Russian-Hebrew): Walk at night under the heavens.

shammes (pl. *shamosim*): Sexton.

sheigetz (pl. *shkotzim*): A Gentile youth.

sheitel: A wig worn by ultra-orthodox married women.

Shevuos (*Shabuot*): Variously known as "The Festival of Weeks" and "Pentecost." It originally was a harvest festival and is celebrated seven weeks after Passover.

shi-shi (*shishi*): Sixth part of the Scriptural portion for the week read aloud on the Sabbath in the synagogue, and regarded as a great honor for the reader.

shkotzim: Plural of *sheigetz.*

shlimazl: An incompetent person, one who has perpetual bad luck. Everything happens to him.

Shma Koleinu (Shema Koleinu): "Hear our voices!" The first words of a Day of Atonement hymn; a popular idiom meaning: "idiot."

Shma Yisroel (Shema Yisroel): The first words in the confession of the Jewish faith: "Hear, O Israel: the Lord our God the Lord is One!"

Shmin-esra (Shemoneh 'Esreh): Eighteen (actually nineteen) benedictions, forming the most important part of the daily prayers, recited silently, standing up, by the worshipper.

shochet (pl. *shochtim*): Ritual slaughterer.

shofar: Ram's horn blown in the synagogue at services on *Rosh Hashanah* and *Yom Kippur.*

Sholom Aleichem: Peace be unto you.

shul: Synagogue.

Simchas Torah: "Rejoicing over the Torah," the last day of *Succoth* (Feast of Tabernacles), celebrating the completion of the reading of the Torah.

starosta: Village elder or "mayor" in Czarist Russia.

succah: A booth made of fresh green branches in which pious Jews celebrate the Feast of Tabernacles. This is done symbolically to recall the forty years wandering—"that your generations may know that I made the children of Israel to dwell in booths, when I brought them out of the land of Egypt."

Succos (Succoth): The Feast of Tabernacles, survival of the ancient festival on which male Jews were required to go on a pilgrimage to the Temple in Jerusalem. Lasts nine days and begins on the 15th day of the seventh lunar month of *Tishri* (September-October).

tallis (tallith): Prayer-shawl.

tallis-kot'n (tallith katon): "Small *tallis,*" a four-cornered fringed undergarment worn by male orthodox Jews in pursuance of the Biblical commandment to wear a garment with fringes.

Talmud: The Corpus Juris of the Jews, a compilation of the religious, ethical and legal teachings and decisions interpreting the Bible; finished c. A.D. 500.

tfillin: Phylacteries.

T'hilim: Psalms of David.

Torah: "Doctrine" or "law"; the name is applied to the five books of Moses, i.e. the Pentateuch.

Troika: A Russian sleigh drawn by three horses.

tzimmes: Dessert made of sweetened carrots or noodles.

vareniki: Fried dough filled with cheese or jelly.

verst: A Russian measure of distance, equal to about ⅔ of an English mile.

vertutin: Cheese or cooked cherries rolled in dough.

Yekum Perkon (Yekum Purkan): Aramaic prayer in the Sabbath service.

yeshiva: Talmudic college.

Yom Kippur: Day of Atonement; the most important Jewish religious holiday; a fast day, spent in solemn prayer, self-searching of heart and confession of sins by the individual in direct communion with God. It takes place on the tenth day of *Tishri,* eight days after Rosh Hashanah (New Year).

yom-tev (yom-tov): Holiday.